PENGUIN BOOKS

the savage crows

Robert Drewe was born in Melbourne and grew up on the West Australian coast. His novels and short stories have been widely translated, won many national and international prizes, and been adapted for film, television, radio and the theatre. He has also written plays, screenplays, journalism and film criticism, and edited two international anthologies of stories. He lives with his family in Sydney.

Also by Robert Drewe

Fiction

A Cry in the Jungle Bar

The Bodysurfers

Fortune

The Bay of Contented Men

Our Sunshine

The Drowner

Memoir

The Shark Net

Non-fiction

Walking Ella

Plays

South American Barbecue

The Bodysurfers: The Play

As Editor

The Penguin Book of the Beach (first published as *The Picador Book of the Beach*)

The Penguin Book of the City

ROBERT DREWE

the savage crows

PENGUIN BOOKS

For Sandy

Penguin Books Australia Ltd
487 Maroondah Highway, PO Box 257
Ringwood, Victoria 3134, Australia
Penguin Books Ltd
Harmondsworth, Middlesex, England
Penguin Putnam Inc.
375 Hudson Street, New York, New York 10014, USA
Penguin Books Canada Limited
10 Alcorn Avenue, Toronto, Ontario, Canada M4V 3B2
Penguin Books (NZ) Ltd
Cnr Rosedale and Airborne Roads, Albany, Auckland, New Zealand
Penguin Books (South Africa) (Pty) Ltd
5 Watkins Street, Denver Ext 4, 2094, South Africa
Penguin Books India (P) Ltd
11, Community Centre, Panchsheel Park, New Delhi 110 017, India

First published by William Collins Pty Ltd 1976
Published by Pan Books (Australia) Pty Ltd 1987
This edition published by Penguin Books Australia Ltd 2001
Offset from the 1987 Picador edition

1 3 5 7 9 10 8 6 4 2

Cover design and digital imaging by Ellie Exarchos
Cover images by Getty Images
Printed and bound in Australia by McPherson's Printing Group, Maryborough, Victoria

National Library of Australia
Cataloguing-in-Publication data:

Drewe, Robert, 1943– .
The savage crows.

ISBN 0 14 100799 0.

I. Title.

A823.3

www.penguin.com.au

Contents

Although some passages of *The Savage Crows* deal with real people and events it should be pointed out that only the characters of Robinson and Truganini bear any resemblance to their *known* personalities. Similarly, though I have drawn on several contemporary documents and newspapers I have allowed myself great freedom of imagination in reconstructing some nineteenth century events. Because of these rather elastic boundaries students of Australian history wishing a factual study of Robinson's expeditions are directed to *Friendly Mission: The Tasmanian Journals and Papers of George Augustus Robinson 1829–1834,* edited by N. J. B. Plomley (Tasmanian Historical Research Association 1966). I must also point out that all the characters in the twentieth century passages are fictitious.

I wish to thank the Literature Board of the Australia Council for the fellowships which assisted me in writing this novel.

R.D.

I

Events at the Anglo-Australian Guano Company

STEPHEN CRISP wrote frenetically of murder, greed and politics, recurrent atrocities. He was young and unstable enough for these topics, dovetailing as they do, to still interest him. He was writing his disordered chronicle in his three-room flat at McMahon's Point where he now lived alone.

He did most of his writing at night, rising sleepless and randy in the humidity and stumbling out to the kitchen to find big dappled slugs gliding over his cutlery and dinner scraps. He prised their shrinking, mucilaginous bodies from the Formica and flushed them, shrouded in Kleenex, down the toilet. It took hot water to remove their slime from the fingers. He worked at the kitchen table among their criss-crossed silver trails. The slugs returned every night, sliding out from dark soapy cracks behind the plumbing. One night he stamped one into the seagrass matting, it infuriated him so much. Next night a leopard-printed slug was grazing on the paste of his companion. A night or two later all that remained of the squashed slug was a faint brown outline.

He often slept late until the harbour and motor traffic noise woke him about noon, then meandered up the hill to the corner delicatessen for bread, fat-reduced milk, oranges and a length of cabana sausage. A weather eye was kept open for the landlord: Crisp was behind with the rent. He also owed miscellaneous sums elsewhere to people who employed threatening collection agencies.

His flat, number 6, was one of eight in a liver-coloured brick building named *Cardigan*, after the town in Wales. *Cardigan*'s narrow front yard couldn't support grass or shrubbery because of the shade and damp and surreptitious gas leaks. The local tomcats sprayed the foyer. Furled and weathered suburban newspapers gradually pulped against the letterbox. Inside, Crisp's bathroom window overlooked Lavender Bay, a small silvery piece of Sydney Harbour. The bay was attractive from that distance but at close quarters the tides could be seen converging, collecting the harbour's plastic detergent bottles, beer cans and old baby carriages. Astride the lavatory he had a panoramic vista of the boatbuilders' sheds, Luna Park's ferris wheel and Big Dipper, the railway shunting yards and the half-hourly Lavender Bay ferries. At night the view was more picturesque: fairy-lights twinkled from Luna Park, the midget train on the Big Dipper rumbled into sight every three minutes. There was a steep downward slope where girls screamed every trip. From his throne Crisp had viewed the nation's biggest celebrations: the fireworks displays for the Captain Cook Bicentenary in 1970 and the opening by the Queen of Australia, Elizabeth II, of the Sydney Opera House in 1973. Forty years earlier he would have had the same box seat for the grand opening of the Sydney Harbour Bridge.

Since leaving his job at the Commission Crisp also researched and wrote his opus in the Mitchell Library. On sunny days he bought cheese sandwiches and vanilla slices and ate lunch in the Botanical Gardens with stenographers and receptionists to gynaecologists and ear, nose and throat men.

Was the task beginning to amount to an obsession with him? Some of his few remaining friends said so. And, if so, was he the full dollar these days? At parties, leaning against refrigerators at 2 a.m., he held forth among the filled ashtrays and dead bottles on Count Strzelecki's *Theory of Decline*, the Siege of Three Thumbs, Drink the Great Destroyer and such subjects.

Why don't you get it all down? people kept saying, some of them half-seriously. So he had decided to go ahead. Lately he had been compelled to try to understand everything, starting with himself and working up to the nation. What caused particular styles of indigenous behaviour, for instance? Like his own. The reaction of Commission executives to him, even those barely above him, made him feel like old William James's crab in PSYCHOLOGY I: filled with a sense of personal outrage at being classed simply as a crustacean and thus disposed of. *I am no such thing*, the crab would say, *I am myself, myself alone*.

Why did the neat and amiable (anal, granted) David Appleyard turn into a prize turd when promoted head of Current Affairs? Why did he imagine Crisp an intractable radical? Why were Appleyard's pencils arranged at 90-degree angles to his desk edge? (Why had Crisp's father always desperately spread the toilet seat with layers of paper prior to evacuation, even in the safety of his own home? Did he imagine the bottoms of his pure babes carried virulent germs?) Why had he left Jane? Why had Anna left him? Why was his fear of death getting out of hand? Why did guilt weigh upon him like a wet woollen overcoat? Why did he care?

He had to put everything—past, present, friends, strangers, the whole obtuse yet complicated place—into perspective. It was very likely that what he was beginning to refer to as his 'thesis' was at the heart of it. It might say it all. (This is an indication of his general condition at the time, though he didn't voice such ambitions publicly. *I'm not that far gone,* he thought, imagining the cynical Commission smiles around the lunchtime wine carafes.)

Now Crisp would have been less than honest if he hadn't admitted to another reason for throwing away his career and embarking on his thesis. The cautious life-preserving Capricorn side of him thought the project might put the brake on his down-hill racing. Give him an all-consuming but *serene* interest, as it were. Job, marriage, health—mental and physical—were all fast eroding. Ease the hypertension by swapping the Valium for his long-service pay and a research grant from the Australia Council. Dispel gouty uric acid crystals from big toe and index finger joints with wine-less meals of Vogel's health bread. Deflate potential hæmorrhoids with exercise and orange juice. So he said shove it—in a civilized way—to the Commission, took the money due him, stepped out from under his office-political cloud and, instead of the Commission, now concerned himself with events at the Anglo-Australian Guano Company. Same thing really, he thought, laughing at that.

This particular day he was writing:

'William Lanney, patronizingly nicknamed "King Billy" by the English colonists, succumbed to "English cholera" on March 3rd, 1869 in his room at *The Dog and Partridge* at the corner of Goulburn and Barrack Streets, Hobart Town. Attempting to dress himself so he could proceed to the Colonial Hospital for treatment he was overcome with the exertion of lacing his boots and fell dead on his faeces-stained palliasse.

'Shortly after his body was decapitated, a white man's skull inserted inside his swollen facial mask, his hands and feet severed and the rest reduced to a wheelbarrowful of blood and grease.'

Since Anna's leaving he made Friday the night for his weekly foray around the traps for alcohol and, optimistically, for sex. These days he regarded himself as sexually deprived and he doubted whether he was actually as predatory as others (Jane, Anna in her way) seemed to imagine.

Cultural and age gaps were everywhere: he spoke a different language to the really young, available girls. And he couldn't be bothered going through the rituals, though he had for a couple of months slept with a twenty-year-old Arts dropout, Megan, who sold cosmetics in David Jones' main store and modelled part-time while waiting for 'something in television'. Although a cosmetician of sorts she had no time for makeup. Pearly skinned and devoid of tanned hip and breast boundaries (she never swam or sunbaked), she clopped in and out of his flat on her Dr Scholl's sandals. She had a vague and neurotic air which had momentarily fascinated him until one night (she'd been raised on a diet of youthful, no-nonsense sportsmen) she remarked, no malice intended, 'Gee, you fuck funny. Wriggling it about like that.' Though he was obliged to laugh with her, that was it. She used to keep a small tortoise in a bowl beside her bed. It spent its life treading water, its nostrils just cleaving the surface.

'Shouldn't you give it some rocks to climb on, or a float or something?' he wondered. Their bed rhythms made waves; the tortoise scrabbled for air. 'Perhaps a little ramp to rest its legs.'

'No, he'll get away. Besides he loves to swim.' Her insecurity, he gathered, stemmed from an earlier misadventure to some North Queensland walking fish. She was cleaning their bowl when they walked right up her arm, ran even, into the sink. The water washed them down the plughole. Every so often she still poured fish food down the drain in case they were hungry, wherever they were.

Megan was remembered also for the fact that after lovemaking and before sleep she had a routine: she always put on a bra to prevent overnight breast sag.

'When you've got good ones you might as well try to keep them nice.'

Where no cultural or age gap existed—with the twenty-eightish journalists, television researchers and so on—Crisp found the women generally even more tense than he. Since his fall from favour at the Commission they regarded him warily, mindful of their burgeoning careers, meeting his closing-time propositions with graceful and flirtatious rejections and half-hearted squeezes of the upper arm. Such incidents usually faded immediately from his mind—especially if he'd been drinking solidly for several hours—and he was therefore sometimes fazed to hear embellished tales of his sexual harassment circulating at pubs and parties. Sufficiently old-fashioned for a youngish man, Crisp could, however, act chivalrously lecherous when reminded of a past proposition by the girl in question. Then they sometimes called him a sexist.

Anna was still encountered at occasional parties. She was always pleasant to him, but to the jaundiced Crisp she was acting out her stereotype: the pivot of the dope-smokers' group, sociable cuddler of English lecturers and coke-sniffing poets, quaffer of hocks and rieslings and, he feared, casual vanisher upstairs with spunky young film makers and serene bisexual organic farmers.

For appearances' sake they were now cheerful acquaintances.

'How's the wife?' she'd banter, wafting past in a transparent caftan.

'Fine. How's your father?'

Her father was a touchy subject, the only one on which the liberated Anna was a snobbish Yugoslav immigrant Upward Achiever. Sam Kubic (Crisp had never met him in all the time they'd been together) was allegedly a swarthy fascist market gardener at Mona Vale. Tomatoes were his *forte.* The tragedy of his life was his daughter's antipathy to both the overthrow of Tito and nice young Croatian boys with good road haulage businesses. Alas, having grown up with Rutherglen bug and spotted wilt her interest in tomatoes was also sadly minimal.

After such exchanges at parties she'd smile and sweetly walk by. She had a tender heart and would be unhappy to learn that he was disintegrating rapidly, he thought on these occasions. Two or three wines and some intimate conversation on the stairs and she might weep gently and maybe come home with him. 'I can almost come just by looking at you!' Hadn't she used to say that? But he held back, gripped by pride and perversity, even while wanting above all to wake up with her, on a Sunday morning, say, and eat strawberries and read the papers in bed among the toast crumbs: *And then as Madame Ilse removed her panties our reporter dressed, made an excuse and left. . . .* And he, too, held back. Besides, what if she smiled sweetly (an arm around the beer belly of a fashionable political press secretary) and told him to piss off?

Not many people (Crisp was an exception) know or knew that Lanney—also Lanne, Lannie and Lannay—was the old Aboriginal verb of the western tribes of Van Diemen's Land (later named Tasmania) signifying to fight or strike. Members of a once fierce tribe, the Lanney family showed little fight, however, when captured while robbing a shepherd's hut on the Cape Grim property of the Van Diemen's Land Company, their ancestral home. They were taken by an amateur quartet of blistered and hæmorrhoidal storekeeper-troopers between Mount Cameron and the Arthur River on the west coast and locked in Her Majesty's Gaol at Launceston before being exiled to the Aboriginal settlement at Flinders Island.

Crisp the imaginative researcher had learned that language difficulties at first prevented the family from communicating with the other exiles on the island. They were a close-knit little group, very attached to each other. The mother, presumably from privation and anxiety, seemed prematurely old and feeble. The father was gentle and well mannered, deferring graciously to his white protectors. The five children, ranging in age from an angular daughter of eighteen to a plump five-year-old boy whom the whites named Billy, made a good impression on the Protector, a Doctor Joseph Milligan, with their docile, affectionate natures.

On the subject of young Billy, it seemed to his teachers that he was a slow learner. An attempt by the catechist, Mr Robert Clark, to instil in him a basic Christian education was a complete failure. He was imperfect in the alphabet, his spelling was weak and his Lord's Prayer miscarried every time. Alongside Billy his friends Neptune, Cæsar, Bonaparte and Nelson fairly shone, their constant phlegmy coughing and wheezing notwithstanding.

'What will God do to this world by and by, Neptune?'

'Burn it, Father Clark.'

'What did God make us for, Nelson?'

'His own purpose, Father Clark.'

'Who are in heaven, Bonaparte?'

'God, angels, good men and Jesus Christ, Father Clark.'

'What sort of place is heaven?'

'A good place. With sugar and shellfish.'

'What sort of place is hell?'

'A place of . . . torment?'

'Yes. What is a place of torment, Cæsar?'

'Burning for ever and ever, Father Clark.'

'Why do you love God, Bonaparte?'

'God gives me everything.'

Billy Lanney only once gave a *really* satisfactory answer in general catechism.

'Do you like God, Billy?' questioned the catechist.

'Yes.' Wall-eyed, he deposited nervous nose pickings on a serge trouser leg.

Bonaparte, Neptune and Nelson could count to one hundred and Cæsar could cypher a little. Neptune and Cæsar could even write and read words of three letters, but then they died before their eleventh birthdays and Bonaparte soon afterwards.

If no student Billy Lanney had sharp eyes and a special acuteness of vision at long distances. Aboard whalers a keen eye at the masthead was worth a good wage, so he absconded from the Christian attentions of protectors and catechists and signed on board the *Aladdin* at Hobart Town. The life suited him and he was popular with his fellow seamen, being a lover of rum, beer and the other wharfside attractions. He was also received with affection, of a maternal nature, by the few remaining members of his race—all old women—whenever he paid them a shore-leave visit. Considering he consorted chiefly with Europeans and had no black friends of his age or sex remaining alive it wasn't perhaps surprising that he found fault with the excellent photographic portraits made by Mr C. A. Woolley in 1866. Billy Lanney complained that they were 'too black' for him. Mr Woolley's photographs, full-face, profile and three-quarter face, nevertheless did him no injustice, showing a strong, heavily-built young man with deep-set, sad eyes.

About this time the *Hobart Town Mercury* published this paragraph: 'At the last ball at Government House there appeared the last male Aboriginal inhabitant of Tasmania. We had heard much before of the Last Man of his race but had never expected to be favored with the sight of such a novelty. In this case, however, the person in question was accompanied by three Aboriginal females, the sole living representatives of the race beside himself, but not of such an age, or such an appearance, as to justify the expectation of any future addition to their numbers.'

As Crisp had discovered, and now noted in one of his Tudor exercise books, the colonists had rather late in the day recognized Lanney's unique position. They came to stare at the living fossil, to poke at him, measure his skull, capture his abject face on canvas and photographic plates.

Government House put him on show yet again, for the colonial tour of Prince Alfred, the Duke of Edinburgh, in 1868. When the two men strolled together in the public gaze along the Hobart Town waterfront the colonial press was enthralled at the 'royal blood' flowing in both circulatory systems. It amused itself reporting the imagined details of their *tête-à-tête* on the Derwent River.

(Royal *tête-à-tête* as imagined by the *Courier*: Prince Alfred—'A fine day Your Majesty, eh? Such a hyacinth sky and the fishing boats, whalers and what-have-you all apainted in their many hues for the occasion!' King Billy—'Oh, I agree Your Majesty. A sky to do credit to the jackets of your own Royal Horseguards. And will you give a wave of your handkerchief to that aged female sable subject of mine spreadeagled on the tavern steps?')

Someone said that Her Gracious Majesty herself would surely have invited King Billy to dine with her next time he visited England but that unfortunately the *Aladdin* did not sail and whale in that vicinity. Nevertheless it was probably some consolation to receive Victoria's smiles indirectly in the warm greeting and gloved handshake of her second son. And he was allowed to keep the blue coat and gold braided cap in which the Ladies' Welcoming Committee had dressed him.

Now, over a hundred years later, Crisp was interesting himself in such matters in his thesis. He thought of it as a thesis in the sense of an act of laying down, of getting it all on paper, *everything*, rather than the advancing of some proposition to be maintained by cogent argument and aimed at receiving some scholastic honour or other. (Not that he didn't advance a few theories of his own.)

On Saturdays Crisp visited his daughter, bouncing along with a hangover in the 190 double-decker bus to Whale Beach, a stuffy ninety-minute ride up the coast. Wendy still missed him and had recently developed asthma. He was having trouble keeping up the mortgage payments on the house. Jane seemed to require vast sums of money for house-keeping, Italian lessons and bikinis. Sodden with guilt he paid up every Saturday, selling the car at a painful loss and manipulating overdrafts and credit union loans like an arthritic juggler. His old neighbours cut him dead, but tossed loud remarks over the fence about the uncut lawn, the untrimmed lantana hedge. Whenever he arrived they were in their driveways vigorously polishing their cars.

He estimated during one idle bus trip that he had travelled the equivalent of two-and-a-half times round the world on the 190 bus. He knew all the advertising slogans over the bus windows by heart (Kinsella Funeral Services: *When Shadows Fall We Are At Your Service With Dignity and Taste and Unobtrusive Decorum.* A Civic Service Extended Over the Past 140 Years by Five Generations.), every shop-front from North Sydney to Whale Beach (P. Valenti—Fruitologist—Fresh Fruit and Vegs; Coleman Bros. Grocers—Cigs and Cool Drinks; SeaView Service Station, Marfak Lubrication, Prop. S. E. 'Stan' Wolfinger). Returning home on the ten o'clock bus after his Saturday visits he was apt to be half sat upon by thickly powdered grass widows who got on at the Dee Why Hotel. One heavily be-ringed matron hicupped, coughed quietly down his right leg and left the bus at Manly Vale. As new passengers climbed aboard at Balgowlah and Mosman they smelled the vomit on his pants and shot off disgusted glances.

Up at Whale Beach all was now quite civilized. Jane had a lover, a divorced doctor called Poynton, a man in radiant health who liked skiing, sailing and such extravagances. He had arranged for Wendy to have some allergy tests which showed a primary aversion to cat fur, a secondary one to general animal dandruff. They didn't have a cat, however, only two Muscovy ducks for the snails.

One thing to be said for Nicholas Poynton's emergence from the snowdrifts and spinnakers, rosy-cheeked, jawed like a Marlboro man: the central trauma of their separation seemed to dissipate. Crisp could be grateful to him for that. The visits from woebegone nuns had immediately ceased. Cousins and aunts of the lapsed Jane, they had sought her out, arriving mysteriously in pairs on the doorstep from obscure Catholic crevices every Saturday, being determinedly solicitous to him, trying to tempt him back with half-hourly offerings of Devon creams and milky tea. Thwarted, they spent their remaining freedom huddled sadly over the sink in rubber gloves. The surprise appearances of concerned Catholic friends had also dropped off (the most agitated being Katy Stackpool, mother-of-three, showing scant recollection of having once or twice gone down on him at the drive-in—small neat buttocks rubbing condensation from the Prefect's steamy windows—in less devout adolescent days). They had an amazing race memory for the licentious evils of divorce.

Hiding in the weekend book pages Crisp was encircled and pounced upon one subdued Saturday in the early stages of the separation. They were well rehearsed.

'We've been discussing things, Stephen,' Jane said. The paper crackled like thunder on his knees. An unusual number of lighted cigarettes were in the room, clouds of smoke. 'We've come to the conclusion you're extraordinarily selfish.'

'Not in front of Wendy,' he said, pleasantly.

'She's playing next door.'

'You do tend to live just for yourself, you know,' Katy offered. 'I hope you won't mind me saying that.'

'What is this?'

'Selfish in every way. With me especially.'

Plenty of innuendo in that. 'What do you mean *every way*? Come on, let's fill Katy in on all our private affairs.' (He meant, of course, let's not, not if you have any sensitivity left for my feelings. There are quicker fellows I bet than I was with you. With every other woman I am fine. I think . . .)

Katy again, for Christ sake. The reasonable approach, even confiding: 'Jane asked me for some help . . . Kevin and I have had our troubles. But we've seen them through . . . Jane has no one else to turn to. If you only realized what she's been put through lately.'

'And I wasn't satisfied during the last year, Stephen!' (Crackle, rustle. The newspaper would any moment explode in his hands.) 'You thought only of yourself.' Katy soaking up all this prime material. (Probable bedtime scene in the Stackpool household tonight: 'Oh, Kevin. Jane Crisp says Steve is bad in bed.' 'Really? A dud fuck, eh! Fancy that, heh, heh.')

Jane said, 'I don't know how many nights I cried myself to sleep,' and wept at the memory of weeping. Surprisingly, the thumping of Crisp's pulse calmed in the neck and temples and he felt like soothing her, certainly not counter-attacking, perhaps smoothing the auburn tendrils from her wide shiny forehead, patting the freckled shoulders. Avuncular, he felt. Jane and Katy, however, lit more handfuls of cigarettes and disappeared into the overgrown garden. His name came murmuring up from under the banana plants and then they passed out of earshot behind the lantana. Cicadas chattered. Lawn mowers hummed. Wendy ran in from next door and played Junior Scrabble with him (moderate obscenities forming themselves on his little wooden stand) and then he went home early. Jane and he rarely fought again and never in front of Wendy. They made a point of that.

And, later, Anna would whisper, pinkly, 'When you come you really mean it!'

Now Crisp took his daughter swimming, for the asthma, fishing, or for hand-in-hand walks through the bush each Saturday, keeping out of the house deliberately. Get air into her lungs, he told himself, stretch her chest cavity, drive out the infanticidal mucus. At North Avalon they sat on a steep sandhill and watched the veteran world surfing champions Midget Farrelly and Nat Young leading a coterie of young surfers through their art. Wendy found a cardboard grocery carton and it became a sled, sliding jerkily down the sandhill until she became over-excited and began wheezing, doubling over and hawking strings of cloudy bubbles on to the sand. Sometimes she was too exhausted to walk home and he piggybacked her, her shallow breaths whistling in his ear. The flushed cheeks and soft cupid lips brushed his face, withdrawing gently from the prickles, and at home alone, sorry for her and himself, he could easily cry remembering the sensation. As he loped along through the sand chanting:

This is the way Wendy rides,
Wendy rides,
Wendy rides.
This is the way Wendy rides
On a cold and frosty morrrrning.

As far as Billy Lanney was concerned, his restless chronicler noted that all the public display and lionizing in 1868 had become a torment to him. Lanney began hitting the rum heavily at *The Dog and Partridge, The Black Swan* and other waterfront taverns. He collapsed in the town's cheapest brothels and burst the blood vessels in his eyes with the force of his vomiting. James Bonwick, the eminent historian and anthropologist, found him too drunk to talk with. As Bonwick said, 'I went several times to his ship in the hope of catching him sober and having a chat with him, but was obliged to terminate my visit to the charming island unsuccessful in that object.'

For a time he rallied and went whaling again in the *Runnymede,* which was short of hands. But, bloated and sick, he returned to port late in February 1869 and was paid off with £12/13/5 in wages. For several days he complained to the tavern girls of stomach pains which went untreated apart from the ingestion of a local brandy sold from her dog-cart by Mary Scrutton and her five children and alleged to have medicinal properties. Copious bleeding followed, from several orifices. He died alone, but was remembered sentimentally almost immediately. Recently he had turned thirty-four.

Crisp was interested to read in a newspaper advertisement for the Tasmanian Timber Promotion Board that William Lanney was commemorated even to this day by the King Billy Pine, 'used in boat-building, joinery and other specialty purposes'. Such fringe items of information, trivia, piled up in his mind and notebooks. He collected a list of various tribal translations from old research books: I love you—*Mena coyetea*, I will go and hunt—*Mena mulaga*; When I returned to my country I went hunting but did not kill one head of game because the white men make their dogs wander and kill all the game and they only want the skins, leaving the flesh to rot—*Malanthana-mena-tackay mulaga pooty nara pamery lowgana lee-calaguna cracku carticata ludarnny parobeny nara moogara nara mena lowgana reethen tratyatetay tobantheelinga nara laway relbia mena malathina mobily worby pua-yunthea.*

Crisp paused in his jottings and wrote *The Anglo-Australian Guano Company* in the margin, underlining it before continuing:

'The body was removed from *The Dog and Partridge* to the dead-house at the Colonial Hospital, the Premier, the Honourable Sir Richard Dry, declining an order for its possession by the members of the Royal Society. The Society's representations to the government set forth at length the reasons why the body should be secured to them. It was of the greatest scientific value. Unfortunately no steps had been taken in the past to secure a perfect skeleton of a male Tasmanian Aborigine. This oversight should be rectified "in the interests of science".

'Sir Richard, however, was intractable. He refused to sanction any interference to the corpse. Further, he sent "positive instructions" to the hospital that it should be protected from the risk of mutilation. The funeral subsequently took place, arranged by Mr J. W. Graves, the leading barrister and a "true friend" of the original Tasmanians. Invitations were issued to a number of Old Colonists and others. Between fifty and sixty citizens presented themselves at the dead-house in readiness for the burial.

'Rumours had meanwhile got afloat that the body had been already tampered with. Captain McArthur of the *Aladdin* and some other friends of the deceased from his whaling days requested that the coffin should be opened to satisfy their minds that the burial ceremony was not a vain show. This was done by Mr Graves and the body was perused by those who wished to see it. (The numbers so desirous were very few.) The lid was then screwed down again. A seal was needed but none could be found in the dead-house. A search of the dispensary finally disclosed an old brass stamp. On being impressed on the wax it left the simple word WORLD.

'The coffin was then covered in a black possum skin rug and overlaid with two native spears and waddies around which were twined the folds of a Union Jack. Four seamen humped it on their shoulders. The pall was borne by Captain Hill of the *Runnymede* and three coloured seamen: a Negro and two Sandwich Islanders. The mourners included Captain McArthur and most of the masters of vessels in port as well as many businessmen connected with the whaling trade and a large muster of Old Colonists. As the procession moved along Liverpool and Murray Streets to St David's Church it gathered strength and was followed by increasing numbers of spectators. The Reverend F. H. Cox read the service and preceded the body to the graveyard, clothed in his surplice. On leaving the church the procession had grown to one hundred and twenty mourners.'

So, Crisp noted (nibbling and spitting out slivers of fingernails as he worked), the cortege left St David's after a fine Anglican service, the sightseeing crowd witnessing the true fellowship of the sea as the sailors carried off Lanney's headless, limbless trunk under the Union Jack and a possum skin rug. As well as a stranger's peeled head.

Not that the seamen realized this, of course. But, after the funeral, some of them were still suspicious of the intentions of the medical-scientific establishment. They demanded a police guard for Lanney's grave. A constable was told to patrol the graveside, but somehow the order miscarried. Next morning the whalers discovered their fears justified. The grave had been robbed and the soil around it was soaked with blood and grease. A skull had been discarded, tossed on the sand heap. It wasn't Lanney's.

During the morning this report spread through the town and hundreds of people hurried to the cemetery, including the Premier and Mr Graves. In their presence the sexton tidied the grave with a rake and reburied the broken coffin, throwing in the skull for good measure.

Unfortunately government procrastination hampered the discovery of the mutilators and body snatchers. Sir Richard preferred no involvement in the affair (there were few votes in it), explaining that he had visited the grave only for legal reasons, because of reports that the complete coffin had been removed. Had this been the case he would have issued search warrants (under the requisite Act) as executor for Lanney, with instructions that should any portions of the body be found they should immediately be taken possession of by the Crown. Sir Richard and his Attorney-General, Mr Dobson, satisfied themselves, however, of the presence of the coffin (empty).

No further steps were taken as it was extremely doubtful whether any legal property existed in pieces of the late native.

Naturally rumours instantly spread on the body's whereabouts. Two grave diggers said they had traced globs of blood and wheelbarrow tracks to the warehouse of the Anglo-Australian Guano Company in Salamanca Place. But there the clues disappeared.

The *Mercury* laid the blame for at least one of the mutilations on the Royal Society. It alleged that some of its members, gaining admittance to the body while it lay in the dead-house, were greatly annoyed to find that someone had already taken the skull, after skinning the head and replacing it with that of a dead school teacher. 'The European skull was placed inside the scalp of the unfortunate native, the facial features being drawn over so as to have the appearance of completeness. Feeling sure that the persons who had taken the skull now intended to take the body from the grave and so possess a perfect skeleton, the Society resolved to cut off the hands and feet and to lodge them in safe-keeping, an operation which was carefully done.'

Popular contemporary opinion sheeted home the blame for the original mutilation to a Doctor Thomas Kater, the honorary medical officer at the hospital and a leading figure in commerce and Government. J. B. Stephens, a colonial versifier and wag, published a long verse entitled *King Billy's Skull* which was taken up in anti-establishment quarters in Hobart Town in the years following Lanney's death. Crisp noted it in his thesis:

Fancy the honour, the kudos, the fame!
A whole museum athrill with one's name!
Fancy the thousands all crowding to see
Skull of the Last Aborigine!
Presented by Asterisk Dash, M.D! . . .

There was a lead. Crisp duly researched and noted that Doctor Kater had been suspected by many townspeople of having conspired to possess Lanney's skull. Aided and abetted by his son Burton, a medical student, he was believed to have severed Lanney's head, replaced it with that of a schoolteacher named Ross, and lowered it from the dead-house window with a long bandage to his son below. A Doctor Sevitt may have been in the conspiracy with the Katers. Sevitt had been particularly asked to watch over Lanney's body in the dead-house but had instead accepted an invitation to take tea that evening with Mrs Kater, a leading social figure in the colony.

There was a document in the Mitchell Library purporting to be an affidavit made by one Charles Williams, the hospital gatekeeper. It alleged that Doctor Kater had sent for a barber, entered the dead-house and locked the door. It seemed the wily Williams had peeped through the keyhole and seen Kater and his assistants bending over a corpse. Later that night Williams claimed to have seen the Katers leaving the hospital grounds. The doctor carried something under his arm. The parcel was *head-shaped*, swore Williams, signing his name in elaborate working-class copperplate.

Uproar followed. Sir Richard Dry summarily suspended Kater from his position though the doctor denied involvement in the various dissections and mutilations. Kater refused to bow to official disapproval, standing again for Parliament and winning his seat. Ten years after the Lanney affair Thomas Kater was Premier of Tasmania. Williams the gatekeeper was sacked six months after putting *his* head on the chopping block.

King Billy's dead, Kater has his head,
Sevitt has his hands and feet.
My feet, my feet, my poor black feet
That used to be so gritty,
They're not aboard the Runnymede,
They're somewhere in this city.

This was a popular song which swept through Hobart Town in 1869, also duly noted by Crisp. He also recorded in his chronicle that gatekeeper Williams has sworn in his affidavit: *Doctor Kater I know had a tobacco pouch made of Lanney's skin.*

Eventually, one Saturday night, Crisp met Poynton, being unable to escape before he arrived to take Jane partying around the northern beaches. They both coped jovially enough, Poynton's eyes disappearing into his glowing cheeks.

'Saw you on television once or twice,' said the doctor. 'Something about trade unions, the greedy buggers. Your face looks fatter in the flesh.'

'Nice to meet you,' Crisp said. More a well mannered mutter. He almost said, inanely, 'Have a good time,' like a teenager's father.

Poynton was tanned, of course, with nice muscle definition. Jane had always laughed at male narcissism, allegedly loathed sporty men. Now she seemed to find it intriguing that Nick worked out in a gym and rowed with the Palm Beach surf club. ('Where does he get the time? What about his house calls?' Crisp had asked sourly. 'He has a partner, naturally. Or a locum or something.' Naturally.) Crisp noticed that he favoured silvery dangling things around the neck and the casual exposure of skeins of blue-black chest hair. The rear window of his BMW carried a faded sticker: *Beware! Nationalized Medicine is a Health Hazard.* The BMW's exhaust coughed most healthily as the doctor disappeared with Crisp's wife.

Thank you for the world so sweet,
Thank you for the food we eat.
Thank you for the birds that sing,
Thank you God for everything.

Wendy recited the old children's prayer that her agnostic father had chanted at his own childhood bedtimes. (*God Bless Mummy and Daddy and make me a good boy tomorrow, Amen.*) 'Aren't you ever going to live with us again or have breakfast with us?' the child asked. 'Nick does.'

Does he now? 'I'll always be where you are, darling,' her father hedged. 'We'll see each other all the time, whenever you want. And when you're bigger we'll go on trips together all round the world.'

The eyes were dark-rimmed and doubtful. Anxious to believe, like her mother's. He kissed her cheeks and blew air bubbles in her neck to make her giggle. She did for a moment, then coughed and turned on her side away from him on her rubber pillow. 'Laughing gives me asthma,' she said.

Until the sitter arrived Crisp drank coffee in the lounge-room among familiar but strangely dated trinkets: wedding present brandy balloons, two paintings they'd given each other, books he'd bought himself. Poynton's after-shave lingered in little clouds.

Crisp the sneak padded into their old bedroom. She still used two pillows, he noticed, but the sheets and pillow cases were new, a slithery material of muted paisley pattern. Stealthily he slid open her dressing-table drawers and rifled through them. Cosmetics. Meds. Letters: from her mother, sister (he, Crisp, mentioned only once, by sister Caroline, having been spotted on television looking 'very drawn') and, from England, a mysterious hand-written envelope with no letter enclosed. Hair dryer. Underwear (new and unrecognizable). Twisted masses of pantyhose. Six months' supply of Neogynon (thoughtfully prescribed by the good Doctor Poynton?). Drawings of Wendy's. Bundle of old greeting cards enclosed by a rubber band. *To my own Jane, wishing you a happy 23rd birthday. All my love, Steve.* And so forth. He replaced everything as neatly as he could, memories included, in their various compartments.

By the time the sitter arrived Wendy was deeply asleep, her breathing less laboured. Crisp rocked back along the coast road towards Sydney in the 190 with a busload of yellow-headed adolescents identically clad in the surfer mode: western shirts, Levis and rubber thongs. His fellow passengers punched each other amiably and flicked spittle at one another with their fingers. The back of his neck anticipated a glob at any moment. The boys got out, cackling hopefully, at the Collaroy surf club dance.

At home at McMahon's Point the slugs were in the fruit bowl and perusing some sweating cheese he'd left unrefrigerated. He flushed the ringleaders down the toilet and turned on the television. His friend Peter Tooth was smoothly taking an objective line on a story about mining the Great Barrier Reef. Spokesmen for the mineral sands development companies appeared urbane, reasonable, community-conscious. Questioned by the adroit Tooth the conservationists came across as scruffy, unreasonable, community-conscious. Nothing to upset Appleyard there. He switched channels to the Creature Feature where things emerged from the primeval slime once a week and tried to take over the world. He fell asleep even before this week's monster had revealed itself, the attractive female scientist and her fiance blissfully unaware of the steaming protoplasm seeping under the laboratory door. At Crisp's elbow an ex-peanut butter tumbler of brandy sat hardly touched.

The thesis continued, on paper and in his head, taking several shapes. Metaphorically truncated himself, he angered over King Billy's dissection, became violently subjective, wrote fast and furiously in his exercise book:

'The Anglo-Australian Guano Company, leading colonial processor of seabird shit, disappearing point for the last shreds of William Lanney, may have been where the gentlemen of the Royal Society hid the remains until emotions cooled. The Society and Government were at loggerheads. These men of the scientific establishment (who had busied themselves classifying flora and fauna over cups of tea while people died) suddenly discovered the dearth of an Aboriginal skeleton. Past neglect should be corrected overnight. A deputation of Royal Society members went over the Premier's head and waited upon the Colonial Secretary to press for Lanney's corpse. The Colonial Secretary was unyielding. He refused to allow the dissection of the body, though he permitted the scientists to examine and measure it, make casts, prod and poke. Beyond this they were forbidden to go. And then Kater beat them to the head! "God rot him and the Colonial Secretary!" said the gentlemen of the Society to one another, sawing off the extremities, later indulging in a little grave-robbing and loading King Billy's trunk and limb stumps aboard their barrow and trundling down Salamanca Place.'

Crisp retained a vision of the headless, limbless Last Man.

2

The Naked Lubra Calendar

CRISP, ALONE AND increasingly introspective, reflected that his father—one hot December night yeast-ripe with the smell of river algæ—came home from work with his briefcase bulging with back copies of the *Saturday Evening Post*, *Life*, *Time* and the *Ladies' Home Journal* and three New Year gift calendars rolled inside brown cardboard tubes. The calendars came with the usual season's greetings and best wishes for continued prosperity for you and yours in the coming year from business contacts at firms like Atkinson Resins, Universal Adhesives Pty Ltd and Swan Flooring (W.A.).

His father, the gregarious company bondsman Murray Crisp, forty-three, was at this stage married fifteen years (wed in Pilot Officer's dress blues in a simple but moving 1941 Presbyterian ceremony at St Paul's, Nedlands, marked by the non-attendance of his new mother-in-law, Maureen 'Molly' Dolan, who cried for three weeks before and after the wedding but then bucked up and though an R.C. thereafter became a 'good scout' in Murray's opinion), the father of two boys (Stephen, fourteen, and Geoffrey, nine) and assistant manager of the West Australian branch of Hallstrom Gelatine. He was therefore second in seniority for the magazines, as for everything else.

From having worked in Hallstrom's mailroom in his school holidays Stephen knew that as the magazines arrived in the post they were opened by a fifteen-year-old apprentice bodgie named Rodney Biven who once drew a face, collar and snappy bow-tie on his penis with a company ballpoint. Biven would paste a printed sticker on each magazine cover showing the distribution order: Mr Hawker (State Manager), Mr Crisp, Mr Wylie (Chief Accountant), Mr Chappell (Sales Manager), Mr Gomme (Factory Manager), Staff Canteen. Murray Crisp's position in the distribution order ensured his copies were never tattered and barely dated. Hawker wasn't much of a reader and generally passed the magazines straight over. Murray Crisp liked to read in bed, especially C. S. Forrester's Horatio Hornblower stories and Erle Stanley Gardener's Perry Mason serials in the *Post*. The *Post* cartoons were also good for a laugh, particularly Hazel.

A summer after-dinner scene: Stephen and Geoffrey are flipping through the magazines, reading the cartoons (featuring pith-helmeted hunters in stew pots, men on desert islands, apologetic husbands returning home frayed from work: 'Honey, I didn't get the raise but the boss says thanks for the Angel's Food Cake!'), then opening the calendars. One shows a Sydney Harbour yachting vista of full-spinnakered eighteen footers, the second twelve oil prints of gnarled ghost gums and assorted charming fishing villages (entitled *Storm Warning*, *First Light* and suchlike) and the third depicts each month for the upcoming New Year of 1957 with its own Kodachrome red-ochred photograph of a central Australian landscape. But one picture is a shade more interesting than the others, illustrating October or some latish month that their father hasn't noticed. It shows a still green billabong dotted with water lilies and overhung by dipping eucalypts. In the foreground, giggling happily for the camera, are three naked Aboriginal women, waist deep in the lake. They are all slim, wide-mouthed and ingenuously cheerful. One lubra has a lily in her dripping hair, another a flower clasped coquettishly before her thighs. The third, less reserved, flashes white gappy teeth and splashes water at the unseen cameraman with a pink palm. Water ripples about their bellies and hips. On the bank of the billabong their crimson Lutheran-issue dresses lie abandoned. The caption under the photograph says *Outback Innocence*.

Stephen is not averse to spotting bare breasts but has scanned enough *Man* magazines at the barbers not to go overboard about it. Even Geoff is only slightly agog. So they are both unprepared for the sudden change in their father's behaviour, his tearing the Inter-Den from his teeth, his controlled, tight-lipped instruction:

'Give me that!' His long upper lip has turned pale. He snatches the Naked Lubra Calendar from the boys. 'Not the sort of thing for children. They shouldn't be allowed to print pictures like that where kids can see them. Get the wrong idea completely.'

He stamps off to his bedroom with the offending calendar and from the ensuing jingling and slamming noises he has obviously hidden it under the penny box in his socks and handkerchiefs drawer. He returns to the dining-room as their mother is leaning over the table, balanced on one foot, clearing away the dinner dishes. He sits down and pours himself a beer in the pewter tankard from the Cottesloe Golf Club. He speaks:

'Your frock is too short, Jean,' he says, addressing the rosewood sideboard. 'Your bottom is showing.'

(Their mother is still in her tennis dress. She is the former Jean Dolan who made the State singles finals every year between 1932 and 1940. Now she plays with female friends of the patacake volley, underarm service variety. She was once virtually engaged to Athol Hedge the Davis Cup player in the late thirties and Stephen has played for years with a Dunlop Maxply racquet Hedge gave her. He reached the Wimbledon singles finals with it, losing to Don Budge shortly before Budge's Grand Slam. It has A.H. embossed on the leather grip and is light enough for a woman because Hedge was one of those neat, suave players who rarely ruffled their hair, relying on elegant place shots rather than a powerful forehand or service. Whenever his name is mentioned Murray Crisp grumbles, 'That siss!')

Her mouth contracts into fine creases around the lips. 'It *is* a tennis frock,' she says. (Murray doesn't really approve of her playing tennis. He has been more successful in preventing her, by a determined lack of interest rather than outright opposition, from joining the golf club as an associate or buying a small car for the shopping. He likes her at home where he knows where she is. 'In case of some emergency or other,' he says. He likes to tell dinner guests over the Drambuie that when Jean married him she married Halistroms, too. 'I told her that right from the outset. She understands that.' At that stage she usually goes out for more coffee.

At forty she is still an attractive woman, with slim legs, a good figure, no visible varicosity or skin blotches and dark blonde hair passed on to Geoffrey. She sighs a lot, her sons sense half-consciously, and stiffens just noticeably when her husband kisses her hello or removes lint from her clothing with elaborately quiet attention. They are therefore amazed, her sons, to see old photographs of the young Murray and Jean at weekend picnics, clowning on ferry cruises and, thin and brown in funny woollen swimsuits, holding hands and smiling into each other's features.)

Their father is not ready to simmer down yet, is driven by personality and events to keep picking away at unsatisfactory silences and vibrations. 'No one ever tells me anything.' He calls out this statement from the dining-room to the kitchen, aims it through the door, around the breakfast 'nook' and past the cupboards and electric stove to the refrigerator, where their mother now hovers with a bottle of milk in her hand. 'I didn't know you were playing tennis today. You could at least keep me informed.'

'You know I play every Wednesday. Do you want a blow-by-blow account? God knows I get out of the house rarely enough.'

'All I ask is a little information about your comings and goings.' He takes a long draught from the tankard. 'I suppose you were gadding about with Beryl O'Brien.' (Beryl O'Brien likes to drink scotch in the daytime and flirts with men not her husband. She is often introduced into arguments, by either side.)

'Don't be ridiculous, Murray. You come home tight and start picking at everyone. First the children, now me. Act your age, why don't you.'

'Thank you very much. Thank you, Jean. I suppose you encourage the children to see filthy photographs. That would be your style.'

'You're mad! You brought the bloody thing home. You're the one with the peculiar mind.'

The father rises to his feet, eyes bulging. The boys are edgy with fear and fascination. The nostrils have dilated on cue, suddenly revealing the gingery hair they look for at such times. He thumps down the Teams Stableford tankard on the table. Beer froths over the rim and trickles down the side of the tankard.

'Don't swear at me, Jean. Don't ever swear at me if you know what's good for you!'

The mother, face crumpled, throws down the tea towel she has been clutching and runs from the room. The scalloped hemline of her tennis dress flicks around her thighs, her rubber soles squeak on the kitchen linoleum. The bedroom door slams.

'Don't play the prima donna with me, Jean. That cuts no ice with me.' He paces the room, sits down again and drains the tankard. Suddenly, his eyes lit by inspiration, he's on his feet again, digging into his wallet, plucking out a handful of notes, striding towards the bedroom door. He pushes open the door and throws in the money.

'Here, buy yourself a dress that doesn't display your privates.'

Presbyterian-trained Murray Crisp never swore in front of his family or told off-colour jokes. Stephen was working in the mailroom at Hallstroms when Biven of the puppet-penis said he'd heard his father was the most popular man in the saloon bar of the Shaftesbury Hotel of an evening, and not just because he was one of the bosses. Always ready with a quip and a beer for the workers and an eye-twinkle and a doff of the Akubra for the pointy-breasted stenographers sipping a Friday night Pimms.

'Funny bloke, your old man. I suppose he's told you the joke about the brothel doctor down at Roe Street?'

'What?' Unbelievable. But then there was the evidence of the *Mirror*, the sex-and-scandal paper his father brought home from the golf club every Saturday night and then burnt in the incinerator every Sunday morning. Stephen was so impressed with this weekly scenario that he began buying it himself, and a packet of Turf to go with it, stretching out in the municipal rose gardens to smoke and read items like:

A 22-year-old socialite is recovering after surgery in Royal Perth Hospital following an unusual assault on her during a three-day champagne orgy with four American airforce officers.

The beautiful redhead, whose father is a prominent grazier and businessman, was lying nude in a champagne-filled bath at her luxury Mount Street flat when the assault occurred.

Naked as the day he was born, an excited Yank airman, inflamed by passion and copious draughts of champagne and bourbon whiskey, chewed off a champagne-flavoured nipple.

The injured girl, who is shortly to be married to an up-and-coming member of the local legal fraternity now visiting London, was rushed to hospital in a taxi by her two equally attractive flatmates and two of the airmen.

One of the girls, a vivacious 21-year-old blonde often seen at charity balls, told a *Mirror* special reporter: 'We were just entertaining some friends for cocktails when the accident occurred. Keep our names out of this or your job won't be worth a brass razoo.'

A U.S. officer attached to the RAAF base, Pearce, was later interviewed by police but no charges were laid.

The heading above the story said:

TIT BIT IN MOUNT ST.

But usually the *Mirror* dwelt each week on events in a less fashionable locale the other side of the tracks. Roe Street was an important part of Western Australia's cultural heritage: grist for the mill of countless farmers, miners, fruit pickers, fishermen, sailors, visiting football teams, randy tourists and Italian, Greek and Yugoslav migrants. The Biggest Quasi-Official Brothel in the Southern Hemisphere. Virtually untrammelled by the police, reasonably disease free, the street was an address burned into the mind of every Perth schoolboy.

'But what do they do there?' Stephen was embarrassed to have asked his friend Harley Onslow in sixth grade.

The world-weary Harley knew it all. 'The wogs put their dicks into ladies,' he said.

Sauntering down the street on the way home from school, peering into the tiny cottages, Stephen imagined the wild carnality going on behind the dusty shutters. Private school boarders regularly broke bounds and—acne-faced sons of farmers and skinny pale progeny of diplomats—strode through Roe Street in their mélange suits and pale blue caps asking the prostitutes politely, 'How much for a do?'

An old madam called Dora sat every afternoon on her front step in a pink chenille dressing gown cleaning her budgerigar's cage. 'Come back when you've got hairs on your balls,' she'd laugh. 'Unless you want to fuck Bertie here.'

The girls of Roe Street would screw anyone but schoolboys and Aborigines. Even so, Stephen wasn't so crazy as to let his father know he'd loitered there.

The first magpie yodel woke him, ululating into his sleep. Sun rays filtered through the Moreton Bay fig tree and the flywire wall of the sleepout and fell on the wardrobe door, dancing lightly on the scratched varnish and reflecting the crisscross patterns of the flywire. Dust motes in these early rays scrambled skittishly from his breath, still coming fast from his usual nightmare: about *teaques*. Not t-e-a-k-s or t-e-e-k-s but always spelled with a Q and U. Even in the dream he knew this was the correct spelling. They resembled dugongs, sea-cows, with rubbery tits and hag faces. But they were no sea-sirens mistaken for mermaids by lonely and romantic sailors. They smiled shyly at Stephen while suckling baby teaques at the breast. There he'd be, wandering along White Beach or fishing from the crabbing jetty and they'd flap into shore on their backs with quick flicks of their tail flippers and flummock joyfully up to him, crooning and rubbing their backs and bellies on his bare legs, adoring as puppies. But their skin was rougher than a shark's and grazed his thighs and calves. And when he shooed them away and ran up the beach, up the hill towards home, thick clods of teaque shit stuck to his feet like cowpats. When he shook and stamped them clean he saw his soles torn away, through to the bone.

Eating dried apricots from a jar he and Harley Onslow lay on their stomachs at the cliff edge of the Onslows' grounds at Peppermint Grove while the Onslows' red and white Collie capered about and a willy-wagtail flicked from the trees and swooped the dog for nesting hair.

'Want to hear a poem?' Harley asked, and recited it anyway:

Abba-dabba pudding,
Green snot pie,
Dead dog's liver,
Squashed blow-fly.
Makes a good sandwich,
Spread it on thick.
Then wash it down
With a cup of cold sick.

They were shaded from the heat by blue-gums that rose without a bark ripple from the Onslows' lawn. Willows sloped languidly over gravel paths, trailed limp fronds on the grass. At the foot of the cliff the river stretched tightly into the far eastern distance. Four or five miles upriver a cluster of small grey shapes moved slowly in formation towards Peppermint Grove. As they glided closer the boys saw they weren't boats but creatures of some kind. They slid speedily through the water with no splashing and half-smiles on their wrinkled faces. Stephen perceived that they were teaques, but had suspected this all along. They gathered at the foot of the cliff and trod water, mumbling to themselves while their flipper-legs fluttered in the river, Then the biggest teaque flopped out of the water onto the Onslows' boat landing and regarded them intently, squinting up into the sun.

'We want you, Stephen,' it crooned in a deep but not unpleasant voice.

'Why?' His throat was dry as sand.

'We've come to eat the rich people,' the teaques cried together, clambering out of the river and hauling themselves up the steep steps towards the cliff top.

'We've come to eat the snobs and nip their dickies off,' they sang, their blubber shining in the sun.

'I'm not rich. This isn't my house. My father was killed in the war,' he lied. 'I'm a Legacy ward, I'm poor.'

Still the teaques flopped across the lawn towards him. Their breath had the stink of an old bait tin and its rankness seared his skin. They encircled him, snuffling and grunting while he clutched his pants with terrified hands.

'Eat him,' he yelled suddenly, pointing at Harley. 'His name is Harley Onslow and he's very rich. This is his house and his father is just about a millionaire. Bite his off!'

And the teaques slowly turned and sniffed the richness of Harley's freckled skin and did as he suggested. They ate his skin off layer by layer and he didn't cry out. He just lay there on the grass reciting *Abba-Dabba Pudding* quietly, like a prayer, until he was gone.

Morning, early and already hot. Padding past his parents' room (and a couple of muffled early morning farts from his father), through the kitchen and down the back steps into the yard where he pissed on the lemon tree as usual, saving some for the moss growing along the damp side of the laundry. The moss hung in dead brown strands where he had already been but the lemon tree seemed to thrive on it. He unpegged his bathers and shirt from the clothes-line and changed out of his pyjamas. He collected his kylies and gidgie from the laundry and walked down to the river, the dry buffalo grass bristling under his feet.

Already at 6 a.m. most of the Claremont homes were awake. Ruffle-headed men in pyjamas or khaki gardening shorts blurrily doused their buffalo and couch grass with enough water to last out the day. Sprinklers whirred and clattered, spreading sparkling arcs of water. Small rainbows flashed and vanished on shrubbery and rose-bush. Rivulets coursed through sparsely covered lawns before sinking into the sand, passing briefly over the bodies of sergeant ants and slate-grey beetles which shook their feelers dry and marched on. Claremont had its taps on full-bore, its water-pressure fully extended. 8 a.m. was curfew and until 6 p.m. the Government forbade all hosing, sprinkling or squirting. Summer in Perth, Western Australia, and the dam was low. Prosecution and middle-class ignominy awaited offenders.

Stephen went kylie-ing of an early morning. The river sat smoothly on its sandy basin and any small disturbance could be seen on its surface. Trumpeters and gobbleguts nibbled weed and algæ breakfasts in the shallows. Mullet snapped at insects, flashing silver whorls. A light air carried impressions of grassy things, lizards and salt bush. A lone inflated condom bobbed near shore. *A French Letter!* Later the Easterly would blow through the city and across the river estuary changing these dead inland smells, desert grit and wheat stalk particles into misty spindrift, whirling out across the ocean towards Africa.

The seasoned fisherman, he thought himself. He waded out to the edge of the seaweed with the kylies to where the trumpeters fed. The river crept up his legs. Twenty yards or so from the fish he stopped and waited for the ripples to disappear and for the river to form smoothly around him. He raised a boomerang-shaped kylie between forefinger and thumb above his head. (It was a design centuries old, being adapted by the local Aborigines, using metal scraps, from the wooden kylies of their past.) He stood like an Aborigine, poised and skinny, waiting for the fish to surface. Then he threw one kylie, and then the other. They sliced into the river, into the panicking school, cutting and stunning.

His mother acted proud of him. She put the four or five small mutilated fish in the refrigerator, promising to eat them for lunch. She really would eat a little of them if he were home to see. Otherwise the cat might get them. But she went to the trouble if he were there.

Awash in random recollections Crisp conjured up his tenth birthday. He went swimming alone at White Beach in the late afternoon. There had been no birthday party again because it was January and all his friends were away on holiday. He felt duty bound to wear his gift yellow satin-elastic Jantzen trunks. Anyway, he wanted to try out his underwater mask and flippers, also presents from his parents. Down the ramp to the beach he went—a towel around the waist hiding the shiny yellowness—noticing on his way a crowd of children and adults shuffling around the cliff top above the beach. The children were anxious and nervy and jumped about uneasily in their wet bathers. Sweating heavily, two men were trying to haul a pony up over the cliff edge. The horse, one of several shaggy plump pets which usually grazed in the bush above the beach, had stumbled over the cliff top while eating lupins and lay four or five feet below with a leg wedged fetlock deep in a rock buttress. It was snorting with fear and pain, frothy mucus dripping onto the rocks and hanging in strings from its jaw and neck rope.

'Piss off you kids!' one of the men shouted. 'Out of the way.' He scattered them with a cursory wave of a tree branch. Stephen moved off around the headland and down to the beach.

All the five o'clock regulars were there, cooling off the day's sweat: Mr Oldmeadow the town clerk stepping floridly down the ramp in his solar topee and flannel dressing gown; the Grundy brothers, three older boys he knew, prodding around the rocks with bamboo sticks, scooping up jellyfish and flinging them at one another. He sat in his yellow satin-elastics under the tea-tree hedge which overlooked the beach, hidden from the beach, until the Grundys waded out of sight around the headland. He wasn't sure if they'd laugh at the trunks. He wasn't too sure about them himself.

Through the tea-tree he saw Mr Oldmeadow throw off his dressing gown and helmet, take three or four deep breaths and charge for the water. Pink fat wobbled down his back. He hit the water with a smack and struck out strongly with a wide overarm stroke. He counted his strokes. Sixty-five, sixty-six. The town clerk was just a flurry of foam beyond the weed line.

He crawled out from behind the hedge, fastened the string of his trunks, walked into the river and flopped down. He sat in the shallows and stretched the flippers over his feet, rinsed the glass of his mask and put it on. Then he slipped down to the river bottom, flapped his feet and drifted into the deep. Waving weed fronds stroked his stomach, blowfish darted between his legs. He surfaced for air, rising slowly up on his side so he could be both in and out of the water simultaneously. Above, the sky was turning pink in the south-west over Blackwall Reach. Below, lettuce-green weeds trembled in underwater currents. The glassy line bisecting air and water divided his face mask in two halves. He bet himself he was the only person in Australia and probably the world doing exactly that at that precise moment.

Mr Oldmeadow swam slowly back to shore, kicking along on his back, his stomach in the air, making popping noises with his mouth. As he churned past Stephen sank down to the bottom and watched him pass overhead. The town clerk's legs were pale, almost luminous, and, except for bald patches on the calves, covered in fine waving hairs. His feet were lemony with horny nails and waxen corns on the toes. Mr Oldmeadow had an appendix scar that distorted the pink globular swoop of his belly. When he reached the shallows he dived a hand into his trunks to rearrange his genitals before stepping ashore.

When everyone had left the beach Stephen took off the mask and flippers and ran back into the river, weightless and free. He swam out to the deep, looked around carefully and removed his bathers. Clutching them in one hand he sank to the bottom and rolled and played. Then he wanted to crap, a tricky business underwater because he found he couldn't squat properly and the waves rocked him off balance. Eventually the turd bobbed up from under and floated off majestically up the estuary. He watched it for several minutes, glad there was no one about to pin it on him. Another first, he bet himself: an Underwater Birthday Shit.

Back inside his yellow Jantzen's he trudged up the ramp from the beach, the flippers and mask strung along one arm, around the headland towards home. He remembered the pony, saw the men still labouring over it in the distance, moved cautiously towards them. The crowd of kids had gone, only the awestruck Grundy brothers still watched. They said nothing as he came up, their eyes fastened on the panting workmen. The men had rigged up a block and tackle around a tree. The horse was dead, shot through the head. The mane was clotted with blood. One of the men, having already severed its legs, was standing with blood on his desert boots sawing off its head. The other man was attaching the pulley chain to the carcase.

'Hey, Snow,' he called to Stephen. 'Want a leg for the dog?'

'I haven't got a dog,' he whispered, and ran home. He must have dropped the face mask—it was missing when he arrived. He retraced his steps but couldn't find it. He wouldn't return all the way to look for it so one of the Grundys probably picked it up. Next day they denied it, naturally.

Why did these old memories concern him now? Why was he so engrossed in himself? Crisp wondered. Self-awareness, the problem of the urban colonial liberal. The trouble with being all that and alone as well was that you had all this fascinating stuff to reveal to people, bit by bit, and it was wasted; went unrecorded. That was no way to get your little slice of immortality.

3

The Savage Crows

THE SUN FELL through the bathroom window, warming Crisp's knees as he ruminated on the lavatory. It struck the blue shower curtain, shimmering over its slime-streaked motif of dolphins and seagulls. Humidity had blistered the paint on the bathroom walls. He picked abstractedly at the bubbles with a dead match from an overflowing heap on the rim of the bath below the bath heater.

Across the bay tiny workmen were faintly and rhythmically tapping metal on the high loops of the Big Dipper. More workmen were suspended like mountaineers on the huge clown's face at the entrance to Luna Park, painting the clown's eyebrows and chipping rust from his spidery steel lashes. From the boatyards below *Cardigan* came the whine of electric saws and an occasional shout or snatch of laughter. Crisp was more agitated than he could remember. He needed a focus. *I'm going round in circles*, he'd realized as soon as he woke, *fragmenting my case.*

What was his case? The thesis concerned aspects of the hunting down, slaughter, rape, infanticide, betrayal, deportation (redemption?) and extinction of a unique race of four or five thousand people. They inhabited a remote, mountainous and heavily wooded island the size of Scotland situated 150 miles south of eastern Australia between parallels 40° 33′ and 43° 39′ south latitude and between meridians 144° 39′ and 144° 23′ east longitude from God knew when until the last death in 1876.

Crisp thought it the most effective act of genocide the world had known.

His stated intention was to finish the thesis in time for the centenary of the death of the last Tasmanian, an old woman named Truganini, in 1976. The anniversary would be a fitting time to publish, even in the confines of a university press, a modern account of a fascinating but unevenly chronicled period of British colonial history. All the more apt because of the analogous current racial strife and so forth.

That was his story, pragmatic enough, for general circulation. He had researched copiously on the subject. He'd studied Bonwick's *The*

Last of the Tasmanians ('the woolly-haired Tasmanian no longer sings blithely on the stringy-bark biers or twines the snowy clematis blossom for his bride's garland. The bell but tolls his knell and the Aeolian music of the she-oak is his hymn and requiem') as well as Bonwick's *Daily Life and Origin of the Tasmanians* and his *Lost Tasmanian Race;* H. Ling Roth's *The Aborigines of Tasmania;* David Bunce's *Twenty-three Years' Wandering in the Australias and Tasmania*; James Erskine Calder's *Some Account of the Wars, Extirpation, Habits Etc. of the Native Tribes of Tasmania*; The Reverend John West's *History of Tasmania.* And others.

The Tasmanians' occurrence on the face of the earth, specifically the chin of it, Crisp had discovered during Australian history class when he was eleven or twelve, about 1955. They were regarded as a sad event, though black, wily, savage, untrustworthy, given to wanton outrages upon white inhabitants and no great respecters of property or livestock. They took up one chapter only in his history book, being noted chiefly as clever escapees from the Black Line, that shoulder-to-shoulder cordon of three thousand soldiers, police, settlers, traders and suckholing ticket-of-leave men which succeeded in snaring an eleven-year-old boy and one adult (sleeping) male called Nichay-manick, known to the authorities for once spearing a lame horse at Emu Bay.

So the cordon, which cost the small colony seventy thousand pounds, wasn't a *complete* disaster, Governor George Arthur possibly told his shaving mirror. And a great morale booster for the lads, who immediately formed themselves into the prestigious Liners' Club and held the first of their periodic banquets at the Macquarie Hotel where they munched imported luxuries and drank themselves comatose. Especially those merchants in the firearms, victualling, clothing and blacksmithing trades.

Dressing quickly, racing through breakfast (sniffing gingerly at a carton of apricot yoghurt, eating an apple instead), he was on a ferry within a half-hour, sitting up in the bow with the sun on his face. The day was warm but he shivered as the ferry passed through the shadow of the Harbour Bridge. From the bridge's pedestrian footway high above the boat an orange whirled through the air and plopped into the harbour. A droplet of water splashed on the seat beside him. Crisp felt single-minded now. He clutched two of his Tudor exercise books and carried a pocket of pens and pencils. He strode up the hill from Circular Quay to the Mitchell Library seeking a new direction.

For several weeks he now absorbed himself in the papers and journals of one George Augustus Robinson. This Robinson had enjoyed the reputation of 'The Conciliator' of the Tasmanians. His name cropped up frequently throughout the story of the Aborigines—and here Crisp was fortunate. Just recently the library had purchased from the estate of the late Arthur P. Robinson of Bath, England, a mass of papers which had belonged to his father, The Conciliator. The Robinson Papers comprised private and official correspondence, memoranda, random observations and other jottings, native vocabularies and a wealth of field journals covering his expeditions in search of the Aborigines.

Crisp's project assumed new significance. He lived and breathed Robinson. He saturated himself in the papers and journals during the day, wrote furiously at night on the slug-streaked table. He saw no one other than on his Saturday visits to Wendy, gave up his aimless Friday nights.

'Are you getting enough to eat?' Jane asked, showing concern for his pallor as he wolfed down coffee and crumpets.

'Certainly. I've been busy,' he said, bobbing his daughter on his knee, changing the subject by making appropriate horsey clip-clop noises, inhaling her sweet hair.

The thing was, he was enmeshed in the unpublished manuscript of a book which he found among the papers. It seemed that Robinson had written it a year or so before his death at the age of sixty-eight (according to his obituary in *The Gentleman's Magazine*) or seventy-eight (reportedly recorded on his tombstone). Taking the tombstone as correct, he'd been born in 1788, the year of Australia's first settlement, in London, the younger son of William and Susannah Robinson of Boston, Lincolnshire. William Robinson had established a small building and joinery business in the Islington district of London.

Of Robinson's early life Crisp could discover little. He did learn, however, that as a young man he was employed by Colonel Robert d'Arcy of the Royal Engineers in building martello towers for the defence of the south coast around Chatham. On 28th February 1814 Robinson, then presumably twenty-six, had married Maria Amelia Evens at Christchurch, Newgate Street. Only the barest of notes related to the early years of their marriage, but it seemed that the young couple continued living at Islington and that by 1818 Robinson had set up as a builder on his own account.

One thing was clear: by 1822 Robinson was restless. He was considering emigration, preferably to the Americas. Among his papers was a letter dated 4th March of that year from a shipping company advising that a passage was available to South America. In August 1923 he travelled up to Leith intending to embark on a ship there for the Poyais settlement on Nicaragua's Mosquito Coast. (In 1819 Sir Gregor MacGregor had bought from the Nicaraguans a land concession near the mouth of the Black River, issued a seductive prospectus and encouraged hundreds of Scots and Englishmen to apply for land and emigrate with their families. On arrival the immigrants found they had been duped. The land was largely swamp. Disease was rife. They died like flies and the survivors were eventually evacuated to Belize in Honduras.) The news of the Poyais swindle reached England in mid-1823. It seemed Robinson heard of it just in time, judging by a newspaper cutting found among his papers. He went to the Poyais office, cancelled his booking and transferred to a ship bound for Australia. On 9th September 1823 he sailed on the *Triton* under Captain Crear bound for New South Wales via Van Diemen's Land.

During the voyage he penned a note to his wife and five children at home at Islington: 'I undertake this voyage to make you and the family comfortable,' he wrote. 'Weather chiefly pleasant, though hazy with mizzling rain off Tenerife. Passengers a mixed sort though amiable enough. Captain Crear faithfully observes the Sabbath. The text on the last occasion was Corinthians II 5:10. All aboard sang two psalms of a seafaring nature whereby the congregation sighted a large school of porpoises to starboard.' The *Triton* arrived in Hobart Town on 20th January 1824.

In Hobart Town Robinson rented a house with other emigrants from the *Triton* and immediately earned some money doing carpentering jobs around the town. As a free settler he quickly obtained a government grant of a block of land in Elizabeth Street on the corner of Warwick Street and extending back to Murray Street. He made some useful business contacts and began to prosper. By October 1824 he was able to write to Maria: 'I am doing well, have all the respectable business in town and employ twelve men. I am worth four hundred pounds.' (Despite this glowing picture Maria Robinson did not come out to Van Diemen's Land until 1826. Finally she summoned up all her courage, gathered young George, Charles, Maria, William and Henry and set sail for Hobart Town on the *Greenock*.)

Crisp could discover only scrappy records for the first five years of Robinson's life in the colony. Jottings in his slanted, cramped hand (sometimes without punctuation, or he might pepper the page with full-stops and dashes; more often a sentence ended with a squiggle that seemed to represent a long trailing etc. etc.) indicated that he took an active part in Hobart Town's religious and charitable work. He became secretary of the Van Diemen's Land Seaman's Friend and Bethel Union Society and a committee member of the Auxiliary Bible Society. He was a regular visitor to the prisoners in gaol and, as he wrote, 'a comfort to condemned felons'. He was active in the foundation of the Van Diemen's Land Mechanics' Institute, of which he was elected the first chairman. By January 1829, at the age of forty and after five years in the colony, George Augustus Robinson had éclat in the small community as an industrious and public-spirited member of the burgeoning middle class.

But, curiously perhaps, at this stage of his middle life, Robinson was still an unfulfilled man. As he remarked in his lengthy introduction to his book:

'My mind became early and deeply impressed with the deplorable state of the aboriginal inhabitants. Although peaceable and inoffensive they struck me as poor and wretched. I saw thirty and forty at a time perambulating the streets of the capital in a condition of near nudity with no-one to watch over their interests. These simple people were thus left prey to the designs of the depraved of the white population, initiated into every species of crime and barbarously and inhumanly treated. They were grossly maligned by these evil-doers to cover their own malpractices. Their docility was attributed to sloth and supineness. (It was never imagined they would have the manliness to resist.) When they did retaliate it was in so direful a form that terror and consternation were spread throughout the colony. Peaceful settlements fell into frantic disorder and the houses of many families were turned into mourning.

'Physical force was advocated by the military, the police and many settlers. (Savages, they said, should be coerced to be controlled.) Armed police patrolled the districts. Military stations were formed. Tickets-of-leave were promised to convicts. Rewards of five pounds apiece were offered for every aboriginal captured alive. But all these repressions were to no purpose. Aggressions continued as usual. Terror spread throughout the colony. Nothing stayed the bloody proceedings.

'Returning home from the services at the Bethel one night I was pondering the problem. I wondered whether the aboriginals could be instructed, whether anything could be done for their moral, religious and material improvement. They were represented as a bare remove from brutes and incapable of instruction or rational thought. I could not believe that man could be so debased. Even brutes were accessible to kindness; how much more man, made after the express image of God!'

Such, Crisp noted, was Robinson's state of mind when a notice appeared in the *Hobart Town Gazette* offering fifty pounds a year, plus rations, to a steady person of good character who would reside upon Bruny Island and 'effect an intercourse' with the natives.

'The appointment was aimed at me,' Robinson wrote. 'Even though there were powerful reasons against my entering such an enterprise (I had a wife and now seven children dependent on me) I could not refuse. I reasoned the matter over with Mrs Robinson and with difficulty obtained her consent. I applied for the post, indicating my strong devotion to the cause. I submitted to the Governor that just as the degraded Hottentot had been raised in the scale of beings and the denizens of the Societies Islands made an industrious and intelligent race, so might the inhabitants of His Excellency's territory be instructed. I also begged leave to submit that the proposed salary be raised. "Should my offer be accepted I do not wish the superfluities, only the necessities of life. I wish to devote myself to these people."

'There were nine applications for the position but the Colonial Secretary informed me that mine was successful. I was elated. The Governor would consent to give me a salary of one hundred pounds a year to serve the natives, instruct them and their children and cultivate a little land for potatoes, etc., etc.

'My friends thought me rash and reckless for a man with my responsibilities to sacrifice a lucrative profession and live among savages for this salary. They set me down as demented and denounced it as a wild and visionary scheme. Happily, there were other friends who took a more favourable view and by them I was encouraged . . .'

The Savage Crows: *My Adventures Among the Natives of Van Diemen's Land*

G. A. Robinson

My endeavours began on 30th March 1829 when I left Hobart Town at 9.30 a.m. in a large whaleboat with six hands bound for Bruny Island lying close to the mainland due south. My official position was Storekeeper, certainly not a title for me to act vaingloriously! As I saw it, however, I had been placed in the vanguard of the movement for the amelioration of the natives. I had a twofold plan to carry out this object: by civilization and by instruction in the principles of Christianity.

I had already decided on the form of my civilization at Bruny. The site should have fertility of soil, proximity to fresh water, be contiguous to the shore and remote from settlers. The village should form three sides of a quadrangle opening to the beach—the mission house to be situated at the upper end so as to command a view of the whole establishment, the married persons to occupy one side, the single people the other. Each native family would have a log hut covered with bark. Each allotment was to be fenced. A school should be erected from logs, this building to answer—in the first instance—as a church for the performance of divine worship. A vegetable garden should be laid out.

How would I accomplish these targets?

By assisting the aboriginal to erect his hut.

By instructing him in preparing a few rods of land as a potato ground (the nourishing properties of the potato had recently been stressed by the Liverpool Institute of Medicine).

By prevailing on him to cook his food in the European manner and to catch fish to eat with his potatoes (the children, if practicable, should eat at a separate table—I am a great believer in the old saw *Children Should Be Seen But Not Heard*, one always observed in my own family).

By instructing the aboriginal in the principles of Christianity, first by public worship, second by public education. The school would open and conclude by prayer.

By adopting the education system of Doctor Andrew Bell (developed so successfully among the half-caste children of Madras) so the children would learn by repetition which took hold of the mind. The children would be taught in English.

In outlining these plans to His Excellency before my departure I had remarked that the formation of such an establishment was of primary importance. The aboriginal would receive Christian instruction. He would acquire sober British habits of industry. The establishment would produce its own potatoes. The natives would be content.

The Governor wished me well in my endeavours and served me tea.

4

Travels with Anna

ANNA, CRISP RECALLED, never used euphemisms. She did not receive *a little visitor* or experience *that time of the month* as Jane coyly had. When she had a period she might mutter, 'I'm bleeding like a stuck pig.' She would not complain of her ever-present monilia as *itchy privates* or somesuch. Paralleling her interest in the feminist movement came an even more direct wave of plain speaking. She felt bound to announce in a stage whisper in restaurants or at the cinema (squirming in her jeans), 'My cunt's playing up.' It often was. She tried and discarded a score of gynaecologists, returning home flushed and angry that the chauvinist male doctors had either put her down or patronized her as a silly girl needing a couple of babies to set her right. She went through every contraceptive pill on the market, IUDs, gels, and found nearly all unsatisfactory. She brought home packets of condoms, some imaginatively coloured, from a new vending machine strongly patronized by her history students at university and presented them to him with a flourish.

'Here, look what I've got for you.'

'Very racy. But why don't you try that new mild pill I read about?'

'You just don't want the responsibility.'

'It's the feel of the bloody things,' he said. A sensitive creature. 'And the whole production of it. Lacks spontaneity.'

On the subject of monilia, she had once published in one of the trendier women's magazines a playful letter headed *Get Your Knickers Off* in which she argued a case against underpants:

> The onslaught of monilia that is currently flourishing amongst women under thirty has been aggravated by certain 'technical advancements'. Dacron, nylon, bri-nylon, acrylic fibres—none of these materials is very absorbent. They create a warm damp climate in which monilia thrive. I am sure the wearing of underclothes results from sexual repression. The healthiest thing to do is to wear no underpants and a long skirt or, if you must, cotton underpants.

The heavy breathers must have had a field day, Crisp imagined, making obscene calls to every Kubic in the phone book. Anna, at that stage living with him at McMahon's Point, escaped molestation (though a sly-eyed English lecturer, laying on a heavy Southern accent, offered some pub advice: 'If it itches Ma'am, scratch it.').

Despite his 'bourgeois sensitivities' as she called them, he missed all this; her recently acquired and rather naive coarseness, her independence and enthusiasms, lusts and fantasies. Dark Anna—she was intelligent, kind, attractive and, he suspected, *a better person* than he was. He missed her company.

Not just around the flat. They had taken three memorable holidays together—one each year they were together—in New Guinea, North Queensland and, yes, Western Australia. In Port Moresby they stayed with the Commission's chief correspondent Tony Charlesworth and were stimulated by the political alchemy at work during the introduction of self-government. While Crisp had long discussions over glasses of South Pacific beer with budding politicians at the University Club, Anna pestered the Charlesworth's *boi* Beni for instructions on where to buy and how to get the maximum kick from betel nut. Beni eventually took her to Koki market and bought some nuts, pepper sticks and a gourd of lime.

'You got to chew with all your teeth,' he said, giggling as she mixed and masticated the fibrous sludge, slapping his thighs as the combination took effect.

Anna relaxed on the steps of the Charlesworth's apartment. 'Quite a buzz. Phew!' Cross-legged, tanned, dressed in a bright cotton shift, she was in close harmony with the tropical landscape and the languid movements of the wharf labourers unloading cargo on the jetty beneath the apartment block. She spat the wad into the poincianas and laughed up at Crisp. Her teeth and gums were as red as those of the old crab sellers in the market.

Anna made a strong impression on Port Moresby. Bra-less, her breasts jigged beneath a *Pangu Pati* T-shirt. Papuan eyes rolled as she strolled through the town. They were drinking milk shakes in one of the trading stores when a fat white waitress behind the counter chastised a middle-aged Papuan plate-scraper. The man was elbow-deep in sink water.

'Hurry up with those spoons, you stupid ape,' the waitress yelled, and licked a glob of icing from her thumb. The man hunched embarrassedly over his suds. A dozen customers perched on stools around the counter peered over their drinks at him.

'You dumb racist bitch,' said Anna in a clear voice. 'Wash your own fucking spoons.'

The waitress appeared apoplectic. She waved a pair of cake tongs at Anna. She clenched at them so they snapped at her like crab claws.

'Get out of here you filthy commos. Causing trouble. I'll call the manager. Get out of here with your dirty street language.'

Anna was also away and shouting. 'Why don't you leave this country to the locals instead of ripping it off?' The other customers clucked and tutted over iced coffees. Crisp took her arm and led her away. The waitress pursued them, still snapping her cake tongs. Black faces looked up in bemusement from menial tasks and watched the procession straggle to the door. On the street Anna gave the waitress the finger sign through the shop window. Crisp was uncomfortable about the whole fracas and embarrassed on several levels.

Serenity, though, was recovered. Tony and Janet Charlesworth gave a small dinner party for them. One of the guests was a talkative anthropologist, Doctor Warren Logie from U.C.L.A. Logie had spent the past six months working in the Highlands and around Port Moresby with an archaeological team from the Australian National University. The team was investigating the old theory that the Tasmanians had migrated south from Asia through New Guinea and eastern Australia during several thousand years of nomadic roaming. Logie supported it. (At this stage Crisp's later obsession was only embryonic but he was nonetheless interested to hear Logie's viewpoint.)

The American was yellow-haired and earnest and, though no more than thirty-five, dressed in the floppy casual tropical gear of a Florida senior citizen.

'We started off with the old premise of T. H. Huxley,' he said. 'Huxley noticed physical similarities between the Tasmanians and the Melanesians of New Guinea, New Caledonia and the Torres Strait islands. He concluded that a pioneering group of these negritoes managed to get to Tasmania by making short voyages down the eastern seaboard. Along a chain of small islands that later probably sunk. Either that or they made the whole trip by sea. But the sea-drift theory doesn't hold water, if you'll excuse the pun. The Tasmanians had no sea legends, few sea skills and only very rudimentary rafts. And they had taboos against eating scale fish.'

'Is that so?' Anna said. She seemed to have a stupid aversion to some Americans.

Crisp, though, was fascinated. He liked to hear specialists talking animatedly of their craft. It had an almost hypnotic effect on him. (His father, a keen do-it-yourself carpenter—a skill learned from Pop Crisp who'd been a *real* builder and carpenter—had once nearly mesmerised him while making a mortise-and-tenon joint. Still when he smelled fresh wood shavings he could hear his father, unusually contented, chatting as he planed and chiselled: 'The mortise-and-tenon is the most useful joint you can have, son. Use it for joining ordinary square-edged pieces of wood. When you've got a special piece of wood—one with grooving or moulding, say—you make a few slight variations and Bob's-your-uncle.' He'd let him use his chisels and even his steel jack plane until he left it out in the rain.)

Logie, sucking on a glass of local beer, warmed to his subject. 'Precious little excavation has been done in New Guinea and Indonesia. But we've turned up a couple of interesting things near Wewak. Crude implements, weapons and so on that we think have Tasmanoid characteristics.'

'How interesting,' Janet Charlesworth said, and munched an after-dinner mint.

Beni padded silently into the room to remove the dinner things. The guests, all of whom were against the idea of servants, said 'Hello Beni' rather loudly and were helpful passing him the dishes.

'Why do you call them boys? It's so demeaningly colonial and racist,' Anna said. Everyone agreed. Beni padded out with the plates.

Tony Charlesworth said, 'It's *boi*. Pidgin is such a bloody ugly language, but the locals use it themselves so there's not much you can do to stop those white supremacist connotations.'

Crisp stretched back in his padded cane chair, vaguely uncomfortable. His eye was caught by a translucent gecko hunting insects on the ceiling. It captured a moth, quickly despatched it. Warm scented air wafted up the hillside from the harbour. Below them in the street young men wearing T-shirts advertising beer and car mufflers sauntered towards the town's excitement. Some were arm in arm or had their arms around each other's waist. A few had leaves or a single feather stuck in their hair. Their feet stirred up puffs of dust. Logie drawled on.

'To students of the Tasmanian mystery perhaps the biggest discovery was made by one of your Aussie anthropologists, Norman Tindale. Back in the thirties he found an old faded photograph taken in the 1890s or thereabouts of some North Queensland Aborigines. He saw right away they were clearly Tasmanoid in appearance.'

'Clever,' Anna said. 'For an Aussie.'

'So he set out to find the descendents of the people in the picture. And he did, helped by a mentor of mine from U.C.L.A., Professor Joseph Birdsell, by the way. The Aborigines of the Atherton Tableland were found to be small and graceful. Some had dark skin, others light brown. They seemed to be the descendants of Tasmanians who'd been assimilated into the tribal structure of the Australian Aborigines.'

The American took an unusually dainty sip from his beer. 'All in all the evidence seems to support the theory of transcontinental migration.'

'But how did they end up in Tasmania?' Crisp asked, curious to know but mostly not wanting to dissipate the pleasant daze induced by Logie's monologue. Anna raised her eyebrows at him.

'You had a situation where a number of family groups found their way down to the bottom of a well-timbered peninsula teeming with game and remained there. Then at some unknown time in history the peninsula became separated from the mainland. With the melting of the polar ice-cap the level of the ocean rose and what is now Bass Strait appeared. The small family groups multiplied and spread into tribes. For centuries this race remained isolated, cut off by the sea, retaining its simple way of life.

'Noble savages,' Charlesworth said, freshening their drinks.

'They stayed in this state of suspended animation, like so many ants in amber, until the European explorers arrived in the eighteenth century.'

'And the trouble began,' Crisp said.

'Now you're wondering what happened to the negritoes who didn't follow their fellows down into what became Tasmania. Well, those who stayed on the mainland were killed by the Australian Aborigines. Between ten and twenty thousand years ago—none of us can agree on a date—the Australians may have followed the same trail across the land bridge from Asia. They were better hunters than the Tasmanians. They had more sophisticated weapons—boomerangs and so forth—and they had dogs, which went wild and became the dingoes of today. They were cruel to their enemies. Those negritoes not killed were assimilated. So the Tasmanians disappeared from the Australian mainland and only the sea barrier of Bass Strait prevented their complete extinction by the Australian Aborigines.'

Logie gave a small smile, leaned back in his chair. 'That job was to be undertaken much more rapidly and efficiently by you fellows. Your ancestors, anyway.'

Crisp heard Anna's sharp intake of breath across the room. He was also about to make the obvious defensive retort, but the American salvaged the moment.

'Not that we've got a perfect record on that sort of thing.'

At night they made sweaty love to the accompaniment of cicadas, shrill night birds and the soft alarming sound of Beni's feet on the gravel outside their louvered bedroom. Beni seemed to hardly sleep at night but wandered between the grey, gaol-like tavern and the cramped fibro *boihaus* behind the apartments with the *wantoks* from his home village. Sometimes, full of beer, a *wantok* would press his face to the louvers and give a blood-curdling yell to terrify the whites. It never failed. The first time Anna clutched at him so frantically her nails tore his chest; his larynx ceased to function, muscles turned to jelly and awaited the headhunter's machete. Only nervous giggling from Beni and the sounds of drunken stumbling in the bushes allayed their white dead-of-night fears. In the morning curds of betel phlegm hung from their windows. They found Beni curled up asleep on the rough cement gully-trap in the back yard. His head rested like a child's on the plastic Pan Am bag in which he kept all his possessions. He was dressed in one of Janet Charlesworth's cast-off blouses. His sinewy black neck bulged from the Peter Pan collar.

Tony Charlesworth said, 'Things don't seem as cut and dried when you've been here a while.'

Crisp sent his father a postcard from Port Moresby. It showed Baiyer River tribesmen shaking their spears in mock anger. During the war Murray Crisp had piloted Boston bombers in New Guinea, carrying his bomb load from daunting mountain airstrips up into metallic rainclouds and dumping them on all things Japanese. He was then lean and brown, sported a handlebar moustache and was pictured in the family album posing bare-chested with comrades in front of tents and coconut palms. He was also shown shaking hands with faithful wartime Fuzzy Wuzzies and bouncing chubby Papuan babies on the knee. The album displayed, in contrast, several photographs of he and his fellow trainee pilots (then paler, younger, more round of cheek) lined up in innocent rows in their blue goon suits at Point Cook, Victoria. A few downy moustaches aside, they looked like schoolboys. As for his father's New Guinea war he gleaned two pieces of information: he'd had a pet marsupial squirrel called Mo (after the comedian Roy Rene) which nested in his shirt pocket, and he refused ever after to wear rubber thonged sandals. They reminded him of the Japs, he said.

On the postcard Crisp wrote: 'Dear Dad, Having an enjoyable time in N.G. You wouldn't know the place. Cheers, Stephen.'

I cannot easily describe the emotions of excitement and curiosity I felt as I approached the island. I regarded it as a mirror in which I hoped to find the reflections of my faith. We were blessed with pleasant weather, the wind was favourable and the men in good spirits. We reached Rat's Bay on north Bruny three hours after leaving the mainland. Here we made our first contact with the natives. Four of them—three men and a girl clad only in kangaroo skins—greeted us most amiably, uttering occasional words of English. Obviously they were used to intercourse with Europeans. The female was named Truganini, the men called Mangana (whom I took to be her father), Wooraddy and Weanee. Truganini was aged about twenty and was very much the coquette. The men deferred quite chivalrously to her, whether because of her vivacious personality, some higher status or simply because of her greater command of English I did not know.

I invited them to eat with us, offering some tea and biscuit. I was curious to observe how these people conducted the ceremony of their meal and my curiosity was soon gratified. The small slender girl produced a woven grass bag from around her neck and withdrew from it a large lump of tree gum. She handed the gum to one of the men who threw it on the fire. He also placed on the coals a small kangaroo or wallaby, ungutted and complete with fur, and the gum and the meat smoked and fizzed together, the stickiness clinging to the singed fur. Shortly Mangana, the eldest warrior, snatched the kangaroo out of the fire and plunged his face into its entrails. He ate happily for several minutes and then threw the carcase back on the embers. It sizzled for a moment before Wooraddy grabbed it up and, ripping the tail and legs asunder and nipping off the choicest portions, satisfied his hunger for three or four minutes. The meat was then passed to the young man

Weanee who gorged himself on the thinner flesh around the ribs and back before throwing the remaining half-picked bones, skin and meat shreds to Truganini. She received these leftovers with a degree of respect and submissiveness which surprised me, owing to the men's deference to her earlier. After they had all satisfied themselves of the meat they gladly shared our tea and biscuit, appearing no strangers to these comestibles.

We set up temporary camp at Birches Bay, a sawyers' settlement, while I surveyed the island to find a site for our civilization. I hit upon the idea of taking Truganini with me as a sable guide, this island being her home and she holding such a strong place in the affections of the other aboriginals. She was a friendly creature, quite unabashedly plucking at the red hairs on my forearms with some curiosity and delight.

"Kangaroo fur,' she said.

Our boat proceeded around the coastline from Isthmus Bay to Little Cove, the men pulling against adverse winds, and then to Great Cove. Here I took two men and surveyed the interior, tramping through an extensive swamp where narrow passages wound in a serpentine fashion towards a central clear space. Truganini informed me the trails had been burnt by the natives so they might hunt kangaroos with their dogs. We traversed a vast extent of clear country interspersed with copses which formed a cover for the kangaroo and returned to the boat much fatigued. After some refreshment we proceeded back to Birches Bay through a heavy sea, arriving back late at night. I was very unwell in the stomach and head. I remained ill the next day though it being the Sabbath I preached to the sawyers at their camp. Seventy were present and very attentive. After the service I returned to my sickbed, too unwell for any journeying.

No more than ten days had passed since my arrival on Bruny before I found there were disadvantages in having settlers and sawyers inhabiting the island. One James Kelly had grants of land at the northern end of the island. I soon discovered that the convict servants at Kelly's farm were enticing the natives with food, clothing and tobacco for which the women were submitting to immoral practices. I proceeded to the farm and cautioned Kelly's men about their improper conduct.

'If it occurs again I will make an example of you,' I warned them, informing them of my close relationship with the Governor. I stayed the night at the farm but was very inhospitable entertained, having to sleep in a draughty outhouse and brew my own tea. Fortunately I had some biscuit in my knapsack. Amazingly Mr Kelly seemed to take his convicts' side in our disagreement.

I returned to camp next morning to find a group of downcast natives at my tent.

'Weanee been sick and die,' Mangana told me. I was astonished at this news. Apart from some sort of scorbutic affliction of the legs the young man had seemed perfectly healthy when I last saw him.

'Where is his body?'

'On the fire,' said Mangana.

They took me to the place where they had burned him. There was a heap of ashes with some grass and sticks piled on top in a small mound. The women were bewailing Weanee's death, tears coursing down their cheeks. That night I wrote off a request to the Governor on the matter of comforts for ill natives.

I found myself assuming a protective nature over the natives on the island. No sooner had I chastised the servants at Kelly's farm about their immoral relations with the native women than I found two of the convicts trying to entice the women away, not half a mile from our establishment. They were chiefly ogling after Truganini. She, in her way, was neither encouraging nor modest in the European style but like most of the aboriginal women had a keen sensual curiosity and a desire for the material luxuries.

'Get back to your farm. Mr Kelly will hear of your insubordination.' I told them their pardons would be far distant if I caught them again interfering with the natives. The men sloped off, mumbling insolently into their shirt fronts. A pair of reprobates.

That afternoon I had similar insolence from one of my own convicts, Samuel Hopkins. The man refused to work in loading the whaleboat with supplies for my journeying.

'This is no work for an Englishman. Acting the slave for the heathen. Bloody savage crows.' A dark-jawed fellow, he had the felon's shifty cast about the eyes. I sent him up to Hobart Town in charge of the overseer to cool his mood in gaol.

The following day, taking two convicts and two natives, I travelled through the bush towards Isthmus Bay to select a suitable site for our civilization. I got benighted sooner than I expected, the evenings falling unexpectedly in these parts.

After mizzling rain at dawn pleasant weather broke through next morning. We continued our journey and after two hours came to the head of Isthmus Bay. Here, on 29th April, I decided to take up my grant of five hundred acres and establish my civilization. I set out the site of the village on a gentle declivity leading down to the bay, the site delightfully pleasant and close to the water. After partaking of a tasty meal of perch and biscuits I left the convicts to erect a hut and departed with the natives for our temporary camp. (I had persuaded the natives to eat some fish only with great difficulty. It seemed they had some aversion to scale fish of which I was unaware when drawing up my sustenance schemes for the mission.)

I was anxious to begin work immediately. I travelled to Hobart Town and arranged for supplies, bricks, sashes and other building materials as well as slop clothing and sulphur medicine to be sent down to Isthmus Bay on the *Prince Leopold*. On 14th May the whole party removed to the new establishment, travelling across from our camp over rocks and through thick brushwood. On our arrival I found the brig unloading the bricks. The convicts had halfway completed a small hut. An aboriginal couple with the white names Joe and Morley and their two small children had made their way overland from Rat's Bay to the new settlement and I greeted them warmly as our first arrivals.

I read to the prisoners of the Crown the regulations for their observance. I also transmitted to all the settlers on the island, particularly Mr Kelly's men, letters from the Governor requesting them not to interfere with the natives.

For the next four days I employed the men in erecting the hut and burning scrub. Hitherto my days had been occupied in superintending the prisoners, but now I had time to converse with the natives and soon obtained upwards of sixty words for a vocabulary. They presented me with some waddies and baskets as gifts. Truganini demonstrated that the baskets were made of rushes of a kind they called *i-ris*. She first placed the grasses on a slow fire to give them a tenacity that enabled her to twist them into threads. Then she nimbly plaited the threads together into a basket of semi-globular shape. The waddy was a most effective weapon, about eighteen inches long and two inches in diameter, of a straight spiral form and made of she-oak hardwood. The men were remarkable dextrous in using this missile and seldom missed their target. They were expert in throwing stones also, able to brain any fast moving creature at a good distance.

Morley, wife of the aboriginal Joe, was much afflicted with some unsightly disease in these first few days. Her lamentations were most disheartening, increasing in intensity day by day. I gave her a blanket and some sulphur ointment. I also anointed her children with ointment for the scabrous sores on their legs.

On the fourth day in our new home, 17th May, we celebrated the Sabbath. I read the scriptures and felt much comfort in the Acts of the Apostles. The small band of natives was most attentive to the service, the convicts less so. That afternoon Joe went in pursuit of game for his sick wife, returning shortly with two wallabies. He skinned the animals with a piece of glass bottle and offered Morley the entrails, these portions being much favoured by the people. She tried to eat but could not swallow. The next morning she was evidently much worse. She appeared in a dying state and looked wishfully at me as if anxious for me to afford her relief. Alas, I knew not how to relieve her.

'What is the cause of her illness?' I asked Joe.

'*Mery-dy byday lidiny loomerday*,' he said. 'Sick head, breast and belly.' On each of these parts he had made incisions with broken glass. Her forehead was terribly lacerated, the blood streaming down her face. Her whole frame was wasted. She had a ghastly countenance and appeared in dreadful agony. Joe was much affected, crying unashamedly. Indeed his affection for his wife and children was very striking. In civilized society he would have been termed a good husband and kind parent.

I made Morley some tea from my supplies. I could not bear the afflicting scene so retired to my quarters. Soon Joe followed me, his cheeks running with tears, bringing his children and kangaroo skins.

'Where is your wife, Joe?'

He pointed to a fire, bigger than the other campfires, on a small hillock about a hundred yards distant. 'She is dead in the fire.'

We walked to the spot. The wind had driven the fire from the legs, which were quite exposed. The stench was intolerable. The body was in a sitting posture. The wind soon extinguished the flames on the chest and head so Joe asked me to assist him in gathering wood to consume the body. My feelings were particularly agitated by the distasteful and melancholy request but I gave an unwilling assistance.

The next week occupied all our energies. I was forced to send another prisoner, Rufus Murdoch, to the authorities at Hobart Town charged with neglect of duty, refusing to work and being insolent to me. His remarks were directed at my personal stature and the aspersions he cast about my relationship with certain of the aboriginal females left me no alternative from the disciplinary point of view. I would not dignify his vile assertions by repeating them in these pages.

Truganini returned from a hunting excursion with two new native women, Dray and Catherine, and another family group joined us. The aboriginal Joe learned to work the stern oar on the whaleboat very efficiently and was adept at catching kangaroo, opossum and wallaby-rats. I had several conversations with the natives on the Being of a God and by 25th May felt that I had fully gained their confidence. The children, who at one time would cry if I looked on them and scream agonisingly if I pointed my finger at them, were now quite familiar with me. Joe was now willing to place his two children William and Mary, aged about six and four years, under my care—a mark of confidence as he was very fond of them.

Little more than a week after his wife's death Joe suddenly appeared ill and weak, barely able to drag his waddies and spears behind him. A day or so later he called me to come to his assistance. I found him lying forlornly on his heap of kangaroo skins.

'Mr Robinson get me wood. Joe *tie*.'

I supposed him to mean that I was to collect wood to consume his body when he died and I began to encourage him.

'Joe no die.' I patted his head and brought him tea and tobacco.

Part of his meaning was made apparent by his daughter coming with a stick to assist him to walk. Then, in the course of the morning, one of the children emptied its bowels on the ground.

'What name that?' I immediately asked.

'*Tie*,' said the child.

Joe's request suddenly became clear to me. I was to get him a stick to help him leave his hut for the purposes of evacuation. (How ridiculous we make ourselves appear when we are only partially acquainted with a language!)

Joe was soon extremely ill. These people were very impatient of pain. He had made several deep incisions in his body to afford relief, so that the *Ragewrapper* would leave his affected parts. Wooraddy sliced the sick man's throat with a piece of glass jar in an attempt to improve his breathing. He avoided the jugular, slicing below the Adam's apple. Perhaps the streaming blood afforded Joe some relief of the spirit if not the body for he at once seemed to drift into a more peaceful sleep. Perhaps leeches would have had a more beneficial result, I thought, without producing such vast quantities of blood. But none could be found, the weather being unseasonally dry.

By the Sabbath of 31st May I had obtained one hundred and fifteen words towards my vocabulary and could make myself tolerably well understood in the native tongue. I performed Divine Service for the natives in front of their huts. Four of the prisoners attended. I decided to preach to the natives in their own language:

'*Motti* (One) *nyrae* (good) *Parlerdi* (God), *motti* (one) *novilly* (bad) *Ragewrapper* (Devil). *Parlerdi* (God) *nyrae* (good). *Parlerdi* (God) *maggerer* (live) *warrangelly* (sky), *Ragewrapper* (Devil) *maggerer* (live) *toogunner* (below) *uennee* (fire). *Nyrae* (Good) *parlerwar* (native) *logerner* (dead) *taggerer* (go) *teenny* (road) *law-way* (up) *warrangelly* (sky) *Parlerdi* (God) *nyrae* (good). *Novilly* (Bad) *parlerwar* (native) *logerner* (dead) *taggerer* (go) *teenny* (road) *toogunner* (below) *Ragewrapper* (Devil) *uennee* (fire) *maggerer* (remain) *uennee* (fire).'

The natives were gratifyingly attentive. Comprehension lightened their sable features.

In the afternoon Joe requested a fire outside his hut and asked to be carried there. He did not survive long. I was writing up my journal in my quarters when his groans ceased, and with them the sounds of the other natives. A solemn stillness prevailed. I went out and saw he had just expired. The others were seated around his fire, busily twisting lengths of grass. They bent Joe's legs back against the thighs and bound them tight round with the twisted grass. Each arm was bent together and bound round above the elbow. The natives built a funeral pile of dry wood covered by dry bark about three feet high. Lengths of smooth bark were laid across the top upon which they placed the corpse, arching it over with dry sticks. Both men and women assisted in kindling the fire, after which they left it and did not approach the spot any more that day.

Next morning I went with them to inspect the remains and found one of the dogs eating an unconsumed limb. I ordered the natives to urgently collect the remains and burn them. I wished them to burn his body on the same spot as his wife's pyre but they refused, possibly through superstition. After the remains were burned the ashes were scraped together and some grass and sticks laid over them.

I wanted to talk with the natives on the circumstances of Joe's and Morley's deaths but they said they did not like to speak about it.

'Where do you go after death?' I asked.

'To England.'

I scarcely credited what I heard. I asked the question again and got the same reply from all of them.

'There are plenty of *Parlerwar* in England,' said Truganini.

Next vacation they had travelled to North Queensland by train, stopping at long-platformed stations overseen by gaunt porters in broad-brimmed hats. At each stop the passengers sprinted for the bar and sank as many beers and Bundaberg rums as they could cram into the ten minutes, reeling back into the carriage to belch and fart, play pontoon and read Zane Greys and Phantom comics. It occurred to Crisp that the railways always managed to assemble the same cast. In his wide low-budget travels across the country he'd noticed that every second-class carriage had its complement of young tattooed soldiers playing cards, reading comics and swigging rum or sherry. There was always a lone middle-aged man—with the look of a widower or a frayed bachelor—in a dark crushed suit. He sat awake all night chain-smoking and coughing and occasionally rubbing his hands through his short, oiled hair. He usually travelled light, with only a brown gladstone bag or vinyl airlines bag, and read only the newspapers he bought at each station and quickly discarded. There was usually a harassed woman with a small child and a colicky baby which slept by day and cried at night. The woman had the mien of the deserted wife, appearing near tears but keeping a grip on herself. Her eyes seemed to search each station platform for a particular familiar face. Often there were two or three girls travelling together, perhaps to visit sisters married to garage mechanics in country towns. They read True Romances and paraded up and down the corridor in front of the soldiers to the water cooler. Generally, too, there was an Aborigine, or a couple, sitting silently in a corner seat out of the way, eating sandwiches and staring out the window.

After one night spent sitting up (there were no sleeping carriages) and another on a fresh train where he shared a sleeper with two all-night smokers and a nightmare-prone Italian, Crisp slipped the conductor two dollars.

'How about letting my wife and I share a sleeper?'

'It's more than my job's worth, mate. You can't have men and women in the same second-class sleeper. Against regulations.'

Queensland, oh Queensland! 'Honeymooners,' Crisp said.

The conductor winked and deftly pocketed the note. 'Sweet dreams. Number 22 should do you.'

Anna heard their exchange and blushed deeply despite herself. Crisp was pleased. She was really a softy, he thought, and though the narrow jolting bunk later made lovemaking difficult (and he bumped his head on the upper bunk at a crucial stage), her unusually shy reaction to their act of bribery made it, for him anyway, a memorable event.

Afterwards they drank a glass of tired water from a dusty railway carafe and splashed some on their bodies, sitting cooling on the bunk as the scenery raced past. As the train rattled from the high rainforest into a wide field of sugar cane, Anna kneeled on the carriage floor and licked and devoured him. Crisp kneaded her breasts while outside the train window in the heat a blue kingfisher flipped from the telegraph wires and dived into the cane, after a grasshopper or cane toad perhaps.

'Symbolism everywhere,' he said, stroking her. 'Keep doing that.'

'I love the way you touch me,' she said. 'I love your hands, all veiny, and your blunt-tipped fingers. Like a tree-frog's.'

'Croak, croak,' he whispered, softly tweaking her with spatulate tree-frog fingers.

They spent a sensual time in Cairns, the somnolent, dry winter heat driving them to a small watercourse called Lake Placid outside the town. Here they swam among tame perch and freshwater tropical fish and played Tarzan games, swinging into the lake from a rope on the bank, shooting small rapids with their bodies, skimming over mossy rocks like canoes. Giant butterflies flapped slowly over the lake and in rock crevices tiny spiders glinted like jewels.

'Let's swim naked,' she said.

'O.K.' But he was suddenly reminded of the film *Deliverance*. Perhaps it was the rapids and the high and thickly wooded river valley bearing down on them. He had momentary visions of them being sniped at by North Queensland mountain men. Not to mention dark hillbilly sexual images.

'Don't be silly,' Anna laughed. 'We're alone.' She removed her bikini, dropped it at his feet and dived into a deep pool. She surfaced and her breasts bobbed white in the shadows and reflections of the valley walls. She lifted back her head to smooth her thick hair and laughed up at Crisp perched on the bank in his trunks. He noticed how big her mouth was—and how square and white her teeth. Her face was profligately European.

'Come in Stephen. Get your gear off!'

He was surprised to realise he felt threatened by her, by her strength and independence. 'We'd better go, it's getting late,' he said, and got to his feet. Anna climbed out of the lake and he tossed a towel to her.

5

Ameliorating the Natives

3rd June, 1829

If Your Excellency pleases I wish to submit my first report on the aboriginal settlement on Bruny Island and the progress I have made towards the amelioration of the native race.

I have taken the important steps of separating the children from the rest of the tribe and propose erecting a dormitory for them. They are destined by Providence as a foundation upon which the superstructure of Your Excellency's benevolence is hereafter to be constructed. I hope to rouse them from that torpid inactivity in which they have so long slumbered. They are by no means deficient in instinct, and fully sensible of what benefits my endeavours may bring them. I seldom speak to the children other than in English; the adults I address in their native tongue, having already studied some two hundred words of their vocabulary.

I have instructed the white settlers to prohibit their convicts from encouraging the natives with gifts of food and clothing as in no instance have the aboriginals conducted themselves immorally without such encouragement. I have asked those with aboriginals in their employ whether they would part with them so that they might come to our establishment.

I have conversed with the aboriginals—those at the establishment are from Southport, Port Esperance, Port Davey as well as Bruny—about leading an expedition to their tribes. They cheerfully acquiesced. An expedition to all the tribes from the Huon River to Port Davey would, I am sure, be attended with beneficial results. I am informed they are by no means hostile and it is only by such an undertaking that Your Excellency's humane intentions can possibly be understood. The natives could return with the expedition or if otherwise disposed they would know that asylum was provided for them at Bruny Island whenever they wished it.

Should Your Excellency approve of such an undertaking I beg to offer my services. I now have a sufficient acquaintance with the language to make myself tolerably well understood, and I believe I have sufficiently acquired their trust and confidence.

Crisp, who had been as far west, south and east as the country extended, had long wanted to travel to its northernmost point: Cape York Peninsula. (He didn't realize it at the time but this enthusiasm for pacing the country's geographical boundaries was probably a harbinger of his later preoccupation with attempting to clarify and explain things in general.) He and Anna bought tickets for the small launch that carried mail and provisions from Cairns to the reawakening ghost town of Cooktown and travelled the hundred miles or so up the coast, sharing the sunny deck with sacks of pumpkins and oil drums.

They played silly games in the sun. 'I spy with my little eye something beginning with B,' Anna said, indicating a clump of passengers—the women in timeless floral dresses, brooches and hats, the men in dark trousers, white shirts, ties and hats—knitting, reading magazines and staring fixedly out to sea from the shade of a canvas canopy. One of the men, tiny and wizened but with huge freckled ears stretching the length of his face, extracted a handkerchief from his pocket, blew his nose, examined the contents, refolded the handkerchief and replaced it in his pocket.

'I give up.' Crisp was trailing a hand in the launch's wake. The boat was heavily laden and low in the water. Sharks and exotic tropical nasties occurred to him and he pulled in his hand.

'Banana-benders of course. Look at that mob of classic Queenslanders over there in the shade.'

'You win.' He lay back in his seat with his head on the gunwale and absorbed the sun. A mile from them the thickly forested shoreline stretched unbroken by beaches or settlements. There were no signs of life other than theirs, no smoke trails or vessels or noise other than the boat's engine, the dull hum of conversation and the clicking of the Queensland matrons' knitting needles.

Through that impenetrable jungle, over the Mitchell River and the Great Dividing Range, had trudged intrepid and foolhardy explorers. Edmund Kennedy and his faithful Aboriginal assistant Jackey-Jackey, the hero of fourth-grade history lessons. How he loved that story: fierce blacks, exhaustion, treachery and clinging lawyer-vines. Spears in the back and hip bones protruding through the intrepid and foolhardy skin of the starving English and Irish expatriates. Storekeepers, botanists, boozers, naturalists, labourers—none of them resourceful beyond eating their horses and sitting under shady trees waiting for death. Only Jackey-Jackey pulled through, of course, doing the right thing by the white master, indefatigable and carbine-waving when threatened by his wild northern countrymen, getting by on grubs, lizards, seeds and roots, plenty of protein and roughage there, turned down by the delicate European palates.'No thanks Jackey, black-fella tucker that. I think I'll wait for the supply ship. You go ahead though.'

That was the story of this place. It took the second generation to feel at home in the wilderness, to adapt. Or it did a century ago. European expatriate Anna Kubic, ex-Yugoslavia, post-war refugee, daughter of leading Mona Vale tomato grower Simo Kubic, Sydney University graduate, lecturer in European History (Modern), women's activist, seemed to find no difficulty in adjusting and assimilating. Less than he did, actually.

She lay beside him on the next seat, her face half shielded by sunglasses, her wide bottom lip protected by salve and the down on her stomach glistening with suntan lotion. A tiny pool of oil had collected in her navel. He scooped it out with a forefinger and smeared it on her belly, spreading it gently with a steady circular motion between her waist and the top of her black bikini pants. She made soft sounds, responsive flickers at the corner of the mouth, began to gently contract her buttocks, undulating under his hand. He wanted to place his hand between her warm oiled thighs (just for some lubricious reassurance) but sensed the Queenslanders looking askance at them over their *Women's Weekly* knitting patterns. So he lay back with a sigh against the gunwale and dozed in the sun.

Cooktown squatted between the rain forest and the flat tropical sea. In the bar of their wide-verandahed hotel drovers, maintenance dodgers, unhung murderers and miscellaneous frontier drifters cracked stockwhips, drank, vomited and sang old favourites to the accompaniment of ukelele, lagerphone and bush bass. Wild whistles and wolfish leers greeted their arrival.

'It would be a good idea to put on a bra,' Crisp advised. 'Or I'll have to fight everyone.'

'Nonsense.'

'What room are you in sweetie?' This came from a menacing dark lounger in a black singlet. He extracted a cigarette stub from his mouth with two finger stumps, blew smoke into the air with movie-western-saloon braggadocio. 'I'll be up for a night cap.'

'Or a Dutch cap,' called a freckled youth. The boy was small and thin with lined eyes and ginger hair. Crisp gave him a level television current affairs stare.

The bar subsided, friendly enough, and by the time they returned downstairs and ordered drinks—Crisp anticipating perhaps a little trouble, Anna brassiered under her shirt—enough other women had arrived, stringy local wives and an off-duty barmaid as well as the passengers from the launch, to take the heat off Anna. They drank schooners of beer with nervous gusto, Crisp broadening his accent (as he did almost unconsciously in such circumstances), shedding dulcet Commission tones, even leavening them with the occasional obscenity.

To his relief the dark singleted man reeled off into the night with an armload of bottles. The ginger youth though stumbled into their conversation just before closing time.

'The name's Andy from the Isa,' he said. 'I want to get married.'

'Good for you,' Crisp said.

The boy clutched a glass of rum and performed a little dance on the spot. 'I wanta get married,' he sang, and broke into quiet tears. No one else paid any attention to his crying. Anna looked fazed.

'Steady on there,' Crisp said.

'I got my girl up the stick and she pissed me off. I thought, shit, I'm lucky escaping the shotgun. But I miss her. Never seen the kid. Rhonda's engaged to a fucking bank teller now. Fucking cuntuver bank teller! Drives a bloody Toyota and goes water skiing. Rhonda pissed me off. Can you beat that?'

Andy from the Isa turned creased and cloudy eyes on Anna, blinking pale freckled lids. 'Will you marry me? You've got nice big tits.' He stretched a hand out to touch her.

'Piss off mate,' Crisp instructed.

They tramped around the town, absorbing its gold rush history, avoiding the long grass (pythons: shy but fond of domestic tabbies), swamps (crocodiles: smallish but sharp-toothed) and coastal shallows (stone fish, box jellyfish and similar fatal stingers). The local Aborigines, they learned from an old fisherman pulling in abundant rock cod on an old gut line from the town jetty, used to prefer the Chinese miners in their cannibal days.

'Stands to reason,' he said, squinting at the tourists with a canny and faded eye. 'Sweeter tasting, full of rice and bamboo shoots. Not like your Aussie miners. Too stringy and full of booze and tobacco. Meat eaters. Their sweat stinks.'

'I didn't know they were cannibals. I've never heard,' Crisp said.

'Wild country up here mate. This isn't your Brisbane, you know. Funny things happen up here. Ask Norm over there.' He pointed to a thin blue-black man in a red T-shirt hunched over a line at the end of the jetty. 'Hey Norman. You used to eat Chows, didn't you?'

'What?'

'Chows. Chinks. Chinamen. You blokes ate them, you black bastards.'

'Too fuckin' right,' Norman muttered, without turning around.

'Good bloke, Norm,' the old man confided. 'Salt of the earth. Not like some of them.'

He sent his father a postcard. It was a coloured photograph of a stone memorial to a local heroine, a housewife who had fought off savage Aborigines while her husband was away from home. They had speared her Chinese servant and pursued her in canoes when she escaped with her baby into the tropical ocean, paddling a water tank. She and the baby evaded the blacks but her breast milk dried up and they died of thirst, the baby first. The tank floated on into the Coral Sea, collecting much rainwater. On the memorial was engraved:

In Memoriam
Mrs Watson
The Heroine of Lizard Island
Cooktown
North Queensland
A.D. 1881
Five fearful days beneath
The scorching glare
Her babe she nursed.
God knows the pangs that
Woman had to bear,
Whose last sad entry showed
A mother's care,
Then—'Near dead with thirst.'

JOHN DAVIS, *Mayor 1886*

It was the only postcard the store carried. On it he wrote, 'Dear

Dad, Cooktown is fascinating. Almost a ghost town. How are things with you?'

In mid-June I left Bruny for Hobart Town, spending three weeks with my wife and family and attending to the business of the establishment. I made a point of attending the Colonial Hospital on several successive days for the purpose of being instructed in some surgical operations.

I was received very warmly at Government House, His Excellency offering me tea, a selection of eclairs and a sort of ginger wafer biscuit freshly imported from London.

'Keep up the good work, Robinson. You're doing the extirpationers in the eye.'

'Your Excellency is generous.' The wafers were so fragile I feared mine would explode in a shower of crumbs. 'Have you given any thought to my going to Port Davey on my suggested aboriginal expedition?'

'Which? Oh, of course. I approve of that, Robinson. Conciliation before extirpation is the mark of the statesman. I feel a great deal of responsibility for our black brethren.' The Governor sighed and flicked a crumb from his tunic. 'You could say the aboriginal problem is becoming one of the chief rigours of my office.'

I could only sympathize with the man. The military mind sometimes finds it difficult to countenance questions of a social or philanthropic nature. Nevertheless, his former appointment as Governor of Honduras should have acquainted him with the difficult task of administering people of colour.

As he farewelled me the Governor inquired after my wife's welfare and asked about my children. 'I love the little folk,' he said.

I took three aboriginal children from the gaol back to Bruny with me, trusting that our numbers would be even further swelled by other arrivals. Alas, I found that a woman named Horatio had died and that four men were ill and unable to walk without help. I issued slop clothing to the sick and gave them tea and sugar.

One of the patients, Bung-ler-the, was much worse next day. I was concerned he would not survive his complaint because it resembled the sickness which had killed the others. At this time the vessel *Prince Regent*, on her way to Hobart Town from England, was aground on a sandbank off Three Hut Point and being assisted by the Government brig *Cyprus*. I manned my boat and went aboard the *Prince Regent* to solicit the opinion of the ship's doctor. This gentleman, name of Fattorini, I had been informed by the ship's master, was once page to Napoleon *le Grand* and a surgeon of some reputation. He was a tall stooped man and fashionable dressed. His grasp of English was commendable.

He graciously returned ashore with me. Monsieur Fattorini viewed the dying man, poking at his chest with a pale finger, then listening to its soughs with the aid of a silver egg-cup affair.

'He has an infection of the lungs, probably incurable.'

'Could you perform an operation, Monsieur?'

'It is too late. His complaint might have been checked by bleeding in its early stages. Now I can do nothing. His throat is filled with purulent matter. There is a difficulty of respiration.'

'They all seem to suffer from that complaint.'

Monsieur Fattorini surveyed the grieving natives around the sick man. 'They do not wear sufficient clothing. Consequently their lungs are chilled. Stout shoes are necessary in these climates just as in Europe. I never travel without a cloak, even in summer.' Here he plucked a small white handkerchief from his sleeve and wiped his hands. 'And Paris can be most humid.'

At seven o'clock Bung-ler-the breathed his last. The usual ceremony was performed and his body committed to the flames. As the head caught fire the widow began a mournful lamentation and raked her nails down her breasts. The doctor was most intrigued, being used to the procedures of higher civilizations. He clicked his tongue at such happenings and held his handkerchief to his nose.

'Their appearance is most unusual,' he mused. 'The hair in coils, the lips broad, the nose flattened. But they are smaller than Africans. And I notice both sexes practise scarification. Does it have a sexual significance?'

'I believe so. Forgive me for asking Monsieur, but what is someone of your station doing in the colonies?' The matter intrigued me.

He ignored the question. 'The women are sadly ill-favoured. Unfortunately. I wonder why they permit themselves to be so dirty?'

'I apologize for my rudeness. I myself felt a need to depart Europe's shores.'

'Not at all.'

For the sake of camaraderie and at their request I accompanied Truganini and Dray on one of their afternoon fishing excursions. They unashamedly removed all their clothing and dived repeatedly for mutton fish while I wrote up my journal on a sunny rock. The water ran easily from their hair (it having more curl and body than European hair and thus lacking that plastered-down appearance) and gleamed on their slender bodies. The ochres, ashes and animal fat with which they adorned themselves were washed away, revealing their skin to be a fine reddish brown rather than black. Wet, they presented a most pleasing aspect, even the cicatrix on their arms and chests observing a patterned harmony with their supple limbs.

(In such a way I gained a knowledge of their mode of existence, which was acquirable only by them making one their companion in their travels. On this occasion I learned, for instance, of their fondness for a marine plant, *poorner*, which they scooped up from the sea bottom and chewed in raw handfuls. Their resources were prolific when hunger craved—herbs, fungi, roots, berries and shellfish abounded; there was animal food of every variety including rats and beetles. They held our luxuries in some antipathy. The only European foods they relished were sugar, tea, potatoes and flour.)

Hiking back to the establishment with my dripping companions (they giggling and struggling with their basket loads of shellfish and *poorner*), I resolved to hasten once more to Hobart Town. Random thoughts of an affectionate nature filled my mind and fixed themselves upon my good wife and children in Elizabeth Street suffering alone the rigours of colonial life. Next morning being the Sabbath I performed a short divine service—both aboriginals and convicts behaving with the utmost decorum—and started for town accompanied by Truganini and Dray. I had clothed them for the purpose most presentably and they twittered excitedly as we set off.

I called upon His Excellency immediately on Monday morning. He looked surprised to see me but was most civil as usual, receiving me this time in a small anteroom off the entrance foyer to Government House. At his request I introduced the women (having instructed Dray to keep her pipe and ship's tobacco surreptitiously hidden in the folds of her frock) and they came forward with alacrity.

'Good morning,' said the Governor to them, presenting his hand. 'His Majesty wishes you to know that he has your interests at heart.' He smiled at the petite Truganini. 'He knows you are loyal subjects.'

I thanked him on their behalf. The women stood stock-still, smiling vacantly.

'And he wants your people to be friendly to our people. No spear anyone. You understand? No spear white man, sheep or cow. No throw stones. No steal flour.'

'King in England good man,' Trŭganini said wisely.

We made our departure, no refreshments being offered on this occasion, possibly because of the early hour. I stayed a week in town (despatching the native women back to the island in the whaleboat), finding Maria and the children in good health and performing in God's name useful tasks for the seamen, the aboriginals and other unfortunates of the town.

Outside their hotel the wind stiffened in the night, tangling and flapping the clothes, long since dried, hanging along the second-floor verandah, rattling a loose beer sign. Inside the bar a prawn fisherman down from the Gulf said, 'It's blowing up a bastard.' The prawning fleet was battened down in Cooktown to see out the weather.

Their boat set off for Cairns at dawn into the fringe of a Coral Sea cyclone. The skipper had a macabre sense of humour. Before they hit the open sea he fed the passengers a breakfast of curried prawns, green peas and rice. Within an hour the decks were awash with colourful vomit.

Crisp, a perpetual worrier, wondered whether they would make it back to Cairns safely. They sat on the open deck at first, to get the wind on their faces. They clung to the edge of their seats until the seats began sliding around the deck and then they clutched at steel stanchions supporting the small wheelhouse. Anna stumbled to the stern and hung over the low railing, violently sick.

He slid down the deck to her, grabbing her around the waist. 'For Christ's sake come back. You'll be washed overboard!'

'I don't care. I'm sick.' She retched hopelessly over the stern. The bile blew back at them but they were lashed clean by the rain and spray. He dragged her back under cover. She shook her drenched head, wiped her mouth on a sleeve. 'I can't vomit in front of these people. I must look terrible.'

High peril on the sea and the arch-feminist was worried about cosmetic appearances! He put his arm around her but she shrugged it off. 'Please don't touch me. I can't bear to have anyone touch me when I'm ill.' She curled up on a hatch cover among sacks of mail and closed her eyes.

With difficulty Crisp stood up. Seawater surged around his ankles, speckled with peas and curry. A deckhand was helping two middle-aged women into life-jackets. One of the women said, 'Oh God!' over and over. The other, one of their stolid Queenslanders from the trip up the coast, sat down in her life-jacket and resumed knitting. It looked like a fawn sweater for a big person, or perhaps a car rug.

No one approached Crisp with a life-jacket. Although he could see the jackets stored behind thin wooden slats above the seats he couldn't bring himself to be the first adult male aboard to put one on. Nevertheless he positioned himself within striking range. The second deckhand was busying himself making mugs of milky tea and cutting thick meat sandwiches. The deckhand flicked a sliver of pink corned beef into his mouth and poured the tea. Bile gushed into Crisp's mouth.

Where the coastline had been he could now see only the crests of giant whitecaps. The skipper was having difficulty keeping the bow into the waves. Every second wave struck like a massive hammer blow. The keel shuddered and threatened to snap in halves. The engine strained and coughed when the screw came out of the water, impotently turning in the air, and Crisp considered praying old Protestant prayers that it wouldn't falter and the waves would not overturn them. If he could remember any . . . As he had done during two or three other crises he did, in fact, promise that this time he would lead a better life (even *believe* perhaps) if they got through. Maudlin thoughts filled his head as they often did, centred about his daughter, Anna, Jane. Jane surprisingly stricken by the tragedy. His father bearing up bravely.

Though invisible the coastline was obviously on the boat's starboard side, perhaps a mile away. Could he and Anna swim the distance in huge seas, supported by life-jackets now temptingly arrayed above his head? In her present mood she would instantly surrender to the waves. Could he drag her to land using a dimly remembered Bronze Medallion lifesaving grip? ('*Right arm over the shoulder and grab the patient by the left tit*,' the instructor said. '*If it's a sheila so much the better.*')

The second deckhand nudged him. The man wore streaming oilskins and a soaked but jaunty beret and spoke with his mouth full.

'Hey mate, do you want a sandwich? Put a lining on your guts.'

The launch arrived at Cairns after thirteen hours. It chugged into Trinity Bay and moored at the wharf. The captain's eyes were blood-shot and sticking from his head. He stood at the top of the gangway and shook the passengers' hands as they disembarked.

'Nice work,' Crisp told him, and they walked jelly-legged into town. He pulled Anna into the first restaurant they saw. 'Let's eat here. I'm ravenous.' Sitting beneath tourist posters for München and Wiesbaden in the Blue Danube Cafe, Crisp twitchily ordered schnitzel and potatoes and a stiff drink.

'Cabbage all gone, sorry,' the proprietor said, exposing a leaden tooth. 'Vhot you vhonta drink, tea or lemonade?'

'Tea.' Aching for a triple brandy Crisp began to twitch all over, tics jumping along his cheeks and eyelids. He flickered and trembled through the leathery meal. On the hard wooden chair his buttocks fluttered like moths. That night Anna slept like a log while he, exhausted, twitched from scalp to feet until morning.

'Delayed shock,' she diagnosed, giving him breakfast in bed: boarding house Weeties and a slice of canned pineapple. 'Food for my hero,' she said, serving it with a nice kiss.

The remainder of their Cairns vacation passed quietly. They returned to Lake Placid once, walking along hot roads through the canefields. Every few yards the body of a cane toad lay flattened on the bitumen. Fetid smells of dead things fleetingly passed over them. At the lake they didn't shoot the rapids or explore upstream but hired canoes and picnicked like anyone else. They had a drink at the Redlynch Hotel because Crisp reckoned that Xavier Herbert, doyen of local writers and author of *Capricornia* sometimes drank there. He wasn't there. Instead he went with Anna to a commune inhabited by some counter-culture acquaintances of hers—a girl, Betty, with a willowy body and irregular teeth, and two bearded boys, Wayne and Danny, who wore chamois jockstraps. They served their guests immediately with dope and a muddy brown drink, thick and sticky, made from bananas. Anna took her shirt off and sunbaked; Crisp kept his pants on and was shown over the commune's crops. Slow purple Ulysses butterflies fluttered among the banana leaves.

'It's a fine food, man,' Danny said. 'What else has got protein, carbohydrates, fats, the works? It keeps body and soul together and it's fucking easy to grow.'

Wayne emerged from a semi-trance. He was the quiet one of the group. 'The banana was here when we came and it'll be here when we go,' he said.

A dim recollection from the sixties occurred to Crisp. 'I've heard the skins are an hallucinogen too.' He offered this politely, like a weather report. 'Like those mushrooms and so on.'

Danny laughed. 'Mellow yellow bullshit. Sixties pop songs.' With a sweeping gesture he presented another agricultural vista: row upon row of sturdy cannabis plants thriving among the bananas. 'Why bother when you've got the devil weed right here on the farm?'

'Any trouble with the police?' The North Queensland police were legendary for their animosity towards 'hippies' and Aborigines. Crisp was willing to commiserate at their victimization.

'We got busted once. One bloke was hassling us but we found out where he drank and Rosemary picked him up. Everything's sweet now. She likes fucking them for some reason. Kinky girl, Rosemary.' Danny laughed.

Betty sat cross-legged on the grass in front of their wood and tin hut in a pair of cut-down Levis passing around joints tailor-made from a small cigarette-rolling machine. Anna was already on the way, smiling happily. 'He's got pimples on his arse,' Betty said. She twirled the machine's handle and another neat joint popped out.

He felt bound to ask. 'Who?'

'Constable Matthews. We caught him swimming in the creek with Rosemary. Uncircumcised and with a bum full of pimples. A grisly sight.' She giggled. 'The question is—does Rosemary squeeze them when he's on the job? Pop, pop.'

Anna was enjoying some private joke or other.

'What's so funny?' he said.

'Nothing.'

'Share the humour.'

'Cunt-stable Matthews,' she snorted. 'Good morning CUNT-stable!'

'Terrific.' Crisp found the heat overpowering. The others, lean and brown, seemed oblivious. Either the grass was affecting him badly or the sweet and viscous banana potion. He moved into the shade. The droning of crickets in the palms was deafening. The clucking of the commune's dusty hens mingled in the cacophony.

'The chooks are in fine voice.'

Danny said, 'They're great little layers, man. Lay beautiful rich eggs. Free-range eggs. It's magic recycling. You chuck them the scraps and out come these lovely orange-yolked eggs.'

Betty said, 'You've got to hunt up the little buggers though. Wait till you hear them cluck, follow the noise and you've got an egg.'

'Borky bork bork,' clucked Wayne.

Anna clucked too, then attempted a rooster crow and began coughing with the throat strain. The coughs turned into giggles. A patent leather fruit bat, awakened, dropped out of a fig tree and flapped over their heads, returning to its sleeping perch. Someone said 'bats in the belfy' and people giggled. Danny eyed Anna's breasts with soft-eyed but uncool lust.

Anna seemed to have a good day but Crisp didn't enjoy himself particularly. She was still slightly stoned, humming to herself, when they sauntered back along the bay to their guest-house. He didn't feel communicative, rather self-aware, lonely and self-pitying. The tide was out and on the wide mudflats left behind small boys skimmed along on sheets of five-ply, their bodies coated in black ooze. Small movements at the corners of Crisp's vision were in fact mudskippers, weird pop-eyed fish that walked on land. Focussing intently on the mud he saw it was alive with mudskippers and translucent soldier crabs, scurrying about, encircling each other.

'Who eats who? That's what I want to know,' he said.

Before they left Cairns they bought some small presents for Wendy and postcards for friends. They scrawled messages on the cards on their last morning, sitting on a park seat at the edge of the bay. The high tide lapped at the sea wall. A passive family group of Aborigines sat on an adjoining seat eating potato chips from a newspaper parcel. The father had a typical North Queensland profile, Crisp thought—broad forehead, nose and mouth; the mother appeared rather Melanesian, with more delicate features and an aquiline nose. Their children, two girls and a boy, sat solemnly at their feet in the sand. The boy picked at a Band-Aid on his knee, eating slowly meanwhile. Suddenly the biggest girl threw a chip to a cluster of seagulls. The mother scolded, 'Don't throw your lunch away Donna!' and slapped her legs.

Crisp addressed one of the postcards to his father. He wrote: 'Weather beautiful up here, Dad. Cairns is certainly a thirsty place. Cheers for now, Stephen.'

My patience was sorely tried. Curiously, the natives seemed to delight in misbehaving whenever I went to town. On my return this time Mangana told me three of the children had run away: William and Mary, the orphans of Joe and Morley, and another orphan boy, Pona. We began a search for them, all the men engaging in the pursuit. Towards dusk the children were spied crossing a sandy beach two miles from the orphans' hut and moving rapidly away from the establishment. Keen-eyed, the six-year-old William climbed a high tree to conceal himself from us; the two smaller children crouched beneath bushes. It could scarcely be credited that children so young possessed such craftiness. I sent three men to catch them, which they easily accomplished despite the wails and struggles. The children's natural love of the bush and propensity to ramble was here clearly exemplified. No other motive could have made them leave a place where they were universally treated with the greatest kindness and regard.

The child William had to be carried back to the establishment, being troubled by wheeziness of the chest. He seemed listless and feverish from his exertions.

Another happening added to my travails. On their return from Hobart Town—and while I was still absent—Truganini and Dray had joined another eight natives and absconded to Adventure Bay, the principal rendezvous for all whalers in the straits. This information came from Catherine, who was too sick to join the absconders herself and regarded her friends' activities most jealously. I was furious. It was obvious that the whalers, who were allowed by the Government to carry on their lucrative business on the island, abused that privilege by carnally occupying and otherwise exploiting the women. I noted in my journal: 'If the natives derive encouragement from these men the objects of my establishment will be defeated and the most prejudicial consequences will remain.' I determined to travel to Adventure Bay to confront the culprits.

Next dawn I was preparing regardless of the mizzling rain to set out for the whaling camp when I heard William the orphan boy groaning in a piteous manner. I found him in apparent great agony. I would have resorted to bleeding but having insufficient light and wanting for surgical experience I abandoned the idea. Besides, the child appeared to be in a dying state and little hope remained for his recovery. At 6 a.m. the lad expired in similar fashion to his late parents, from a severe oppression of the chest. A coffin was made for him from tree bark and at 9 a.m. I summoned the men and the orphan children Mary and Pona to attend his funeral. I spoke on this occasion on the frailty of human life and called the children's attention to the importance and necessity of being prepared to die.

6

The Whalers

After the funeral of William the orphan boy I proceeded in the whaleboat to the whalers' settlement at Adventure Bay. I took four prisoners with me. We reached the neck of land which connects north and south Bruny but here the heavy seas and periodic squalls forced us ashore. We hauled the boat up the beach and started across the Neck by foot to Adventure Bay.

Rounding the western corner of the bay we spotted Emara, Wooraddy's wife and her three small children. Sores of a scabrous nature afflicted her body. She appeared feeble and forlorn and was entirely naked except for a white gull feather stuck in the forepart of her hair. She sat on a small scrap of blanket. Her children played listlessly in the sand.

I interrogated her. "Where are the other *parlerwar*, Emara?'

'Some sick, like me. Others hunting kangaroo.'

'Where is Truganini? And Dray?'

'They stay with the whalers. And another woman, Pagerley, as well. They sleep plenty night with the white men. They give them plenty tea, sugar. Tobacco sometimes.'

'Take me to them. Then return to your husband.'

'Too sick. Whalers push me out. No sugar, no tea.'

I was furious. Disgust engulfed my emotions. 'Carry her,' I ordered the convicts and we marched down to the camp.

The stench of rotting meat was overpowering, hanging over the whole camp. Whale carcases were drawn up on the beach breeding flies. The shallows were streaked and glistening with oily putrescence, tidal pools congealing in the sun. I could barely control an involuntary retching. 'Emara, where for God's sake?'

The woman pointed out the slab hut where Truganini and Dray were staying. I strode forward and banged on the door, calling their names, kicking aside shards of broken glass. There was no answer, nor was there any movement inside. The women it seemed had spotted us and absconded.

I sought out the camp overseer, a big red-faced American with a turned eye. Name of Crawford and worked for Messrs Kelly and Lucas, one of the three firms working the whaling industry there. (There were from eighty to ninety men employed there, two schooners, two sloops and about twenty whaleboats.) Crawford came out of his hut testy and ruffle-headed, tucking his vest in his greasy trousers.

'You have some of our women here, Mr Crawford. Leading them astray against the Governor's wishes and their better welfare.'

'By their own free will, Robinson. Free as the wind to come and go as they please. We don't work them like the sealers.' He fastened his bad eye on me with some menace. 'It seems we feed 'em better than you do. All bones most of 'em.'

'Don't cross me Mr Crawford. I have the Governor's ear. Your licence is in his hands. Your conduct will be reported to him immediately.'

'Jesus, what harm do we do? A bit of female warmth for some tea and sugar. We don't share our grog with them, I can tell you. No harm done as I see it, just good humoured fun like in Owhyee. Them darkies like a bit of fun whatever the climate.'

'You make them subservient to their own carnal appetites, Mr Crawford. That's what you do.'

Hallstrom was going multi-national, his father wrote from Perth. In a small way of course. Hallstrom Gelatine was becoming Hallstrom Industries. Gelatine would now be only one of its interests (though naturally a primary one for the time being). Management had recently initiated a diversification programme, negotiated several canny take-overs—one, Massey-Morgan, previously a competitor in epoxy resins, caulking compounds, sealants and grouting; the others in widely diverse industries. Would he (Stephen) believe Magna Plastics, Cornish Alloys and Lance O'Meara Swimming Pools? Secondary and subsidiary companies now existed in Auckland, Suva and Kuala Lumpur. All this activity meant that he was being promoted to national plant manager based in Melbourne and operative immediately. (Luckily he'd been able to sell the house to Laurie Wylie, his replacement, who now needed a bigger home for entertaining. Not that he was able to make much on the deal.)

On another matter could Stephen tell him whether he was still on television because he hadn't seen him on-screen for several months.

Everything O.K. at the Commission? Also, without prying, what was the score now between he and Jane? All couples had their ups and downs. For goodness sake think twice before doing anything final. Those marriage guidance people were supposed to be quite effective. By the same token, while his mother and he had had the usual number of ups and downs they would never have considered *divorce*, for the children's sake. Give Wendy Grandpa's love.

I went up to town on August 18th, staying ten days. The only good tidings that met my return to the island were that the whalers were leaving Adventure Bay for the season and my new cottage was progressing satisfactorily. Most other circumstances were dismal. Wooraddy, his face and body daubed with mourning ashes, arrived at the establishment with his two eldest children, one of whom was so weak his father had to carry him. Wooraddy himself was in a very diseased condition.

'*Emara piggerder logerner nene*,' he said. 'Emara and my smallest child are dead in the fire.'

I inquired after the other aboriginals.

'Plenty dead in fire.'

'And Truganini, Dray and Pagerley? Where are they?'

'Dray's baby dead.' Wooraddy looked sheepish, rubbing a finger along his ash-caked forehead. 'The women are gone to Bull Bay with white men.'

My state of mind was depressed at his remarks. My anger grew an hour later at finding two white men with muskets passing through our vegetable garden.

'Where are you from? What is your business here?'

'Just looking for stray cattle, Mr Kelly's cattle,' one man drawled, looking up with a sly confidence. 'Couple of young heifers, all black, no particular markings.'

'Get out or I'll have you sent back to gaol!' I whistled up the dogs and the men shambled off. Snatches of coarse laughter drifted back from the track.

I welcomed the Sabbath next day as seldom before. I performed divine service and preached an admonitory sermon to my prisoners. I concluded by impressing on their minds such truths as were necessary to their eternal salvation—the danger and deformity of sin and the never-failing retribution of a Deity offended by man's overwhelming depravity.

They were all most attentive. I allowed them the following day to work for themselves as an inducement to good behaviour.

To stir Wooraddy from his bereaved state (and to improve my vocabulary) I spent several hours over the next few days conversing with him. His own illness seemed to be improving. He told me interesting facts: that the kangaroo ate the prickly mimosa and native fig whereas the farmers generally supposed it fed only on pasture land. The natives could thus be well supplied with game even in rugged country where the European could scarcely travel and where sterile soil made agriculture useless. I surmised that as other parts of the country were settled, that extensive tract of land around Port Davey to the southward must become the natives' stronghold. From here they could descend on the peaceful settlements and devastate the surrounding country unless they were prevented by prompt measures. It was now established that the Port Davey tribe was in league with others in committing those dire atrocities which had spread so much alarm throughout the territory.

When Wooraddy was fit enough to travel I instructed him to find where the women were staying. He should report back to me which white men were responsible for their seduction. He gave me a quizzical glance.

7

Happy New Year

IN THEIR THIRD YEAR TOGETHER Crisp and Anna had made one further trip, just before the breakup. Soon after he left the Commission —his past under a cloud, his future shadowed by the thesis—they flew to Western Australia, his old stamping ground, for what precise reason he wasn't clear. He hadn't been back since he and Jane left on the Transcontinental, sharing a tiny second-class cabin with a diarrhoeic baby. They'd bumped their heads whenever they moved a muscle, the air conditioning had broken down in the middle of the desert. Behind them the Nullarbor Plain was strewn with soiled disposable diapers. Their garbage chute was choked with them. Little Wendy had defecated her way across the continent.

He floated on his back on a Li-Lo in the swimming pool of his brother Geoffrey's home in Dalkeith, a salubrious riverside suburb of Perth, watching swifts dipping and gliding in the upper airs. As he cruised gently from one end of the pool to the other his brother's two Great Danes, Lady and her son Cheyenne (Shy for short) hurtled around the pool's quarry-tiled sides barking excitedly despite the heat. There was just breeze enough to ruffle the leaves of the silky oak bordering the pool and to tinkle the oriental wind chimes dangling from a branch. The Li-Lo had a special fitting at the front to take a glass of refreshment so you could sip as you floated. It could also hold a can of Aerogard spray as protection against the March-flies. It held neither at the moment. Occasionally Crisp slapped a thigh or shoulder where a fly landed but he was too lazy to fetch the spray. When he became too fried in the sun he slid off into the pool, swam a couple of laps and remounted the Li-Lo.

He had a hangover, a dull champagne headache, from the New Year's Eve party at the Royal Freshwater Bay Yacht Club the night before. It had been quite a night. They'd joined a party organized by Geoff and Denise, his sister-in-law: Bob and Carolyn Hart, Tom and Fiona Bishop, Peter and Helen d'Arcy, Jim and Claire Oakes, and five or six other people he'd known dimly in the past.

Geoff and Denise had gone to considerable trouble over his return to Perth, especially as he was visiting with a woman not his wife—an unusual situation for them and one made potentially more indecorous by their friendship with Jane. (Denise and she still wrote regularly.) But they had welcomed Anna warmly enough, redecorating their spare room as a bedroom for them and, with Geoff's sense of humour predominating, hanging novelty posters on the walls: a dejected knight with a broken lance (*Once a king, always a king. Once a knight's enough!*), two ducks copulating on the wing (*Fly United*) and a man and woman showering (*Save water. Shower with a friend*). There were also two big framed press photographs of Denise, in happy tears, sash and evening gown, being crowned as Miss Western Australia a decade before, and one of Lady and Shy in the *On Guard* position (Geoff and Denise had no children). On the dressing table Denise had arranged in a Tongan palm-leaf basket a display of colourful match books gathered around the world while enjoying her prize as Miss W.A.—including matches from three communist countries. Crisp hadn't fully appreciated the exhibit and was using them with abandon until informed of their significance. He kept spilling the match books on the floor when he stumbled out to the bathroom in the middle of the night, so he put the basket on top of a wardrobe.

But the best example of the thoroughness which his brother and sister-in-law had put into their holiday preparations was the party they'd organized for the yacht club dance on New Year's Eve, a big annual social occasion. Geoff had even gone back through old copies of *The Reporter*, their school magazine, to make sure he hadn't left anyone significant out of the party. Crisp had nothing in common with any of them these days but he was touched by his brother's intentions. And curious enough to see what had befallen the former football stars and cadet camp masturbators.

They had drinks first at the Harts, where the women had a chance to scrutinize the girl who'd usurped Stephen Crisp, eyeing her backless black dress, straight black hair. The men chatted amiably, joking at each other's receding hairlines and spreading paunches, and also paid Anna polite but close attention.

'We've been dying to meet you,' Fiona Bishop said to Anna. 'We've heard so many nice things. And to see Steve again.' She circled him with a brown arm. 'How's my old lover?' she said. Harley Onslow's sister. Perhaps he'd once or twice taken her to the movies or to a school dance; a shy, pale and overdressed convent girl with a damp handkerchief in the palm and a darting cheek peck at the front door.

'Terrific.'

Anna raised an eyebrow, took a sip of gin and tonic and turned her bare back on them. A small raised mole on her right shoulder blade brushed his sleeve. *Oh, oh.*

Helen d'Arcy collared Anna. 'Where are you from?' She smiled widely, showing a tiny smudge of lipstick on an upper tooth. With a deft gesture she flicked her long blonde hair behind her shoulders.

'What do you mean? From Sydney—but originally Yugoslavia.'

'Sorry.' The smile was apologetic. 'I meant what area. The North Shore? Double Bay? I love Double Bay. I always shop there when I'm in Sydney.'

'Lavender Bay actually. We're living together at the moment. They call it Lavatory Bay because all the harbour rubbish collects there.'

'Oh, I don't know it. What school did you go to? I know most of them in Sydney—Abbotsleigh, Ascham . . .'

Anna turned back to Crisp and linked arms. 'I'm pushing thirty and the lady wants to talk to me about school. Isn't that an interesting phenomenon?'

Oh Christ, Crisp thought.

'Doesn't he look well?' Fiona said. 'You get better with age, Steve. Tom loses handfuls of hair every day. He says it's the state of the market doing it. The fault of the bloody socialists.'

'You said it baby,' her husband said. 'And the left-wing media.' He clapped Crisp goodnaturedly on the shoulder. The others laughed—he'd gone Bolshie of course but seemed the same old Crisp underneath. You could blame it on the Eastern States, the left-wing attitude.

Crisp was intrigued at Bishop's bossy, confident manner, which he carried off even in a casual reefer jacket and white slacks. Twenty years before he'd been known as Diesel Bishop because his flat mandibular profile resembled that of the Southern Aurora. The dormitory matron had electrified him against nocturnal wetting.

They drove to the yacht club in his brother's Volvo, along winding, cliff-hugging streets, through tree-lined suburbs where coloured lights indicated other New Year parties in progress. Crisp pointed out features of interest to Anna, his arm around her shoulders. Her skin was taut and cool and aromatic with oriental spices. The sea breeze was stiffening, shaking the peppermint trees and roughening the river.

'I hope you know what to expect,' he whispered.

'Are you kidding?' she said.

At the yacht club the party was well advanced. Tables had been set up on the wide sloping lawns overlooking the river and red and green striped marquees, dispensing food and drink, and a dance floor had been erected nearby. Waiters hurried from marquee to table with ice-buckets of champagne and plates of cold chicken. A rock group of conservative appearance was resting between brackets, the musicians sharing a jug of beer and smoking cigarettes. Beneath a high white gum strung with lights youngish men with modish clothes and hair of medium length laughed confidently and competed enthusiastically for the drink waiters' attentions. A phalanx of girls with pleasant, open faces and well tanned shoulders chatted happily at the edge of the crowd, their eyes skipping over each new arrival. Several pairs of eyes, some of them vaguely familiar, met Crisp's, made notes and passed on.

He was desperate for a drink. He snatched a passing bottle of Great Western and poured several glasses. He downed his quickly, but not as quickly as Anna, whose uptilted jaw and determinedly upright carriage he thought signified either nervousness or trouble. Or both. She was sticking close to his side. A small movement flickered over her face as Fiona came over, holding out her glass for refilling. He filled it with a quip and sinking spirits, setting Fiona off into peels of giggles which shook her brown cleavage. Her tan was actually made up of masses of tiny freckles crammed together. She had filled out in the breasts.

'You're a clown Steve.' She turned to Anna. 'He'd laugh a girl's knickers off in the old days.'

'I didn't know you wore any,' he said.

Anna said, 'He's still a card now.' She gave him an intense eye. 'Another champagne please.'

He clawed at his hair which was flying in the sea breeze. 'Go easy, it's only ten o'clock.'

'Fuck the time. I'd like another drink.'

'Wow,' Fiona said. 'I'll leave you two to it.'

Crisp poured the drink. 'Her brother was a friend of mine,' he said.

'That's all. By the way, he's dead.'

Anna drank her champagne, said nothing. Near them a marquee fly flapped noisily in the wind. A waiter secured it with a quick granny knot.

The complete evening passed through Crisp's mind as he floated on the Li-Lo in the late afternoon sun, lying on his back, his horizontal vision extending not much beyond his body, past the stomach hair and appendix scar, along the thinly haired shins—serrated by old blows from football boots and hockey sticks—to the left big toe where gout waiting to get a foothold was kept at bay only by the valiant Benemid.

He'd kept her from the champagne for an hour, walking with her down to the marina among the Dragons and cruisers, sitting quietly on the river-wall picking flakes of rust from the handrail as the amplified salvo of the band carried over them across the river. Before midnight they returned to dance, moving closely together and then joining hands with Geoff and Denise and the Harts for *Auld Lang Syne*. On the midnight stroke they kissed: Crisp felt her teeth pressing forcefully through her lips, then cold against his tongue and mouth like stones.

'Happy New Year.'

'Happy New Year darling. Are you aware how much I love you?' she asked. Though smudged her eyes were round and penetrating. Looking into them made his eyes water. She was dishevelled in the wind and he smoothed back her hair from her forehead. The gesture seemed too paternal to him. He kissed her lightly, stroking the dark strands at the nape of her neck.

'I love you the same.'

Beyond her head he saw Fiona and Helen looking at them, chatting animatedly. He drew Anna closer, his hands on her hips, fluttering over her buttocks.

'Why do you behave strangely sometimes?' he attempted.

'Because I'm mad. Crazy as a loon.'

They went to the bar, out of the wind, and hot from the dancing drank more champagne, drained their glasses dry. Jim Oakes came up to them, effusive, very much the budding gynaecologist and social lion.

'Let me get you both a drink.' He patted Anna's stomach familiarly.

'Three and a half month's gone I'd say. Who's your gyno?'

Crumpling, she ran weeping to the toilet. Crisp drew deep breaths of surprise and urged his sister-in-law after her. *What was this?*

He inhaled rather than drank two glasses of champagne, being past sipping. It was warm and sweet. They were on to the late night cheap stuff. Bile rose in his gullet with a hiccup. 'Happy New Year,' he said to Doctor Oakes, raising his glass. He felt decades, not a year, older. 'You dead shit.'

'What did I say?' Oakes asked everyone loudly.

Fiona materialized at Crisp's side, drunk and playful. 'Oh you devil,' she said, playing to the crowd. 'Stephen the rat with women. Time for a New Year kiss lover.' She pounced on his mouth, darting in with a sour champagne tongue. Diesel Bishop stood benignly and mandibularly by. Crisp grasped her lightly above the waist, in self-defence. Finding it bare there he moved his grip to a safer, clothed area. It was probably bad manners to urgently dislodge New Year kissers, even voracious lamprey-like ones.

Out of the toilet sped Anna, appearing like a dark avenging angel beside them. She turned furious and disappointed green irises on him. Tears streamed through her eye makeup.

'Fuck you Stephen! She pushed him heavily in the chest. 'Fuck all you bourgeois piss-ants! Let me through!' She brushed past Fiona and ran down the clubhouse steps clutching her silver purse. She was bolting through the parking lot as he gathered his reflexes and hurried after her. He reached the car park but couldn't see her among the Rovers and Lancias. He tripped over a Jaguar's tow-bar and fell to his knees on the asphalt.

'Fuckingshitchrist' up into the peppermint trees. A knee was grazed and small stones were sharply embedded in his palms. He yelled after her but she had vanished down the dark overgrown path through the veldt grass. A headlight shimmered briefly on her purse and she was gone. There were no street lights or nearby houses to illuminate her path.

He returned furious to the clubhouse. Everyone looked up as he arrived, smoothing down his windblown hair, and the women changed their conversation. Oakes sauntered up to him, glass in hand, and deposited the other heavily on his shoulder.

'Perfectly normal behaviour Steve. Highly strung is she? It's obviously her condition.'

'She's not.' A triangular flap of cloth lay open at one knee. His sweat rose in stale waves. The band was playing its last bracket for the night, an amalgam of numbers including a Western Australian interpretation of a rock version of *Brazil*, featuring two pairs of maracas and a harmonica.

They searched for her in two cars—retracing all routes from the yacht club—Crisp directing operations from the Volvo, abject and angry simultaneously. He peered into dark parks and shrouded lanes. Images flooded in of Anna slaughtered by drunken drivers, pack-raped by Hell's Angels revellers. Or, more likely, of her stepping testily over an unfamiliar cliff into the black river. He would have driven around in circles all morning—it was now well after three—but Denise suggested driving home to see whether she was there.

She'd better be, he thought darkly, and she was, in her anticlimactic fashion, sitting at the edge of the pool paddling toes in the water and petting the Great Danes. Cheyenne was worrying one of her shoes with flaccid lips. Crisp couldn't speak he was so relieved. Strangely, the next thing that occurred to him was her uncharacteristic ease with the big dogs. She was usually afraid of them, and of all dogs, and would cross the street to avoid a Pekinese. 'I'm more of a cat person,' was a saying of hers. Some women liked to say that.

'You're a character aren't you?' Denise said. She threw off her own shoes. 'We've been looking everywhere for you.'

Anna looked up with a small embarrassed smile, almost shyly, fondling Lady's jowls meanwhile. 'I rang someone's doorbell and they drove me home. They were very kind. The man was a judge though not at all authoritarian. His wife writes books for children.'

They sprawled, deflated, at the poolside while Denise made coffee. They drank it as the New Year dawn came up, the colour of tangerines. The sea breeze had dropped already and a warm dry easterly was shivering the thin leaves of the silky oak. The wind chimes tinkled lightly.

Anna asked, 'Can anyone tell me why Lady has only five nipples? Cheyenne has six even though they're rudimentary in the male.'

'Nature does funny things I guess,' Geoff said.

Underwater lights illuminated the pool, casting a chlorinated glow which had attracted moths, small crickets and black night-flying beetles. The moths had fluttered and drowned quickly and the beetles too eventually succumbed after struggling to climb the slick tiled walls. The crickets, however, did not surrender easily and scudded across the pool's surface, from one side to the other, with a futile energy that caught and held Crisp's attention until the others had left him and gone to bed.

8

Mortality Reports

16th September 1829

If Your Excellency pleases I wish to submit a report on the serious rate of mortality among the aboriginals.

Ten deaths have occurred up to this time. The mortality is not confined to the settlement; those aboriginals visiting the establishment only infrequently are also succumbing to disease in large numbers. I have, of course, no way of tabulating these numbers of fatalities.

The fatal complaint seems to generally originate in cold, due no doubt to the severity of the season and the natives' apathy to European shelter and clothing. There are more fatal effects among the adults than the children.

On an autumn Saturday afternoon as Stephen was mowing the front lawn Harley Onslow called for him solemnly in his mother's car to go surfing. It was early April, between heat and cold. At the beach the aftermath of Cyclone Tessa had tossed heaps of kelp on the shore. Massed banks of leathery brown weed and branches of sea-grapes lay dry and crackling in the sun. Sand fleas and slaters flicked around their feet as they stepped gingerly through the piled weed and headed for the water's edge. A gull picked optimistically amongst the storm debris—broken toys, orange peel, plastic containers—hoping for the eyes of a dead fish. It hopped away as they approached, with some difficulty: one of its feet was missing. The lame leg, thin as red thread, ended just below the joint, unbalancing the bird and giving it a personal trail of single footprints.

Harley and he weren't talking, because of Julie Stumm's behaviour the night before at a party at Harley's house—Harley's farewell party, actually. She'd been going out with Harley for a year or so, then last night at a party for Harley because he was leaving school to go jackerooing at Bruce Rock for three years, she'd played the tease, throwing her brown limbs around Stephen all night. *She's using me for some purpose to get at him*, he'd thought at the time, but had gone along happily with the slow, close dancing: Fats Domino, Buddy Holly and all that, the laughing embrace at the end of a frenzied Jailhouse Rock. (*When he'd cracked a fat against her, for Christ's sake. 'Hey Stiffy,' she'd whispered in his ear, and giggled.*) Another erection was stirred in his bathers by the memory. He sat on a heap of weed putting on his flippers, feeling vaguely treacherous and misunderstood. But wishing to be friendly, they'd been friends for years for God's sake. Between his toes were chopped snippets of grass blades.

Sitting on their boards out beyond the line of breakers six surfers were waiting for the swells to mount. The easterly was blowing and the sun carried strength enough to pleasantly warm their shoulders. They'd spoken only a handful of words before they walked into the sea, backwards, to lessen the drag on their flippers. They dived under a breaking wave, kicked through the white water and the sea clasped them like an icy hand. They surfaced together, snorting and blowing with the cold, but there was none of the usual frozen brass-monkey camaraderie.

Tides had scoured a narrow channel parallel to the shore about fifty yards out and filled it with a tangled mass of weed. It writhed in the broken water, raising spiky branches like drowning hands. And rasped against their bodies, scraping their sides, winding tentacles around frenzied feet like a sea creature seeking body warmth. Some of the weed stems left small scratches. Thicker lengths clung flaccidly like slabs of wet tripe. They kicked fiercely through the channel and reached a sandbank—beyond it they were into clear unbroken water.

A moderately high wave reared up and they both struck out in front of it. Stephen caught the wave and was well positioned on its slope; looking up he saw that Harley had caught it too, but not so well. So he tried to beat him by a little more and kept his head and shoulders down, streamlining his body, and it carried him almost to the beach.

Elated for some reason he swam out again through the chop, over the weed channel, under the breakers to where the waves were mounting. Harley was there waiting for the next one. His head was turned away facing the horizon. Another bigger wave rolled in and Harley was too eager to catch it, swimming out to meet it, getting too deep and missing it altogether. But he caught it cleanly. It picked him up like a balsa boat and he rode it all the way into shore.

More waves passed that were too small to consider. Then came a fine big wave, rising out of the horizon in a powerful glassy swell only seen at the change of seasons. It sucked up the undertow of the previous wave to bolster its strength, mounted high and unbroken behind them. They kicked wildly and were plucked up like corks and thrown down the chute before it, arms out-thrust for balance to avoid being dumped and rolled on the bottom. Two of the board riders caught it too, and speared down the slope between them.

He knew this much (because he was raising his head for a desperate gulp of air): one of the board riders wiped out, lost his balance and fell from his board. The freed board spiralled high into the air and sliced back into the wave not ten feet from him. He fought to keep buoyant and streamlined while the tearing currents wrenched at his stomach muscles. White water slapped him across wind-blown shore waves and finally bounced him into the shallows. He waited for Harley. The surfer retrieved his board from the beach and paddled out to sea again but Harley didn't appear. Another wave broke heavily, snapping at the sand bank. The remaining surfers rode in on the cloudy yellow froth. Harley wasn't on this wave either and he could not see his head, red and taciturn, bobbing beyond the breakers.

He shouted for him, walking into the sea, and the surfers turned briefly around, then re-faced the horizon. He swam out to where they had been, beginning to panic now, weak and ineffectual in the legs, lacking wind. A wave dumped him and rolled him on his back. When he gulped air pain shot the length of his spine. Sand and weed fragments clouded the water, swirled in his eyes and mouth.

Perhaps because he could see nothing he gave up diving too soon. He yelled at the surfers for help. Very cool fellows, they looked at him askance until persuaded by his panic to join the search while he ran to the surf club for help. A boat crew eventually stroked up and down the beach in the rising seas before they ran into trouble of their own, almost submerging beneath the pressure of waves on the sandbank. They found nothing.

He was there the next afternoon, Sunday, had been there since dawn, when the water police brought Harley's body up with hooks. Half a mile north it had been, twisted naked in the kelp channel. A blue flipper remained fastened to one foot: the ankle had puffed and swollen around the heel strap. The weed around the body was much the same colour as his hair, the reddish-brown of rusted iron. The reef and the police hooks had scratched and gouged the limbs. 'Fucking shame,' said a sergeant from Cottesloe station, covering the body with a grey tarpaulin carrying a lifebelt and anchor trademark. The tarp said *Jensen Marine—Evinrude, Stebercraft, Mercruiser Inboards.*

Vaughan Onslow, Harley's father, never got over it. In the street later, or in a store, he'd come up to Stephen saying, 'I ensured this sort of thing wouldn't happen. You know that, young Crisp?' He was referring to his insistence that his son rise at 5 a.m. every morning for six years to be trained by Olympic swimming coaches. (Consequently Harley had become a very good swimmer though not surprisingly turned off competitive swimming by the age of sixteen.) His father had donated a new surf rescue boat, the *Harley Onslow*, to the surf club in his son's memory and aged ten years overnight. Harley's mother and sister Fiona had also taken it hard. Julie Stumm had behaved decorously for several months and then left for secretarial school in Melbourne where she eventually became involved with a married accountant, suffering facial injuries when his car left the road on a hairpin bend after a weekend's skiing at Fall's Creek.

As for Stephen, he felt certain guilts, on different levels, as well as sadness. His culpability quotient had in fact risen ever since. It unfortunately showed no sign of levelling off as people around him were hurt in varying degrees.

23rd September 1829

Your Excellency, it is with feelings of the utmost sorrow and concern that I am called upon to report an increased catalogue of deaths which has come to my knowledge a few days subsequently to the transmission of my last report. I have cause to believe that death hath visited with dire havoc a great portion of the aboriginal population.

The number of deaths has now risen to twenty-two. There are now remaining of the Bruny tribe eleven persons, consisting of two men, four women and five children. I am informed by one Wooraddy, the chief of the tribe, that its original size was above twenty families, between eighty and one hundred people.

I have not seen people die so quickly. The average time from the first observable signs of illness to the last breath is thirty-eight hours. I am not sure of the significance of this.

9

A Loathsome Disorder

The day I despatched my second mortality report to the Governor saw Wooraddy return from Bull Bay bringing news that Truganini, Dray and Pagerley were at Kelly's farm.

'Plenty white men there. Women very sick.'

From his description of their illness it seemed they were afflicted with a loathsome disorder contracted during their cohabitation with the whalers at Adventure Bay.

'What conduct could be more palpably atrocious and debasing than this (I immediately penned to His Excellency) in men who vainly assume an ascendancy over this benighted race! The circumstance of these forlorn beings cohabiting with the whalers was bad enough, but any encouragement calculated to seduce them away from their dependence on me is a direct offence to Government. I presume Your Excellency will wish to take immediate action.'

Wooraddy was anxious that I should send for the women. I guessed that he harboured a strong predilection for Truganini. He had become very dejected since his wife's death and constantly bewailed his widowed state. (I had observed that a native without a wife was a miserable being. His main object in life was finding a woman to provide him with shellfish, herbs and fruits as well as wifely affection.) Thus he was delighted when Mangana, Truganini's father, left suddenly of his own volition for Bull Bay in quest of the women. That day, the Sabbath, I performed divine service, descanting on some of the principal passages in the 28th chapter of St Matthew. The convicts were most attentive.

After an absence of seven days Mangana returned with Truganini and Pagerley. The women were in an afflicted state, walking with the aid of crutches and strangely loath to meet my gaze. Truganini leaned on her stick, fidgety and tense, peeling bark strips from it with her fingers.

'Tea and sugar for us?' she asked grumpily.

Pagerley flopped down on the ground and picked at a callous on her heel with a muttonfish shell. 'Dray burn in fire soon,' she mumbled into the sand.

They had left Dray behind as too ill to walk: on a sandy beach with a fire and a pile of limpets for food. Truganini and Pagerley said they had been 'very sick' but were now recovering. I could see no outward signs of a loathsome disorder but they were much reduced in flesh. I sent a boat for Dray and issued the others with provisions and slop clothing.

The change in Wooraddy was remarkable. He become animated and cheerful. He hugged me, danced around me calling 'Good Mitter Robinson'. That evening I noticed some fresh decorative incisions on his chest, the blood barely congealed, and a renewed application of plumbago-like ochres and animal grease.

At nightfall the boat returned with Dray. She appeared exceedingly debilitated and near starved. Her eyes were glazed and seemed not to recognize me. She complained of a pain in her loins, the area of which was very swelled. Wooraddy and Mangana laid her down on a bed of skins and I attempted to take her pulse. She gave a sly little coquettish grimace and with a wasted hand like a brown claw snatched at my private areas.

'Good white mans. Biscuit, sugar, tea?'

As the women recovered their strength over the ensuing weeks I tested my growing fluency in their dialect by conversing with them, and with Mangana and Wooraddy, about their tribe and life on Bruny before my arrival. These discussions generally took place in the evening around their fires when the natives were sated with meat and shellfish, hence very garrulous and content. They brought me sweet berries, bush honey and a wild fruit resembling the greengage which they called *num-her*. They would roast some plant roots and *poorner* in the ashes and munch them, I would eat my fruit and we would drink tea together. Behind us the sea rolled placidly onto the beach shelf and the murmur of voices sounded from the prisoners' quarters.

I was interested to observe at these gatherings that Mangana and Pagerley had soon become partners, or as our society would have it, man and wife. Mangana forced his suit for several days. At first Pagerley, who was aged no more than twenty, showed some repugnance for him. He was, after all, probably fifty and no oil painting even by sable standards. Eventually, however, she yielded to his wishes.

Possibly she was a realist. With Wooraddy's infatuation for Truganini becoming evident Mangana was the only available male on the island.

Wooraddy had been equally assiduous to possess Truganini, but so far had not met with Mangana's success. Whenever he approached her—or rather jumped at her with piercing screeches, displaying himself quite overtly and zealously—she yelled, '*Ragewrapper, Ragewrapper*' and bewailed her fate with lamentation and weeping. No way discouraged Wooraddy laughed at her tears and renewed his wooing, presenting her with choice opossum entrails and intricate decorations—necklaces and wristlets—made of polished green shells strung on fibrous twine. He danced attendance on her, encircling her with slow jigging steps, shaking scarred limbs and offering his red-ochred and charcoaled body to her. This situation disturbed me, I must confess, but I decided it was a peculiar characteristic of savage life—that there existed a mutual dependence and one could not exist without the other. Still, my feelings were agitated by the fact that if a native held in fear fixed his attentions upon a particular female she was compelled to submit and become his partner for life or risk the violent consequences.

This eventually happened in Truganini's case. Suddenly one evening the lithe and wily girl, wearied no doubt by the constant barrage of her suitor's attentions, slipped across to Wooraddy's fire, crouched on her heels, pulled one of his fur cloaks about her shoulders and hunched over the coals. That night she entered his hut, becoming, by their lights, his wife. Wooraddy's happiness was boundless. He had a fit of giggles that lasted into the night.

During our nightly conversations (made more serene by the lessening of tensions between these two) I sought personal details for my journal of those few remaining members of the Bruny tribe. The more information I gleaned the more I came to the realization that in the person of Truganini stood the blueprint for the larger tragedy of her people.

She was the daughter of Mangana—as I have mentioned—who had been chief of the Bruny people, giving way to Wooraddy as he reached middle age. Her mother, Mangana's first wife Thelgelly, I discovered had been stabbed to death by white settlers before her eyes. Her elder sister Leena had been raped and carried off by sealers to the islands of the straits. While still a young girl Truganini had been the intended wife of a young warrior, Paraweena. Wishing to return to

Bruny from the mainland one day, the young lovers and another warrior, Pogenna, were offered a ride across the channel by two sawyers known to them, Watkin Lowe and Paddy Newall. In mid-channel Lowe and Newall threw the males overboard and dragged Truganini to the bottom of the boat. As the natives swam to the boat and grasped the gunwale, the whites chopped off their hands with their hatchets. The helpless men waved their arm stumps and drowned before Truganini. The Europeans were free to do as they pleased with her. Such were her first encounters with our civilization.

I prepared for my expedition to Port Davey, proceeding to Hobart Town to select the convicts who were to accompany me and to receive the written approval of the Governor for my journey 'for the purpose of endeavouring to effect an amicable intercourse with the aboriginals in that quarter and, through them, with the tribes in the interior'.

The final escort party was Alexander McGeary, Alexander McKay, Samuel Hopkins, John Tunnicliffe, John Simpson and William Stansfield. McKay held a ticket-of-leave and was to receive a conditional pardon after two years' service with good character. In the case of the other four any indulgence to be extended to them would depend on their good conduct in my service.

By mid-January of 1830 my preparations were nearly complete. Clothing was issued to the escort party and provisions for ten weeks were loaded on the government schooner *Swallow*—this vessel and the Bruny whaleboat were to provide our transport.

McGeary and Mackay mumbled darkly about the inadequate supplies of their rations compared to the quantity given to the natives. Their comments roused the overseer of the schooner, one Thomas Sutton, to insubordination and the use of improper expressions.

'I won't move a bloody inch without more ration. And if this boat don't move you don't get your precious blacks.'

I made known his behaviour to the port officer, by whom he was sentenced to twenty-five lashes. For the moment all complaints ceased.

Before setting sail I visited the natives in the colonial hospital and in Richmond gaol. Those in the hospital were confined with the lunatics for greater ease of their administration, not a situation I favoured. One boy of about ten had been thrown down, had his teeth knocked out and been otherwise maltreated. (Living with lunatics was not only calculated to create a prejudice in their minds against the white inhabitants but must also have militated against the Governor's good intentions.)

On 30th January we started on the expedition, sailing with fair winds. I instructed the schooner to anchor off Bruny and we took on board Wooraddy, Truganini, Dray and Pagerley, all much pleased to see me.

That night we camped on the shore, all the white men grievously tormented with sandflies and mosquitoes, though in good spirits and anxious to proceed. Truganini, Wooraddy and Pagerley visited my tent, bringing a gift of a basket of lagoon tubers called *lo-ity*. We shared a pot of tea.

By way of conversation I asked Pagerley, 'Where is Mangana?' Munching her *lo-ity* stalks she pointed silently to the brazier on which my potatoes were roasting. I noticed she wore a new amulet of hair and skin.

Eventually Truganini said, 'My father is dead on the fire.'

Mangana had died from the effects of the loathsome disorder.

Geoffrey Crisp collected bigot jokes in an exercise book (his brother was amazed to learn). They went down well at the golf club and on lodge nights and bolstered his reputation as a wit and raconteur. (Sample: What's the definition of gross ignorance?—One hundred and forty-four Pakistanis; What do you call a boong who marries a pig?—A social climber.)

He had it made, Geoff: the Dalkeith house and pool (on which his brother presently glided on a squashy Li-Lo reversible mattress—green one side, blue the other—absorbing the ultra-violets and cogitating, a fallen gum twig between the teeth, on such matters as Geoff's genial bigotry, moderate wealth and local social cachet), clubby and undemanding business interests, a pretty ('best in the State!') and doting wife, the affection and respect of his peers. Such as they were.

'How do you do it?' Stephen had asked him early on. 'How does everyone do it? Why are you all so bloody rich?'

'Rich! This is W.A. my boy. Personally I haven't got much dough but this place is rich in every mineral under the sun. This is the biggest quarry in the southern hemisphere. We support the rest of the country.'

'Oh, come on.'

'We could be the biggest at everything in the southern hemisphere if the East didn't bleed us dry. No bullshit.'

Actually, Geoff owed nearly everything to his wife. Or to his father-in-law, Clive Gerrard, for conveniently having only one child, a three-State earthmoving business and a lymph nodal system eventually overrun by Hodgkin's disease. But Denise's profession had been most useful. She was a former model and, as readers of every newspaper in the State were aware, one of the most photographed (though *never* in a bikini) Miss Western Australias in the history of the competition, raising heaps of money for spastic children and losing out in the Miss Australia finals to Miss New South Wales (the 22-year-old home economics teacher Dianne Baker) only by a whisker.

And Geoff, still in his brother's mind's eye a small kid whingeing along behind him on his tricycle, had married this long-legged El Dorado and never looked back. Denise's reputation had launched the Claudia fashion boutique into a sound proposition; buying Spiro's, the wine bar next door, had been his idea but its close proximity to the University made it a sound one. He spent only two mornings a week in his city office, leaving the land speculation (the main money spinner) to his manager. He might play a round or two of golf at Lake Karrinyup or sit around drinking beer with Bernie Caravousonos, who trained his two geldings, in Bernie's kitchen at Belmont. Or he might drive over to the Claudia-Spiro complex, run an eye over the accounts and take the salesgirls from the boutique next door for *quiche lorraine*, sending them reeling back to work full of the house hock. Geoff might stay drinking with a few regulars until the bar filled with students at four o'clock and then take Lady and Cheyenne for a surf and a run along the beach. At night, if there wasn't a lodge meeting, he and Denise usually ate out, either at a favourite steakhouse at Fremantle or at a seafood restaurant built over the river bank where the oysters were flown in daily in ice-packed crates from the East. (The creatures refused to grow locally.) Every Saturday there were the races—and regular mid-week country meetings. There were parties and balls and friends popped in with convivial armloads of bottles. There was never a spare moment.

This was the *milieu* which enveloped Crisp and Anna. As far as he was concerned he felt surprisingly relaxed. The easy predictability of the place soothed his post-Commission tensions. Sun basted the body. The swimming pool washed away hangovers. Furry parameciums swam unmolested back and forth across the vision. Swifts and swallows held the attention, skidding high in the sky.

She commented, 'They're sucking you in with all that luxury.'

'I'm copping it sweet,' he said.

'They're such smug bloody chauvinists.' But she rolled over on her back, sighing with comfort, seduced by summer ease, the serenity of the river and the pollution-free skies. 'There are stars here I haven't seen for years,' she said.

'Just take it easy,' he said.

But he had brought up the matter of the bigot joke book. 'Why do it?' he asked, sipping one of Geoff's tawny ports. 'Isn't it a shade racist?' The women had gone to bed. The dogs lay comatose at their feet, trembling at busy dreams.

'Just for a laugh. Where's your sense of humour?' Apropos of nothing, or something, Geoff said, 'Ever rooted a coon, by the way?'

'I beg your pardon. No, actually. Isn't that an offensive question?'

'Me either. Bob Hart has.'

'Really? I couldn't be less interested.'

A dark and confiding moment, obviously. Geoff lowered his voice, casting a cautious glance down the hall towards the bedrooms. The former Miss Western Australia slumbered on.

'Bob nearly got us into all sorts of trouble.'

'How's that?'

'About two years ago after a company pissup. We were driving home in Bob's managing director's 280 SE. The boss was flaked in the back and Bob starts cruising through East Perth offering women wine. Two jump in the car. Bob's into one like a flash and the other's spilling wine all over the upholstery.'

Crisp sat silently sucking sweet mouthfuls of port. *Company men at play.*

'The girls finish the wine and want money, you see. One starts yelling, "Five bucks a fuck" over and over. I couldn't come at mine. I don't play around as a rule, anyway. Bob got shitty and refused to pay and they start screaming like maniacs. Can boongs yell!'

'Can they?'

'Can they ever! Bob shook one, you know, to quieten her down and the other one screams out the window for the whole bloody tribe. Then the boss wakes up in the back and wants to know what's going on.

"Can we give you ladies a lift home?" he says. Christ, and we're fighting the Black War. One girl grabs the keys and Bob's got to just about twist her arm off to get them back. They're biting and scratching us, the horn's blaring and their mob's running towards us picking up handy bricks and tearing palings from fences. We got them out of the car just as the first rock hit the roof. That Merc took off like a bloody jet.'

Geoff grinned boyishly into his port. Was that the trace of a blush? 'We had scratches all over our arms. Bob lost a few bits out of his face. The boss stank of bloody perfume and muscatel. What a night!'

Crisp wanted to go to bed. 'And what do you feel about all that now you're not young and foolish?' he asked. Barely hopeful.

'I still think Bob was lucky not to get a dose.'

In Geoff's opinion it was at this stage that his brother went peculiar, began to come on very heavy. Lounging around the pool after a Sunday evening barbecue (the d'Arcys and Oakes were also there, sipping claret and picking steak shreds from the teeth) Crisp bridled —as did Anna he noticed by her eye-rolling—at yet another slighting reference to *coons* and *boongs*, this time in an anedcote by Peter d'Arcy. D'Arcy the pharmacist was relating how he'd been forced to stop serving an Aboriginal woman with medicine because she wouldn't pay her bill. Geoff glanced sideways at his brother, seeking his confidence about the pickup episode, but found him unreceptive, staring distantly away from the group, drinking quickly.

'You can't run a business on handouts,' d'Arcy was saying. 'I had to push her out of the shop in the end. I told her straight. I said, "Listen Mary, lay off the plonk and spend your booze money on medicine for bub." They won't listen to reason.'

The story didn't strike a particularly responsive chord with the women, even Helen d'Arcy. Their identification was with the mother.

'Poor thing,' Claire Oakes said. 'Those lubras must have a terrible time. I read in the paper their babies have a mortality rate ten times that of white children.'

'Unfortunately,' said her husband the sage gynaecologist, 'these people won't help themselves. All the government handouts and health care don't mean a thing without self-help.'

Helen d'Arcy said, 'You can't blame them for being prostitutes, can you? I mean if it was a choice of that or your child starving.'

'Oh, I could never sink that low,' Denise said.

In jumped Crisp, the neo-lefty from the East. 'It's not generally taught in schools that some pillars of pastoral society used to distribute poisoned flour to the blacks in their locality. And organize shooting parties like fox hunts on Sunday afternoons after a roast dinner.'

'Really?' d'Arcy said, looking over at Oakes.

'I dispute that,' Oakes said. 'And anyway they were savage bastards in those days. Spear you as soon as look at you. Kill all the best stock, cut off one leg and leave the rest of the carcase to rot.'

Crisp's eyes fixed on the silky oak's swaying wind chimes. 'For that matter it was popular among the graziers to distribute typhoid infected blankets to the Aborigines in winter—a neat trick which saved valuable bullets and carried off the women and children with much more approbation.'

'How terrible,' Denise said politely. 'Would anyone like some dessert? There's only fruit and cheese I'm afraid.'

'What bullshit,' Oakes said. 'Typical left-wing propaganda based on legend and hearsay but with no facts to back it up.'

Crisp was unremitting, began gesturing with his wine glass. 'Not that your ruddy-cheeked farmers minded dealing with women and children as a rule. They'd snatch up babies by the feet and dash their heads against rocks.' Struck by inspiration he tossed the T-bone from his steak to Cheyenne. 'Or throw them to the dogs.'

Oakes got to his feet, angrily brushed grass from his trousers.

'Or into their parents' camp fires,' Crisp said.

'Let's go home Claire,' Oakes directed. 'I've had enough communist remarks for one night.'

Geoff and Denise saw them off. Crisp sensed vaguely that excuses were being made for his behaviour. Anna was surprisingly silent through all this, quietly sucking grass blades. The d'Arcys finished their drinks. Crisp helped himself to more claret and sat down heavily beside d'Arcy on the lawn.

'Did you know that the kylies we fished with as kids were essentially the same weapons used by the Swan River tribes thousands of years ago? And with the same name?'

'I didn't know that.' D'Arcy looked at his wife.

'They were a variety of boomerang, though differently shaped to those of southern and eastern Australia. Mostly they were about three-tenths of an inch thick in their thickest parts and with knife-like edges. They weighed between three and five ounces and their length varied from twenty to twenty-three inches. They carved them from a type of acacia. They flew further than the boomerangs of the east.'

Crisp took a draught of claret. And swallowed a small floating gumleaf, coughing a stream of red bubbles over his shirtfront. 'In weapons as thin as these,' he said, wiping his chin, 'a very small deflection was enough to ensure their true flight and their return to the thrower.'

'Is that so?' d'Arcy said, glancing at his watch. 'We really must be going.'

'And this is interesting. You remember those fishing spears we used to make from broom handles and two-inch nails? (d'Arcy nodded blankly.) We called them gidgies. The original gidgie was eight feet long and thrown by the woomerah. When threatening a stranger a warrior would say something like "*Gad joll nye darnaga*"—I will spear you.'

The d'Arcys both said that *was* interesting, looked at one another, made their farewells and left.

Kylies and gidgies, Crisp mused in his wine glass, were the only weapons deadly enough to kill the crafty teaques. To pierce their rough hides, penetrate their blubber and bring serenity to the coastal regions and river estuaries of guilty dreams.

And, searching through his pockets, he found a folded sheet of paper on which he had copied an energetic war and love song of the extinct Ben Lomond tribe of Tasmania. He wished he knew the translation but this had been destroyed by colonial linguists, the subject being not very select. He read aloud:

Ne popila raina pogana
Ne popila raina pogana
Ne popila raina pogana.

Thu me gunnea
Thu me gunnea
Thu me gunnea.

Thoga me gunnea
Thoga me gunnea
Thoga me gunnea.

Naina thaipa raina pogana
Naina thaipa raina pogana

Naina thaipa raina pogana.

Naara paara powella paara
Naara paara powella paara
Naara paara powella paara.

BALLAHOO, BALLAHOO, HOO HOO,

This was their massacre/climax whoop, a guttural shout. Slaughter and lust, death and love. After it, Crisp had a dry throat. He drained his glass.

10

Mother's Baked Beans

HE THOUGHT HE KNEW where to find his mother's grave, remembering himself on a hill dotted with stunted banksias overlooking a raw yellow hole with his tight-lipped father and a crowd of his father's business associates. (On his penultimate day in Western Australia he was visiting the grave for the first time since the burial.) Some friends had also been there, and some family, listening to the Reverend Clyde Woolhouse's maunderings on Jean Crisp the loving wife and mother (that, in fact, was what Murray Crisp later had engraved on her headstone: In Memory of Jean Audrey Crisp. A Loving Wife and Mother). Geoffrey had been too upset to attend the funeral, still a youngster. For most of the male mourners—women weren't encouraged to participate because of their slim grasp on their emotions—it had not been an entirely wasted day. While the bereaved cruised home in the undertaker's black Humber to receive Jean's red-eyed friends and neighbours with their offerings of casserole steak and stewed plums for the motherless, Murray's business associates adjourned to the Highway Hotel and clinched a few deals over scotches.

As it happened Crisp was mistaken. He couldn't find the grave and after an hour trudging through the heat and dust of the cemetery, peering at endless rows of headstones, he sought assistance from the cemetery's main office.

'Afternoon mate,' said a ginger clerk in khaki shirt, shorts and long socks. 'Name and initials of deceased, date of death and what religion?'

'Crisp J. A. March 29th 1962. Presbyterian. It's on a hill near some banksia trees.'

The clerk produced a thick book of burial records, found the entry and wrote the required information on a card. He handed it to Crisp. His mother was now grave number 184, compartment BC, burial registration number 119004, denomination *Presb.* No monumental work was to be erected on any grave without application to the Cemetery Board. Wooden kerbings, crosses, etc. were prohibited. (Nothing flashy, so you Micks go easy on the angels and Virgin Marys.)

'Turn left at the crematorium, hard right past the Garden of

Remembrance and you can't go wrong.' The clerk snapped shut his book of deaths.

'Thanks.'

'Hot day for it,' the clerk said.

He found the grave eventually. Bulldozers must have razed the hill he remembered because the grave now lay in a shallow treeless gully, its identification number overgrown by weeds. It was a plain grave with no monument and its surface was covered in small gravelly pebbles to deter weeds. By its scruffy appearance it had never been tended. Either a bushfire had swept over the Presbyterians or gardeners had tried to burn back the weeds for the grave was fringed with a beard of charred grass. A scattering of singed dandelions sprouted from the pebbles. Crisp tugged them out and began to tidy the grave's surroundings with his hands. He scratched in the earth and uncovered the identification number. One Eight Four. The inscription on the headstone was still clear enough, the granite untouched by the fire. Pottering about the grave, plucking and smoothing, he suddenly felt it the most futile task he'd ever done. Up would pop the dandelions again tomorrow. Winds would blow, sands would shift, bushfires would singe. Through all this weeding and tidying he permitted himself a tear or two, but none came, only the familiar ache at the back of the throat—the sensation he got when he dwelt on Wendy who would never live with him. Perhaps only self-pity moved him sufficiently these days.

Worse. He couldn't prevent himself considering some very macabre questions: such as her probable state of decay after numerous years in the yellow sandy soil. This was a perversity in itself. Mothers did not decompose. Mothers lay eternally in white nighties, size SSW, chosen by tearful Thelma Dengate, arms folded displaying wedding and eternity rings and with maroon lips, sharply defined eyebrow arches and purple eyelids turned heavenwards in mummified grace. Well remembered characteristics like the fair, barely greying, hair; the tiny translucent mole at the left jawline or the freckled, tennis-tanned shoulders didn't rot away into the sand, surely, any more than did a Mother's only artifice—two capped teeth which had allowed her to grin unembarrassedly again, shy no longer at what she'd long imagined was her smile's dingy greyness. (It was his fault. 'You drained all the calcium out of my teeth during the war, dear. I fed you the full fourteen months because of the cow's milk shortage. Trust you to be an early teether with a full set of choppers at nine months! A tiger, squeezing and pummelling at me! "What's this then?" Dad said when he came home on leave, saw you for the first time, "A devil for the breast!" Poor Dad with dreadful tropical sores all over his body and thin as a rake. I could hardly bear to touch him. There was a bit of jealousy there, I can tell you. You were the little man of the house. Bossy! What a tantrum when he'd give me a bit of a cuddle! I thought you'd never wean, then you'd not touch a skerrick of food but Mr Ladyman's eggs and rhubarb. Old Mr Ladyman'd call from his fowlyard over the back fence, "Want some eggs today Mrs C? Lovely googs. Delicious roobub? Good for the little soldier. Put hairs on his chest".')

In the next row from his mother's grave—still in the C section—Crisp noticed a big handsome monument resting on a marble plinth. Though not ostentatious it stood out by its size from the other spare Presbyterian graves. It was the tomb of John Curtin, wartime Prime Minister. No dandelions grew in its vicinity and no bushfire had been permitted to lap at its marble. Tending it, a swarthy gardener coughed, hawked and spat on the ground, then glanced up shyly to see if he'd been spotted. He wiped his mouth on the back of his hand.

'Pardon me gentlemans,' the gardener said.

My party reached a wide bay in the afternoon of the next day and set up camp by a creek flowing into the bay. The natives amused themselves by frolicking in the water. Truganini and Dray gave me two presents: a good luck amulet containing the ashes of Mangana (a questionable gift but given with the best intentions) and a flint for sharpening spears. By evening I was swelled from gnat and mosquito bites, the insects especially relishing the skin of the palest in the party—myself.

The following morning the men ran to me with the news that they had discovered some human remains. I inspected the body with the natives. It was a woman, only recently dead.

'Been sick,' Truganini said. 'Left here by her tribe, the *Toogee*. *Ragewrapper* kill plenty *Parlerwar*.'

So the mortality attacking the Bruny natives seemed to be general among the tribes. (For some reason this fact brought me a degree of relief.) My natives all backed off from the body, viewing it with some alarm.

From the southward and westward came strong winds. These adverse winds and the shortage of room aboard the vessel convinced me we would be better to travel overland to Port Davey. (Though designated a schooner the *Swallow* had been built originally as a ship's longboat, then lengthened at the stern instead of amidships making her very crank.) So we set out overland: eight blacks, five whites and four dogs. I estimated we should make Port Davey in three days. Little was known of the country: the distance by longitude was sixty miles.

Following the tracks of the *Toogee*—the Port Davey tribe—over the next days we passed through dense forests, crawling on hands and knees through holes in the rough foliage and scrambling over slick moss-covered rocks. We travelled through swamps, in places up to our thighs in mud. We descended cliffs so steep I worried for the safety of the convicts carrying our knapsacks, and ascended a rugged mountain range composed of white and variegated marble. Broken rock fragments rolled from the leaders' footsteps and fell on those following behind. While descending we had to cling to tufts of grass to check our headlong tumbling.

Harassed by strong winds and driving rain and hail from the southwest, we had still not reached Port Davey after a week. We forded eight rivulets, many of them breast deep, and crossed another mountainous tract before reaching the coast again. Our food supplies were almost exhausted: the natives had eaten nothing substantial for thirty-six hours and the dogs were near starved, so the sea was a welcome sight. The natives caught crawfish and stoned to death a large seal marooned on the beach. They flitched the seal meat and carried the flesh back to camp. They ate hungrily of the seal but I could manage only a skerrick, feeling poorly from the cold and improper diet. Nevertheless we pressed on westward over a wide marsh, flooded by the recent rains, towards Port Davey.

Three more days passed. Our provisions were now eight days gone. Three of the convicts went hunting with the guns but returned empty handed. Two of the men, Platt and Hopkins, lay prone on their blankets from weakness. McGeary was so weak he could not walk unaided. In desperation I sent McKay and Stansfield back to the *Swallow* for emergency rations while we subsisted on mussels, a few crawfish, roots and berries brought in by the natives. The mussels were bad and made all the white men sick. Platt moaned constantly on his bed, 'We'll die sure enough. And we'll be the lucky ones.'

McKay returned on 19th February with some welcome provisions. We rejoiced. But he also brought the unhappy news that the schooner had parted her cables and run aground. Most of the stores had been gotten out but the potatoes were spoiled by seawater: she had run aground on a sandy beach and was filled with sand. 'She's wrecked, she'll never be made seaworthy,' McKay said. I sent all the men back to carry the provisions off before they spoiled. I should have gone too but I was troubled by boils on the legs arising from the bad and frugal diet which rendered me quite lame.

My people left me, black and white together, and I was alone in the wilderness. During the night the creatures of the bush made sport of my situation. They ran brazenly about my bed and the birds screeched endlessly in the thicket. As the wind dropped to a zephyr the mosquitoes rose in clouds from the swamps and feasted on me.

My men returned with the provisions, some dragging the whaleboat across the marshes. They brought further news of the *Swallow*.

'You've been done,' Stansfield announced boldly. 'A useless hulk the Government's got you. Nine feet of keel without a single bolt, timbers quick-cemented with lime. Tight enough while laying at Hobart Town but her seams are a mile wide now.'

McKay smirked. 'The water in the hold's as clear as that alongside. His Excellency's given you a bleeding sieve.'

(But even here was an example of the Lord's aid. The way I saw it the boat's coming ashore was most fortunate. Had she struck bad weather at sea we would have been lost. Every black and white soul perished—a tragedy indeed.)

My illness worsened as we continued on. Now I was stricken with a painful and violent action in the bowels, occasioned, most likely, by eating rock oysters. At the time I was taking a course of calomel pills—prescribed for all sensible explorers in this part of the globe—but even this strong purgative offered no relief. Rather it desperately hastened my movements.

Stansfield offered advice: 'You best cure the dysentery by taking some fine flour, boiling it for five or six hours and eating it hot. The lumpier the better. Corks up the gizzard.' I followed his recipe, there being no alternative. The nights were excessive cold, my boils turned to wide-cratered pustules. But neither the cold nor my decreasing flesh surface deterred the mosquitoes.

Though excessive weak I had no alternative but to travel on. I left some men with the whaleboat and the bulk of the provisions and we climbed a lofty tier of mountains—hills of white quartz rising to a great altitude. We slept alongside deep ravines dangerously close to Nature in her most pristine character: perpendicular cliffs, immense chasms through which dark rivers roared, mountain peaks hidden by clouds. Piercing winds rushed up the ravines.

McKay and McGeary could not be relied upon. While crossing a deep chasm—the slope so steep I was lowering myself gingerly down by clutching stems of plants—I found myself suddenly alone. My party was not behind me as expected. I wanted to return though felt too weak to recross the ravine. Turning about desperately I saw McKay and McGeary about four hundred yards from me. I gathered my strength and *cooeed* to them. They turned around, saw me, hesitated for a moment and then walked on.

Shaking with emotion and illness I was forced to climb back up the mountain and wait to fall in with the natives, who had not yet passed me. Finally they found me, Wooraddy and Truganini forcing a way through the thicket and, half-carrying me, helping me along a high mountain ridge whereby we could avoid the deep ravines. We stumbled over thickly timbered gullies, the trees slick with black moss: we slipped and fell constantly. That evening we camped on the side of a bare rocky knoll. I was excessively ill and cold. During the night I rolled into the fire and it caught hold of my clothing. Flames burned my hands, lips and cheeks before I extinguished them. The natives with me also felt the intensity of cold and wished for morning.

At forty-six Jean Crisp had succumbed to a cerebral haemorrhage. She had always been a well woman, as they say. She'd exercised regularly, drunk only socially, smoked moderately and eaten sparingly. Murray Crisp, on the other hand, was a classic type-A character (as the heart men like to classify his sort of personality) who drank enthusiastically, ate heartily (he was twenty-five pounds overweight), smoked seventy cigarettes a day, lived for work and Hallstrom Gelatine and hadn't exercised beyond once-a-week golf in twenty years. He was therefore mystified as to why she had gone first.

Everyone was. Everyone was edgy, peculiarly unsettled.

'If only I'd been taken instead,' he moaned once to his elder son during the bereavement period, though not again. 'She was so young, so well. Not a grey hair. And I'm ready for the scrapheap.'

He seemed to be right. His eyes were dark-circled and rheumy from grief and Dewars. His face was almost transparent, its broken veins prominent. The shoulders had lost their rigidity and a thick flesh fold spilled over his belt.

'One in a million, Jean,' he'd say into his whisky glass of an evening. 'She was one in a million, your mother. I don't want you to forget that.'

They had been difficult times for the Crisps for several reasons. Six months before her death Stephen had gathered his courage and the attractive and personable Jane Wittaker from a Chekhov tutorial and bearded his mother in the kitchen. Peas and carrots simmered on the stove, lamb cutlets browned in their egg and breadcrumbs.

'Jane's pregnant,' he announced. He and Jane smiled thinly. She carried an armful of books as well as *The Cherry Orchard* and wore a fawn sweater and very collegiate check shirt. Nothing showed yet.

'What!' said his mother and clutched at the oven door handle for support. Fainting seemed a possibility. 'Oh my God,' she groaned, and said so many times every day until they were married in the local registry office four weeks later. She took the news badly—in such a way that she said some surprising things:

'I would rather it had been your father,' she said once, her face ravaged by the precariousness of parenthood and other emotions. 'This is worse than adultery. My first child!'

And: 'Where did you do it? In the car? At the beach? Was Jane a virgin? This is a sordid affair and will ruin your life. What about your studies?' She cried and moaned that her trust had been abused and left half-smoked cigarettes burning all around the house.

She also announced (with the air of a Holmes): 'I should have realized this was going on. There have been less semen stains in your bed recently.'

At other times she would say implacably, 'I'm taking this very well. It's your father who can't cope with it. From the business point of view. I mentioned it at the Dengates the other night and he hissed at me to shut up. He's funny like that, quite narrow-minded.'

She informed him she was under Doctor Williams' care. 'For

nervous exhaustion over this whole affair. I asked him if he could terminate the pregnancy. Because of your ages and so on. He said no.'

'You had no right to do that. No right at all.'

'What would you know?' she cried, staring through the venetian blinds across the lawn to the neighbours' superfine couch grass and orderly rosebeds. 'You are a child and your brain is in your penis.' (*Penis? In the bath when he was small she had always called it a doodle.*)

His father actually said very little. He seemed extraordinarily embarrassed, making an appearance in Stephen's bedroom the morning after the pregnancy announcement while he, equally uncomfortable, feigned sleep. His father cleared his throat. He was fully dressed for management duties: charcoal grey, even the hat.

'Son, your mother tells me you and Jane are in some trouble.'

'Yes.' Though he wouldn't accurately describe it as trouble. Confusion perhaps.

And then his father asked, 'Will you get the sack? What will they say at the Commission? Will it affect your promotion?'

Good God. 'No. Why should they care?'

'Some firms would take a dim view of that sort of umm, behaviour. By the same token management likes to see a stable home life and decent moral standards.'

'Not every organization is like Hallstroms.'

Murray Crisp took this ultimate rudeness well. 'Don't speak to me like that. Jane's father—is he in business? He and I will have to sort this thing out.'

'He's dead.'

'Oh, pity.' He did not mention the matter to his son again.

So he and Jane married despite everyone and went to live in a tiny green fibro flat surrounded by tea-tree hedge up the coast. Dank but romantic. Grasshoppers came down the bathroom flue and the kerosene bath heater roared like a Boeing. The kitchen window opened on the Indian Ocean a hundred yards away and Jane fed seagulls on her first cooking attempts, scones heavy as grenades. They cooked on a primus stove and kept their food cold in an ice-chest. They felt like pioneers in the cool, cement-floored flat. Winter was centuries away. He dropped out of part-time university and sold his books. Before the baby came they swam most days before he left for work, he pushing her rapidly thickening body up the steep sandhill from the beach to the flat. Early on she had morning sickness. He'd stand behind her, his face against her back, gently rubbing her stomach as she puked pale lemon bubbles into the toilet. Next door a red-haired used car salesman named Ron Malloch could be heard nightly through the paper-thin walls refusing his wife permission to shave her legs and armpits and pluck her eyebrows. He belonged to some extreme branch of Protestantism: another of their tenets was against radios.

'I won't have you interfering with nature Elaine and flaunting your body in public,' he'd yell. Then the Mallochs' bed would pound and squeak away into the night.

'Malloch the hair fiend strikes again!' Stephen would say and, arms about each other, they'd giggle themselves to sleep.

So came the denouement (like a classic tragedy): his mother's death twenty days after Wendy's breech birth. Jane a week out of hospital and convalescing at the Crisps with the baby, Stephen there too in his old room, Jane and the baby in Geoff's room and Geoff sleeping on a camp stretcher in with him. (The day after Jane left hospital Stephen had snuggled in with her, nestled up to her in his pyjamas. His mother's face at the door: 'Get out of that bed, Stephen. I won't have you two canoodling in this house with your brother to see you.'

'We're married, after all,' he complained, but did as he was told. The chastened smutty child.)

On her last morning he'd passed her in the corridor outside her bedroom. Sallow-faced, she had a hand to her forehead and steadied herself with the other. She wore small brocade slippers from Hong Kong and a bunch of pink Kleenex, for a slight cold, overflowed the pocket of her housecoat. She said, 'I have a splitting headache, dear. I'm going to lie down.'

People went about their 8 a.m. business. Jane was changing the baby at the far end of the house. Geoffrey left for school. His father read *The West Australian* on the toilet—muted farts and the rustling of newspaper sounded from the bathroom. Stephen showered quickly and dressed for work, keen young trainee on the Commission's news staff. Today he was assigned to cover the police courts, the minor criminal courts where swollen-eyed Aborigines and old lags filed before Stipendiary Magistrate A. C. Cusack on drinking charges and for saying 'shit' in the sensitive hearing of policemen. (Magistrate Cusack was popular with the Press for his sense of humour. He would crack most of his quips twice, with a wink in the direction of the Press table.

'You're looking off-colour this morning Don,' he'd say as an aged and hungover black man shuffled into the dock.

'Yes Mr Cusack.'

Or: 'This is the record of a blackguard, Sam,' he'd remark, waving a sheaf of prior convictions for park drinking. 'A blackguard.'

'Sir, I was only celebratin' me birthday.'

'Many happy returns Sam. One month.')

Before he ate his breakfast he took his mother two Disprin and a glass of water. She was in her housecoat lying on her side and her eyes were half open but had become milky blue, opaque. Her mouth lolled ajar. He was struck by the strange hunched posture of her body. He touched her shoulder and it had lost all tone and elasticity.

'Mum?' In fear reverting to childhood. 'Mummy?'

There was a small movement. She enunciated slowly and thickly, her tongue negotiating tiny distances only with great difficulty. 'Stephen,' she said, her last message to him, or anyone. 'Your baked beans are on the stove.'

Down the corridor his new daughter gave bubbling cries and his father ripped many handfuls of toilet paper—being fastidious in such matters—and flushed the toilet. Then came a hissing sound as he sprayed the room with the scent of eucalypts.

His mother's friends brought strong opinions with their casseroles and queen puddings in the ensuing weeks. They made themselves at home in Murray's absence, sitting smoking and drinking coffee around the blue Formica table in the breakfast corner, smiling sadly when tiny Wendy was displayed and shaking a head or two. A couple of them brought the baby squeaky toys, soft-bristled hairbrushes and pink balaclavas and jumpsuits. Jane bustled about, hiding in the techniques of young motherhood. Stephen, on night shift, moped uncomfortably about the house the rest of the day.

Beryl O'Brien helped herself to scotch and ice blocks, talking around her cigarette and thawing ice trays under the tap. 'All this killed her,' she said. 'The disgrace and so forth. Not that Murray was an easy man to live with, but he tried to do the right thing by his family. You've got to give him that. Sent them both to a good school.'

Thelma Dengate said, 'I played tennis with Jean the day before . . .

she passed away. I thought she looked tired and drawn. I won a set for once. Her mind wasn't on the game. I said, "Look dear, worrying won't help," but her mind just wasn't on the game.'

'Whose would be?' Beryl O'Brien said. 'Whose would be?' She drained her whisky and topped up her glass. A thought occurred to her in mid-stream. 'Anyway, they're right for this week if Marion brings the oxtail.'

By 13th March my fever was overcome, my spirits much improved. My party climbed the highest mountain range we had yet encountered, a colossus of white quartz which at a distance appeared to be snow, and on the summit espied a good luck omen—a rare white mountain kangaroo.

'*Dray*!' Wooraddy exalted, pointing to the bemused creature. It stood nibbling moss from the rock crevices, making no attempt to escape us. The natives, however, would not kill it—its spiritual value was fastened on their minds. Dray the native woman—named after this species—was especially excited with the animal, dancing up and down, pointing first at the kangaroo and then at herself and making soft squeals in her throat.

Eventually it hopped down the mountainside whereupon the natives all ran to its grazing place and gathered up its faecal pellets in their hands. They bound the droppings in grass and wore them as good luck amulets, appearing so cheerful and optimistic that I desisted from any lectures on the Only True Spirit.

Descending the mountain I noticed McKay and McGeary hurrying from me again. 'Here, you men!' I called. 'Apologize for your conduct. Why did you desert me? You are here to help me.'

They stopped. McGeary looked to McKay to reply. McKay came up to me, thick-browed and headstrong.

'I'm Sandy McKay, a ticket-of-leave man. So I obey the law. But I'm me own man. If I fall down the mountainside I have no person to help me up. I expect no assistance.'

'You intractables harm this undertaking. I don't require you or any man to do what I wouldn't do myself. God blesses this enterprise but we must help each other.'

'Does He now? Well He can help you up when you fall down then.'

Shortly we came to a serpentine river which I felt must link up with

Port Davey. We followed its course to a small bay where, to our pleasure, we found our whaleboat anchored. On this coastal plain the weather was warmer and wildlife abounded. Swans and geese flocked along the river bank, screeching and squabbling over wild fruits and marine creatures. We ate heartily of provisions and fresh waterfowl. I raised the Bethel flag and held a service on the Sabbath. The convicts and natives were moderately attentive.

That afternoon Wooraddy espied smoke rising from the mountains from whence we had come. '*Parlerwar!*' he said. It seemed the *Toogee* tribe had spotted us before we discovered them.

'The *Toogee* have fled to the mountains,' Wooraddy said, 'They set the plains on fire as they go to warn the women to hide and to cover their tracks.'

My feelings were intense. 'Go after them,' I urged. Wooraddy, Truganini, Dray and Pagerley stripped off their European clothing and ran off towards the smoke.

At eight o'clock all but Dray returned and informed me they had made the hostiles understand the nature of my mission.

Truganini said, 'They want you to come to them in the morning.'

At dawn Dray, who had remained with the *Toogee* all night, returned to camp accompanied by two young *Toogee* women, Time-me-ne and Wy-yer-rer. They were not the least timid. Time-me-ne was a fine healthy girl about eighteen years of age; Wy-yer-rer was equally healthy though slightly older and not so stout. They showed their pleasure and excitement at the variety of objects new to them, walking around my tent and studying it curiously.

'*Wore-rae line-ne*,' they giggled. 'Cloth house.' Everything they saw underwent a close scrutiny. I played my flute for them and they were entranced at the sounds.

I asked the women to effect an interview with the whole tribe. They led me and my natives about nine miles over hills and through thickets to their camp. Their fires were still burning and skins and odorous portions of animals lay about. But there was no sign of the *Toogee*. Suddenly Time-me-ne and Wy-yer-rer vanished into the bushes. I was apprehensive; Wooraddy even more worried. '*Ragewrapper*,' he mumbled. 'They are evil people. They will spear us.' Truganini hunched fearful between us. I sought confidence from that God whose service engaged me, instructing Wooraddy and Dray to follow one set of footprints into a thick scrub and call on the hidden native to come out.

'*Nyrae num*,' Dray cried. 'Good white man here.'

There was a profound silence. Dark bushes and leafy ferns ringed the camp clearing. In the thicket there was no sound from either bird or insect.

Stephen had a telephone call from Doctor Williams. "Will you call in at the surgery after dinner?' he asked.

He tapped his blotter with a little scimitar-shaped letter opener, caressed the silver knife in physician's fingers. 'I asked you here as a friend of the family. I don't want you to think that your behaviour necessarily killed your mother.'

Stephen's eyes fastened on a kidney dish of instruments catching and reflecting the light on a glass cabinet behind and above the doctor's neat oiled head. His heart pounded chokingly somewhere in his gullet. Methylated spirits hung in low clouds, swept up into his sinuses.

'It could have been a combination of several things. Apoplexy was the old term for it, a burst blood vessel. In a youngish person like your mother occasionally a berry aneuryism occurs. A small berry-sized blown-out balloon due to a congenital defect in the vessel. Perhaps shock or worry might precipitate the bursting, perhaps not. I've had patients of thirty-five die in their armchairs watching *Gunsmoke*,' he said generously.

Stephen sat speechless. Doctor Williams deposited his scimitar on the desktop and rose from his chair. His long thin throat was speckled with razor nicks. *Physician heal thyself.*

'That's all,' he said. 'Look after that family of yours. And Stephen (he turned), keep an eye on your father.'

He did so, awake and asleep. He sat with him in the lounge-room until after midnight watching obscure westerns night after night, pouring him beers which made him less rheumy and excitable than scotch.

'The children's welfare is my main concern,' his father would address the Axminster. And then look up at his elder watchful son. 'Your mother would want it that way. One in a million, Jean.'

He dreamed regularly that her death was a mistake, a dream itself, a non-event which would crumble and disperse on his waking, like any nightmare. His dream doctors diagnosed earnestly (fingering their stethoscopes and slim nostril torches): 'Just a run-of-the-mill cerebral haemorrhage. Three phenobarb a day before meals and tell her to wear a shady hat while gardening.'

Or, quite often, he would dream that his father had died instead. In these dreams his own role as the harbinger of parental death was understood but unspecified. He was never actually *asked* to make the decision, to reverse the result, to pull the trigger, but he knew he had done so and it seemed yet another act of treachery.

11

Conciliating the Natives

There was a rustling of ferns and shortly one old woman crawled from the thicket, followed by Time-me-ne and Wy-yer-rer, the young women who had accompanied us back to camp. Then came the rest of the women and children, about fifteen in all, silently emerging from the bushes and squatting by their fires again.

I seated myself amongst them, offering gifts of biscuit, beads and mirrors. Mouths full of biscuit, the women hooted a signal for the men to come home. Presently the men strode into the clearing carrying their spears and waddies. Several had kangaroos and opossums hanging across their shoulders. They were robust warriors between five feet nine inches and six feet in height, broad-shouldered and well proportioned. Cicatrices like thick welts covered their chests. Their features were like the European rather than the African, being intelligent of countenance and sensitive about the mouth and nose. Surprisingly their beards resembled those of the Poland Jew, growing long and to a point at the chin's extremity and leaving the underlip bare. Majestic moustaches decorated their top lips. The men came and stood around the fires, behind the seated women. There were twenty-six natives in the tribe, including two babies, two little girls, one pubescent female and one stout lad about fourteen. Dogs of the cur breed cringed at their masters' feet.

Dray told them how far I had travelled seeking them, that I wished to befriend them and that if they chose to follow me back to Bruny they would be happy and comfortable. There the Governor would protect them from bad white men.

'Mitter Robinson *nyrae num*,' she said. 'Good white man.' They laughed heartily, eagerly snatching the ornaments, ribbons, buttons, knives and looking glasses I distributed among them. The mirrors fascinated them and they each searched behind the glass for the images confronting them. Both men and women examined me and my clothes, felt my hair, hands, legs and stomach and determined with prodding fingers to which gender I belonged. Time-me-ne and

Wy-yer-rer told them of my cloth house and how I played the flute. I was an object of wonder.

The *Toogee* were anxious to inspect these mysteries and though evening was approaching when we set off for our camp they accompanied us, laughing and dancing along the track. As we made our slow way across the coastal plain we spotted Stansfield trudging towards us, carrying a gun in full view of the natives. I had no doubt he did this intentionally. The *Toogee* became restless and murmured among themselves. I signalled to Stansfield to return to camp lest he scare the tribe away but he kept walking towards us.

'*Nyrae num*'. Wooraddy told the *Toogee* that Stansfield was another good white man, but they had their eyes on his weapon and were not convinced. They said they would remain where they were for the night and that I should return to my camp.

'Make a fire and I will stay with you till morning,' I suggested, but they were unwilling for me to stay, glancing in a sidelong fashion into the shrubbery. They would remain there but I should return to my people.

Wooraddy, Truganini, Dray and I set off, joining the stupid Stansfield after two hundred yards. We stumbled into creeks in the growing darkness, scratching ourselves in thorny thickets. We made a torch but the rain was gathering over us and it soon extinguished it. Approaching midnight we arrived back in camp overcome by fatigue, cold and hunger, and collapsed on our blankets. Next day I returned with my natives to where I had left the *Toogee* overnight. They had gone.

We had no further sight of the tribe the next week. The weather was fair and I led several parties in search of them, but in vain. I had much to contend with. The convicts were becoming obstreperous. They were anxious to make captives, to kill if necessary.

'My object is to conciliate and tranquillize,' I told them. 'If the natives want to return with us it must be of their own will.'

The sniggering McGeary suggested, 'We could capture them all and send them back to Hobart Town in the schooner. If it sank no matter.'

'I will not be their gaoler.'

'I would rather capture them than have five pounds,' he said. 'What a thing that would be to talk about.'

Even the idiotic Stansfield offered a suggestion. 'We could make them drunk and then we could take them anywhere.'

To my astonishment my blacks were just as eager to capture the *Toogee* as the convicts. Wooraddy bore a malice to the tribe which I found hard to suppress. 'Give me a gun and I will bring them back,' he urged me. (These people attributed magic qualities to firearms. Loaded or unloaded they appeared the same to them. Give them *par-lene-ne* and they would face anything.) I refused to carry weapons on a conciliatory foray, keeping them securely at base camp.

'These people are your brothers,' I said. 'Go and hunt wallaby and birds, not your brothers.'

'*Ragewrapper*,' he sulked. 'Eaters of scale-fish. They will spear us.'

My bedding was crawling with vermin. Even though my blanket was quite new I gave it to the natives—as I had several others on which I had caught lice—and slept in my boat cloak. I found it almost impossible to keep clean of vermin while associating with the natives and lying around their fires, but I was obliged to do so while I wished to be successful with them. I went bathing in the shallows to relieve the vermin bites and was instantly surrounded by Truganini, Dray and Pagerley, curious to see my bare skin.

'The water is cold,' I shivered. '*Lia tunnack*.'

'No, no,' the women laughed. '*Lia pyoonyack*. It is warm.' They splashed me with their palms, delighted to see their protector knee deep in the ocean, his trousers unceremoniously rolled above his calves. Angry red weals on my flesh showed where the cursed lice had bitten me. I abraded the bites with handfuls of wet sand to relieve the itching. Truganini watched this performance with interest.

'*Tia reea lugungana*,' she suggested. 'Go naked. You must submerge yourself to remove the lice.'

The other women intently surveyed my reaction to this idea. Dray giggled. '*Wayanna*. White-belly seal.'

'Go ashore,' I ordered them. 'Keep a long way off.' They splashed away behind a rock outcrop, tittering and fluttering their hands in the waves. I removed my blouse and trousers and washed myself thoroughly in the brine. Vermin lumps spotted my person in unlikely places. The salt water gave a satisfying stinging sensation and I wallowed unashamedly for several minutes before donning my clothes.

The women reappeared, chirping and laughing. I have mentioned how they were great adepts at swimming, most experienced at diving into heavy breakers among the rocks for crawfish and mutton-fish. Now they stood poised naked on the rocks, oscillated their thighs in a rather obscene movement, chanted a guttural song together and plunged into the sea.

On 25th March we espied the *Toogee's* smoke again and hastened after them. Again they set the plains on fire as they fled and the smoke ascended in black clouds. I urged my people forward through the hot charred grass, up a sloping hill, towards them.

Abruptly two tall aboriginals stepped out from behind a she-oak. They were sent to waylay us: each at least six feet tall, stout and sinewy warriors. They stood on the crown of the hill clutching their spears. Over their shoulders hung kangaroo skin mantles. I called a greeting as we approached but they did not heed me. A sullenness spread over their countenances. They called to Truganini: 'Are there any more *num*, white men, with you? Do they carry guns to trick us?'

'There are no more white men. Mitter Robinson has no gun. Good white man.'

Immediately the warriors became less suspicious and approached me to shake hands. I enquired after the rest of the tribe. 'They are hidden in the bushes.' The warriors, named Neen-ne-vuther and Tow-ter-rer, hooted for the tribe and they crawled out from hiding.

Neen-ne-vuther and Tow-ter-rer were the biggest men in the tribe and apparently its leaders. They led my party into a thick forest where their new camp was centred by a swift-flowing river amid a grove of kangaroo-fig trees. We were to stop with them for the night. The *Toogee* were cheerful hosts and we spent the night in great conviviality, eating wallaby and wombat followed by figs from the trees that sheltered us. The tribe sang and danced until a late hour, their bodies sweating from the exertion despite the cold. My blacks sang and danced in their turn.

When I reflect now on how these people were calumniated and had every vice attributed to them, when I muse upon the dire alarm that pervaded the settlements on account of them, it may appear a matter of surprise to my readers that I should sojourn with thirty of them for nights together, the only Briton in the recluse of the forest, far from my people and the means of protection. It should not be so. I took comfort from a nightly prayer: *Oh, Thou preserver of all men, it is to Thee I look.*

Rain soaked us during the night. Several of the *Toogee* crawled into my bed, under my boat cloak, together with their dogs, so that with my knapsacks and the natives I was so crowded I could hardly move. I dared not order them away without annoying them. I wished heartily for morning. Examining my clothes at daybreak I found them covered with vermin.

I conferred with the *Toogee* at nine o'clock, feeling a need to act promptly before Wooraddy's mutterings and threats antagonized them. He was busy agitating my natives by telling them the tribe would spear us all by evening. He constantly urged me to capture them. 'I will kill Neen-ne-vuther and Tow-ter-rer. Smash their scabby heads with my waddy. We will tie up the others and drag them to Hobart Town.' He made my role very difficult. I told the *Toogee* I came not to injure them but to do them good.

'You may accompany me back to Hobart Town or stay where you please.'

Neen-ne-vuther said, 'We will follow you,' through a mouthful of figs.

Tow-ter-rer was more distrustful. 'We are the *Toogee.*' Squatting thoughtfully in the cold ashes of the previous night's fire he crunched kelp strands, popping the seaweed berries with his teeth. 'Whites have always killed us before.'

'My purpose is friendship. *Lapoile lu nagreenah moolanah.* I wish to be your friend and look after you.'

Tow-ter-rer shook his head in bemusement.

While the *Toogee* considered my suggestion—a drawn-out procedure needing the support of the whole tribe—I explored their tribal lands, crossing their river in a bark canoe. Wooraddy had gloomily warned me I should drown if I attempted the crossing. I instructed Truganini, Dray, Time-me-ne and Wy-yer-rer to swim across and tow me to the opposite bank. The women were very careful, steadying the boat whenever the river surged against its sides. When I was on the other side the knapsacks were brought over similarly, and then the children. The men swam clumsily over holding up their kangaroo skin mantles with one hand while they paddled with a sidestroke, each trying to beat the other to shore.

They led me to another of their villages at the other extremity of the river's sea-mouth, this one also surrounded by fig trees and near some fishing rocks. We made a fire and the women dived for shell fish. The men brought in kangaroo and edible toadstools. We all ate well, the *Toogee* appearing in good spirits and singing their usual songs. My natives took their turn and also sang. The most friendly intercourse seemed to have been established. I made my bed in a large bark hut about ten feet in diameter and seven feet high and in the form of a circular dome all stuck full of swan and cockatoo feathers.

Mizzling rain swept over the village during the night, gradually becoming heavier. The stout warrior Neen-ne-vuther forced himself into my bed at midnight and commandeered my blanket.

'*Tunna tunna*,' he grumbled, 'the night is cold.' His breathing rasped in his chest throughout the night and filled my hut with the stench of sea things and rancid meat. I could hardly move, such was his muscular breadth. He was infected with the cutaneous distemper and next morning his skin flakes covered my clothes. I found it impossible to keep myself clear of vermin.

The tribe was content over the next several days to remain in camp and consider my mission. While they talked, squatting on their haunches munching bunches of kelp, I gave them more beads and other trinkets they seemed to prize. They insisted on giving me five wallaby skins in exchange. Neen-ne-vuther and Tow-ter-rer went hunting and speared three kangaroo and numerous pink and white cockatoos. Every night they sang and danced and the sounds reverberated through the forest. Each night now the weather was colder Neen-ne-vuther came with his scaly infection to share my bed. On the third night I dared to order him away. He was angry and departed muttering.

The 28th March being the Sabbath I spent the day reading the 15th and 16th chapters of St Matthew. Every so often while I sat reading or writing my journal the *Toogee* would come up to feel my hands, legs, arms etc. to see whether I had bones. I found myself severely infected with the cutaneous distemper as well as vermin bites and, following the local remedy, had my face, arms and feet painted black with ashes and ochre to try to relieve the complaint.

The morning after the Sabbath I was wakened by a dog yelping in the distance and found the *Toogee* gone. My people could not believe it when I woke them. 'We did not hear their children or their dogs,' they said.

'They are *Ragewrapper*. Evil,' Wooraddy said.

I could do nothing but return to my camp and await the arrival of the whaleboat. Waiting for the boat was an agony. We were again out of provisions. The cutaneous distemper broke out over my whole body, my skin erupting in scores of weeping ulcers. I rubbed myself with gunpowder mixed with urine as a desperate measure. The application was a painful and malodorous expedient and had little effect except to stay the infection's progress.

Truganini tried a joke. 'Mitter Robinson a *Parlerwar*, not white man,' she said, seeing my blackened face and body. I had become rank and evil smelling, more so than the natives whose own sores, less restricted by clothing, healed in the open air.

I considered my plight: infected with a scabrous distemper, riddled with vermin and out of provisions. I told Wooraddy: 'I would sooner face a thousand hostiles than have this infection. It came from Neen-ne-vuther.'

He was unsympathetic. 'Neen-ne-vuther *tagant-yaryak poon-yer-lon gran-ler-ther*. He is a diseased man who eats kangaroo droppings and rotten scale fish.'

I wrote in my journal: 'Such was my fate and that of any person desirous of making himself useful to these unbefriended people.' As I wrote, imagining my situation at its lowest ebb, mosquitoes rose from the damp bushes and settled on my tortured body.

Nursing a cold riesling Geoff said, 'You can't live in the past forever. I don't have time to look after graves what with the businesses and everything.' He was relaxed in the fastness of his study, embedded in a deep soft chair. His brother also sipped wine. 'You're very sentimental all of a sudden,' Geoff said. 'Hey, you're not a Comm are you, to change the subject. All that business the other night about cruelty to Abos a hundred years ago. Jim went home pretty annoyed you know.'

'I'm nothing. Anna says I'm a Tory chauvinist and the Commission thinks I'm a screaming radical. Jim's a pompous prick.'

'Yeah, well let's forget it. All water under the bridge. You know, I think I'll be cremated and have my ashes scattered over Ascot. The bookies have got most of me as it is. And the bloody taxman. I'm supporting the bloody Abos, not shooting them. Giving them money to piss up against the wall.'

'You want to drop it or go on with it?'

'Settle down.' He filled his brother's glass. 'Everything O.K. with you? I mean if you need some sort of help . . . You seem sort of agitated.'

'I'm fine. A few things on my mind, you know how it is.'

'Sure. Listen, Denise and I have always been fond of Jane, so we were wondering . . .'

'Naturally. I'm fond of her myself.' Geoff was becoming the image of their father, something about the eyes perhaps. A superiority in the raising and lowering of the eyelids.

'Of course.' What had come over him lately? Obsessed with Abos and death and smart-arse social issues. Screwing up his marriage, tossing in a good job, not much money in it but a secure job and his face on TV every week. You could do a lot worse. All those liberated women he knocked around with, tits bobbing everywhere most likely. Probably getting more bangs than breakfasts, the sly bastard. Though he seemed to have lost his shrewdness, too.

'You always were a silly bastard,' Geoff said, summoning memories and an affectionate smile.

'Meaning what?'

'You remember that tree-house in the mulberry tree? You up there reading all the time. Comics. Captain Marvel, Tom Mix and all that stuff.'

'What was the name of Tom Mix's horse?'

'Christ. Silver?'

'No, that was the Lone Ranger. Tony, it was. Tom Mix'd say *Dig dirt Tony*. Meaning gee-up. Hopalong Cassidy's horse was Topper. Roy Rogers had several Triggers actually, all palominos.'

'You remember that stuff?'

'Who was Lash LaRue? No one remembers him these days.'

'I'm buggered if I know.'

'King of the Bullwhip. Black cowboy clothes from head to foot.'

'Sounds kinky.' No doubt about it. Around the twist.

Abruptly Denise burst into the study. The ex-Miss W.A. was distracted and moved from one foot to the other in the doorway. Anna, bemused and towelling her wet hair, hung behind her.

'Geoff, Cheyenne has a worm,' Denise announced, 'A *tape* worm!'

Her husband hurried outside with her. Grimacing at each other,

Crisp and Anna were drawn after them. Outside in the sunset the dog was scraping its anus along the patio tiles. Denise ran to the animal and made ineffectual dabs at its rear with Kleenex tissues.

'Poor Shy, poor fellow,' she crooned, dabbing away. 'Has he got an itchy botty? Geoffrey! I can see a section of *tape* worm!'

'Charming,' Anna said. 'Are those things catching? God, and I've been patting him.'

Crisp said helpfully, 'When those worms are stretched out they're as long as a tennis court.'

'Truly?' Denise was wide-eyed with concern. 'Poor baby.' She patted the huge beast reassuringly. 'Denise make Shy's botty better.'

... aged five, first week at school, little Stephen enlightens Mummy on delights of learning process: 'Trevor Rumble pokes his finger in his bottom and smells it.' Mummy says: 'Dirty little blighter. If you do that you get tape worms inside you eighty feet long and they eat out all your innards.' After that Stephen wouldn't have touched his with gloves. And they said if you played with your doodle it dropped off ...

An hour later they were packing for the flight back to Sydney. Crisp mooned about sluggishly, rolling socks into balls, hunting cuff links, gathering up loose change into heaps.

Anna rustled in the bedside bookcase, collecting their paperbacks. 'Look here,' she said. 'Would you believe it? The great danes have got their own movement. The W.A.G.D.O.B.A.! And even their own publication called *Wagger*. That's neat.' She waved a slim magazine.

'Wag what?'

'The West Australian Great Dane Owners' and Breeders' Association. It's their Christmas issue. Listen to this—"Geoff, Denise, Lady and Cheyenne Crisp wish all their friends a Merry and Alcoholic Christmas and a Prosperous New Year".'

'Let me see that.'

'There's a photo of them, too. Dogs and all. My God!'

Crisp picked up the magazine. There was Geoff posed at the edge of the pool, hairy stomach overlapping his trunks; Denise as photogenic as ever in a bikini and sunglasses pushed back on her hair. And the dogs' great heads slobbering in the foreground. 'I suppose it's an interest for them.'

'It's pathetic.'

'Easy. They're my family.'

'Aren't they though.'

'Perhaps you feel superior because of your tertiary education and legendary high-mindedness?'

'Whose acting superior? I've had about enough of your playing the small-town boy made good.'

Hardly good. From golden mean to near disaster. Crisp closed his eyes and inhaled deeply. *Here we go again.* He opened them, facing the wall. A poster flapped lightly in the draught. *Once a king, always a king. Once a knight's enough!*

'Slyly checking on all your old conquests. Boring middle-class housewives that they are, giving me a close scrutiny for the whole three weeks.'

'I thought you were all sisters. You ought to be raising their consciousness to your own exalted level.'

'Very amusing. Very deft. And the men are worse, if anything. Smug chauvinists chasing the almighty dollar. I've had a gutful of them.'

'And I've had your aloofness and jealousy. Anyone would think I was screwing these women the way you've treated them.'

'You wouldn't have the guts.' She snapped the locks on her suitcase, which had a worn tartan covering and stickers from Bali and Katmandu (that he now savagely imagined she had retained purposely, the *poseuse*). 'Or the stamina.'

Crisp paused, his chest heaving. His temples tightened. Hands compressed his head and the constriction nearly overcame him.

'But what really floors me,' she said, suddenly softer and very low, appearing surprisingly near tears, 'is your attitude to me.'

'How's that?'

'Well, it's obvious the first thing I'm going to have to do in Sydney is have an abortion. I'll be cutting it pretty fine, too.'

'You're not really pregnant?'

'Boy, you really are a live one aren't you?' She sobbed softly. 'And thanks for finally enquiring.'

He burst out into the night air. *Tinkle, tinkle* went the ubiquitous wind chimes and he was standing by the pool. Denise sat calmly alone in a deckchair, serenely regal now, sipping soda water. The dogs lay around her, loose-lipped and foolish.

'There's nothing to worry about,' she said. 'No panic.'

'No?'

'I looked it up in *You and Your Dog* and rang the vet just to be sure. Tape worms are common enough and not harmful to dogs if they're treated. Geoff's gone for some pills and Shy'll be right as rain.'

'That's good.'

'Yes. Oh Stephen, you can tell Anna she's in no danger.' His sister-in-law stared at him intently and he realized they'd been fighting at an open window. 'Unless they eat dog turds where she comes from.'

'That remark isn't worthy of a Miss Western Australia or a dog lover,' he said, and turned wearily back to the fray.

McKay arrived in camp on 2nd April, having concluded that bad luck had befallen us. He brought a small supply of salt pork, tea and biscuit. I sent him next day with Wooraddy and Truganini to the penal settlement at Macquarie Harbour for medicine and more food. (My infection was spreading fast despite assiduous applications of the gun-powder and urine mixture.) Against my wishes McKay took a carbine with him. Like the other convicts he was very much afraid of the *Toogee* and dared not venture the shortest distance without a weapon. I despatched all other hands to the wrecked schooner to return with as much provision as they could carry. (If the Government had furnished me with a proper vessel in the first place all this time and effort could have been saved!)

On 6th April I set out with Dray, who knew this country well, through forests and morasses towards Rocky Point in the north. Dray soon spotted smoke and we hurried forward though she was hampered by a heavy load of provision. Shortly we heard children's voices calling '*loinah! loinah!*—snake! snake!' and we concealed ourselves in the trees. Almost at once there appeared Neen-ne-vuther and his wife, Tow-ter-rer and his wife and small child, an old man about seventy years and an old woman and her young daughter.

We came out of hiding slowly, and with welcoming gestures. The *Toogee* showed not the slightest surprise at seeing us and immediately kindled a fire from materials in the women's baskets. They invited us to sit down like old friends. Tow-ter-rer carried a brown snake which he threw on the fire. The old man I had not seen before. He was the oldest aboriginal I had yet seen and excited my curiosity.

I addressed myself to him. 'How do you live with no wife to catch you shellfish?'

'Nnnh? I live on kangaroo-figs and roots from the ground.' He was nothing but bones and could scarcely walk. He came and lay down by the fire where Neen-ne-vuther's wife was crying from a pain in the head. The old woman sent her daughter with a relic of the dead enclosed in a kangaroo skin bag. The sick woman took it, placed it against her temple and lay down by the fire. Shortly she rose up, seemingly without pain and handed the bag to its owner. Neen-ne-vuther and Tow-ter-rer espied an opossum in a she-oak above us and Neen-ne-vuther scrambled up the tree and brought it down alive. '*Pawtella*,' he laughed and dashed out its brains on the tree trunk. He threw the body on the fire for a moment, then plucked it from the coals and ate from it. I saw his infection was almost gone, most of his scabs healed. He passed the opossum and snake meat to his companions, the children receiving choice scraps and the dogs the bones. The old man got nothing. I gave him some biscuit which he ate without interest. I settled down by the fire, drawing my blanket over my scabrous body. The natives as usual came and lay close to me.

I awoke at 5 a.m. to find the *Toogee* gone without a sound and without giving me the least intimation of their intentions. Dray had left me and gone with them. The forest was still, the sun not yet arisen, and I was alone.

I climbed a yellow sandy hill spotted with clumps of dry gorse. A small sand-tunnelling creature scrabbled away from me beneath a bush. The marks of its nails remained in the sand. Thuddings and boomings reverberated from the earth: the foot poundings of kangaroo and wallaby. I felt brown and yellow eyes upon me. My own eyes were almost closed from the angry pustules on my eyelids, boils covered my body. But worse than my personal difficulties was the fact that yet again I had missed an opportunity to civilize this wild tribe. Was the Lord humbling me for placing too much dependence on others?

The day was dawning fine, the sun warming. Small parrots flashed in the bushes. On the hilltop I kindled a fire and cooked some potatoes from my knapsack. Then I arose, trudged down the hill and headed back along the track ten or twelve miles to whence we had come, opening my shirt so the sun and breeze might dry my sores.

Back at our last camp all the people were scattered, most still not back from the schooner with provisions. I decided to make a final effort to conciliate the *Toogee* while they were nearby—within two or three days they might be miles away. I had spent much time with these people and my patience was sorely tried. Loading myself with what provisions I could muster I hurried on for Rocky Point. I was now alone again but the hope of meeting the *Toogee* buoyed my spirits. There was no time for eating or resting. I scrambled over eroded gullies and high rocks, frequently stumbling under my load in the advancing darkness. Night was well fallen when I sighted a fire on the verge of a she-oak forest bounding a small bay. I was afraid to halloo in case I alarmed the natives and they ran away, so I walked towards them, emerging from the forest upon a rocky ledge above their camp. The moon had now risen and I was quite visible to them. They set up a shout of alarm but quickly realized it was me and greeted me cheerfully.

It was the same party I had recently visited. Only the very old man and Dray were not with them. I asked after Dray but to all my questions Neen-ne-vuther gave vague answers and looked beyond my eyes.

'We saw you on the sandhill making fire and watched you go away,' he said. 'We saw white man, Wooraddy and Truganini go to the settlement.'

I gave them tea and biscuit while I pondered how to act. Capturing Neen-ne-vuther and Tow-ter-rer suggested itself to me, these men being the finest in the tribe, but I could not manage this alone, unarmed, and the other *Toogee* would then alarm the rest of the natives along the coast. Instead of making friends I should have enemies. They would arm themselves against me and for aught I knew might kill me. I therefore resolved on another idea. I would use my knowledge of the nature and function of the human mind on them. This time I would be the first away, before they could depart. They knew I wanted them to accompany me but I would leave them. They would be confounded. I rose from the fire, packed my knapsack and said, 'I am unhappy that you run away from me. I will not spend the night with you at your fire.'

Neen-ne-vuther and Tow-ter-rer were at a loss to account for my strange conduct. All along they had made the decision to leave and now I was doing the same. '*Oo-eeta poona*,' they said. 'The moon is risen. Why do you leave when it is time to sleep?'

'I do not wish to stay. I will tell the Governor you have run away from me.'

'No, no. Tell him we will not spear white man.'

They were truly nonplussed and saddened at this turn of events, like disappointed children. As it was about midnight they gave me a firestick and offered to guide me through the forest to the sandy beach where I wished to camp. 'Will you come again to see us?' Neen-ne-vuther asked anxiously. 'We will come with you in friendship tomorrow. We will bring other *Toogee* from along the coast.'

I was overjoyed. My plan had enabled me to fully gain their confidence. I said I would meet them at Rocky Point. I would take them to the Governor and tell him the *Toogee* were a fine people. Neen-ne-vuther smiled happily and I left their camp in a state of good humour and satisfaction.

By morning my land parties had not caught up with me. Luckily my journey seemed near fruition: my wheatmeal was nearly gone. I had not tasted meat for six days and the cutaneous infection flamed and chafed along my limbs. My clothes by this time were completely dismantled, my trousers torn off above the knees. I opened the ends of two wheatmeal bags and bound them around my legs with kurrajong bark. My shoes had long fallen in tatters—I tied pieces of leather around my feet to protect them from sharp rocks. I pushed quickly forward for Rocky Point nevertheless, following an obvious native track—bits of firestick dropped by the *Toogee*, scraps of shell and crawfish, small shrubs broken down—and by afternoon came to a spot where they had recently been, their fires still smoking. I was hurrying on towards the sounds of children playing when I was spotted by a warrior who gave the alarm. It was the full *Toogee* tribe, upwards of thirty people. They ran into the forest leaving all their belongings—puppies, shellfish, skins, baskets—behind. Dray was with them, running naked as the *Toogee*. I called to her, 'Dray! It is me,' but she fled past me, wildeyed. Neen-ne-vuther also showed no sign of recognition. They disappeared into the depths of the bush and it closed silently around them.

12

Certain Forms

BACK IN SYDNEY, alone, Crisp worked long hours on his thesis. Writing, reading, occasionally lapsing into stupors of self-absorption. From the lounge-room window (he worked there in his underpants, crouched over a small sideboard, when the sun made the kitchen too hot) he looked out to his left on similar liver-coloured apartment blocks—*Edinburgh, Killarney, Harbour Lights.* To his right he looked down on an overgrown bed of white daisies. There were no other scenic diversions like he had in the lavatory. He ate and drank while he worked: beans eaten cold from the tin, grilled cheese on toast, cups of black Nescafé. He was treating two stubborn boils with Pluravit vitamin capsules and packets of sultanas. A worrying pins and needles sensation had lately tingled in the fingers so he upped his vitamin dosage to five capsules a day and observed his faeces turning black, his urine an elfin leaf-green. His notebooks and manuscripts carried circular stains from his coffee mug, the odd speck of dried tomato sauce. Crumbs lodged in the binding of old histories from the City of Sydney Library. He missed Anna.

On the plane from Perth she'd said, 'I think we should give it a rest. A clean break. We're stultifying each other.'

'Not seriously? You're just tired from the strain and travelling. And the other business.' He did not refer to it directly.

'The other business! That's a nice little euphemism.'

'You should have told me about it sooner,' he whispered, and faintly said it: 'Being pregnant.' Ever the conspirator he squeezed her nearest knee. Affectionate as all get-out. 'We'll work it out.'

'We will, will we? The royal plural. Who carries the can?' The words were tougher than her expression: sad and puzzled. 'I've been thinking, I'm too dependent on you. Especially in unfamiliar surroundings. It's disastrous to be like that.'

It was true she had become a homebody at his flat—cooking racks of spiced lamb, making bowls of taramasalata, buying him lambswool sweaters and Modigliani prints for the wall. She'd ironed his shirts, whistling old show tunes at the time. She had come home flushed and talkative from *Women in Education* meetings and brought him cups of hot chocolate in bed.

And now it was guilt time.

Above Australia he stared at her. She peered out the window at strings of cloud vapour wisping over the Nullarbor Plain. Below them was saltbush, red dust and desolation. Her full lower lip was drawn tightly inwards. She wore no makeup though smelled of patchouli oil, spicy and enigmatic. He looked at her thoroughly while seeming to be staring past her through the window. Her body was peculiarly gathered upwards in the breasts and shoulders under her red cotton T-shirt. He thought she must be wearing a bra. Pinkness showed at her cheekbones from emotion. Her hair was lustrous and freshly washed.

Wriggling closer to her in his seat, he said, 'Change your mind.' She held his hand loosely on her thigh. It was denimed and taut but contained warmth and softness beneath the fabric and, he knew, swept upwards in a gradual silken curve of soft and faintly rippled skin.

'That would be a mistake.' She studied his eyes. They were, as usual, sympathetic and unrevealing. 'You know, sometimes I've been tempted to ask where do I stand, what's in it for me, just like all the little secretaries eventually ask their married lovers. But I didn't.'

'And now you are?'

'Not really. I've made my decision, you see. I'm on my own again.'

'But I want us to be together,' he said. He was always ill at ease with lines like that.

As far as she was concerned, she clasped his hand, the hand resting on her leg, and held it tight. Her face was pushed almost into his. 'Oh Christ, you use people! You take me for granted.'

'Nonsense.'

'You always get your way, or try to. This time no dice. We'll see each other I suppose but we're not living together.'

'But why?'

'You might well ask.' She had raised her voice. A hostess hovered, raised an eyebrow and backed off up the aisle. Anna almost hissed, 'Because I like looking after you.' There were tears in thin trails down the womanly European cheekbones. 'And frankly I don't think you're worth it.' She turned away from him, back to the window and the plain below.

They had remained silent for the rest of the flight, Crisp sinking into his seat with an airline magazine from the seat-pocket. Anything could draw his attention: he read an item concerning some 'centuries-old rock engravings by the now-extinct Tasmanian Aborigines'. The engravings were soon to be 'imaginatively presented as a tourist attraction at Devonport, Tasmania'. A museum was in the planning stages following the recommendations of a Government-sponsored feasibility study. A special advisory committee had been appointed to protect, develop and promote the engravings. An information centre staffed by 'attractive young women in smart uniforms' would shortly direct tourists to the engraving sites, where displays showing tribal habits, hunting and fishing activities, nomadic camp life and historic burial sites would be installed. Authentic scenes would be portrayed by the use of life-sized figures of Aborigines made of coloured fibre-glass and acrylic.

When they'd landed at Sydney she'd kissed him and taken a separate cab to a friend's flat in Glebe. The next day she'd come for the rest of her things, gently refused to make love, eaten an apple and left, her bold stride hampered by a long Indian dress and two crammed plastic laundry bags.

'What are you doing?' he'd said, loitering unhappily around the wardrobes and cupboards. And alternatively, 'Do you want some help?' But she'd smiled sadly and purposefully and tossed her apple core in the sink. Two thin silver bangles jingled around a wrist as she went out the door. Crisp was thus left alone to his work and fantasies, though her hairs remained twined around the taps in the bathroom basin and clogged the plughole in the bath.

Two nights later came a raucous banging on the door. Without light-sleeping Anna beside him he slept heavily on, the thudding infiltrating his dreams but not rousing him. He was flying, breast-stroking gently off the ground, above the rooftops and electricity wires of a small, unfamiliar country town. Details were in monochrome—he didn't run to coloured dreams—but in black-and-white he could see the slate roofs and weathered sandstock buildings in the finest clarity. Below, on a grassy football oval, his mother and Wendy were breast-stroking too, running through the dandelions, making little ineffectual jumps, struggling for lift-off. In frustration Wendy cried, 'Just because I've got asthma I can't do anything.' His mother began breast-stroking faster and faster, her arm strokes becoming frantic dog-paddling movements. 'Stephen!' she called, her jerking body growing smaller below him, 'Stephen!'

Awake, blurry, he walked towards the name-calling; opened the door to find Jane crowding the jamb with a small, sandy, neatly-clipped man. The man clutched both camera and torch. Jane, bright-eyed and agitated, abruptly moved into the room. She was strangely overdressed for three a.m. in a white suit and shoes; her hair was pulled back severely with a narrow ribbon but escaped in brown wisps to form sidelocks. The man's suede boots had crêpe rubber soles which squelched busily on the parquetry floor.

'I'm sorry Stephen, I had to do this,' she said. 'There are certain forms to go through.'

'Where's the co-re?' asked the sandy man, poking his head into the bedroom. His torch flashed into the room, darted over the crumpled bed. 'Come out Miss Kubic. Nothing personal, just doing a job. Don't enjoy this any more than you do.'

'Oh let her put something on first.' Jane perched nervily on the arm of a chair. Her lipstick was brighter than usual and some was on a tooth. Her glance flitted anxiously into the dark expanse of the bedroom.

'Steady, steady,' the man warned. 'No collusion.'

Crisp gaped, at the mouth and pyjama pants. He tucked himself back inside. 'Christ, the private eye and all.' Drained of surprise, he sat down himself. 'Am I supposed to hit him or do you want a cup of tea?'

'Oh yes.' Jane's eyes still roamed the room. 'We've been outside for hours.'

'You've been wasting your time. She moved out on Saturday. I would've thought your detective friend would make sure of that.'

The man fiddled uncomfortably with the strap of his Canon. 'Mrs Crisp checked in a phone call to Perth that you and Miss Kubic had returned here together on Saturday. We understood Miss Kubic was living on the premises.'

'Good old Denise. Miss Kubic's flown the coop. Tough luck.'

Jane discovered the kitchen and made tea. Crisp and the private eye sat heavily in the lounge-room, Crisp with his legs crossed out of modesty. He surveyed the private eye with a fake man-of-the-world glance: the man wore a tweedy sports coat, green woollen tie and corduroys. He looked more like a country doctor.

'Just doing my job you understand. Frazer Investigations. We act for Cowan, Stuart and Blennerhasset, your wife's solicitors. Nothing personal against you or Miss Kubic, though if you don't mind me saying so you've got a lovely little wife there. A man could do a lot worse. These days young chaps often don't realize what a good thing they're on to.'

'Really?'

'Especially when there's a child involved. Sex rears its ugly head and the kiddies are left up the garden path. My wife and I have had our barneys but our boys mean the world to us.'

'I'm a fond father myself.' Nevertheless the old guilt juices flowed anew. Even a three a.m. homily from this avuncular idiot started them off. 'No problem there,' he added defensively.

Jane brought in the tea and some gingernut biscuits on a saucer. The hostess role always suited her. Those well-spoken W.A. girls were bred to it.

'Nice drop,' Frazer said, sipping thirstily. He dunked a biscuit, ate it in two bites and submerged another.

'I'd be careful with those. I've had them a long time,' Crisp warned.

'Stephen, did you know there are hideous slugs crawling all over your kitchen?'

'Just grazing. They feed at night. We have a truce these days. They have me beat. At least they can't open the fridge door yet.' He sipped his tea. 'You know, this is quite pleasant. We must do it more often.'

'Don't be flippant.' She perused a carved lime gourd from New Guinea. 'Does Anna's not being here mean you've broken up?' She traced the gourd's whorls and patterns with a fingernail. Long and painted, like the others. In his day she'd bitten them.

'Sort of.' *Give nothing away*, he thought, *in front of the private eye*.

'Oh. You realize that some adultery evidence would speed things up.'

'Careful. No collusion,' Frazer said, dunking another gingernut. His timing was out and the biscuit disintegrated into his tea. He smiled foolishly and spooned out the mush into his saucer.

'You're in a rush all of a sudden.'

A cool eye from Jane. 'You'd like it to draw on indefinitely, wouldn't you? Never having to make a decision.' She smoothed back an escaping sidelock. 'We're going to Britain shortly for Nick to study. The Royal College of Surgeons. We'll probably marry in London.'

Marry! 'I can't imagine him as a surgeon,' he said. 'Don't have to go overseas to learn that, anyway. What about Wendy?' *And me*, he thought. *Me, me, me.*

'Please don't be impossible about this. It will make things easier for you. Financially. I'll be looked after. You'll have only Wendy's expenses to worry about—education, clothes and so on.'

'I want to worry about her.' *The significance of all this!* 'She's my daughter, too. What plans have you two made for her?'

'We'll stay in Britain and Europe for two or three years. Nick wants to do some skiing in Austria. Wendy will go to school. It will be a valuable experience for her, the travel and everything.'

'I'll miss her.' *Thank you for the world so sweet, food we eat, birds that sing, everything.*

'Naturally. And she'll miss you. But this is the best thing for her.'

'Three years! She'll forget me.'

Jane stood up, brushed crumbs from her skirt, ran her tongue over her teeth. She was now perfectly composed; perhaps the procedures with the crockery had relaxed her. 'You sell yourself short, Stephen,' she said.

Frazer the investigator yawned in the corner, set down his murky cup and saucer, gathered his camera and torch. 'Time's money, Mrs Crisp,' he said. 'Thanks for the tea.' They left, Frazer politely gesturing Jane through the door.

Crisp went back to bed with his teeth full of gingernut crumbs but could not sleep for an hour or more.

On 21st April I reached the heads at Macquarie Harbour and trudged on to the penal settlement. Wooraddy, Truganini, McKay and McGeary met me outside the settlement on their way back to me with medicine, a small amount of provision and welcome clothing and shoes. Our boat had arrived that morning. I made the decision to continue my mission of conciliation, necessitating an immediate call on the gaol commandant, one Captain Briggs. I took Wooraddy and Truganini with me. I gave Wooraddy an old red coat from the fresh supplies, and clean trousers, and he appeared very martial and lordly. I loaned him a fowling piece and gave him a broken carbine to carry. He was remarkable proud, marching about like a cocky sergeant.

Captain Briggs was a disappointment. The man had a vulpine, taut bearing and was not fully conversant with the importance of my mission. Obviously he was not mature enough for the responsibility of his duties.

'Robinson, eh. Tomfool idea traipsing about tranquillizing the blacks.'

'His Excellency doesn't share your opinion, Captain. By his authority I desire accommodation and provisions for my party.'

Briggs raised his eyebrows and surveyed my weather-beaten features with some derision. (I had applied yellow ointments to my pustules and my face was shiny with unguents and spotted with scraps of rag.) 'I have been authorized to indulge your hobby, Mr Robinson. You can have what you need. Mr Schofield the chaplain will tend to you.'

'Thank you,' I said, very formally. The man was a martinet.

'Goodbye Mr Robinson. Please ask your blackman to remove that travesty of a uniform. It insults us all.'

The Reverend Mr Schofield was a different stamp of a man, warm-visaged, distinguished and resolute in his religious attentions to his incorrigible charges. He invited me to dine in his barracks, serving a choice shoulder of lamb, brandy and even some lime juice for my infections. He presented me with a letter from my wife dated 3rd March and forwarded on to him:

My dear husband,

I begin to fear something has befallen you. I would be happy to hear that you are in good health. I have had my health very bad since you left; I may say that my house has been a place of mourning. Three weeks after you left I was confined to my bed and two days after that my youngest child Alfred was taken ill. He lay in strong fits a day and a night. I am sorry to say he departed this life 21st February. Dear husband, you may guess my trouble of mind, my dear baby dying and you away from home in the wilderness.

The blacks staying at our house absconded but were captured by the soldiers. They were taken to Launceston in a bullock cart chained neck to neck, two constables going with them.

My dear husband, return home as soon as you can. I am very dull. I have the dear babe continually in my thoughts and I am longing to see you.

Your loving wife,
Maria.

My feelings were overcome at the news. The splendid Mr Schofield was most sympathetic, offering prayers and condolences for the infant and my family. He was also keenly aware of my mission and more perspicacious than many of my acquaintances as to my aims. He toasted my expedition with cognac. 'Your cause is God's will and He will prosper it if you keep close to Him. A noble race will rise up and call you blessed—as their friend, patron and spiritual father.'

'You are too generous, Mr Schofield.'

'Nonsense. The object of your expedition lies near to my heart. It's one of the most glorious beneath the canopy of heaven.'

'I believe that's true. But I want no praise or honour for doing God's work.'

'Your humility does you credit,' he said, administering to my cognac glass. 'If you only play the man and the Christian you will immortalize your name on history's pages.'

'Granted, there are certain dangers of course. Certain tortuous decisions to make. In any such hazardous undertaking . . .'

'Indeed. You've already shown your bravery. But I think the dangers are nothing when the object is taken into consideration. I mean the conversion and salvation of these wretched creatures.'

'I see we are in complete harmony Mr Schofield.'

I determined to write to Mrs Robinson while at the settlement, but pressure of organization prevented me. Mr Schofield provided me with writing paper, three pencils and sealing wax so I could correspond while on my journeys. Captain Briggs, though still displaying sour disapproval of my expedition, was forced by my signed authority from the Governor to provide for us. We left Macquarie Harbour laden with salt meat and flour, tea, sugar, half a gallon of lime juice and some preserved soups. I had asked Briggs to supply me with a trusty convict as a servant-clerk. He looked down on me from the garrison steps, high-coloured and pompous.

'There's no prisoner fit to be trusted,' he said, and turned on his heel.

A noise diverted Crisp as he worked in the hot afternoon—like a cardboard carton of old shoes or a bundle of newspapers dropping from a height onto cement, scraping and clattering against walls and waterpipes as it fell. He worked on, the harsh buzzing of cicadas filling his ears again until, fifteen or twenty minutes later, faint moans rose from the asphalt courtyard below the window. Out in the heat mirage of the afternoon a waxen face and a set of curiously angled limbs lay beneath him. Down the back stairs, two flights, he ran—surprisingly noticing absurd elements of trivia along the way: a heap of magazines discarded near the stairwell, a grease-eroded electric frypan, an ant-encrusted pet-food dish. The top magazine on the pile displayed a cover photograph of Princess Grace, older these days but still serene. On the asphalt lay an old man. His skin was hot and sallow; flies and ants crawled around his lips. A bone piece protruded at the elbow of his shirt and one leg was strangely doubled under him.

Kneeling there in his Y-fronts, Crisp despaired. He had nothing to shade him with; obviously he should not be moved. The old man wore a small pectoral cross, now twisted on its chain around his neck, but if he wanted prayers Crisp was equally useless.

'Hang on old chap. I'll call an ambulance.' First he had to brush the insects from the face. The flies were lethargic and persistent. The asphalt was sharp and burned Crisp's bare knees; the cicadas grated mercilessly in his head. In the sun it approximated a hundred and fifty degrees easily.

Then, responding to some cue of his own, the old man clutched abruptly at Crisp's wrist, dry-fingered and urgent. He looked up bleakly like a shot gunslinger in a classic western and said two words.

'Barbara,' he whispered. 'Christmas.'

The ambulance men had trouble getting the stretcher out into the courtyard through a bottom-storey window. Someone thought his name was Parslow. Parsons? A pensioner, he lived in *Killarney* next door. Second floor; tore his faded net curtains as he fell. Barbara may have been a daughter who lived in Adelaide.

Shocked, Crisp couldn't work further that afternoon. He called one of his few remaining friends at the Commission, Peter Tooth, and arranged to meet him at the 729 Club. He drank a double brandy to Tooth's gin and tonic. 'I saw a man die today,' he announced.

'Christ,' said Tooth, uncharacteristically stylish in summerweight blue seersucker. 'How?'

'Fell from his window. Or jumped perhaps. Old-age pensioner in the next block of flats. Lived by himself.'

'Terrible.'

Crisp sucked at his brandy. 'I couldn't do much; I was only in my underpants. His bones were sticking through his clothes. And the heat was awful.'

Tooth said 'Christ' again. 'We're doing a programme on pensioners,' he said. 'By the way, congratulate me. I've been given *Counterpoint*, starting next Wednesday. Big research team, five reporters.'

'I wondered about the new suit. Congratulations. What about management interference? How will you get on with the lovely Appleyard?'

Tooth gave him a long ambiguous glance. Crisp was tieless, his desert boots scuffed. 'There shouldn't be any trouble,' Tooth said, crunching ice, draining his drink. 'I'll play it as it lays.'

'As the saying goes.'

'Right.'

Tooth left early for a producer's dinner party in Paddington. Crisp drank more brandies into the evening. Presently a fairly attractive dark girl, a TV research assistant, came up to him at the bar. 'Don't I know you from somewhere?' she asked. She smiled, revealing irregular but sexy white teeth. She had olive skin, a wide mouth, interesting Continental features. 'The old Newcastle days?'

'Very possibly,' Crisp said, buying her several drinks, accepting one in return and taking her home in a cab to her Balmain terrace where the combination of several factors prevented him from retaining an erection.

We headed northwards along the coast from Macquarie Harbour. Now that my full party was together again it was not long before we had nearly exhausted our provision. By 11th May we had nought left but wheatmeal, and this in a coarse sack carelessly dropped by the natives on the ground so that the sand mixed with the flour. Luckily the kangaroo was plentiful and the fig trees abundant.

Pleasant weather assisted us in espying some fresh *Toogee* tracks and we soon noticed smoke to the north. Following a path along the coastal cliff-face we eventually came to a dead-end hard up against a wall of granite. A tall well-made warrior of about forty years and a pubescent girl squatted on the path eating mutton-fish. They saw us, started up and were trapped against the rock face. The man had no weapons but grabbed up a handful of stones and faced us, shivering with tension. The girl screamed, '*Num! Num!*' and plunged heedlessly over the cliff, a distance of about forty feet, into the sea.

I stood motionless, neither advancing nor retreating, and offered the man a haunch of kangaroo. He trailed through the dust towards me, trembling with anticipation, preparing to throw his stones. In his nervous state he had puddled the ground at his feet; moisture streaked his thin greased legs. I placed the meat on the path before him and with it a blanket and some beads. He bent over the meat, sniffed it, then picked it up, unsure of himself.

Beneath us the girl struggled in the choppy tides to reach a small outcrop where the waves were breaking heavily in plumes of spray. I feared she might drown. 'Swim after her!' I instructed Truganini and Pagerley. They clambered down the cliff, dived into the sea and, being strong swimmers, soon reached her. They brought her, protesting, from the water. Her breast was gashed and her temple severely abraded. They asked her to come to me, speaking in her dialect, '*Tawe loccato. Puggana tareetye.* Come ashore. He is a good man who will give you food.'

The girl shook her head and dived once more into the sea. Again the women swam after her and brought her struggling to land. The man, apparently her father and imagining her soon to be stolen and violated, began wailing, '*Legara loggatale meena!* Run away my daughter!'

The girl was shaking with fear, still looking anxiously towards the ocean, so I backed away several yards and requested my natives to follow me. Immediately she ran into the bush and concealed herself. Our generosity astounded her father, who approached me and shook hands. His name was Lee-ther. I put the beads around his neck and hung some buttons on them. (Wooraddy made a disgusted face.) Lee-ther came and sat down by us. I gave him some bread as well as the kangaroo haunch. He was pleased with the meat but would not eat the bread, saying, '*Toogee* have been poisoned with white man's food.' This was the first time whites had visited his territory with the purpose of doing good. 'They kill us and steal our women. Sometimes they shoot everyone—women and children too—and throw the bodies in the fire.'

After a long parley, his confidence in us satisfied, Lee-ther hooted loudly and an older woman, his wife Peegooner, emerged from the bushes holding a small boy by the hand. She joined us by the fire. She was not as frightened as her daughter and conversed cheerfully with me, pleased at the baubles I gave her. I handed Lee-ther my telescope. '*Numerick.* See through it.' He thought it was a gun and drew back afraid. '*Parlene-ne!* Do not shoot us!' I unscrewed the instrument, removed one of the lenses and demonstrated the power of the sun's rays through the glass. 'Eeah,' he laughed and focused the ray on his wife's leg so she felt the pale autumn warmth. They were delighted with the game.

Truganini drew me aside. 'Wooraddy has stolen Lee-ther's mutton-fish,' she said. 'He has hidden their food basket because they are evil.'

I ordered him to return it. Wooraddy grumbled deep in the throat but offered no opposition. The *Toogee* appeared not the least surprised at his behaviour but received their property back gratefully. 'We must join our tribe,' Lee-ther announced after an hour's socializing, and hooted for his daughter. With a cracking of twigs she plummeted from a gum-tree not thirty feet from us and joined her family. Blood still showed at her breast and forehead but it aroused no comment from her parents.

We left them in good spirits and journeyed on a mile, passing several other scattered *Toogee* before camping for the night. Everyone we saw ran up the hillside and hid in the bushes from us.

We camped by the side of a well-worn *Toogee* path in the midst of a thick forest. All night I was afraid the various groups of *Toogee* might amalgamate and ambush us while we slept. My blacks were exceedingly nervous, curling up to me like children. They would go to sleep only after I had left a heap of biscuits and presents in a prominent position as a peace offering. Next morning the gifts were gone without us hearing a sound.

We kept to the same path next day, emerging at noon on a wide rocky beach. My natives espied traces of smoke and eventually, in a small hidden cove brilliantly coloured by orange, yellow and green lichens, we came upon twenty natives standing in earnest discussion. The men were heavily armed with spears and waddies. We watched them from cover at the edge of the forest. Several of the women climbed down to the rocks to shellfish, taking the children with them. I decided to approach the rest of the tribe. 'Halloo,' I called, moving slowly from cover. 'I am your friend. I have food and gifts.' The warriors scuttled over the rocks like crabs and ran into the bush; the women all dived into the sea and swam out to a small reef about one hundred yards off-shore.

In their panic they had left behind all their kangaroo skin robes, mutton-fish, crawfish, whelks, baskets and puppies. I filled a reed basket with bread and put some handkerchiefs, beads, knives, scissors and blankets nearby. Wooraddy and Truganini wished to steal their fish but I would allow nothing to be disturbed.

As Wooraddy moped about sullenly he espied two children hidden in a crevice—a baby girl wrapped in skins and a boy about six years old, pretty featured and well formed, crying silently beside her. As we approached the boy tried to escape down the rocks to the sea but Wooraddy brought him back, scooping the terrified child up by the ankles. I patted him, giving him a shiny japanned box, but he treated it with the utmost contempt, pushing it from him. He looked mournfully toward the reef where the *Toogee* women were now clambering from the ocean. I wrapped the baby in a blanket as she was trembling with cold. I put a skin over the boy's shoulders to keep him warm and, after placing beads and ribbons around his and the baby's necks, hurried away lest their parents might become desperate and charge us.

Hazy weather set in, with mizzling rain. We camped several miles away from the coast. The cold was intense, it now being early June and into the Antipodean winter. We made our camp on a wide plain resembling an English park: beautiful grass like a bowling green dotted with honeysuckle trees. I saw the tracks of a large tiger or hyaena creature and many scratches on the ground where Truganini said the *Toogee* women had raked up the sand with their fingers to catch ground mice. Being the Sabbath next day it was apt for me to read St Matthew and write in my journal: 'The Lord is very good to me and I am in good health.' Wooraddy entertained us with tales of the heroic exploits of the Bruny men in battle. As I have recorded he was the last of them.

That afternoon I journeyed out with Truganini and Wooraddy to reconnoitre. I estimated we were two miles or so from Mount Norfolk, inland from Sandy Cape. Just off a track well trodden by the *Toogee* I found a neat mound about eighteen inches high.

'What is this?' I asked them, scraping the earth with my fingers. 'A sign of some sort?' My hand suddenly clasped some splintered pieces of human bone.

'*Ragewrapper!*' Truganini shrieked. 'Dead *Toogee* bones!' Wooraddy too trembled as though his dissolution was near. They both fled up the track and would not relax until we were more than a mile from the funeral mound.

Farther on we discovered two big and deserted native huts, built as usual near a water cascade and a grove of kangaroo-fig trees. Hanging from one roof was a grass basket filled with shellfish and house-leek.

With difficulty I persuaded Wooraddy and Truganini from stealing the food, giving them a Christian lesson by placing beads, knives, buttons etc. in the basket as we left. Wooraddy shrugged, clearly thinking me mad. On our way back to camp two hours later we passed the huts again. The *Toogee* had fetched their presents. They had left in their stead some mutton-fish lined in rows, two for each of us (they must have observed us) and a masticated grass ball taken from a kangaroo's stomach.

'*Nemone!*' Truganini exclaimed. 'Good luck grass. You must eat it.'

I mimed the act of eating. 'You eat some,' I instructed (though properly against such superstitions), dividing up the bilious sludge between them. They chewed their portions avidly, crunching them like cabbage. Truganini smiled. '*Ragewrapper* gone now. Dead man's bones happy.'

At the right of his loungeroom view the bed of white daisies grew thicker and wilder as the thesis grew. Unkempt plants straggled over the garden edge into the courtyard; their white blaze filled half Crisp's vision when he looked up from his exercise books. Lizards moved amongst the stalks and darted momentarily into the sun; sometimes he thought he saw them.

Back fifteen or sixteen years he could not look for long at fields of white flowers, stretches of white sand or whitewashed walls or fences without becoming dizzy and nauseous. Unless he turned quickly away into the shade his head would pound and he'd vomit, eyes rolling, right where he stood. This was an after-effect from a youthful illness. At first his parents had thought his listlessness some sort of adolescent sham to avoid school exams, then flu. By the time paralysis had reached the neck and spine and he screamed from the pains that flashed inside his skull they realized it was neither. Doctor Williams was nonplussed. Murray and Jean sought a second opinion from Doctor Goodwin, Hallstrom's company doctor, whose advanced alcoholism didn't prevent him from recognizing meningitis when he saw it. An ambulance ride to hospital, spinal drainage, isolation ward and 'wonder drugs' followed. Paralysis proved only temporary, the blinding headaches vanished. Young Stephen left hospital three weeks later able to touch chin on chest again, fifteen pounds lighter, seemingly inches taller and with a downy brown moustache. After-effects were the aversion to glare and whiteness and deep spinal aches in times of stress, over-fatigue and, years later, general dissipation.

(A month after his mother died he woke up alongside Jane one morning completely numb down one side—eyelid, cheek, tongue, arm, chest, leg. Doctors found nothing really amiss—the numbness remained all morning until he vomited.

An appointment was made for an encephalogram. Electrodes were taped to the skull while flashes of lightning were induced to explode behind the eye sockets. On a cylindrical graph spidery ink lines recorded no abnormalities and the girl working the machinery flirted slightly as she removed the sticking plaster. Machines had been wrong before, was all he could think.)

But he hadn't let his mother forget he could have died, basking in self-righteousness for a month or so, occasionally dropping a question on her at the dinner table: 'Why didn't you believe me?' he would ask. 'I knew I was sick. Why would I pretend something like that, for God's sake?' Her eyes showed her guilt, unwarranted as it was what with her own troubles—at that time worrying breast lumps soon to be surgically removed and scrutinized and the family's moving to a new and bigger house. Here there would be waves of entertaining on behalf of Murray's career. He had become State manager just the month before, on Hawker's retirement. '*You know I'm married to Hallstrom's first, Jean.*' Because of his attractive grin she hadn't taken him seriously at first; she had learned to since. But the breast operation was a success, mastitis and not what she'd dreaded, and the move into the new house, a mile away in Dalkeith, accomplished fairly effortlessly.

Handyman Murray did some of the tasks himself. He painted the facing boards for the roof with pink primer, landscaped the sloping front garden into three terraces and planted a lawn of superfine couch mixed with bent. On the bottom level under the main bedroom window the grass grew only sparsely in the shade of the house and he had to mix in some buffalo to strengthen it. Jean was against having rosebeds in the front garden—too hackneyed—but she liked roses in the house, so Murray dug the beds in the back yard, preparing the soil beforehand with a mulch of sheep manure and old *Women's Weeklys*. Below Stephen and Geoffrey's rooms, built beneath ground level, was his workshop. He called it his 'dog-house' (and he often did retreat there during squabbles) and lined its walls with shelves to hold his tools, Black and Decker electric drill, nails and screws in old Vegemite jars and lengths of dowelling tied together with electrician's tape. A machinist's vice and a carpenter's vice were bolted to a big central workbench. The dog-house was also used as a storeroom for old tea chests, furniture, the lawn mower, gardening tools, the boys' bikes and summer inner tubes.

Murray's old RAAF kitbag and uniform were down there growing mould: moth-nibbled dress blues, peaked cap, tropical khakis and pith helmet. He still wore the khaki shirt for gardening every Sunday (Saturdays he played golf). In the dog-house he built a portable bar for the back patio, a bookcase for Stephen, several coffee tables, a homework desk for Geoffrey and a hall lamp whose base was three blocks of wood, inset with coloured counters, in the form of large dice. With Fred Hill, an employee from Hallstrom's flooring department, he laid the vinyl tiles on the kitchen, bathroom and toilet floors. In the second outside toilet, a humorous touch, they laid two black tiles cut in the shape of feet in the approximate position where men stood to urinate. When young Geoff stood on the footprints, however, his stream splashed on to the floor.

It was Geoff who brought up the matter of the Naked Lubra Calendar again. Looking for bus fares, he was raiding their father's penny box—an old Dunlop-65 golf ball box into which he dropped his loose change each night—when he came across the calendar. He ran smugly with it to his brother.

'Look what I've got! Natives showing their titties.'

'You'll get a belting. He hid that especially.'

'See. They've got no clothes on. You can see their bosoms.'

'So what?' He could though, even the nipples which were always covered by coy hands or strategically draped curtains in *Man* or the *Mirror*. The lake reached their waists and was so clear that the outline of the girls' thin legs was clearly visible. They were also naked below the waist. He looked closely at the photograph but could not make out the furry black triangles he knew were lurking down there below the waterline.

By 13th June we were out of provision once more, the people exhausted from their exertions and lack of food. We reached Mount Cameron, climbing to the peak up a hillside thickly timbered with large gum and peppermint trees, and looked out over the Strait. We could see Robbins Island, Pelican Island, the Doughboys, Black Rock, the Petrel Islands and Cape Grim. Cold and hungry, I welcomed the sight on our descent of three shepherds, all armed with muskets, overseeing a flock of dun-coloured sheep on the high grassy plains where Cape Grim ran into the sea.

The shepherds were weather-beaten, roughly-dressed men employed by the Van Diemen's Land Company which occupied all this land with its sheep. Hospitable enough, they invited us to share a meal at their cottage, motioning me to sit at a thick wooden bench among a heap of fleece. My people squatted on the floor. I ate heartily of mutton-bird and tea, my natives likewise though the shepherds regarded them suspiciously. One of them was a rosy-cheeked Scot from the islands who spoke mainly Gaelic; another, also a Scot, a scrambled mixture of Gaelic and English. The third, a solid sandy-headed Dorsetman with protruding eyes, joked at the expense of the ruddy islander as we finished our meal.

'Old Jim here's just beginning to speak English. He saw the blacks for the first time and thought the bleeders'd understand Gaelic.' Snorting with laughter, he stamped tobacco into his pipe with an oil-ingrained thumb. 'He went up to them speaking his gobbledegook. Amazed when they didn't catch on to it. Gaelic! The savages are too bloody thick to understand English.' The Scot glowered embarrassed over his tin plate, his cheeks scarlet.

The Dorsetman, name of Charles Chamberlain, leaned confidentially towards me, indicating the natives with his pipe stem. 'Find them trustworthy, do you?'

Greasy-lipped, Wooraddy glanced up from a mutton-bird carcase.

'Most.'

'Worse than the crows around here. Bloody birds pick the eyes out of the lambs soon as the ewes drop 'em. Bloody blacks throw our sheep over the cliff.'

'Unusual. Exerting their territorial rights perhaps.'

'I know nought about that. Bloody-minded savagery is how I see it.' The man grew expansive, glad of a comprehending listener, puffed importantly on his pipe. 'Tell me, you're a gent looks like he knows the doings in Hobart Town. Is that Arthur a bleeding conciliator or what? A-babying the savages, putting pressure on the company and so on.'

Before I could answer Chamberlain leant towards me and resumed his monologue. His voice had a sly edge. 'Let me tell you something to keep under your hat,' he said. 'The company surveyor came around here last week offering us some poison to destroy the hyaena. They'd been worrying the sheep dreadful last summer. I said, "We don't need it now but we could find a use for some come December." He said, "You don't understand. A different species of hyaena," he said. "You put it in the blacks' flour."'

Truganini looked up at me, alarmed. Wooraddy too had caught his meaning. Another extirpationist if ever I'd seen one, this shepherd. I was keen to leave the sheep-run without delay. I disliked its cloying smell and the idiotic bleating of its creatures.

'Thank you for the food,' I said. As we moved off two crows were at work on a lamb's carcase, drooping heavily over the eyeless body like ugly umbrellas. The lamb's mother stood stupidly by.

We encamped at the edge of the cape, near some fishing rocks for the natives and close by a wild orchard of the greengage fruit. The night was bitterly cold; the natives as usual huddled about me till morning.

A barrage of sounds woke us; to my ears musket fire. The natives were exceedingly fearful, hovering about me and touching my shirt hem for reassurance. I hurried in the direction of the shots, my people unhappily running behind. Truganini moaned softly, then swallowed her sounds at a fierce glare from her husband.

Around the headland we hastened, following a *Toogee* track that wound erratically at the lip of the high cliff face and disappeared into a copse of she-oak trees. Again the guns sounded.

'*Ragewrapper, Ragewrapper,*' Wooraddy murmured.

Sporadic musket shots rang in the distance and now we could hear streams of piping sound, high screams carried to us by the sea breeze. My natives stopped in their tracks, terrified, and refused to go further. Isolated shots still reverberated in the near distance and I hurried, alone, towards them, the salty crust of the sand track squeaking under my feet. A low ululation rose from a cliff ledge below and ahead of me and an old *Toogee* woman crawled to her knees from behind a lichened outcrop. Blood gushed from a vast black cave in her cheek. The woman turned her half-face to the sea and struggled to stand upright. She attempted to steady herself, preparing to dive down into the sea, but her stick-legs wavered and shook as if palsied. Then her tremors ceased and slowly she raised a surprised hand to her cheek-cavern and stepped forwards to the cliff edge, appearing to be solemnly contemplating the breakers below. Her other hand was fingering a charm tied to her gaunt waist when the ruddy-faced Gael rose silently from behind a boulder, aimed his musket and blew her body like a bunch of black feathers over the cliff.

'You murderer!' I was near blinded with rage. 'I witnessed your crime. You'll hang for that.'

The shepherd turned his glowing face towards me in surprise, mumbled something unintelligible, shrugged and ducked back behind the boulder. I leaped up the path after him, heedless of the risky footing. My eyes streamed with tears of anger; spittle ran down my chin. Wind gusts snatched at my hair and clothes, howled up the sandy track, blew grit into my eyes and shouting mouth.

Around the boulder from the sniper's nest the track widened into a grassy clearing which overlooked a ledge dotted with fig trees. A narrow path led down to the ledge; at its farmost reach was a dead-end —a high rock wall. Beneath the ledge was a drop of a hundred feet or more on to angular rocks stippled with brightly coloured lichens. The ledge was strewn with *Toogee* bodies—men, women and children lying amongst their scattered food baskets in a morass of blood and ripe fruit. The Dorsetman and the second Scot moved among them, swinging bodies over the cliff on to the rocks. Blood ran down the cliff face, congealing in the sand and probing like fingers into porous crevices. The split bodies of the *Toogee* sailed over the cliff edge and flopped like oozing sacks on to the golden, green and orange-hued rocks.

Dray, Neen-ne-vuther, Tow-ter-rer! I collapsed on the clearing, near to suffocation from the spectacle. My heart hammered at my ribs, pulses fluttered over my body. I remained there, gasping out prayers, as the shepherds flung the last mutilated bodies over the edge, collected their carbines and muskets and sauntered up the path to me. Below them lay the object of my endeavours, the *Toogee* tribe. Chamberlain led the way. 'Morning sir,' he said. 'A bit of crow hunting for the company.'

'What? What?' I was nigh on speechless.

'Like I mentioned, the savages drove thirty sheep of ours over the Cape. Bit of luck getting them on the cliff while they was picking figs.

Couldn't fade away into the bushes like bloody shadows ...'

'Murder! Cold-blooded slaughter! Those people are protected by British law.'

'Oh, no. Not murder, British justice. We threw 'em down on the rocks like they threw our sheep. On the company's instructions. Company's policy is tit-for-tat.'

'You have slaughtered a complete tribe.'

Chamberlain plucked out his pipe, stoked it with thick fingers blood-stained around the nails. Its bowl gleamed with the grease of fleece and mutton-birds. 'I didn't know we did that good,' he said.

Emu Bay
26 July, 1830

If Your Excellency pleases I wish to inform you and the Colonial Secretary that I have been most successful in making friendly contact with the tribes of the west coast of the colony, as was my object.

Had this attempt been made some few years ago I have no hesitation in saying that ere this time a most perfect system might have been established and our communication kept up with every aboriginal throughout the island.

At present I am of an opinion that all those aboriginal natives inhabiting the settled districts ought to be removed, for although tranquillity on the part of the aboriginals be restored, yet such is the character of the men employed in the interior in sheep herding that at every opportunity fresh outrages are perpetrated and the defenceless aboriginals are thereby goaded on again to retaliate. The Original Inhabitants have been cruelly treated; not one aboriginal that I have visited but what they have dire wrongs to complain of. I enclose a report on the recent behaviour of three shepherds in the employ of the Van Diemen's Land Company. ...

We stayed at Emu Bay for several days enjoying the hospitality of this small surveyors' establishment. I took the opportunity to send off letters to my wife and the Reverend Schofield as well as my letter to His Excellency. On Sunday 1st August I hoisted the Bethel flag and, because of the bitter cold, conducted a pleasant service inside the Emu Bay store amongst the sacks of flour and sugar, the preserved meats, biscuit tins and tea chests. I took my text from Corinthians II 13:5: 'Examine yourselves whether ye be in the faith; prove your labour.'

I felt I had expounded one of my finest sermons (and recorded later in my journal): 'A short time has elapsed since none but the wandering savage had this desert and the country was unknown; when on those hills the heathen was wont to roam, and after the toil of the day in hunting they would sit round their fire and recount their history, sing their war and love songs and join in the dance; when its Original Inhabitants had not heard of Christ; when if the thunder rolled or the vivid lightning darted they were wont to crouch beneath their wigwam, imagining that the evil spirit *Ragewrapper* was ready to destroy them. But, oh how different on this occasion! Let us pray to God that they be brought to know him, the only true God.'

The local people, surveyors, storekeepers and labourers, were most attentive, it being the first time the gospel had been preached in these parts. The natives unfortunately were rather diverted by the foodstuffs surrounding them. Truganini, I discovered later by her tell-tale trail, had stealthily picked a large hole in the sugarbag on which she sat and concealed a fair quantity in her grass basket. A peculiarly heavy fall of snow took place during my service. Running outside at its conclusion, my natives laughed and shouted '*turrana!*' and played at snowballs.

Emu Bay
28th July, 1830

My dear Maria,

Your letter sorrowed me more than I can express; sorrow at the departure of our infant from this mortal coil and sorrow at your bereavement and unhappiness. I hope by now your natural serenity has reasserted itself; your emotions secure in the knowledge that Alfred has joined the Kingdom of the Lord Almighty where tiny souls find everlasting happiness.

As to myself, I have had numerous adventures and travails doing His work during the past half-year but I must say that my mission has been accompanied by much success. Everywhere I have gone, over mountain, forest and swamp, I have endeavoured to conciliate and befriend our sable brethren and at this date the situation is much improved.

My dear wife, as to your request for me to return home I cannot meet it for some months. I am persuaded by my success so far to continue my conciliatory expeditions in the interior and outlying islands. With His Excellency's approval I shall continue my attempts to ameliorate the condition of the poor benighted savages. I know that the upbringing of our children and the maintenance of our home is safe in your hands. If you lack anything contact the Colonial Secretary's Office and assistance will be forthcoming.

I am,
Your loving husband
G. A. Robinson.

Emu Bay
28th July, 1830

My Dear Mr Schofield,

Your kind thoughts on my behalf and your encouragement to my mission have helped me through many a dangerous and forlorn moment since I left you. Alas, there are not many, even in your calling, who show the benevolence and paternal kindness of your attitudes to the tragic race. I am sure the felons incarcerated at Macquarie Harbour bear testimony to your firm but sympathetic control of their spiritual lives.

My mission is proceeding exceedingly well. Everywhere I go I am greeted by the aboriginal natives as their friend and companion. Indeed, I feel my reputation is preceding me from campfire to campfire. Lest I become too conscious of my importance I must aver, however, that at this present it is only necessary for me to change my complexion to black and walk the bush to be shot at. The most wanton cruelties are still being practised upon these people—I myself witnessed the massacre of the *Toogee* tribe most recently by three employees of the Van Diemen's Land Company—and the flame of aboriginal resentment blazes fiercely. It can only be extinguished by British benevolence. We should fly to their relief. We should atone for the misery we have entailed upon the aboriginal proprietors of this land. But who is there to whom they can make their grievances known? At this moment Mr Schofield, only yourself, myself and a tiny handful of others.

I am
Yours sincerely
G. A. Robinson

Hallstrom Industries,
1231 Collins Street,
Melbourne, 3000.
13th February.

Dear Stephen,

Just a quick note to say we're opening the world's first fully automated gelatine extraction plant (built at a cost of more than $1 million!) in Sydney next Wednesday. I'll be coming up for the opening and be pleased if you can make it, Son. Might be worth your dropping the word to your TV contacts. It's an exciting breakthrough. The entire process has been automated. Not only is it controlled by computer but the process is monitored by a supervisor on closed-circuit television screens! An invitation is enclosed which will admit two to the opening ceremony (to be conducted by the Premier) as well as to the extraction plant and evaporating unit.

Cheers,
Dad.

Wednesday came with its obligation. Crisp felt he should put the thesis aside and attend, resuscitating a suit and a red tie and catching a taxi to Hallstrom's Sydney complex. It sprawled on twenty or thirty acres of bushland north of the city. He paid off the cab and caught a whiff of gluey steam, like semen. The brothel smell was animal proteins, he thought, a million dollar knacker's yard. Yet there were no animals to be seen. The plant was spacious and immaculate, with an efficient looking overlay of steel pipes, glistening metal cylinders and narrow gunmetal ladders. The company was conscious of the environment, it seemed, and had engaged landscape gardeners to plant numerous clumps of regularly spaced native trees and to erect several free-ranging groups of rough shaped boulders where there had not been boulders before. A small waterfall gurgled over the planted rocks. A sign beside the cascade said DO NOT DRINK. THIS WATER IS RECYCLED FROM THE EVAPORATING UNIT. Workmen in neat white boilersuits directed the limousines of the official party to parking spots beside the reception area.

His father waited in an inner reception room near a sideboard of whiskies and gins already poured. A plump drink steward hovered sweatily. His father's handshake was warm but distracted. His taste in clothes appeared to have undergone modernization. He wore a wide-lapelled suit and blue-on-blue shirt. His hair was a fraction longer about the ears and collar, though still parted with the old Brylcreemed precision. Though anxiously cheerful his face was drawn and seemed to have melted under the chin. 'This is my elder son Stephen,' he told the assembled gelatine executives and their wives. 'He's in television.' *Was*. He handed his son a drink. 'You could have brought someone,' he said, smiling but perhaps disappointed. 'Did you tell the TV people? Where did you get that tie?'

'No one was free.' But his father wasn't listening, sipping a scotch and darting his eyes back and forth to the door, awaiting the Premier's entrance. His excitement had flushed his cheeks, even pinkening his ears.

The Premier arrived, smiling genially, and was soon shaking hands with the hierarchy. He nursed a scotch and laughed masculinely several times, raising good-humoured, quizzical brows and gripping major personnel by the elbow. Stephen was led by a junior gelatine executive to a seat in front of a dais set up in the entrance to the extraction plant. The man sat next to him and offered a hand. 'Ken Cornell,' he announced.

'Steve Crisp,' said Crisp.

'I know,' Cornell said.

The official opening was about to occur in the vicinity of fourteen large, round, stainless steel extractors—big, 2500-gallon vats all joined by a long blue ribbon. There was a lectern placed on the dais near the central extractors. Along the front of the dais ran a stainless steel flume which would load the extractors with their raw material of puréed hooves, horns, bones, skins and trotters from the preparation section. The Premier would sever the ribbon, thereby symbolically freeing the extractors for business.

'Well, how else do you officially open a gelatine extraction plant?' Cornell said.

The official guests were first welcomed by K. G. Synott, Hallstrom's general manager. Then the chairman, Sir Austin Parker (elegant despite his limp), called on the Premier to perform the official opening ceremony. This he did without mishap, first praising Hallstrom's consistently vigorous policy of free enterprise, which represented a splendid asset not only for the company's shareholders and employees, but for the State, which (he was proud to say) led all others in the country in attracting new industries. He warmly congratulated the company, personally and on behalf of the Government and citizens of the State, for having a new gelatine extraction plant. With dignified animation he then read a long list of Hallstrom's manufacturing and export achievements, including its progress in the fields of glue, tallow, bone flour, fertilizer and neatsfoot oil. He severed the ribbon with scissors, to enthusiastic applause.

Murray Crisp was to make a speech of thanks to the Premier. He walked to the lectern, clapping the Premier's severing operations as he went. His ears and cheeks still glowed, somewhat embarrassing his son crouching in the front row. To Stephen his smile seemed peculiarly strained and his eyes to be concentrating on some point in the mid-distance beyond the seated guests, out the open doors of the extraction plant, near the high wire fence separating the factory from the surrounding bush.

He thanked the Premier with as much effusion as was necessary. 'This is a proud day for all of us at Hallstrom,' he said. 'As previous speakers have mentioned, this magnificent, fully-automated extraction plant will lead to improved qualities in gelatine, greater technical efficiency, a wider range of applications on local and overseas markets and better utilization of available raw materials.' He drew a hand across his forehead. His flush had vanished, his face now appearing drained and sallow. 'I wish to make brief mention at this point of another important fact. The company has always maintained a progressive policy of technical development. This is why its specialized technical knowledge is so much sought overseas.'

Crisp saw his father make one small step down from the lectern, still staring into the middle distance, then appear to change his mind and return to his speech. A round-faced woman near Crisp, some executive wife or other, made a clucking sound of apprehension. His father continued, gripping the lectern with both hands. 'I am pleased to be able to announce at this ceremony, before our distinguished guests, as it were, that this week the production of gelatine began in a new factory at Manizales (he stumbled over the pronunciation), Columbia. At an altitude of 7064 feet on the slopes of the Andes!' There was a perfunctory clapping of hands. His father's voice was becoming fainter, slurred. 'Hallstrom Gelatine—rather Hallstrom Industries—designed the modern plant, *umm* supervised its installation and supplied the process knowledge.'

There was a burst of applause, led by the Premier. Murray Crisp gave a small childlike gasp, stumbled from the lectern towards the dais steps, in the direction of the door and the freedom of air and space, and fell over the edge of the dais. His body fell first over the metal flume, like a sack over a log, then slid down heavily, legs first, against the side of one of the extractors. Some hard object, a shoe heel or his watch, must have struck the extractor because a high metallic note rang out clearly above the hubbub, remaining in his son's ears for an interminable time. Executives took command.

We set off across the Surry Hills, the party trudging in single file through the snowdrifts past the skeletons of sheep killed by cold, excessive wet and attacks by hyaenas. We journeyed over the high part of Bluff Mountain, a north course, following the native track of broken boughs and footprints, with much exertion reaching the first ridge of the range. We trudged up to our thighs in snow, facing into a sharp bleak wind, thick slate-coloured cloud and frozen rain. Wherever we placed a foot there remained a complete model of the leg. It became greatly wearying to have to pull the feet out of these snow boots and thrust them back into the snow, and so on alternately over the mountain. My feet became so numb I had to plunge them into snow water to obtain animation. Descending the mountain we were almost trampled over by six big white mountain kangaroo. They bounded past us at great speed, leaping over the rocks and along shelving precipices slick with ice. 'Dray!' I said, pointing to the kangaroo, and immediately felt saddened for their namesake, perished with the *Toogee*.

For several weeks we saw no fresh natives. All slaughtered in this part of the country too? The weather cleared as September came but my luck did not improve. I twisted my knee savagely crossing a shallow ravine and the warmer weather brought tiny purple-winged gnats to pierce my European skin with their stings.

While my knee healed I wrote up my journal, read *Peveril of the Peak* (a gift from Mr Schofield) and improved my native vocabulary. (There are only three numerals in the Bruny language—*marrawah*, *piawah* and *luwah*.) Fowler the coxswain showed me a point near the mouth of the Leven River where he, whilst in the employ of the Van Diemen's Land Company, found the head and hands of an escaped prisoner from Macquarie Harbour. 'Two of 'em escaped. His mate killed him and ate his body and when captured was wearing moccasins made of his skin.'

'A most economic murderer,' I ventured.

'Hungry, I reckon,' said Fowler.

On 20th September we continued journeying along the western bank of the Eastern River, passing through marshes and forests of high reeds. Pelicans, gulls, ducks and black swans flocked around us in their hundreds; my natives gathered their eggs and ate them raw, twenty and thirty at a time, yolks dripping from their chins, until their eyes rolled and their stomachs heaved from the onslaught.

We had proceeded a mile or so along the river when Wooraddy heard a dog bark in the distance. Then faint voices carried across the water to us—at last we were within reach of another tribe of hostiles! I welcomed the thought and set off in quest of them, instructing Platt, the only white man with me, to stay with the guns and knapsacks and conceal himself. Wooraddy, Truganini and Pagerley stripped off their European clothing and we continued unarmed, taking some trinkets as friendly offerings.

The forest was now silent and only some recently barked peppermint trees showed that this was native territory. Wooraddy whispered that we must take care. 'These men kill everybody. Hate other *Parlerwar* as well as white men.' Nestling near some deep thickets of edible berries, in a small clearing, were their huts, only recently deserted. The fires where they had been hardening their spears were still burning. From the footmarks they had numerous dogs. Several small heaps of wood in the shape of little houses had been erected by the children in their play.

With Wooraddy leading the way we followed their tracks for about three miles. They led across an upland plain of stunted forest and over a moderately sloped hill. Cautiously approaching the crest we saw a dozen armed warriors running rhythmically along in single file about one hundred yards ahead. They were all big men, quite naked, and painted in war ochres and charcoal. Silently, we followed after them, our path winding around sloping granite outcrops which hid us from the natives but, if they became aware of our presence, would have enabled them to easily ambush us.

Abruptly we heard the sound of voices coming from the hilltop: the rest of the tribe, the women and children, were behind us. We were now caught between the two parties. I saw plainly that the warriors were heading towards our camp of the night before, planning to attack us. (Had not an over-ruling Providence ordered that I should leave that camp, the first indication I would have had of the natives would have been a volley of spears. Thank God for this deliverance and for all His mercy vouchsafed towards us!)

I had to decide quickly on a course of action. The hostiles were now approaching our old camp. We hid among the she-oaks watching them angrily comprehend that their prey had flown. '*Nummer tawé*,' they cried. 'White man gone.' They picked up our tracks and loped off again with long rhythmic strides. One of the warriors had tucked in his belt one of our discarded provision sacks. The bag flapped over his bony buttocks. It read *Crown Sugar*.

I sent Wooraddy, Truganini and Pagerley forward to intercept their path and in an effort to befriend them. I was concerned my sudden approach should affright them and remained a short distance behind, anxiously awaiting the result. My natives approached them gingerly, unarmed and smiling in a passive fashion, though I saw Wooraddy especially was tensed in every muscle of his back and shoulders.

'*Yah! Nun-oyne!*' he greeted. 'We are friends who wish to talk.' His voice was husky with anticipation and fear.

The warriors stopped and raised their spears at him. '*Man-her-ner dracker!*' they shouted. 'Throw spears!' and my natives turned and fled into the bushes back towards me.

I ran back to the hill where I had heard the voices of the women and children, believing the warriors would make all speed to protect them. I reached the hill unobserved to within ten yards of the tribe and peered from behind a granite pile. The warriors hurried to the tribe and began to relate their exploits in agitated whispers. At once their dogs caught my scent and began barking and howling hideously. My natives had meantime caught up to me and were hanging about my sides, anxiously wringing their hands.

'We soon burn on fire,' Truganini whispered pessimistically.

I decided to confront the hostiles. I stepped out from behind the rock and thrust forward my hand in greeting. 'I am Robinson,' I said. '*Tuttah wuttah onganeenah*. Come along, I want to speak to you. I have food.'

They stared at me in amazement: warriors, women and children all incredulous. One of their gaunt yellow dogs ran up and savaged my shoe; the other twenty or so curs howled and rolled back their eyes. The hostiles stood rigid with uncertainty (as if influenced by that Austrian Mesmer!) while the dog got his teeth caught in my ragged leggings. I tried to kick him loose, all the time beaming pleasantries upon the tribe. 'I have biscuit, beads, tea,' I was announcing, when Wooraddy jumped out from behind the rock with a shrill scream and brained the dog with his waddy.

Howling, mewing, the tribe fled, shrugging off their skins and blankets, scattering in all directions over the rocks and into the bushes. Babies, children and adults slipped into crevices, slid down cliff faces and tunnelled into shrubberies, leaving their yapping dogs running in circles in the dust.

'Tell them I will not hurt them!' I shouted to my natives. Wall-eyed with shock they hooted this message into the she-oaks and honeysuckle but the bushes were silent. Nothing remained but the hostiles' skins and possessions and a few aimless dogs sniffing at their dead companion.

I was heavy-hearted. Perhaps I could have captured them under force but this was against my aims as well as my instructions of conciliation. I left some beads as a forlorn token of friendship, gathered my natives and trudged wearily back along the trail to Platt. Kangaroo droppings lay in small black pyramids on the track. Small movements flickered at the corners of my vision. Dun-coloured animals hesitated, drew quick breaths and scampered from our path. Feet thumped and drummed. Twigs cracked. My natives drew near to me, like children. Odours of sour fat and moist earth swept over me, and then a swampy marine smell of shellfish and lagoon tubers. It was Truganini, pressing close to me, holding up a thin hand for my examination.

'*Rié poyé puening-yack*,' she whined softly. 'I have cut my finger.' I pressed it with my hands. My own right leg throbbed with pain—in his enthusiasm to beat off the dog Wooraddy had split open my shin with his waddy. The trunks and branches closed around us as my will ebbed from me suddenly and treacherously. *Maria, Maria, where am I going*? As we filed quietly along the trail I cried for our dead baby and for various reasons.

The next few days passed in their fashion, sluggishly and without features of interest. Even my appreciation of our surroundings, normally keen and enthusiastic, was dulled by pessimism and lethargy. By 23rd September we were travelling in a south-easterly direction through a swampy forest, eventually coming out on to a dry and extensive plateau, the Avenue Plains. Wooraddy pointed out in the dust the tracks of wild cattle. At the eastern end of the plains a stockade had been built to catch them. In the stockade I found an aboriginal skull shot through with a bullet hole. That sort of discovery by now almost went without comment. That night Truganini came quietly to my tent to inquire after my shattered shin, on which an abscess had formed, bringing a poultice of ashes and animal grease, as well as fresh myrtle branches for my bed. The nights were dark here and the hard-packed ground, despite the season, almost frozen. Under my boat cloak and blanket the mattress of myrtle, though rudimentary, helped to keep out the cold.

13

A Multiplicity of Evils

OUT OF THE INTENSIVE CARE unit at St Vincent's Murray Crisp looked well enough, though larger-eyed, thinner and exposing delicate amethyst bruising on both pale arms from intravenous probing and electronic connections. He had moved in with his younger sister Eileen and her family for three months. They were his only relatives in the East apart from Stephen and could be relied upon to administer a multi-coloured mixture of stimulants and tranquillizers, diuretics and anti-coagulants, to restrict alcohol, curtail cigarettes and lace his food with polyunsaturates.

Stephen had largely ignored his aunt and uncle since coming to Sydney; completely so since the separation. Frank Surtees, Eileen's husband, was a bank executive prominent in the community. As a key member of the relevant committees he had taken an influential role in the introduction to Australia of decimal currency, natural gas and Vietnam war refugees. Their children, his cousins David, Peter, Kerryn and Craig were, respectively, training to be an accountant, a lawyer, a teacher and an actor. The first three lived at home in Pymble, but their studies kept them so occupied that the Surtees' home was quiet enough for their uncle's recuperation.

Stephen called three afternoons a week to see his father, finding him off-handedly watching television, flipping through *Readers' Digests* or sipping a rationed brandy and soda in a deckchair under the Surtees' sweet moulting frangipani.

'How're you feeling, Dad?' he'd ask.

'Not bad. How's your work going?'

'Fair enough,' he'd lie.

Those preliminaries over Aunt Eileen would pour herself a sherry, him a beer and a watery brandy for her brother. 'I don't know what the world's coming to,' she said each visit. When the North Vietnamese swept over the South she said, 'They'll be in Telegraph Road next.'

His father moped in his deckchair. 'We kept the Japs out once, we could do it again with B.24s and a viable defence policy.'

Aunt Eileen said, doubtfully, 'Those Toyotas are supposed to be good cars, aren't they?' Snipping flowers from over and around them, she said, 'They're behind the teachers' strikes,' and dropped blossoms in a basket.

'Who?' asked Stephen. For God's sake.

'The communists. I hope Kerryn's not being influenced by them at teachers' college.'

'I doubt it.'

His father said, 'They take things too seriously these days. We knew how to have fun when we were young, no politics. No one plays tennis now or goes on picnics.'

His aunt said, 'I'm worried about Craig. So many of those actors are pansy boys.'

One afternoon Crisp took a Scrabble set with him on the train to Pymble. (Anna and he'd enjoyed playing on Sunday afternoons. Lying about semi-clad provoking each other with words like xebec—a small three-masted Mediterranean vessel—and zax—a slater's chopper, with a point for making nail holes. Once they'd fucked there on the floor among the wooden letters. At the finish, pink and grinning, she'd fumbled around the carpet and made a word on her wooden stand: WOW.)

His father agreed to a game, anything to break the monotony. Though his vocabulary was narrower than Stephen's he showed greater aggression and a more effective use of the premium squares. 'Let's make it interesting,' he suggested, and they played for money—five cents for a double letter square, ten for a triple letter, fifteen for a double word, twenty for a triple word, the winner to get ten cents for each winning point. His father won $1.85 the first game and roses bloomed in his cheeks. 'Haha, there's life in your old man yet,' he said, and lit up one of his rationed, three-a-day cigarillos a couple of hours before time.

'Murray!' Eileen scolded. 'Behave.'

'I'm not inhaling, I'm not inhaling,' he snorted, drawing deeply, savouring the smoke and competition. Thereafter they played a game each visit, always for money. As soon as his father was allowed to drive again he borrowed Eileen's Mazda and met Stephen instead at the Greengate Hotel for a regular couple of drinks and a Scrabble game. When he arrived in the bar his father would be there before him reading the *Financial Review*. He'd fold up the paper saying, 'Minsec's in big trouble,' or 'That's a funny debenture issue of JAC's.'

A couple of times they got drunk together. Once Frank was sent down to the hotel to bring his errant brother-in-law home. 'You're a pair of villains,' he said, breasting the bar in his pin-stripe and ordering a scotch. Crisp felt a sudden bar-room camaraderie, an affinity with his father against his uncle. Murray, in his convalescent check shirt, a crew-neck pullover like his own and suede shoes, seemed of a different, more relaxed generation than neat banker Frank. Even his sideburns had inched down his cheeks.

'I've been watching him,' Crisp said. 'He's had only two weak brandies all afternoon.'

'Quite right,' his father agreed.

Frank kept his observations to himself. 'Eileen's been worried,' he said, drinking his scotch quickly. 'We'd better go.'

'We're on our way,' Murray said, with a backhand stroke sliding money across the bar for another round.

Hallstrom's hadn't forgotten him. The company was gracious about his illness. 'We just want you to get well, Murray,' Kevin Synott told him. Even Sir Austin Parker made the time to take him for a quiet lunch at the American Club.

'Take up gardening,' he advised. 'You can't beat the camellia. *Camellia japonicus*, the queen of winter flowers. The purest colouring of any bloom, a perfect piece of sculpture.'

'I expect to be back at work shortly. As soon as I get the doc's go-ahead.'

'Of course,' said Sir Austin, scooping into his avocado *vinaigrette*.

'I thought I might take a cruise first. Relax a bit, get lots of sleep, sea air.'

'That's the shot.'

Murray smiled guiltily. 'I shouldn't be eating these oysters.'

Sir Austin said, 'Then again, you can do a lot worse than the azalea. What sort of soil have you? Must have good drainage.'

The regular visits to his father instilled some rare symmetry into Crisp's life. He began rising earlier to work in the mornings so he could have the afternoons free. On Saturdays he took Wendy to see her grandfather, who taught her to play poker, gin rummy and dominoes and allowed her to play hairdressers with his hair, teasing it into a sparse grey Afro. This sense of order carried over into the thesis. For the first time his feeling of outrage didn't overwhelm his work. There was less of himself in it. He appreciated subtleties more readily, began to savour ambiguities, discovered an awareness of the other point of view. He bought a leather coat, casually smart, and contemplated growing a moustache.

'Nice piece of hide,' his father commented, fingering a sleeve.

'Why did you always side with your mother?' his father suddenly asked, sipping a thin brandy, turning sad but artful eyes on him. They were standing at the saloon bar of the Greengate. 'I always wanted to ask you that. Geoff never did. He played it straight down the middle.'

'Did I?' He was stunned as a mullet.

'You used to be a little pimp as a kid. If we were in the car and I stopped off for a quick beer you'd always spill the beans when we got home. Now why should you do that?'

'I don't know.' But remembering lounging bored on the Vauxhall's front seat with the Saturday sun burning down on the car roof and bubbling the tar of the hotel car park under the sign that said, for some reason in German, *Bier Garten*.

There was a hot, dusty upholstery smell those Saturday afternoons when they languished in the car sipping lemon squash carried out from the bar, reading Shell road maps from the glovebox instead of swimming, while Geoff whined slackly in the back seat and the river glimmered in a heat haze through the trees beyond the pub.

'I guess I used to feel chivalrous towards her. That's normal in the eldest son, surely.' *Oedipal? Kinky?*

His father shrugged. 'I suppose so. Never could understand why you two ganged up on me, though.'

And one Saturday when the waiting in the heat emboldened him, he had walked gingerly into the bar to get his father, carrying their empty squash glasses, and among the smoke and frightening beery hubbub and Turf calendars on the wall and droning race callers on the radio there he'd been leaning jovially across the bar while a yellow-haired barmaid with fat arms leaned across from her side and combed his hair. And all he could think of now, given his adulthood and their new relationship and the opening to ask possibly any question of Murray Crisp's life, was, 'Why was that blonde barmaid combing your hair?'

'What barmaid?' his father said. And then this drawn, ill and fifty-eight-year-old man, pinking slightly in the hollows of his cheeks, gave a wink and, to preclude further conversation, slowly downed his brandy.

My people and I sought the shelter of a stock-keeper's hut next day as we reached a cattle run at the edge of Quamby's Bluff. The stock-keeper's name was Punch, a ticket-of-leave man and a former constable, very civil in his greeting to me as we trudged up to his hut in the late afternoon.

'Afternoon sir. Have some refreshment and a tot with me? And will your natives have some tea?'

Punch was a black-haired Londoner, about five feet four in stature and most hospitable. He gave Truganini a pair of his shoes and brought me copies of the Hobart Town *Courier* of the 23rd and 31st August to read while his wife, a stout half-caste person, made the tea and his two handsome children played with our collection of trinkets on the floor, piling the buttons into small heaps and adorning themselves with the beads and ribbons.

In the *Courier* of 23rd August I read:

Government Notice No. 160
Colonial Secretary's Office,
20th August, 1830.

It is with much satisfaction that the Governor is at length able to announce that a less hostile disposition towards the European inhabitants has been manifested by some of the aboriginal natives of this island with whom Mr G. A. Robinson has lately succeeded in opening a friendly intercourse.

As it is the most anxious desire of the Government that the good understanding which has been happily commenced should be fostered and encouraged by every possible means, His Excellency earnestly requests that all settlers will strictly enjoin their convict servants to abstain from acts of aggression against these benighted beings, and that they will themselves personally endeavour to conciliate them wherever it may be practicable; and whenever the aboriginals appear without evincing a hostile feeling that no attempt shall be made to capture or restrain them but on the contrary, after being fed and kindly treated, that they shall be suffered to depart whenever they desire it.

If, after promulgation of this Notice, any wanton attack or aggression against the Natives becomes known to the Government, the offenders will be immediately brought to justice and punished.

By His Excellency's command,
(Signed), J. Burnett.

My gratification at this notice was short-lived, however, for in the *Courier* of 31st August I was astounded to read:

Extract from the Minutes of an Emergency Meeting of the Executive Council held on Friday the 27th August 1830, at 2 o'clock.

Present: His Excellency the Governor, His Honour the Chief Justice, the Colonial Secretary, the Colonial Treasurer.

'The Governor informed the Council that reports had just been received from Major Douglas of the 63rd Regiment, Captain Vicary of the 63rd Regiment and Captain Donaldson of the 57th Regiment on behalf of "various settlers" expressing their alarm in consequence of Government Notice No. 160 by which it was announced that Mr G. A. Robinson had succeeded in opening a friendly intercourse with some of the Natives; by which the settlers were urged to conciliate wherever possible with the Natives; and by which it was intimated that if any wanton attack or aggression were committed against them the offenders would be immediately brought to justice and punished.

Major Douglas, Captain Vicary and Captain Donaldson in their communications expressed their firm opinions that the aboriginals are now irreclaimable and that the ensuing Spring will be the most bloody we have experienced unless sufficient military protection should be afforded.

The Governor stated that, feeling the extreme anxiety from the state of alarm in which the settlers were thrown, and being aware of the great reluctance of Sir George Murray in Downing Street for further offensive measures to be resorted to against the Natives, he had assembled the Aboriginals Committee, comprising Archdeacon Broughton, the Reverend Bedford, the Reverend Norman, the Chief Police Magistrate, the Colonial Treasurer, the Colonial Surgeon, the Port Officer and the Secretary, and referred them to the reports received during the week.

The Aboriginals Committee had unwillingly concluded, after mature deliberation, that all Natives were actuated by the love of plunder joined with the most rancorous animosity, and that it had therefore become essentially necessary to adopt the most rigorous measures and to repel them from the settled districts by every means that could be devised, both on the part of the Government and the community, as all efforts to conciliate the hostile tribes had proved quite ineffectual.

In such a state of things it appears to the Executive Council that the time is now arrived when a vigorous effort on a more extended scale than has hitherto been practicable should be made for expelling these miserable people forthwith from the settled districts, His Excellency may rely on having the hearty co-operation of the settlers, and the Executive Council trusts that the volunteers which they may be expected to furnish, joined to the troops in the field, will form a force sufficient for the accomplishment of this most necessary measure.

In advising His Excellency to adopt such a measure the Executive Council is well aware of the responsibility it incurs and of the painful situation in which its advice may tend to place His Excellency, but we see no alternative.'

(Meeting broke up at six o'clock.)

'You look astonished, sir. You haven't touched a drop of tea.' Punch was quite solicitous. The incredulity I felt at discovering this new turn of events in Hobart Town must have been obvious. I was devastated.

'The Governor has recanted, Mr Punch. And on the advice of the biggest bunch of boobies in the colony. The Aboriginals Committee knows nothing about aboriginals. It has not for one minute ever considered the outrages perpetrated upon them by the settlers. It whitewashes European cruelties, it hinders my work of conciliation. It gets in *my way*, Mr Punch.'

'Ah, you'll be Mr Robinson then. I'm very friendly with the natives myself sir. I know of every slaughter of the blacks on these plains since they was first settled.'

I was overcome with anxiety to reach Hobart Town and ascertain what folly the Government was enacting upon the natives. Punch offered to guide us to the edge of the Western Marshes, knowing the quickest and safest route. We set off, Punch carrying a musket as tall as himself, a brace of large pistols, a bayonet at his side, cartouche boxes and a horn of powder.

'I thought you were friendly with them, Mr Punch,' I queried him.

'Very friendly, sir. But are they friendly with me? They're getting all stirred up because of the killings and the soldiers. Where will it all end, sir?'

We camped that night in a clearing between some ghost gums and a patch of silver gorse. The natives brought me four red-bill eggs and eight wild duck eggs and Pagerley gave me a neat basket she had plaited from bottle-green reeds. Truganini seemed jealous of the gift and disappeared for an hour, returning with a young opossum which she presented to me, freshly killed and half roasted, I suffered to eat a portion, not wishing to offend her above all my people.

Against Eileen's wishes Murray booked a cabin on the *Oriana* for a fortnight's cruise of the South Pacific—Noumea, Suva, Pago Pago, Vava'u, Nuku'alofa were the ports of call, all tranquil enough tropical hideaways he assured his sister. 'It's not as If I'll be chasing after wahines or whatever they call them,' he grumbled.

'It's not the fuzzy-wuzzies, it's the gay divorcees that worry me,' she said. 'Those cruise ships are full of them, getting suntans on their alimony. Frank and I sailed in seventy-three. The standard of passengers has dropped dreadfully since they brought in those cheap fares—it's all football teams and boozy divorcees on the make.'

'Really? Sounds interesting.'

'You just watch yourself, that's all.'

'I'd better take my dinner suit.' Murray seemed to be looking forward to the cruise.

Crisp's solicitor wrote to him. He advised that a *decree nisi* had been granted to Jane on the grounds of his adultery. The lawyer enclosed large accounts for 'fees, costs and disbursements' for himself, the barrister and 'the other side'. Payment would be appreciated immediately. A copy of the terms of settlement was enclosed:

Matrimonial Causes Act, 1959–1965

IN THE SUPREME COURT OF NEW SOUTH WALES

MATRIMONIAL CAUSES JURISDICTION. Number 8062

BETWEEN *Jane Priscilla Crisp* Petitioner

AND *Stephen Murray Crisp* Respondent

AND *Anna Kubic* Co-Respondent

BY CONSENT ORDER THAT:

1. The Respondent to pay to the Petitioner for her maintenance the sum of $60 per week during the joint lives of the Petitioner and Respondent or until the remarriage of the Petitioner.

2. The Respondent to hand over full ownership of the home presently jointly owned by the Respondent and Petitioner at Whale Beach to the Petitioner.

3. The Petitioner to have custody of the child of the marriage with reasonable access to the Respondent.

4. The Respondent to pay to the Petitioner for the maintenance of the child

of the marriage the sum of $20 per week until such child completes her secondary education or becomes self-supporting, whichever event shall first occur.

5. (a) The Respondent to pay the reasonable hospital, medical (*Ha*, thought Crisp) and dental expenses of the Petitioner during the joint lives of the parties or until the remarriage of the Petitioner.

(b) The Respondent to pay the reasonable hospital, medical, dental and schooling expenses incurred by the Petitioner in respect of the child of the marriage.

6. In regard to the matters referred to above it is noted that:

(a) The Respondent alleges that he is in receipt of a net weekly income of $132.80 in the form of a Government grant to write 'a book on the slaughter of the Tasmanian Aborigines, tentatively titled *The Genocide Thesis*' and that he is no longer receiving financial assistance from Anna Kubic, the Co-Respondent named herein. His present chosen form of occupation is viewed by the Petitioner as 'doubtful in the extreme' though the Petitioner says she has faith in the Respondent as 'an honourable man'.

(b) The Petitioner undertakes to notify the Respondent through her solicitors of her remarriage or any employment she may obtain during the currency of the order referred to in paragraph 1 hereof.

7. The Respondent to pay the Petitioner's costs of and incidental to the Suit.

8. Liberty to either Petitioner or Respondent to apply.

Out Crisp travelled to Whale Beach next day, uncertain of their new relationship, his new status. Enveloped in one of his old T-shirts, Jane was vigorously snipping the lantana hedge with grass clippers. She also wore jeans and a pair of wafer-thin Indian sandals that gripped each big toe in a leather loop. The brown hair tendrils at her ears were lank with perspiration. Her small tanned hands working away with the clippers bore faint scratches from the lantana—and no wedding ring. She had a live cigarette resting on a rockery terrace he had spent two weekends building four or five years before.

'Hi,' he announced.

'Hello Stephen.'

After he'd been squatting on the grass for several minutes assuming a pleasant attitude and sucking grass blades she put down the clippers, picked up her cigarette and drew on it. She sat on the rockery's edge.

'Well,' she said. 'Here we are then.'

'How do you feel?' he asked, half concerned for her, half for something to say.

'What?' She drew on the last quarter-inch of the cigarette and snapped it into the garden. She glanced at him curiously and reproachfully. Eventually she said, 'Fine, thanks.'

'How was court?' (Harrowing? Terrifying? Depressing? Had she been a wan female figure overwhelmed by authoritarian male legal personalities and mystifying court procedures? His heart could easily go out to her.)

'You didn't miss anything, if that's what you want to know.' Impatiently she brushed hair from her eyes. 'I guess it was melancholy, a serious business. (At least that!) But a piece of cake, really. Very efficient and matter-of-fact. Nick came with me. Afterwards we got sloshed and went to Beppi's for dinner.'

'Bit of a celebration, eh?'

'Whatever you like to call it. I got drunk as an owl, drunker than I've been for ages.'

He couldn't help himself today. 'Drunker than at the wedding?' He smiled bleakly and nostalgically.

'Much.'

'How's Wendy taking it?'

'Well, nothing's really changed for her, has it? You can see her whenever it's convenient until we go abroad.'

' "Abroad"? That's very worldly. You used to call it "overseas".'

Jane lit another cigarette and drew on it. The rapid jerkiness of her movements made it seem she was smoking several cigarettes at once. 'Well, now I'm a sophisticated divorcee, you see.'

Abruptly she stood up and brushed minute grass and sand particles from her jeans. 'You've come too early to see Wendy. She doesn't get home from school till 3.30. If you're going to stay you can make yourself useful and clip that bloody hedge.' She dropped the grass clippers at his feet.

'How's my baby?'

Wendy allowed herself to be scooped up and nuzzled on the cheeks. She was hot and grubby, her green checked school tunic limp and wrinkled, but she kissed him innocently and amorously on the lips and he drank in her childish primary school fragrance—of bananas, apples and plastic reading book covers.

'I got a stamp,' she announced, exposing the back of her hand for inspection. 'For being behaved.' A smudged purple elephant overlay the network of milky blue veins.

'That's terrific!' he enthused, kissing the elephant, the hand, the forearm all the way up to the chubby neck creases. 'How's my baby, my own girl?'

'I'm not a baby. We're doing cuisenaire rods.'

'You're my big girl then. Daddy's big girl. Ticklish girl.' He dug his nose into her side until she giggled and squirmed away.

'You'll break my inhaler,' she warned him gently, patting her tunic pocket, filling him with remorse. His face to her chest, he hearkened to the rasp of tortured, clogged bronchial tubes but heard only the faintest whisper of a breeze through net curtains. Again she wriggled away, but kindly patted his nose.

'Daddy, Nick can play the guitar. Can you play the guitar?'

'I can play the trumpet. Boopoopoodoo,' he burbled through his lips. Daddy the great musician and competitor for filial affection.

'I know you don't sleep here any more. But why don't you have showers here any more?'

'Showers?' Aching inwardly he nevertheless jollied her with smiles and nose tweaks. 'You want me to have a shower here? I'll have a shower here any day. Next time after I've had a swim.'

'Nick has showers here. And shaves, too.'

Virtually on the premises, eh. Soaking under his shower, scraping at his old bathroom mirror.

'And Daddy,' she snickered, 'hasn't he got a big weewee?'

Good God, a flasher as well. Crisp could easily enough imagine a wet and priapic Poynton, all muscles, soapy pubes and tuneful baritone, leaving the bathroom door ajar in the ostensible interest of steam release and good healthy broadmindedness. *Come in darling and pass Uncle the soap*. But perhaps he went too far. Poynton registered more as the vain show-off given to nonchalant display. The change-room football heavy who spent more time untrousered than otherwise, constantly sharing the miraculous vision of his cluster with the chaps from the team; the sly-eyed ball snatcher, the gooser ('I don't suppose you can carry a wet towel on your fat?' asked Biven of long-ago Hallstrom's mailroom puppet-penis fame), the ostentatious farter.

He asked Wendy, 'Do you like him? Is Nick nice to you, sweetheart?'

She looked at him curiously. 'You *know* Nick,' she chided him. 'He's funny and gives me shoulder rides to the shop. He buys us American ice-creams, the 50-cent ones, even double-headers.'

'And is he nice to Mummy?' He sneaked the question in. To further thrash his frayed nerve ends.

'Course! She has passionfruit and banana, always passionfruit in one cone and banana in the other.'

'Does she?'

'Daddy, he's going to be sort of my second father, Mummy said.'

'Only sort of. I'll always be your main first father, darling.' Now he was actually near tears, the spiky throat-ache of self-pity almost choking him.

'We're going to London where the Queen lives. Why can't you come too, Dad?' She hugged him suddenly, but as he groped for an answer she said, 'I'm giving the ducks to Lucy Palfreyman because she hasn't got any pets.'

'That's a good idea.'

'Mummy says there's plenty of ducks in London. And animals like deers and things.'

'She's right. Ducks everywhere.'

'I don't really care about the ducks in London, Daddy.' She patted his cheeks and he could have eaten her up with hopeless love. 'I *seen* ducks.'

'What's this Wendy tells me about Nick parading in front of her? Playing the Greek god in the bathroom? Do you think that's to be encouraged?' He was nonchalantly browsing through the bookcase in the lounge-room having decided that Doctor Poynton wasn't going to inherit his books. There was nothing in the settlement that gave Jane *The Times Concise Atlas of the World, The Great Movie Stars* and Webster's *New Collegiate Dictionary*. ('Take what you like,' Jane had said airily, 'though I do think you could leave them for Wendy.' 'Jesus, she's still on *The Magic Pudding*.' 'Please yourself,' she'd said.)

Now she looked at him oddly as he rifled through shelves of Penguins. 'What did you say?' Her sharply defined brows arched up her forehead. She had a deep etched crease between her eyes that used not to be there. The eyebrow arching flattened it out momentarily, then it settled again.

'Nick showering in front of her. Naked. With the door open.' The words immediately sounded ridiculous to him, prissy, not his own. But he couldn't escape them. He stacked the paperbacks in a cardboard carton, hefted it for weight.

'Are you suggesting he exposes himself deliberately in front of Wendy?' She moved rapidly across the room towards him. She carried a cigarette like a weapon.

'Not necessarily. Just the fact of the exposure. Spock says it's not advisable, seeing nude males around the house. Those that aren't the the father, I mean.'

'What do you mean, "nude males"? Nude male singular, thank you very much. And he does have a rather special place in our lives, I thought you'd realize.' She inhaled angrily, tapped ash on the floor recklessly. 'You're really sick, aren't you? What's it matter if the child sees an actual naked man? She's seen you. The sight of another cock's not going to stunt her growth or anything.'

Hadn't he once been the liberated one of the pair, the partner without the hangups? Long ago. He said nothing, feeling foolish and miserable. The paperback titles were a blur of spidery hieroglyphics. He shuffled the books like cards.

'I think you've got some absurd male penis fear going here,' she intoned. She seemed years older than him, mature, authoritative in her every cigarette puff. 'It's most peculiar, really.' Then she directed a grey glance at him of such intensity that he didn't recognize her, might never have seen her features before. 'You might be interested to know that it's no bigger than yours.' She spoke in a dry, low voice. 'But it's a whole lot more considerate.'

We traversed the river on the outskirts of George Town and journeyed into the town in search of a letter of instruction for me from His Excellency. There was nothing, indeed the people in this place seemed to take little interest in the important affairs of the colony for they knew nothing of me or my pursuits and offered me not even a glass of cold water.

The inhabitants were guarding the town, all the military having ridden to Launceston to join the crusade against the blacks. Big handwritten posters were stuck up everywhere calling upon all settlers and their servants to volunteer. I found George Town a dull, lifeless place, few people remaining there except those connected with the Government. There was a good wooden jetty and a gaol but no church. The only other major buildings were the lunatic asylum and the female factory, both swarming with inmates. From the road the shrieks and gibbers of the asylum's unfortunates could be heard a hundred yards away, along with the shouted orders and whipcracks of their disciplinarians. The India ship *Nimrod* lay at anchor in the harbour. Rumour said her captain and mate had mischievously agitated the townspeople by claiming to have seen upwards of seven hundred armed blacks near Cape Portland and bearing down on the town. A stupid falsehood, but enough to addle the wits of the George Towners. I was unable to get the least information here so proceeded up the Tamar River to Launceston.

Arriving at Launceston I cleaned myself and called upon the town commandant, a Major Abbott. I felt pessimistic immediately upon meeting him. He was a large bristling jobbernowl who personified the military mind in its inability to come to terms with matters requiring a degree of humanity.

'I have no instructions for you. As far as I'm concerned there's nothing more for you to do, Robinson.'

'What do you mean, Major? I am performing a most valuable task.'

'I mean we're going to catch all the savages by driving them like sheep to Tasman's Peninsula, and I dare say you know where that is.'

'I am afraid I don't understand your remarks.'

The major handed me a proclamation. 'Sit yourself down and ingest this broadsheet then. No smoking.'

The document said:

By His Excellency Colonel George Arthur, Lieutenant-Governor of the Island of Van Diemen's Land and its Dependencies

A PROCLAMATION

WHEREAS the black aboriginal Natives of this island have of late manifested, by continued repetitions of the most wanton and sanguinary acts of violence and outrage, an unequivocal determination indiscriminately to destroy the persons and property of the white inhabitants whenever opportunities are presented to them for doing so; And whereas it is scarcely possible to distinguish the particular tribe or tribes by whom such outrages have been in any particular instance committed, it hath now become necessary to adopt immediately, for the purpose of effecting their capture if possible, an active and extended system of military operations against the Natives generally throughout the Island, and every portion thereof, whether actually settled or not.

Now, therefore, by virtue of the powers and authorities vested in me, I declare and proclaim that from and after the date of this Proclamation, Martial Law is and shall continue to be in force against all the black or aboriginal Natives within every part of this Island, excepting such tribes or individuals as there may be reason to suppose are pacifically inclined and have not been implicated in any such outrages. And all soldiers and other His Majesty's subjects, civil and military, are hereby required and commanded to obey and assist their lawful superiors in the execution of such measures as shall be directed to be taken.

To give time for the necessary arrangements and to meet to the utmost the convenience of the community, I direct that the Colony shall form a Line against the Natives and that its General Movement shall commence on Thursday the 7th of October next. Further details shall be forthcoming in subsequent Government Orders.

All minor objects must for a time give way to this one great and engrossing pursuit. Should success crown the contemplated measures, I earnestly enjoin that the utmost tenderness and humanity may be manifested toward the Native Prisoners and, when in custody, that they may be dealt with as beings who have been deprived of the blessings of civilization, and have been actuated in their hostile attacks by a distressing misconception of the amicable disposition entertained towards them by the white population.

Given under my hand and seal at Arms, at the Government House, Hobart Town, this ninth day of September, in the year of our Lord One Thousand Eight Hundred and Thirty.

George Arthur
God Save the King!

Major Abbott peered up from a table stacked with charts, manuals and blue-grey government portfolios. A tic played under one eye. He twiddled with a bayonet scabbard lying among his papers.

'Satisfied, Robinson?' The commandant was doltish and not fit for the office he held. Now he attempted to exert his flimsy suzerainty over me, pointing the scabbard at me and asking, 'You have three natives travelling with you?'

'Indeed, all trusted and courageous servants of the Crown.'

'They must go to gaol. I will have no natives at large in my region.'

'I'll go to gaol myself first!'

'That can be arranged. These are complicated times.'

The commandant tested me sorely. Time was to pull my own rank and end this languid play acting. 'I don't think you appreciate the responsibility the Governor has allotted me, Major. Besides, we are on the most friendly personal terms. I shall report this conversation to him, naturally. There is no question of my natives going to gaol or for that matter my not receiving the utmost support from the military.'

The scabbard tapped abstractedly on the table top for perhaps twenty seconds. The major was not a risk taker. 'Well, if you oversee their behaviour I suppose no harm is done.' He turned back to his papers with studied attention, rustling his brown maps and shuffling government orders around his frown.

I was not finished, however. 'Another thing—'

'Yes, Robinson,' He glanced up impatiently.

'I want a boat and supplies to visit the sealers of Bass Strait.'

'Whatever for, man?'

'To rescue their stolen native women. To save them from slavery and debauchery.'

'Good God!'

An ugly reception befell me everywhere in Launceston. The townspeople and men of influence either ignored me or treated me with derision. By some disreputable sailors on the *Dragon*, a barquentine in port, I was jeeringly disparaged as 'The Black Parson'. On important matters relating to the aboriginals my opinion was not sought. I had great difficulty in preserving my natives from the insults and physical violence of an exasperated rabble. My anxiety was relieved only when a humane Christian named Robert Packer—connected with the local Bethel—took Wooraddy, Truganini and Pagerley under his roof. Nothing was to be heard in the town but that they were going to kill the 'black crows'. Every town lout and gutter cringer strutted about like a colonel. I noted in my journal: 'Empty men love war.'

My natives were terrified, afraid to move outside Mr Packer's house but equally unhappy in their state of rare confinement. They mumbled dejectedly to themselves.

'The major is *tagant-yaryack*,' Wooraddy said, 'a piss-drinker.'

'The major will put you in gaol,' I threatened, to test their reaction. They whimpered and clutched at my sleeves. Truganini ran to the window as if expecting to see massed troops approaching us. Her new shoes retained a nervous squeak.

'Don't be frightened. You are safe with me. But leave me and you will be locked in a small room, very cold, with no kangaroo, no shellfish.'

'Eeah! We will never leave you,' they cried, 'You are our father.'

They sat around me on the floor, pressing so close their haunches touched my shoes, not permitting me out of their sight. I felt they had learned a useful lesson.

The first postcard came from New Caledonia, showing a Noumean street scene—three demure Melanesian girls in white convent dresses and with hibiscuses in their hair strolling arm-in-arm along Rue Anatole France.

The postcard said: 'Having a relaxing time now after two rough days on the fringe of Hurricane Val. The *Oriana* is a happy ship, they're looking after me pretty well and I'm taking it easy. Apart from the stock market lectures I'm spending the time sleeping and reading. Saw *The Tamarind Seed* at the cinema, not bad. Looking forward to Casino Night. Cheers, Dad.'

In Launceston I recruited an assistant, an enthusiastic young man from the local Bethel recommended by Mr Packer. His name was James Parish, a conciliator, he assured me, after my own fashion. I also employed a medical dispenser, Archibald McLachlan. Through Mr Packer's good offices two more native women also joined me before the commandant could gaol them. One was called Jumbo, the other Sal (though their native names were Bullyer and Tanleerboneyer), both escapees from the sealers camped on Preservation Island in the straits.

Jumbo had been stolen by an Englishman, James Munro, and had lived with him for ten years. She was now aged about eighteen and had escaped from him a year before. (Cohabiting with children was common in these depraved parts.) She was attractive, usefully intelligent and spoke English well enough. Sal had been the property of Jack Browning, one of his five women. Her aspect was not so pleasing because of heavy facial hair and she was more advanced in years. I had recruited the women to lead me to their former masters. Now I aimed to rescue their unfortunate companions.

The poor creatures were objects of great compassion. Jumbo told me, 'Munro and the other men rushed at us at our fires at Cape Grim and took six women and girls. I was a small girl, was with Munro ever since. The sealers tied us to trees and stretched out our arms and flogged us. Some sealers beat their women with seal clubs and make the blood run down the face, and cut them with knives.'

Sal had likewise been flogged many times. Her body was very scarred, both from the whip and from self-imposed cicatrix cut into the flesh in the shape of the sun and moon.

'Why did the sealers flog you?' I asked.

'For taking food—biscuit and sugar. Otherwise we lived on limpets, mussels and crawfish. Sometimes mutton birds. Not enough food for the children. Plenty of children killed.'

'The sealers kill children? Which men are these?'

'No, the women. Kill them in their belly, beat their belly with their fist. Don't want the sealers' children. Take the big children into the bush and kill them, put sand in their mouths, bury them in the sand. The men get angry, want the children to work on the boats, kill seals and mutton birds for money.'

That night I noticed Jumbo and Sal in secret whispered conversation, pointing in different directions and watching that we were all asleep. I felt their intention was to run away, and charged them with it. I made them sleep apart and put a watch on them.

Begrudgingly, Major Abbott provided me with a patched red five-oared whaleboat, I set off from Launceston and landed at Preservation Island. James Munro, the retired sealer who had kidnapped Jumbo many years before, met the boat, showing no sign of recognizing her. He was a middle-aged man, short and sandy-headed, and had recently been appointed the Constable for the Straits' islands, a sort of go-between for the Government and the sealers. He was also supposed to report the removal of escaped convicts by overseas vessels.

'Your servant sir,' he said.

'Well, Munro, how do you do?'

'Well enough sir. I have contentment. What more can you ask?'

'And do your native women have contentment, Munro? Living under bondage.'

'What women? They've all left me, vanished to the mainland. I've only got me two children with me. I live by breeding pigs and rabbits and selling them to the ships. I grow some vegetables, sir, and read me Bible.'

'But what about the cruelty, Munro? The floggings and knifings and carnal debauchery?'

'There's none of that on Preservation, sir. Oh, one of me wives used to be a bit wild—a New Zealander. And there was a bad-tempered

New Hollander with a salty tongue. But since they've gone I have contentment. The cutter *Industry* brings me the papers, spelling books and some testaments from the London Missionary Society. Me children help in the garden. Apart from the vegetables we've got wild indigo and the local geranium. On sunny afternoons I take me pistol to the rats and badgers or catch quail and mutton bird for the pot.'

I proceeded in the boat to Woody Island where clouds of birds hung over the tussock grass. One end of the island contained an immense mutton bird rookery. There were moorhens, quail, magpies and geese as well, and grasshoppers chirping in their millions. An old sealer, Geordy Thompson, lived here. He was upwards of sixty years of age and blind in one eye; a native of the Clyde. He had also been industrious, cultivating two acres with wheat, potatoes, onions, cabbages etc. He kept fowls and pigs. He proudly served me some bacon he had cured himself, very tasty and the first made in the straits. He was most civil, giving me hen's eggs, two pieces of crystal and some beads made from local gemstones. He had two black women remaining out of six.

'I shall have to take away one of your women,' I told him. 'I will leave one to look after you because of your age. You must use her well.'

Thompson looked sorrowful but said nothing. He brought the woman, Tooger-nupper to me, patting her reassuringly on the shoulder. His other woman, Ploorer-nele, he kept by his side. She was the elder of the two and by her he had a little boy, a fine child. I took Tooger-nupper away. She seemed frightened and crouched down on the sand between Thompson and myself. Jumbo and Truganini helped me place her in the whaleboat. I felt it wise to fasten her hands to the gunwale until we were a long distance off shore.

In light airs and pleasant weather we sailed to Gun Carriage Island, landing in the early a.m. I found only one person, an invalid named Charlie Peterson, who was most alarmed at our visit, and two half-caste children. The other sealers were away hunting in the straits. Peterson was sallow with illness and afflicted with an ulcerated syphylitic infection of the upper lip.

He said, 'The women are at the mutton bird rookery. If they saw your boat they'll be hiding.' I sent Jumbo, Sal and Truganini to find them.

'If you take my woman I don't know what I'll do,' Peterson moaned. 'I can't look after meself. I've had Poll since she was eight or nine.'

'An evil admission, Peterson.'

'My Poll loves me like a daughter,' he whined.

My native women returned in an hour with four of the sealers' women, all anxious to leave with us while their masters were absent. It was a singular sight to see the women strolling down the hill from the bird rookery with their dogs bounding about them. It would have made a fine coloured illustration. I counted forty dogs.

I left Poll with the feeble Peterson and we loaded the other women aboard the boat. Most of them were reluctant to leave their dogs, but once the boat had put some distance between them and the island they sang and laughed, delighted at their liberation from slavery.

We set up camp on Swan Island, the nearest to the mainland. Here I resettled the sealers' women and began an establishment after the style of my Bruny Island mission. The cutter *Industry* brought us provisions and the newspapers for October and November. According to the *Colonial Times* upwards of three thousand persons were in the field against the natives in the first week of October. The 'Black Line' seemed to be composed of a curious *mélange* of masters and servants. So far it had been unsuccessful, the papers reporting, however, that the whole island 'appeared in commotion'. Two natives had been taken, one of whom had escaped, and five troops had been killed by accidents.

A Captain Hicks was aboard the *Industry*, a pompous young officer bound for George Town. I discussed the manœuvres with him over tea, voicing my puzzlement at how rigid military detachments could operate in country so bisected by rivers and crowned by rugged mountains.

'Oh,' said the captain, playing with his moustache ends. 'This is a military manœuvre which you civilians couldn't understand.'

'Perhaps not, but if you plan to capture the blacks by mere military manœuvres they'll make gowks and dizzards of you. These people are more shadow than soldier.'

'Is that so? You're not suggesting that the 57th and 63rd can't handle some simple skirmishers? Stone throwers, they are man. Without a firepiece between them and no leader worth the name.'

'I wouldn't think they could be driven into a corner by a strange band of amateur beaters advancing in a broken line. These are a wily people, captain.'

'Wily! There is no more debased race in all the earth.' An arrogant tilt to his head exposed his wide nostrils, flared like a pony's. 'It's a proven fact they form the connecting link between man and the monkey tribes.'

'You cannot win this war, Captain Hicks.'

A supercilious smile was the reward for my accurate and knowledgeable prediction.

Gradually my forays and those of my new assistant Parish into the various sealers' camps were accomplishing something. Our settlement on Swan Island was growing in numbers, both from the rescued women and from the arrival of a dozen fleeing natives from the mainland of Van Diemen's Land. Parish had removed five women from Penguin Island, three from Flinders Island and three from the Capisheens. Two had small half-caste children. The women said others would have joined us but for the terrifying tales told them by the sealers. They had said I would send them to gaol with fetters on their legs.

Among the mainland blacks was Woreter-lette-larn-ne, a big man and chief of the Poor-rer-mair-rer nation at Piper's River. He told me that he and five other men and women had seen the soldiers and had slipped back and forth inside the 'Black Line' several times. Woreter said the soldiers stretched for miles and fired their muskets all the time.

'They shoot at tree stumps and at possums rustling in the trees. They light fires everywhere and talk loudly to each other out of fear. They are scared they will find us.' He laughed, a high-pitched nasal guffaw that shook the cicatrix on his broad belly. 'They should take care or they will shoot each other.'

My new natives observed Truganini eating penguin, tried it and approved. They then all set off and slew a great number which they ate and also gave to their dogs. Numbers were killed wantonly and blood and feathers lay over the island and stuck to their legs. I was forced to ration the kills or one of our food staples would have been dissipated.

Truganini acted proprietorial of me before the recent arrivals, bringing me mutton bird eggs attractively displayed in a reed basket.

'*Tridder*,' she said. 'Eat.' All the people then set off to catch mutton birds and gather their eggs. Truly, they fastened upon new ideas like so many sheep.

Each night the men without partners painted themselves in ochre, brandished their knives and chased the women through the bushes. The women screamed and ran continually to my tent for protection, blood streaming from superficial cuts on their breasts and arms, the panting men close behind. This scene of bedlam occurred every night until I was being driven to distraction from lack of sleep and fears that violent murders would occur.

Truganini and Wooraddy watched the regular performance stony-faced, Wooraddy occasionally breaking into a sly grin.

'When will they stop?' I complained. 'Those women will be killed.'

'When everyone has a partner, man to woman,' Truganini said. 'It is the best way.'

Wooraddy lay smugly by the fire picking his teeth with a splintered fowl bone. 'It is the quickest way for them to come together. Otherwise it takes a long time for the women to surrender. Besides, the women like it. A woman with many scars is sought after. Her *parraganna* will swell and fill with milk if they are cut many times.'

Eventually the nightly mayhem abated, the women appearing, if not content, at least sullenly resigned to their new spouses. Now around the evening fires the men performed dances of great hilarity, pretending to be horses or kangaroos. One dance consisted of a continued jumping on the one spot for at least half an hour. Occasionally the women joined in, their dances featuring several obscenities of great imagination.

'What is that dance?' I asked Wooraddy of one explicit performance of lewdness by naked men and women.

'That is the Beginning Dance,' he said, his eye slipping sideways back to the proceedings.

'You mean the Creation?'

He regarded me patiently. 'The first man was Moinee who was hurled from the sky. Shortly a woman, Pup-per, joined him but they could not sleep together properly or make children no matter how they tried. Hee Hooh,' he snickered. 'Then Lal-lor, the small piss-ant, crawled into their kangaroo skins and bit the hole in Moinee's penis.'

I was delighted to receive a letter via the supply boat from Launceston communicating the Governor's pleasure at both my opening of 'an amicable intercourse' with the whole of the black population of the colony and at my procuring the sealers' women.

'You have manifested the most daring intrepidity, persevering zeal and strenuous exertion,' His Excellency wrote, and he would inform the Prime Minister in London accordingly. (Parish and the crew of the supply boat said that similar views were now beginning to surface among many people of sensible intellect in Launceston. Every person they'd met had given them drink or a meal and the commandant had issued orders that neither the constables nor civilians were to molest any blacks proven to be in their company.)

While the obvious failure of the Government's military manœuvres in catching natives no doubt had much to do with this change in attitude I felt that a scale had been lifted from the vision of the One-Eyed Extirpator and that for the first time my methods were being seen as effective as well as benign.

His Excellency's letter concluded with an invitation to visit him at Government House as soon as the rigors of my tasks made this possible. He wished to personally express his deep approbation.

I had hoped to reach Hobart Town and spend Christmas Day with my family, but it was not God's will that I should do so. Instead I supervised the arrival of another six native women from Penguin Island brought away by Parish. We now had thirty-five natives collected together on Swan Island, I hoped the prelude to many others. I was not altogether content with one turn of events, however. An India ship, the *Bombay*, from Hobart Town to Launceston under Captain Lee, called in to spend Christmas Day ashore. On board was a passenger, a Mr Haselhead, a merchant specializing in hides and tallows and familiar with my name and work.

He shook my hand most amiably. 'I have heard you have been of inestimable help to Mr Parish,' he said, 'in helping him capture the blacks and so forth.'

'Sir?'

'The news has spread down to Hobart Town from Launceston that Mr Parish has been singularly successful of late—rounding up a savage tribe on the mainland, reuniting the stolen women of the straits with their families. I would be honoured to meet him.'

Parish had obviously tried to claim credit for my many successes. The man had apparently widely related a story in Launceston that he was the instigator of our recently successful expeditions. If so, he had practised a fraud upon me, endeavouring to rob me of that reputation which I had so dearly purchased at the extreme hazard of my life. Why did everyone associated with me try to rob me of the fruit of my labours?

'You have been misinformed, Mr Haselhead. I do have a Parish in my employ as a boatman, but all men belonging to my expeditions are equal. This Parish has joined me only recently. I have allowed him to handle the loading and unloading of my supplies, a task he performs quite diligently.'

The rest of this festive day passed equally unfortunately. After the *Bombay* had sailed in the afternoon (leaving us rice, pork, beef, tea, sugar and tobacco and taking on board eight Cape Barren geese and six big black swans) Truganini told me three of the women, including Tooger-nupper whom we had removed from old Geordy Thompson, had hidden themselves on board, aided, no doubt, by the sailors. She also informed me that the chieftain Woreter was forcing his attentions on Jumbo, much against her will.

'He too strong for her, cut her all over.' Woreter was an evil man—there was not a woman but he was endeavouring to cohabit with despite his having found a partner during the early mating ceremonies. These mainlanders were an abandoned set, and with such an example as Woreter what could be hoped for?

I found him and reprimanded him. 'You leave Jumbo alone. Stay with your wife or you go to gaol.'

'Weeh,' he grumbled, his thick fleshy brow dividing in a frown. 'She is a whore with sealers' disease and a pouch like a kangaroo.'

'I will take all the women away unless you behave,' I warned him. Even as I spoke he was abusing himself beneath his wallaby frock. Nerves jumped in the furrows of his cheeks.

He grunted, 'Eeh-ooh. Soon it won't matter. We all be dead on fire.'

That evening the men, headed by Woreter, set the bird rookery on fire at the east end of the island. I sent four boatmen and had it put out. Again I threatened to put Woreter in gaol and reprimanded him about his cohabiting with the women. He fixed me with a red and agitated eye and cleared his nose on the ground. I had him tied up for the night and next morning his behaviour was more pacific.

In the mail came another postcard from his father, in every sense the only bright point in Crisp's day. Leaden skies pressed humidly down on him. Across the harbour the city lay bathed in smog. Dun-coloured vapours blurred the horizon. 'Greetings from Suva,' the postcard announced in gold lettering embossed on a scene showing Fijian firewalkers padding barefoot across red-hot coals before an awed, tropically-clad white audience at the Grand Pacific Hotel.

On the back his father had written: 'Fiji hot and tiring but managed to pick up some good bargains in the transistor line—radio, tape recorder, etc. Cleaned up at Casino Night on roulette and Joker Seven but lost a packet on crown-and-anchor. It's "Ladies' Night" tonight—the girls pick up the tab for the drinks! Should be more of it! Cheers from the *Oriana*, Dad.'

Also in the mail was a letter from his bank manager, requesting urgent settlement of his overdraft. 'I wish to discuss this matter with you at the earliest opportunity,' he'd written. 'We cannot allow the present situation to continue.' Crisp pocketed the letter and the card and strode up the hill to the main road to take his mind off the bank manager. He bought the morning paper, discovering to his horror and fascination that an 83-year-old woman in the next street had been battered to death with a mattock. Agnes Burnside. Police were bewildered. Neighbours had heard nothing amiss. She had always turned the television up loud because of her hearing. Bonnie, her Australian terrier, hadn't barked, strangely enough—the murderer must have been known to her, no sign of forced entry. She'd lived alone for twenty-seven years since her son had sold his business and moved to Dubbo. Blood had been observed through the front window by 45-year-old Mrs Gwen Krause, a volunteer driver for the Meals-on-Wheels organization, who was delivering Mrs Burnside's midday Irish stew. Mrs Krause had been placed under sedation.

Crisp abruptly turned the corner, rounded the block and, his heart hammering in his chest, strolled towards the murder scene, affecting the casual air of the *boulevardier*, the same demeanour he presented whenever he walked into a bank. He felt guilty then, too: the dive of his hand into an inner pocket for his cheque book was really the lunge for the hold-up pistol. He half surprised himself when all he came out with was the thin grey book of increasingly rebounding cheques. Now, as he approached a row of neat semi-detached cottages flanked by pale blue police cars, he carefully avoided the gazes of the gossiping neighbours hanging seriously over their front gates, the nervously active children riding skateboards and scooters up and down the pavement.

It was easy enough to find the actual murder house—detectives were huddling grimly on the front porch, a police photographer, no doubt having photographed the grimmer stuff yesterday, was now snapping off shots of the yard, the rear lane, the street. The old lady had called her house *Mafeking*. Its name shone from a brass plate. In the small front garden a plaster stork propped one-legged beside a waterless cement pond. Crisp gave this scene a passing glance and continued on up the street. Four or five houses further along, however, the street suddenly ended in a cul-de-sac hard up against a high wall of natural rock. There was no exit; he could only turn on his heel, very casually, and walk back again past the police.

He became instantly guilty: his shirt and jeans weighed him down like prison overalls. A fair child on a scooter bore down on him outside the murder house. He stopped short as the boy speeded towards him and, anticipating the scooter's direction, sidestepped to the left just as the boy steered in that direction and ran into his leg. The child fell lightly on one knee, the scooter clattering in the gutter. Surprisingly, the child began crying loudly. The police looked up.

'Gregory!' yelled a fat young woman leaning over an adjoining fence. 'Come in off the street or the policemen'll lock you up.' Crisp dusted the boy off and picked up the scooter. As he walked towards the corner he sensed the detectives' eyes following from under their snappy hats. Sauntering the final two yards he felt his cheeks glowing with a peculiar self-consciousness. His shoulder blades and spine anticipated a barrage of homicide squad bullets.

The humidity weighed down on him. He had got into the habit of rising early while his father was convalescing at the Surteeses, now it was still only 9.30 but the day seemed to have been limping painfully along for hours. He went home to change into his bathers, then walked down to the North Sydney Olympic pool, near the northern pylon of the Harbour Bridge. A section of the pool was roped off with orange floats for school swimming lessons. Crisp sat in the empty stands watching adolescent girls racing, squealing and splashing each other. Ogling away, he noticed that the girls' style of swimwear denoted their type of education. The Protestant private school girls wore uniformly styled blue racing costumes, the State high school girls a free-range assortment of multi-hued, miniscule bikinis, one-piece affairs (chosen by the fatties) and racing costumes (worn by the conscientiously sporty girls). The Catholics, on the other hand, ushered and herded by nuns with neck whistles, forlornly paraded with cotton T-shirts and blouses over their bikinis, so lascivious chest, waist and upper arm portions were safely hidden from perverts like Crisp, lurking in the stands. He was more turned on by the convent girls than the others.

Why? Surely not because the young Jane had been one of them, plumply pink in her sky-blue Loreto tunic and thick brown stockings in the days before she learned to smoke dextrously, before childbirth pared down her body to its present lean and whippy dimensions. Long before she said 'shit' in public. (But still had not attempted 'Christ!' or 'Jesus!')

Whistles blew, gym mistresses shrilled and beckoned and stamped around the pool on tanned stumpy legs. The girls left the water, high-breasted, sleek-haired and tittering, rushed towels around their shoulders and chests and scampered for the change-rooms. (A few years and Wendy would be one of them, hipped and breasted and watched from the stands by dirty old men.) When the pool was empty and slick-surfaced Crisp did a racing dive and swam several laps of short stabbing strokes until the chlorine began to savage his eyes. Tears streamed down his cheeks as he climbed from the pool.

It was not until 17th January that I was able to travel to Hobart Town and wait upon the Governor at his invitation. My reception at Government House was worth waiting for, nevertheless—a generous private interview attended by all the Governor's family (except Mrs Arthur, unfortunately indisposed with what my wife had heard was thrombophlebitis caused by constant child-bearing) and accompanied by the most civilized hospitality: sherry served from a crystal decanter and delicate jam pastries prepared, I was fascinated to learn, actually in Hobart Town, by a recently arrived Swiss.

'We are becoming quite a sophisticated hub of civilization, Robinson,' declared His Excellency, waving forward a servant carrying a platter of thin slivers of bread spread with a fawn-coloured meat paste. 'And your services have helped to make us so. Taming the blacks, soothing their predations and what-have-you.'

'Thank you your Excellency.' Emboldened, I went on. 'And the Line? What were the successes of the military these past weeks?'

'Oh,' he surveyed me over his sherry glass, a touch wearily. And warily. 'The operations of the Government, and of the community generally, have had an important effect. Deterred the savages in great measure from their usual aggressions. Bound together every class in a cordial feeling of striving for the common good. That sort of thing.'

I nibbled at a pastry. The jam ran deliciously through my teeth. 'But did they capture any tribes? Did they drive them before them, your Excellency?'

The Governor sighed. At his feet his small daughter had smeared herself with jam and crumbs and was now trying to pull herself up on his red-seamed trouser legs. 'Up, up, Papa,' she begged.

'Oh, do take her Mrs Humphreys,' he instructed the child's governess, brushing pastry from his knees. He adjusted his trouser creases. 'That part of the campaign was a partial failure, Mr Robinson.' His private secretary and aide-de-camp exchanged glances. 'But let us talk about your efforts.' He patted the child's seat as she was carried away whining and kicking, and turned his intent eyes upon me. 'I hear your man Parish is acquitting himself very favourably these days.'

'If I may say your Excellency, the man is a dangerous fraud and not to be trusted with command.'

'Is that so?' He gave me a quizzical look. 'I had received only encouraging reports of his work. I had taken him to be a conciliator after your own heart. Going unarmed into the blacks' camps, sleeping at their fires and all that carry-on.'

'Unfortunately the man is a compulsive self-aggrandizer. I may have to prevent him serving as my coxswain if his behaviour continues.' I felt quite unable to finish my savoury bread. That Parish's boasts had reached even Government House!

His Excellency smiled. The creases beneath his jawline ran like river tributaries into the high buttoned collar of his black frock-coat. 'You are very jealous of your reputation, sir.'

'Well, I . . .'

'Unnecessarily so. I asked you here not only to express the Government's appreciation for so effectually conducting your mission to the savages but also to reward you.'

I was stunned. 'To serve God and the Crown is reward enough.'

'That may be. But what would you say to two thousand five hundred acres of land free from restriction and a bonus of one hundred pounds as well as a salary of two hundred and fifty pounds per annum?'

'Your Excellency is very kind.'

'You have earned it, sir. However I wish you to undertake a last expedition. I want you to effect the voluntary removal of the entire black population. The Aboriginals Committee wants me to place every last one of them on Flinders Island.'

'Really?'

'But they wish to be guided by your expert and first-hand knowledge. They are fully aware that you alone are the recipient of the blacks' confidence and wish to offer you their cordial support and encouragement.'

'I would be delighted to meet the gentlemen.'

Another of his daughters, a pretty, boisterous girl of about seven, romped into the room and snatched a piece of savoury bread from a platter.

'Your children are delightfully natural, your Excellency.'

'I try to fit them into my official duties,' the Governor smiled. 'We have a Children's Hour every evening. They repeat several hymns they have committed to memory and twenty verses of scripture.'

'An encouraging habit in these uttermost parts of the world.'

My stay in Hobart Town passed most agreeably. I spent an interesting afternoon with the Aboriginals Committee, most of whose members were very appreciative of my services. One or two of them, notably the Reverend Mr Bedford, the Colonial Chaplain, seemed to have a keen idea of the native problem. The gentlemen told me they had decided on expatriating the natives to Flinders Island on the following grounds: (1) that escape was quite impossible, so far was the island from the mainland; (2) that game, water, shellfish and mutton birds abounded; and (3) that the communications from George Town and the anchorage for vessels was good. Further, as Mr Bedford put it, 'Though it is possible that the natives may pine here to return to their native land, the Committee imagines that religious instruction and the amusement of shellfishing and kangaroo hunting will occupy their minds.'

That evening I took tea with Mr Bedford at the Church of England residence, quite a grand establishment, after which I accompanied him to the gaol for his midweek service. (The Anglican Church seemed to me to be becoming much more relevant to the life of the colony.) After we departed the gaol (Mr Bedford leaving the felons with the wise words of Ezekiel: 'The Lord hath no pleasure in the death of the wicked. Turn ye, turn ye.') we returned to the manse for roast duckling and turnips, Cape wine and sweet biscuits. The fowl was domestic, a tender change from my familiar stringy wild birds, and stuffed, so Mr Bedford kindly informed me, with four tablespoons of blanched almonds, one Spanish onion, sage, salt and the duck's own liver, heart and gizzard, finely chopped.

Sitting up in the stands Crisp stretched out his limbs to the sullen sun. People were now arriving for a lunchtime swim: fitness enthusiasts from nearby offices, several teenagers, young women who could have been off-duty nurses, a couple of bikinied mothers with toddlers. A tall young man in some sort of ersatz military uniform also made an entrance. He marched briskly from the turnstiles to the edge of the pool, felt the water temperature with his fingers and headed for the change-room. He was dressed in khakis and black boots and wore a type of officer's cap. Emerging from the change-room several minutes later in a tight pair of black trunks, he headed up into the stands near Crisp, passing close enough for him to notice there were no visible hairs on his body—his head, chest, arms and legs were all shaved smooth. The man had a weightlifter's well-defined biceps and triceps, bulging pectorals. He sprang on to all fours on the seat below Crisp and performed fifty pushups. Then he rolled back on his shoulders and, supporting his hips with his hands, cycled in the air with feverish energy. The blood ran to his glistening skull.

Nutty as a fruitcake, Crisp thought. A home-made commando. But the man wasn't done. He turned back on all fours and did twenty more pushups, refining the exercise by adding a hand clap between each pushup. Then with a spring he was on his feet, down the stairs and sauntering towards the high springboard, swinging his arms vigorously to loosen his shoulders. Two teenage boys razzed him. He cracked his knuckles at them and glowered: wrinkles rode his hairless brow.

After some elaborate testing of the board, adjusting the spring, bouncing concernedly, he poised himself, struck a heroic stance and ran with surprisingly delicate steps to the end of the board. He sprang into the air—and jumped like a child feet-first into the water. Crisp had expected a flashy jack-knife at the very least. So had the teenagers: their jeers rang across the pool. The pointed head surfaced and the man loudly cleared his nostrils. He went through the same routine ten or twelve times until he had long exhausted his audience's interest, then left the water. As he was leaving the pool enclosure a while later, dressed again in his uniform, he received a final ironic cheer from the teenagers. He snapped his heels together, gave the Nazi salute and goose-stepped towards the turnstiles.

As Crisp was leaving the pool himself, queuing up for a Hawaiian Delight at the ice cream shop, one of the previously jeering teenagers, a skinny boy of about fourteen with pustuled shoulders, pushed in front of him to buy cigarettes. When the boy turned around, ripping open the pack, Crisp saw that his white chest was emblazoned with the most gaudy and no doubt expensive tattoo imaginable. It was a Disney-style cartoon, highly professional, of what was unmistakably a turd. Only the lump had a little set of horns, cute hoofs, a devilish grinning face and clutched a pitchfork. All this was painstakingly worked into the skin with bright red inks, highlighted by blue flames and smoke and green cross-hatching. Beneath the tattoo was imprinted a slogan in black ink on the pale flesh. It said HOT SHIT!

Crisp sauntered home, rounding *Cardigan*'s corner feeling, if anything, hotter, more rattled than before his swim. A pale blue car cruised up behind him, stopped at the kerb.

'Come over here,' ordered the detective in the front passenger's seat. 'Want a word with you.'

What? Caught at last? A lump constricted his breathing. 'What's the trouble?' he asked, walking over to the car.

'I seen you somewhere, haven't I?' The cop was dark, with pointed features and sharply angled sideburns. 'Apart from this morning I mean, hanging round the Burnside place. I know your face from somewhere. Where is it? You tell me, Sunshine.'

'Possibly. I've got a television programme.' Had. And not his, anyway. 'The Commission has very good relations with the police. Always has,' he crawled.

'What's the name?' During this questioning the detective was smiling casually and humourlessly, one elbow resting nonchalantly on the window ledge. *But poised ready to strike, grab, arrest, shoot.* There were two other plainclothes men in the car. Their faces were expressionless. They stared at him, took in his saggy T-shirt, wet trunks, chlorine-reddened eyes.

'Stephen Crisp.'

'Never heard of you. I know plenty of reporters—the *Mirror* and *Telegraph* blokes, never seen you at the C.I.B. Where do you live? You a family man, Crisp?'

'Just here,' he said, indicating *Cardigan*'s liver-brick frontage. The detective gave the block of flats the once-over. He seemed unimpressed. 'I've got a house as well up at Whale Beach.' Crawling again. 'My wife and daughter live there. Fifty thousand dollars' worth,' he gushed. Mortgaged for thirty years—and no longer his.

'Separated, eh. Everyone's doing it.' The detective pulled his arm back inside the car. Evidently the interview was over. 'Keep away from murder scenes, son, or you'll be in the shit.' The driver started the car and it moved slowly off. It did a U-turn at the bottom of the street and passed him again, the dark cop calling out to him, smiling savagely: 'Hope some tough fucker's looking after your ex-wife. We've got a handy little couple of rapists up Whale Beach way.'

Before I prepared for my final expedition inland after the natives I determined, counting on the support of the Government and the fact that the Governor had been pleased to appoint me as a Special Constable for the island of Van Diemen's Land and its dependencies, to rid the straits of slavery once and for all.

I had decided that those miscreants the sealers ought to be removed immediately from the islands. It was a disgrace that the wretched men should have been allowed to thrive there so long. The British Government had expended thousands of pounds to abolish the slave trade at home; that it should exist in one of her colonies was disgraceful.

Accordingly I embarked on the government cutter *Charlotte* at Hobart Town on 10th March with six soldiers under a Lieutenant Merrett, intent upon exerting the Government's will. We anchored first off Swan Island where we disembarked all the aboriginals I had gathered from the Hobart Town gaol. Their meeting with old friends and relations was truly affecting—a mother encountering her sons, and sisters their brothers. The scene was so moving that I was forced to turn away to suppress the involuntary lachryma.

I found that three natives had died in my absence: a tall young woman named Teekartee, a little girl with the white name Mary and a middle-aged warrior, Loon-mare. Their illnesses had been short and, according to McLachlan my medical dispenser, only the child had appeared to suffer pain during her acute attacks of fever and coughing. All three bodies were interred in the Christian fashion (McLachlan having kept them, at a far end of the camp, for my surveillance), though I offered no remarks on this occasion. At the graveside I was severely tormented by a cloud of gnats and mosquitoes which had flown in from some stagnant quagmire, the worst attack I could remember since my first expedition in 1829, a fact I remarked upon to Lieutenant Merrett over dinner that evening.

'Have you tried eau-de-luce?' the lieutenant asked.

'Eau-de-luce?'

'It's an excellent remedy for mosquito bites,' he asserted, savouring his roast cygnet. 'Colonel Porter in his military reminiscences says he's several times in his life cured snake bite with various doses of eau-de-luce, never exceeding half a bottle.'

'How interesting. I've heard of eau-de-cologne as a remedy, but never eau-de-luce.'

'Once in Ceylon when an enormous cobra bit a sentry the man was almost dead with lockjaw and asphyxiation. The colonel forced him to down half a wineglass of eau-de-luce every quarter hour for three hours and restored him to convalescence.'

'Amazing.'

'Though he spat blood for some time afterwards from the strength of the medicine.'

'On occasions in the field when nothing stronger could be procured I have administered brandy and once a large amount of Madeira, but I find my men fake snakebite to get the liquor.'

'Is that so?' The lieutenant leered a slippery grin. 'In the 57th we use eau-de-luce on the pox. Paint their rogers with it, Robinson, that's the ticket. From bunghole to breakfast.'

'You are my guest, lieutenant,' I said severely.

'My apologies,' he said, resuming his meal. 'This is a fine fowl. Tastier than pelican.'

On 18th March in the early afternoon we landed in the *Charlotte* on Gun Carriage Island. I ordered the soldiers to prevent any sealers' boats from leaving and summoned the sealers to assemble on the beach before their huts.

There were thirteen of them, all but two Englishmen: Thomas 'Jew' Beadon (formerly an apprentice to a London goldsmith), William Proctor, John Biddle, Thomas Tucker (a man with a violent record of abductions and, some said, murder), Edward Mansell, Richard Maynard, John 'Black Jack' Mirey (a native of Otaheite and a man of colour), the invalid Charles Peterson, John Smith, Thomas Bailey, William Day, John Taylor (an American mulatto from Richmond, State of Virginia) and John 'Abyssinia Jack' Anderson. They had sent all their women away to hide when they saw the *Charlotte* coming down the sound. When I had noted their names, personal details and status I read the following notices to them and had a soldier nail them to the wall of the hut nearest the beach.

NOTICE

To all Concerned

All persons residing upon or resorting to any of the islands of Bass Strait and having aboriginal females in their possession I hereby charge and require in the name of His Majesty's Colonial Government to deliver up all such women to me accordingly that they may be placed by me under the care of the Government at my Establishment.

And I further notify to all such persons that the act of carrying off or detaining these unhappy people is a flagrant offence for which the parties guilty of it are punishable by law.

If after this notice the women are not immediately delivered up but still detained then in such cases warrants will be immediately issued for the apprehension of all such offending parties whom the Government is resolved to bring to exemplary punishment.

G. A. Robinson
Superintendent of Aboriginals

NOTICE

To all Concerned

All persons sealers or others will hereby take notice that it is the determination of His Majesty's Colonial Government not to permit any residence upon or resort to any of the islands in these straits unless by express written licence to be obtained for this purpose.

All persons therefore sealers and others residing upon or resorting to any of the islands are warned by me to quit those islands which are solely the property of the Crown.

Such persons therefore who are found residing upon or resorting to any of those islands after this notice are trespassers and will be expelled accordingly.

G. A. Robinson
Superintendent of Aboriginals

There was a general sullenness when I finished reading the notices, then a low mumbling from the sealers.

'You have my permission to remove those belongings which you can carry,' I told them. 'You will leave by tonight.'

They protested, cursing loudly, damning my name. Lieutenant Merrett and his troops stood noticeably by. I gestured towards the musketry. 'Do not incite the soldiers. It would be foolhardy to disobey me.' The sealers cursed under their breath. Most of them were middle-aged or elderly and, though wiry and weather-beaten, not the muscular ruffians they had been.

Anderson, a man in his fifties, complained, 'Gun Carriage produces twenty-five tons of potatoes in one season! We've got pigs, goats, fowls and our vegetable gardens, We make our living here.'

'Very well,' I conceded, purchasing for my people's use seven tons of potatoes and all the sealers' pigs for twopence per pound. 'Load them on to the cutter and leave.'

We saw the sealers off in their packed and overburdened boats and I sent my men into the hillocks and tussock grass after their women. They returned with six women and four children, all wide-eyed with fear at what their masters had slyly warned would befall them. One of the children, a boy of about twelve, had a grossly scarred and misshapen face, his mouth twisted into a perpetual grimace so his right side teeth remained visible.

'What happened to this boy?' I demanded. Embarrassed, the child skulked down behind the women, his face downcast. He played nervously with a broken pink shell.

A withered woman with a tiny, taut face and missing front teeth said, 'The sealers cut the flesh off his cheek for misbehaving.'

'That is abominable!'

'He wouldn't catch enough mutton birds, wouldn't poke his arm into the nest-holes because of snakes. Then he ran away. They made him eat his flesh.'

'Atrocity! Are you his mother?'

'No. They tied her to a tree and cut off her ears and made her eat them. They then cut her woman's parts from her thighs to her belly and she died on the tree. Her name was Been-gunner-rer. She ran away with her son to Cape Barren but the sealers there brought her back.'

'Who are the men who did these outrages? They will hang.'

The wrinkled woman shook her head, screwing up her eyes deep into her tightly drawn cheeks. 'You must tell me,' I insisted, but she would say no more. I searched the faces of the other women, but they were blank as the rock slabs behind them. They shivered with fear in their wallaby skin frocks.

A heavy weight lay upon me, pressing down on my head and shoulders, constricting my breathing. The lieutenant had overheard this exchange. He came up to us, crunching shells under his boots.

'Shall we force her to talk?' he asked. The woman fell back behind her friends, stricken. I dismissed the lieutenant with a curt gesture.

'Don't be frightened,' I soothed them, handing out the usual baubles. 'I am Mr Robinson, the Father.'

We pursued the same course of action next day on Woody Island, ordering off the two resident sealers, Jem Everitt, a ginger-headed Englishman (reported to have killed and buried his black mistress Woreth-male-yer on the island), and old Geordy Thompson, one of whose women, Tooger-nupper, I had previously removed. Now I asked him to surrender his remaining woman, Ploorer-nele, and her small child.

'You are going to a happy place,' I told the weeping woman. 'Your son will be educated in Christianity and the basics of civilized life. You will be safe from the sealers and there'll be woollen clothing for the winds.'

Old Thompson's good eye swept over his little wheatfield and vegetable gardens. He made a cursory inspection of his crops, plucking a few cabbages here, some onions and potatoes there. He stuffed five or six hens in a hessian sack, looked mournfully at his pigs.

'Twopence a pound for the lot, Thompson,' I offered. He nodded slowly. As his woman Ploorer-nele was taken from him he stroked her cheek and gave her five beautifully cut pieces of the local crystal and three sides of his home-cured bacon. Before we sent him off in his boat he carefully stacked his remaining supply of bacon on the rock steps in front of his cottage and urinated on it.

'Steady on there!' shouted Lieutenant Merrett. Musket butts rattled indecisively on the stony beach. Thompson fastened his clothing, climbed into his boat without a word and cast off. Considering the previous character of these abandoned individuals I suppose this depraved and wasteful behaviour should not have surprised me.

On Preservation Island I followed the same procedure, assembling the sealers and reading the notices. However, here James Munro confronted me, questioning my authority.

'I'm a special constable,' he insisted, 'by Government appointment, I have not been informed. I have nowhere to go.'

'Just a courtesy title I'm afraid, Munro. These are my orders and Lieutenant Merrett's men shall support them. Though I shall avoid violence as far as possible. You'll find there's work aplenty on the mainland. And a certain amount of charity at the Bethels.'

'What about my children? They look after me. You can't have them for your bloody Jesus-stinking mission.'

'They would be better off living with those of their own colour, but you may keep them if that is what they want.' The man was florid and emotional, mumbling crude threats. Despite his blasphemy it did no harm to accede to his request. He left in a whaleboat with two other sealers, Jack Browning and Joe Harrington, shaking with anger and keeping his two half-caste sons close by him.

Laden down with cane and palm leaf laundry baskets and tapa-cloth shopping bags, Murray Crisp, harried and sweating, emerged from the Customs shed, cast an anxious eye around for a familiar face and, much relieved, saw his son waiting for him at the edge of the crowd. Offering a damp handshake, he said, 'God, what a nightmare.'

'The cruise?'

'No, no, the disembarking. No wretched porters, no proper organization anywhere. Need a bomb under them, these fellows.'

'How are you?' Stephen asked, though he noticed the tension around the baggy eyes, the added weight under the chin. He carried the heavier luggage to the taxi he had waiting, leaving his father with the lighter but unwieldy native handicrafts. Glassy-eyed sixty-year-olds struggled from the terminal weighed down by similar woven, carved, plaited and lacquered knick-knacks, shouted nervily for cabs, snapped at their wives and appeared suddenly self-conscious at hitting the city street in tropical shirts emblazoned *Bula Bula Fiji Wonderland*. 'Have a good time?' he asked.

'Not bad, not bad. Went to the captain's cocktail party, got a thousand dollar suntan. Met some nice people from the motor trade.' He collapsed wearily into the cab, loosening his navy striped tie, patting his stomach guiltily. 'Must have stacked on some weight,' he said. 'P & O is big on roast beef and Yorkshire pudding. Ice cream every morning around the pool.' His tan was fading to a beige shade, spidery red lines like road map routes glowed on his cheeks and nose. The shoulders of his yachting jacket seemed to overflow his own. 'God, I'd love a cigarette. You don't smoke, do you?' he remarked absently. He tapped the cabbie on the shoulder. 'Can you spare a cigarette, driver?'

'Sorry mate, given them up. The brother died of emphysema.'

'Oh.' His father blinked, then reached into his jacket pocket, took out a tube of Lifesavers, peeled the silver paper off a couple and popped them into his mouth. He offered the packet to his son, then to the driver.

'Never touch sweets, thanks,' the driver said.

The taxi headed north for Frank and Eileen's. 'I'll unload this native stuff on Eileen,' his father said. 'One of the lasses on board talked me into buying it. Not bad stuff, though. I got them a nice duty-free radio too, for looking after me. I must get back to Melbourne this week, get back to work.' He lay restlessly back on the seat munching Lifesavers. 'The holiday's over,' he said suddenly. 'Oh, I got you a typewriter. Little Olivetti, hope it's O.K. Thought you might like a new one for that project of yours.'

'Thanks Dad. Terrific.' He smelled the peppermint on his father's breath, from the side of his vision watched the pink, well kept fingers drumming distractedly on the gaberdine knees all the way up the Pacific Highway.

The Charlotte's captain shaped her course for George Town. We were running short of supplies and water—what with the extra natives on board and the animals I had bought from the sealers—and I was anxious to discover the latest news. But the supplies I wanted could not be obtained at George Town (I needed seven thousand pounds of flour and the commissariat hadn't enough ground) and the *Charlotte*'s captain insisted she needed repairing at Launceston, so we proceeded up the Tamar. I was unprepared for Launceston, not having my best clothing with me and being spotted with unsightly insect bites, but the weather was pleasant and my spirits high nevertheless.

Next morning I breakfasted with the commandant, Major Abbott, who congratulated me on my 'enterprising spirit' (a change in his previous attitude: the man was obviously not so stiff-backed as I had thought) and commented that every person spoke of me. A certain John Batman, an ambitious cattleman and erstwhile aboriginal conciliator (whose inflated importance seemed based purely on his capture of the bushranger Matthew Brady), was in town, the major told me, spreading a story that my men were going to Hobart Town to complain of my incompetence in command.

'The phrase "pompous martinet" was used, I believe.'

I could barely control my anger. 'The man Batman has invented the story to my prejudice. No doubt he is extremely jealous of me, like so many others.' Conduct such as this deserved the severest censure. Not only did it wrongfully damage my standing, but it deceived and misled the Governor.

'Yes, that is probably it,' the major said thoughtfully.

As I prepared for my final expedition, ordering stores, recruiting servants and crew and planning my *modus operandi*, I received a summons to Government House, a rather more peremptory invitation than I was accustomed to get from His Excellency. On arrival I was surprised to see Munro the old sealer there before me, engaged in animated conversation in an ante-room with the Governor's secretary. He was bent over a mahogany table, busily riffling through a sheaf of papers fastened loosely with binder's twine. As I walked into the room he snatched up his papers and stuffed them into a worn leather satchel.

'What brings you here, Munro?'

He smirked at me, tucking the bag under an arm. His long sandy hair had been recently plastered down with water. Moist patches still showed on the shoulders of his jacket.

'You'll see, Mr Robinson. Most likely the Governor will tell you. You're a mite unpopular, Mr Robinson, in some quarters. They say you think you're king of the straits these days. And the inland as well.'

What calumnies! While I had been intent on removing the native women from slavery, the sealers had moved to circumvent me in their sly fashion, going about their plan with skill and cunning. They had sent Munro to Hobart Town as their spokesman.

We were ushered into the Governor's office. 'Good morning gentlemen,' he said. I was astonished. There was no preference to me over this superannuated old lag. The proceedings which followed still remain in my mind as an example of gross unfairness and misunderstanding of my intentions on His Excellency's part.

Munro presented two petitions which were read aloud by the Governor's secretary. The first asked for him to be allowed to remain on Preservation Island: to this His Excellency immediately consented.

'Constable Munro has always conducted himself with propriety, reporting the removal by foreigners of our escaped convicts and so on,' he drawled, while the sealer sat smugly at the vice-regal desk edge.

The second was a petition from Thomas 'Jew' Beadon for the return of the woman I had taken from him—the shifty felon had been wily enough to get a receipt from me for her. Beadon told a pathetic tale of how I had expelled him from Gun Carriage Island without giving him time to find a new home or remove his property. He alleged that he had a clearance from the Port of Hobart Town to work the islands of the straits for seals, that five years ago he'd come upon a homeless native woman and out of a feeling of humanity had taken her under his protection and had since supported her and 'used every effort to instruct her and our two children in a proper knowledge of right and wrong.'

'Your Excellency, that is a lie! The woman does not want to return to him. None of them do. These are evil men actuated by motives of self-interest.'

'There is no need for acrimony, Mr Robinson. We are all united in our aims, after all. I believe Constable Munro has some further suggestions on the natives' general welfare.'

Munro stood before the Governor's desk, found his spectacles and read haltingly from a prepared sheet.

'As constable for the Straits islands I think it is an impolitic plan to take the women from the sealers. With those women they might induce whole tribes to give themselves up, but without the assistance of the women little or nothing can be done. The sealers themselves will volunteer to assist the Government to go out after the natives.' (Here I drew some deep breaths to save myself from an undignified outburst.) Munro continued reading in his flat, unconvincing monotone. 'Most of the women taken by Mr Robinson want to return to the sealers. The natives of his establishment are sickly and discontented; only roaming at will makes them happy.'

The unctuous rascal then removed his spectacles and fixed his watery eyes on the Governor. 'Your Excellency,' he wheedled. 'We've always treated the women kindly, so kindly that they'd hardly do any work. I read the Bible to my children. The youngest is here today, sir, waiting outside to recite his prayers to you. He knows them by heart, and only six years old.'

'Does he now, Munro? My own children are expert on the Psalms.'

'Oh, he's very good on the Psalms too, your Excellency, for a child of his colour. Knows them like the back of his hand.'

My preparations in Hobart Town continued under the cloud of my Government House confrontation with Munro. I was still interviewing likely candidates for my expedition into the interior when a messenger arrived on 3rd May with an urgent despatch signed by the Colonial Secretary which said:

'I am directed to inform you that Constable Munro has represented to His Excellency the severe deprivation felt by the sealers in the Straits since you removed the native women with whom they have long cohabited. His Excellency is led to understand that not only do the sealers feel this, but the women themselves are greatly distressed. Under these circumstances it is impossible to expect that either the women or the sealers will make themselves useful in endeavouring to tranquillize any of the hostile tribes, or will induce them to migrate to the asylum provided for them.

It is therefore suggested that you should make immediate arrangements for returning the females to those sealers who are not known to have treated them with barbarity. You should endeavour at once to engage their services in proceeding to the mainland to co-operate with you in producing a friendly feeling on the part of the tribes.

As the sealers will in all probability know more of the habits of the coastal natives than you do yourself, it will be prudent not to restrict them to any particular plan, but to allow them to exercise their own judgement to a great degree, holding out the expectation that if they are successful the Government will confer rewards upon them and make such regulations for the protection of their occupation in the Straits as will be conducive to their future comfort and health.

You will be pleased to read this letter to the sealers immediately.'

There came a thumping on the door, waking him, and this time it could be no divorce investigator, though at 9 a.m. there were other feared callers (landlords and summons servers were shortly anticipated), the way his finances were going. Crisp called testily, 'Coming, coming,' and pulled on some clothes. One of the last people he did expect to see was Uncle Frank Surtees, surprisingly sloppily dressed and with ginger stubble sprouting from the lines of his mouth.

'You're not on the phone, I couldn't ring,' Surtees said accusingly, stepping into the room. Then, in an abrupt change of mood, he gripped Crisp by both arms. 'Better sit down Stevie,' he said. His breath was not good. *Stevie?* Surtees steered him unnecessarily towards a chair. 'I've got bad news for you.' They always said that. Why? To increase the drama? Heighten the impact? And it seemed you always knew what next they were going to say. *Déjà vu*. 'It happened during the night, Steve, from what I understand from the housekeeper. Her night off, found him early this morning. As soon as we got the call from Melbourne I came to let you know. Dad's passed away.'

Say 'died' for Christ's sake! They never said 'died', these people.

'It's probably a blessing,' Surtees said.

Wrong.

A further despatch arrived at my home.

Swan Island
10th May

Dear Mr Robinson,

I beg leave to acquaint you that during your absence two of the aboriginals have died; one, a female, of fever on the 20th April; the other, a male, of dysentery on the 23rd inst.

I beg also to inform you that several of the females and men are in a morbidly sick state from the bleakness of this place and the want of proper habitation. I also consider that the water on the establishment is prejudicial to their health and I apprehend there will not be a sufficiency of it in the dry season.

Archibald McLachlan — Dispenser.

I arrived back on Swan Island from the mainland and almost immediately strong westerly gales blew up and continued for six days without abatement. When the gales set in the situation was truly bleak. The establishment was exposed to the sweeping winds without any protection, The island's formation, consisting of wide, dark sandhills and little natural timber, caused the sand to whistle over the face of the island, blowing into our every orifice and creating widespread opthalmia. The sand was so fine it was impossible to prevent it mixing with our food, and so black that we were constantly filthy. Adding to my discomfort and that of the other Europeans were the swarms of fleas and immense quantities of flies which infested the island, the flies so voracious they would blow salt pork and even plain salt on which a greasy knife had laid.

Nor should I omit to mention the rats which plagued this and all the other Straits islands, as these loathsome animals made regular nocturnal visits to the stores and to every part of the encampment, and though packs of the natives' scabrous dogs were continually prowling about, the rats were not at all intimidated. Snakes, too, were numerous, and what with the screeching of the penguins at night and the howling of the gritty tempest, everything combined to engender in me painful and gloomy forebodings of my mission.

McLachlan informed me that while I had been absent on the mainland three of the crew had together frequently cohabited with Truganini while Wooraddy was out mutton birding. Woreter had again been menacing Jumbo and, on being chastised, had taken his weapons and speared twenty of the dogs out of temper.

I told numbers of the women I would have to return them to the sealers. They commenced wailing and their new husbands looked upon me suddenly as a turncoat, and worse. I forced my mind to combat this multiplicity of evils.

14

The Last Expedition

My journeys began again on 10th August. This time my instructions were, as the Governor had put it, 'to effect the voluntary removal of the entire remaining black population', a daunting enough task even for a man with strong evidence that God was with him and that the cause was also His.

Guided by an old chief, Manna-largenner, whom I had recruited from the Hobart Town gaol, we travelled south-east from our base camp on the mainland opposite Swan Island, crossing the main branch of the Tomahawk River and its adjoining lowlands of heath mixed with iris and sword grass, and then fording the Montagu River and pursuing a course towards the Mount Cameron Range. This time leeches proved a source of irritation to both black and white people. The blood trickled down our legs as we walked and our leggings were soon congealed with it. I found myself still troubled by the psora and had to constantly apply the yellow sulphur ointment.

My first aim was to capture Umarrah, a warlike chieftain wise to European ways (and the perpetrator of many white murders) and his Stoney Creek tribe would then hopefully follow him to civilization. My second, final intention was to bring in the legendary Oyster Bay and Big River tribes under the two most sanguinary of all chieftains, Montpeilliater and Tonger-longter, who had always acted in unison. I had thus instructed Manna-largenner, explaining the kind and generous views of the Government towards himself and his people. He had cordially acquiesced.

'You give me things, I will help you,' he said. 'I need a woman for the shellfish and night time. You stop white man from shooting me.' He pumped up his chest. 'I have fought Umarrah, defeated him. He was frightened of me and begged for mercy.'

My party numbered fifteen persons this time: two white men apart from myself, Joe—a coloured native of Owyhee as a servant—and eleven aboriginals, including a Big River woman known as Woolyay, also from the gaol. I had limited our provisions to flour, tea and sugar, trusting our three dogs to help in killing kangaroo for meat (Wooraddy had sworn they would not bark, and there was a possibility they might even have to provide us with subsistence!). Nevertheless, everyone apart from myself and Manna-largenner had to carry a heavy knapsack—some of the strongest native women carried forty pounds weight and each man sixty pounds.

Manna-largenner believed the Stoney Creek tribe was nearby. He saw some blurred footprints and animal offal and remarked that the natives were eating as they roamed.

'The spirits tell me so,' he declared, shaking his left shoulder and breast like a palsied person, the shoulder moving round to the country indicated. The rest of the natives wondered greatly at this, and as the spasm was quick they said it implied we should waste no time. Manna-largenner was gratified at the attention paid him. Everyone was most impressed except Wooraddy who grumbled to himself.

'I have fought Umarrah too,' he said. 'The enemy surrounded me and threw abundance of spears at me but they could not hit me. I speared two of them and escaped. I have raped Umarrah's women and stolen his shellfish and cloaks.'

'You have not told me this before,' Truganini said. 'You dreamed it.'

We proceeded, guided by Manna-largenner, in a south-southwest and southwest by southerly direction; then southwest, west by north, west-northwest and west, and then to the northward of west.

'Are you sure we are on the natives' trail?' I asked Manna-largenner, wondering whether it was time for me to produce some prognostications of my own.

He showed his breast, which displayed a violent palpitation over the heart and to which the other natives paid marked attention. 'Umarrah's tribe was down in these parts and hunted and went back again,' he said solemnly.

'Nnh,' Wooraddy grunted.

But it seemed the chief was correct because that afternoon we came upon a heap of kangaroo bones and some waddies, evidence that the tribe had recently camped there. Then, towards the end of the day Wooraddy found a wallaby wedged in a tree fork, placed there by the tribe after hunting. It was tolerable fresh, about two days killed.

Around our fire that night I spent some time explaining the purport of this final mission and the benevolent intentions of the Government.

'Then why did you deceive us and allow the sealers to take away the women again?' Wooraddy asked. He was sorrowful—confused rather than surly. He picked at his toes with a splintered kangaroo bone, keeping his eyes averted from my face.

'That was against my will.'

'Why weren't the sealers put in gaol for killing our people?'

'I am angry too that they were not punished. When we have captured these hostiles you can go to Hobart Town and tell the Governor.'

Manna-largenner stood bolt upright by the fire, throwing his wallaby cloak from his chest. The palpitations began again, slowly and lightly at first, then more violently, so his flesh quivered over the length of his body and tremors ran like pool ripples to his extremities. When he had allowed his body to become still again he said, 'I will go to the Governor himself. I am not afraid. I will tell him which white men to kill.'

'Eeahh!' exclaimed my people, greatly impressed.

'Boastful old turd eater,' Wooraddy muttered to Truganini and myself.

She shot a scornful glance at her husband. 'You are a coward born from a white woman's belly. That is why your waddy is soft,' she said.

'Nnh!' he growled. 'Fish-breathed whalers' whore . . .'

'Ssh, ssh.' I soothed them with a pannikin of sweet tea.

Bored with our flour rations and needing fresh meat I instructed the natives next morning that we would go hunting. We took the dogs Rupert and Mungo after a big boomer we espied near a rill of water about a mile from our camp. Manna-largenner and Rupert encircled it from behind while Wooraddy and I followed Mungo over a wide heathy plain where he raced towards the big animal, now bounding ahead at a great pace.

Mungo soon outdistanced us and reached the kangaroo. It had decided to stop and fight whereas it could have easily outrun us had it chosen. The dog darted about, nipping the boomer on the haunches and tail, whereupon it would turn and stand upright, tall as a man, raking at Mungo with its claws. The dog was fearful of close attack and leaped back just in time to avoid a slashed throat, then resumed barking and nipping at the animal's tail. This confrontation gave us time to draw closer, but on seeing us the kangaroo fled with Mungo slavering after it. Again it stopped and faced the dog, slashing at its snout with its claws, and then leaped away and paused again until, panting with exhaustion, it leaned back on its tail and stood waiting for Wooraddy and me to approach.

The badly clawed Mungo was too weak to master the kangaroo. I yelled to Wooraddy, 'Spear him quickly. Before he attacks us.' Wooraddy stood motionless, poised for flight.

'Quick. Throw a waddy at him.'

'By and by,' he said, his eyes large. 'He is a big wild one.'

Anxious to put the beast out of its misery I crept closer and threw a waddy at its head, striking it on the forehead. Abruptly it made a jump at me, lunging at my chest with its claws, ripping my blouse.

'He will tear out your insides!' Wooraddy yelled. This would have been the case had not Rupert, attracted by Mungo's frenzied barks, run across the kangaroo's path and fastened on to the animal, allowing Mungo to catch it by the throat and bring it down. Exhausted, the kangaroo collapsed, frothing at the muzzle with the dogs on top of it, and at this juncture Wooraddy stepped up and caved in its skull.

Manna-largenner came up to us and pulled his dog off the corpse.

'See, we have killed a kangaroo,' I said. 'The biggest boomer I have seen.'

'I have been watching,' he said. He indicated with a faintly twitching shoulder a low rocky ridge overlooking the plain. 'And so have Umarrah and his tribe.'

The chief seemed sanguine of us meeting the hostiles immediately. 'We had better,' he grunted, 'for I dreamed last night that they came upon us and speared us.' (It was quite singular that during the night I had heard the cracking of twigs, and it had occurred to me in the mist of sleep that it was the tribe.) Now it seemed that Umarrah's tribe had encamped about a quarter of a mile from us on the same evening and had been observing us from a hill near the camp ever since.

At first light next morning I sent Manna-largenner and three women in pursuit of Umarrah and his hostiles (the women as evidence of my pacific intentions and not as 'decoy ducks' as some of my critics alleged later) with instructions to approach them with the utmost diplomacy and tact, stressing that they were friendly emissaries of Mr Robinson, whose reputation among the native peoples was one of generosity and kindness. The chief permitted a slight rippling to pass over his chest and shoulders, gave two quick hoots and ran into the trees, followed by the women. His ululations rang in my ears as the forest closed over them.

When they were an hour gone I took Wooraddy and Truganini and followed the tribe's tracks from the ridge where they had watched us kangaroo hunting. No more than five hundred yards from my encampment we descried some trees where the blacks had peeled the bark to construct their huts, and, on passing through a thick copse of tea-tree came abruptly on their old camp. It was made up of one huge circular hut built of a framework of bent logs overlaid by sheets of bark and green boughs. (I measured its dimensions and found it to be twelve yards in length, sufficiently big to contain from thirty to forty people and the biggest hut I had seen in all my travels.) The ground in front was thickly strewn with emu feathers and splintered emu and kangaroo bones broken by the warriors for the marrow to anoint their bodies.

I had no doubt that these were the warriors who had committed the recent outrages in the vicinity of Launceston and on the east bank of the Tamar.

Four days passed while we remained around our central camp awaiting the return of Manna-largenner and his party—hopefully in the company of Umarrah. The general opinion of my natives was that the chief had been speared by Umarrah's men and that they had raped and abducted the women. What seemed to have confirmed them in this belief was the shadow of the earth on the face of the moon, it having not yet arrived at the full. They insisted this was Manna-largenner.

'The tribe has killed him and he has gone up into the moon,' Truganini muttered gloomily.

'They will kill us too,' Wooraddy grumbled, squatting on his heels above a bandicoot's hillock. He pressed the small mound with his hands and when the animal squirmed he thrust in a hand and pulled it out. Nonchalantly he crushed in the tiny creature's brains with his fingers and threw the body into Truganini's reed bag. 'They don't like me. We are enemies,' he insisted. 'They are savage people. They hate white men.'

Natives are bad politicians, I thought. They had no idea of persuasion. Their ideas extended only to force.

Smoke was sighted by my natives early on the 29th while out hunting.

Truganini said the Stony Creek tribe was making smoke as a signal of its approach. 'God grant that it may be so!' I exclaimed.

My expectation was great throughout the day as I saw the smoke nearing my encampment. In the late afternoon we heard voices and a *cooee* call. I told Wooraddy to *cooee* in return. Another call was heard in answer. Shortly we heard much talking and through the tea-tree swamp, heavily laden with belongings and trudging in single file, came six red-painted men and one woman led by old Manna-largenna and his party and followed by fifteen or sixteen gaunt dogs.

'Umarrah is with them,' Wooraddy whispered.

The man himself then approached me. 'Umarrah,' he said, prodding his scarred and ochred chest, and gave my hand a hearty shake. He was a polite young man, smallish and sinewy, as were the other five warriors. The woman was very old, wizened and naked apart from her worn skin cloak and a necklace of human bones, including the skull of a child drilled cleanly through with a musket ball.

Umarrah noticed my surprise at her age. 'The sealers have stolen all our women,' he said. 'Old Merlooner is the last.' The woman sighed and hunched down by our fire, pulling food scraps from her reed bag and throwing them into the embers.

'Is this your whole tribe?' I inquired, thinking of its savage reputation. I handed around the usual beads, buttons and blankets. 'From the size of your hut I imagined at least thirty or forty warriors.'

'To trick our enemies. Most of the men are killed, the women stolen. We have no children, the tribe will soon die.'

I told him, 'The Government wishes you to be content. If you will not spear white men you may come with me, get food and clothing'. At this Umarrah and his people lifted up their hands. 'Yes, yes,' they cried. So far from being mortal enemies, they embraced my natives and spent the evening in song and dance, a spectacle so joyously colourful it would have entranced any artist. I took a small part in the hilarity, dancing a couple of steps, such was my happiness. My natives were fascinated by the novel sight.

Manna-largenner alone did not join in the festivities, but sat stolidly against a stringy-bark clutching his spears and observing the merriment. The old major-domo watched over the camp all night, refusing to sleep.

'I will watch that the strangers do not knock out your brains,' he muttered, allowing a zealous series of tremors to pass over his body.

Now to find the Big River and Oyster Bay tribes! Umarrah offered enthusiastically to assist us, being familiar with the people and the country. 'You must tell the Governor Umarrah is a good man who found the *Parlerwar,*' he insisted. He was vastly enjoying himself in our party, not the least reason being the sudden increased supply of sable females. Before long he had cohabited with Woolyay, the Big River woman, and she became his 'wife', bringing him tree roots and catching him eels from the fresh lagoons in the region.

Woolyay was also our guide in these parts, leading us over stony hills and across grassy gullies, taking the normal path of her tribe towards the Big River. At a small plot of cider trees she pointed out the ashes of an old fire.

'We danced here,' she said, 'and sang songs of how we beat the Line of soldiers.' Evincing much feeling at the memory, Woolyay danced the victory dance again and hopped on all fours, mimicking the regimental horses.

'Hee-arr,' cried the natives, much amused.

She went then to a big fallen tree about forty yards from the dead fire and, reaching her hand into its burnt-out hollow, withdrew several bundles of spears tied around with pieces of woollen blankets and shirts, six waddies, a fowling piece, a tower musket, a leather bag containing bullets, slugs, buck and small shot and powder. The weapons were all in a tolerable condition.

'Montpeilliater's spears,' she said. 'He speared whites with them and hid them during the Line. The gun was stolen from the soldiers.' I felt that if any further proof were needed of the natives' confidence in me this revelation alone would be sufficient.

That night the locality of the two tribes was the subject of earnest deliberation. Manna-largenner said, 'I will ask my devil,' and threw his body into a paroxysm of tremors, rolling himself about and biting the ground. For several minutes his spasms raged until abruptly they left him, panting, deflated and moaning quietly. Grass and sand stuck to his lips.

'Well, where are the hostiles?' I asked. (I would have treated their superstitions with more contempt had I not wished their utmost co-operation in this enterprise.)

'Long way away. Near the banks of a river,' he gasped.

This was hardly a revelation. 'Tell your devil if I see him I will grab him by the ears and throw him in the fire.'

Umarrah too was the centre of attention, entertaining the others with stories on this and every night, many of them so long as to take upwards of an hour in relating, keeping them awake with the suspense until twelve or one o'clock in the manner of the Eastern storytellers.

Near the Peak of Tenerife we came to a river which ran from the mountains to a wide lake, from south to north. We paused so the natives could hunt the platypus on the river bank, digging out the animal from its nesting burrow.

After they had eaten the platypus I urged them to proceed in the southward direction indicated by Woolyay and Umarrah as being the likely resting place of the hostiles.

'We walk by and by,' Wooraddy yawned, stretching in the sun.

Manna-largenner sat in the soft ooze of the river bank plucking leeches from his ankles. 'My devil says we won't catch the warriors. Too far away.' The others agreed, flopping inert on the ground, suddenly perfectly indifferent to my aims.

I could not suppress my feelings at their languid unconcern. It now seemed clear that they regarded my crucial journeying as an attractive and protracted hunting excursion, one that they could undertake indefinitely while they were under my paternal safekeeping.

'We will leave here now,' I ordered. They did not move. A savage grin of satisfaction sat on their countenances.

'The hostiles will kill us,' Wooraddy said. 'It is better here.'

'If you don't come the Governor will be angry. You will be beaten and gaoled without food or blankets. I will tell him myself.'

Grudgingly they gathered their belongings and followed me. They mumbled husky complaints. Woolyay stifled a sly giggle and dragged her toes in the dust. I thought: No man can know my feelings. No one can know the intense anxiety of him whom God has called upon. But then all men have not the same ambitions, are not driven by the same forces.

'Come on,' I urged the natives in a gentler tone. 'If we walk far today I will give you sugar.'

On we trudged through gum and peppermint trees, frequently meeting animal bones on which the hyaena and other voracious beasts had preyed upon and finally halting for the night near another big lagoon. During the night I was ill, bilious from the peculiar wild game that had lately formed my diet. My mind was much perturbed, which added to my indisposition.

A small opossum-mouse woke me, scuttling across my neck. Quite unafraid, it allowed me to clasp it and I nested it in my blouse from where it could survey the scenery. The day was fine and warm. The sun's heat caused the mellifluous cider tree to send forth its sweet juice and my natives filled pannikins and drank deeply. As usual the people then went hunting, but shortly after ascending a hill above the lagoon they returned hastily and informed me of a big plume of smoke to the south-west.

'It is them,' Wooraddy said.

I despatched him with Umarrah and Woolyay towards the smoke, giving them all the counsel I was able. Manna-largenner elected to stay with me and the remaining natives.

'I will protect you,' he offered. Already a pulse was throbbing at his neck. 'I have fought the Big River tribe on this plain and they ran away up that hill.'

Truganini kept close by me. 'They will rape me,' she said matter-of-factly. I was incensed at her heathen nonchalance, her dispiriting lack of confidence. 'Not if your husband looks after you properly.'

'What if he is killed? You will not defend us with guns, shoot our enemies.'

'You must have faith.'

She looked at me in wonderment. 'Will he stop the enemy's penis? The God in England?'

I kept my attention on the smoke. It grew larger and my impatience increased. With three of the remaining natives I walked towards it hoping to meet the scouting party returning. Eventually Woolyay, Umarrah and Wooraddy came down the hillside appearing much pleased with themselves. Wooraddy chewed a wad of tree gum.

Umarrah said, 'We went to the fires and saw the tracks of their warriors. It is the Big River tribe.'

'I saw the tracks of my brother Popplena,' Woolyay said, 'and those of the chief Montpeilliater. We will go to them tomorrow.'

We returned to camp, agreeing that they should follow the tribe at first light next day. I felt somewhat dispirited but hoped for the best. 'You have exerted yourselves well,' I told them. 'The Governor wants us only to reach the tribes, then your work is done. You do not have to fight anyone.'

Again my stomach was gaseous and unsettled. I slept in the open within a ring of acrid natives, suddenly heartily tired of this sort of life.

A letter arrived. It began with a printed preamble which said:

The following letter should be regarded as a collector's item because it was posted on board the Oriana *during the course of Cruise No. 454 and went ashore from the ship off Niuafo'ou Island in an unusual manner on 6th February 1975.*

Niuafo'ou is one of the outlying islands of the Kingdom of Tonga, 400 miles from Tongatapu Island on which Nuku'alofa, the capital of Tonga, is situated. It is about three and a half miles long, three miles wide, and is of volcanic origin. An interesting point is that a large lake which lies in the old crater of the island contains islets which themselves have craters, and hot springs are found in various parts of the lake. The last volcanic eruption took place in September 1946. When this happened the homes and properties of the 1300 inhabitants were almost wiped out, so they were resettled on Eua Island, south of Tongatapu. About 200 villagers returned to Niuafo'ou in 1958 and the population is now about 600.

What is so unusual about the way this letter went ashore? Well, Niuafo'ou Island is better known by its nickname of 'Tin Can Island' because, as there is no good anchorage, at one time the regular means of mail delivery was for the ship's carpenter to seal the mail in 40-pound biscuit tins and throw them overboard, to be towed ashore by waiting 'postmen' in canoes. Hence the nickname 'Tin Can Island'.

The outward mail was made up ashore into several parcels and tied to the ends of sticks about three feet long. Two or three natives usually swam out, each with a stick topped by a parcel of mail, supported by poles of fau *wood of six to seven feet in length. These poles were very buoyant and easily carried the weight of a recumbent body. The parcels of outward mail were placed in buckets lowered from the deck of the steamer.*

This letter was included in a sealed canister which was thrown overboard off Niuafo'ou Island, picked up and taken ashore for forwarding to this address. As the government vessel in which the mail is conveyed to the Tongan capital sails only at five weekly intervals, it is likely that this letter could take up to four months to reach its destination.

Dear Stephen,

They say this will take up to four months to get to you, but can't pin a firm date on it because—according to a couple of officers I was chatting with over a few drinks last night—it depends on which of the Niuafo'ouan (did I get that right? The silly apostrophe confuses me every time!) canoeists picks up the 'tin can' containing the letters. The crew always stick a few packets of Players and some sweets in the can for the natives and this acts as incentive to encourage just about everyone to act as 'postman'. Apparently some of the older chaps take their time making the final mail drop in port. Then again the weather etc. can hamper the mail drop from the ship—and it might be too rough for any canoes to put out to sea and eventually the cans just wash up on some remote Niuafo'ouan (there's that word again) palm-fringed beach. Anyway, whatever the situation, I'm sure of one thing: this is going to take at least three months to reach you at the earliest.

I'm writing this in a far corner of the Princess Room. Stan Simpson is playing 'Morning Melodies' at the piano—bits of *Carousel* and *South Pacific* (naturally)—and a Cockney steward with a badly fitting jet-black hairpiece has just served me coffee. They say they're all queer as nine bob notes, if you know what I mean, but I must say they've looked after me very well. It's a beautiful day, balmy and sunny, and all the boys and girls are playing deck tennis, lounging round the pool etc. We crossed the International Date Line and they advanced the ship's clocks 24 hours at midnight, making today Thursday 6th February 1975. I must say it's nice to feel timeless and placeless for once and even though the news in the little one-page *Oriana News* I've got here is like news everywhere (Little Progress in Sadat-Gromyko Talks, Man Kicks Puppy to Death, Gas Explosion in High School, Danish Ham to Blame for Jap Food Poisoning) somehow out here it doesn't weigh you down quite so much.

What I'm trying to say is that I'm in a surprisingly happy and relaxed mood in case you think otherwise when you read this. I know I've never had the time to write much (or perhaps to spend as much time with you and Geoff when you were kids as I should have). I always had something on my plate at Hallstrom's. I know it wasn't easy for your mother being a company wife—she not having the sort of personality for making 'business friends' easily—so this is by way of an apology for all that. While I've been convalescing I think I've got to know you pretty well, playing Scrabble, having our few drinks at the pub, and I want you to know how thrilled it made me, our becoming friends for the first time.

When I think about it, this is the first letter I've written like this since the war when I used to send off long screeds to your mother from Wau just before going up in my old Boston. The attack route from Mubo to Salamaua and Lae where we eventually forced back the Japs (helped by the blokes in Beaufighters and some big-noting Yanks in A20s and Mitchells) was along narrow valleys walled by mountains over three thousand feet high. The path was so narrow two of us couldn't fly abreast. Each sortie was like a blasted switchback! There were plenty of natural hazards but cloud was the worst. A couple of good mates flew into cloud before my eyes and never came out the other side. And it's funny—none of our actual low-level swoops through the ack-ack over strips, oil dumps, installations and what-have-you (with the Japs crouching in their camouflaged gun positions under the mangroves) ever worried me half as much as flying into that grey-blue fleecy stuff and expecting to come up short against a mountain.

While you were being born I was in a 'tea party' near Buna being shot at by destroyers. The party began at dawn (about the time your mother went into hospital in Pop's Mercury!) and we caught the Jap warships with their pants down trying to reinforce Buna with troops and supplies. When I got back to base we all got drunk because of our luck and I didn't realize I had cause for a double celebration. I didn't hear the news for four days and didn't see you, of course, for several months. You didn't seem too sure about me for a while until my strangeness wore off.

Well, Stan Simpson has packed up his 'Morning Melodies' and now some peroxided popsy called Maureen is assembling the old boilers to demonstrate how to make gingham sunhats. Gingham sunhats are very big on board with the ladies of my age group. I must say I've been rather rushed by them during the voyage. Single men over thirty are rare as hen's teeth here. There's not many married ones over fifty or so, either. They're all long since 'coronaried', 'cancered' and 'stroked' while their widows travel the Pacific making gingham sunhats. I had to beg off quite a few fascinating invitations I can tell you, until the word flashed around the decks that I was 'not a well man' and the pressure eased up a bit. Now deck chairs are produced whenever I appear on deck, room is made for me at the bar, the entertainment hostesses flirt safely with me. I am in danger of getting a reputation for being 'brave'.

I didn't tell you before I left but when I get back to work I'm being shunted off on to a branch line where they put all the executive crocks. 'Manager of National Operations' they call it. They make it sound pretty dynamic and important, don't they? Actually it means you meet visiting VIPs at the airport, prepare Synott's Chamber of Manufacturers' speeches and take people to lunch and the management keeps you on the payroll. Until the next credit squeeze. Well, at least I won't be 'nationally operating' long enough for it to get me down. I don't blame Kevin Synott for taking the attitude that I've passed it, that I'm over the hill. (Just quietly, he's not in the pink of condition himself. I hear he had a nasty turn in the dining-room of the Atheneum Club!) You can't carry people in business today, not even if they've been with the firm forty years. They'd melt down their grandmother's shanks, some of the cut-throats in the gelatine business these days. And good luck to them.

I reckon this rambling screed will be the last letter you get from me, Stephen. Without making a song and dance about it, I won't last out another four months and don't particularly want to. It makes me angry that I feel like a frail old dodderer these days. I'm so pumped full of blood thinners and sedatives I can't keep my eyes open after 7 p.m. The blood pressure pills have other bad physical effects too, and I'm not *that* old. On the boat I've deliberately stopped taking half the junk so I can stay up and enjoy myself for a change. The old pulse has been doing a ton and I've had a couple of funny turns in the cabin but I've made it this far. And Ronnie, my cabin steward, a nice little bloke from Edinburgh, keeps an eye on me, brings breakfast in bed and so on.

I've named Frank executor of the will. I know you've never been too enthusiastic about the Surtees family but Frank's the sort of fellow who's handy to have around in matters of probate and what-have-you. I'm afraid I won't be leaving much—the house in Melbourne isn't paid off and my shares aren't worth the paper they're printed on. I never managed to save any money. You never do on a salary. Eileen will get a few bits and pieces, Geoff and you can divide up the rest after the Government's taken its whack.

I'm not sure how to finish this letter, keep it nice and light, say all the things it's hard to say in person. (That's right. You don't know how forbidding you can be sometimes. You could make me feel quite stupid with one of those 'intellectual TV interviewer' stares. I always felt more on Geoff's wavelength, I must admit. You're more intractable, less easy-going—or so it seemed until we began to hit it off over these last three months.) But I must finish now. I've got to write one to Geoff too and they've just announced over the loudspeaker that all 'Tin Can Mail' must be posted at the purser's office right away so it can be 'canned' ready for dropping at 3 p.m. off Niuafo'ou. Must finish. I hope you and Jane get back together again for yours and little Wendy's sakes. A divorce never did anyone's career any good. I also hope that 'Aboriginal Project' of yours, whatever it is exactly, works out for you. But what's at its foundation? I hope it's not as airy-fairy as it sounds. You know you can waste a lot of your life spitting into the wind and all you're left with is dribble on your face. By the same token you should try to sort things out in your mind. You seem pretty confused for someone your age, with your responsibilities. (At your age I'd fought a war, built a brick home, started a family, paid off a car—you wouldn't remember the old Austin A-40—and was doing well with the company.) What exactly do you want? That's what you've got to ask yourself. If I were you I'd be skedaddling back to the Commission and asking for my job back while I had the chance. Settling down like your brother. Pussyfooting around never got anyone anywhere.

Cheers—and love,
Dad.

P.S. I hope this doesn't shock you, coming well after the event, as it were. Arriving with my handwriting on the envelope and those funny yellow Tongan stamps shaped like bananas.

At dawn I woke determined that this day, 31st December, my arduous and harassing undertaking would be finished with the old year. We were camped at the foot of Frenchman's Cap whose grim volcanic cone rose four or five thousand feet above the plain. The Big River tribe was camped in thick forest ahead of us, two or three miles distant, their smoke still spiralling from the treetops. We advanced towards them along one of their hunting paths. Careless, or perhaps just confident of their strength, the hostiles were keeping no lookout and we were able to approach to within two hundred yards of their fires. I halted my people and sent Woolyay their tribeswoman, Umarrah and Wooraddy forward to inform the tribe I was nearby.

The hostiles had not yet seen us. They were sitting around their fires eating and conversing when my people appeared before them. There was a cacophony of yells and the warriors leaped to their feet and seized their spears, advancing menacingly towards Umarrah and Wooraddy.

The country was thickly wooded and overgrown with ferns. We instinctively ducked for cover in the underbush as they sounded their war whoop and rushed along the path towards us. I heard the rattle of spears and their agitated muttering as they drew nearer. At this moment my old guide, the chieftain Manna-largenner, jumped to his feet in great alarm.

'They will kill us!' he moaned, and urged me to run away.

'I must stay.' When I did not move he abruptly took up his spears and wallaby rug and fled, scuttling low and crab-like under the bushes.

From their warcries I believed they were rushing to spear us as they had probably already killed my advance party. 'Oh Lord, grant me strength,' I called aloud and stood upright amongst the ferns.

The tribe appeared before me on their hunting track. At the head was a stout and very tall man, obviously Montpeilliater, who carried a single spear at least eighteen feet long. His tribesmen surrounded him, each with three spears and a waddy. They were wild and wiry men, bullet-creased and glowering. With them was the biggest pack of dogs I had ever seen, more than a hundred bony, growling curs. The men quickly surrounded us, shouting their battle whoops and menacing us with their spears. Truganini crouched behind me, plucking at my trouser legs. I patted her head, caressed the soft and vulnerable nape of her neck. A single thought occurred to me: 'I think we shall soon be in the Resurrection.' I must have spoken aloud because my people turned to me in alarm, each quivering low on the ground. My intestines, gurgling loudly, gave up their grip.

Whispering prayers, befouled, I brushed off the clinging fingertips of my people and advanced towards Montpeilliater. I forced my arms to reach out in welcome and my throat to croak pleasantries.

'Who are you?' he shouted, waving his spear.

'We are gentlemen,' I answered in his dialect.

'Where are your guns?'

'We have none.'

Astonishment showed on his face. Still suspicious, he cried out, 'Where are your picaninny guns?'

'We have no pistols.'

Here there was much surprised discussion amongst the tribe. Amid the consternation Truganini recovered her will and sidled around the tribe to speak persuasively to her wilder sisters who were carrying fresh weapons in the rear. Woolyay appeared among the throng of naked, agitated bodies and did likewise, whispering earnestly with the old women. The men aimed their spears at us in watchful guard but during this seeming eternity of indecision made no further threatening moves towards us.

It seemed that the women were the tribe's true arbiters of war—being most threatened by any encounter with Europeans—thus it was with them that Montpeilliater deliberated on our fate. Suddenly the women threw up their arms three times.

'Keen-lee pug-ger,' they cried, the signal for peace. The spears were lowered. I approached Montpeilliater and offered my damp hand. He slapped his ochred chest twice, drawing my eyes to a long shiny scar—the work of a knife or bayonet thrust—then smiled and shook hands.

When I had first perceived the hostiles there seemed to be scores of them. Now, in relative tranquillity, I counted only twenty-six—sixteen men, nine women and a child—including the celebrated chief Tonger-longter of the Oyster Bay tribe, whose remnants had joined the Big River mob for security against the soldiers.Among the tribe I now also noticed my advance party, all unharmed and cheerfully greeting the tribesmen; Woolyay tearfully embracing her relatives, Wooraddy grasping the hand of Montpeilliater.

I spoke again in their dialect, distributing baubles to their delighted hands and explaining the purport of my visit. 'Sit down and drink tea,' I invited. 'Eat biscuit. Soon you may follow me if you wish, to a place with plenty flour, sugar, blankets. The whites will not molest you again. Otherwise ...' I shrugged my shoulders, 'the soldiers will hunt you.'

Montpeilliater considered my suggestion. He sat cross-legged, his stomach lapping his thighs, while he licked at a handful of sugar. The grains stuck to his lips. 'We do not want to be killed,' he said. 'Most of our people are killed.'

'You are right.'

'The soldiers are stupid but we are too few.' He licked his lips. 'Lead us to this place.'

They placed themselves entirely under my control and the evening was spent in mutual good humour, each party dancing and chanting alternately around the fire. I slept a dreamless sleep. My stomach, at last, was still.

Next mid-morning we set out for Hobart Town. We had not proceeded far when Montpeilliater led me from the track to the top of a thickly wooded hill where stood a newly erected hut decorated with crude paintings of emus, kangaroo and human forms. Adjoining the hut was a huge hollow tree from whence the chief handed out three excellent fowling pieces and three muskets. They were primed and loaded and in good condition, with pieces of blanket thrust in the muzzles.

'Take them,' he said.

'You may carry them.' A nice touch, I thought, that he might bear them back to civilization and surrender them to His Excellency as a symbolic gesture. Walking back down the ferny track towards my big throng of blacks I felt the sun playing warmly on my shoulders, heard the chattering of parrots, and a sweet thought struck me.

I had—through the blessing of the Almighty—brought tranquillity to the Colony.

My story concluded, as an Afterword (and rather than be seen to be blowing my own trumpet) may I quote, with all humility, from the Hobart Town *Courier* on the events of 7th January 1832?

On Saturday Mr George Robinson made his triumphant entry into town with his party of blacks, amounting in all to forty, including fourteen of his domesticated companions, with the twenty-six of which the Big River and Oyster Bay tribes was composed. They walked very leisurely along the road, the warriors still with dangerous spears in their hands, followed by a large pack of dogs. Shouts of welcome rose from the gathered crowd, which received the procession with the most lively curiosity and delight. They walked up to Government House and were introduced to His Excellency who evinced much pleasure at the meeting. Before the Governor's feast came presents, sweets, toys, pretty pictures, trinkets and, of course, dresses for the women. All were showered upon the savage ones in the hope that they would now be tamed.

Colonel Arthur pleased them with his courtesy and kindness. He ordered the band (under Captain Logan) to strike up a jolly refrain but unfortunately the wild aboriginals screamed with terror and rushed to Mr Robinson for protection. It was many minutes before they calmed down, but eventually they did and were even persuaded to touch the drums, though they did this as if testing the power of a growling animal. (This incident clearly showed the numerous spectators the power which the *Courier* has all along pointed out of this agent of communication in the savage breast. Much time, money and blood might have possibly been saved had the Government sent bandsmen into the wilder districts to tame the inhabitants into domesticity with trumpet and cymbal.)

A grand feast followed, during which their confidence increased, and after personally being decorated with gay ribbons by His Excellency they were persuaded to go through various feats of their wonderful dexterity with the spear and waddy. The chief Wooraddy put a crayfish on a spear and at a distance of sixty feet brought it down with another spear. Thus hours passed pleasantly in the Governor's garden, which was open to everyone for the occasion.

The blacks were one and all delighted at the idea of proceeding to Flinders Island where they will enjoy peace and plenty uninterrupted. After the celebrations, clutching their new toys, they proceeded on board the *Tamar* where they will be housed until the vessel is ready to carry them to Flinders Island.

On the sober question of the Flinders Island settlement—and whether the expense of the sable colony will ultimately devolve on the Mother Country or on us—it behoves the authorities to take especial care that the work of education and civilization is duly carried on. It is only by such means that the aboriginals can be rendered a productive people, so as to meet the exigencies of their own support. This may be considered a mercenary view of the case, seeing that the simplest ties of humanity would call upon us to discharge our part in the care of these benighted creatures. But independent of the burdens and difficulties of the settler on whom the expense of such a charge would fall--being already more than he can well bear—it would be alarming to contemplate a rapidly increasing colony of savages ignorant and incapable of providing for themselves, and depending solely on us for support.

The removal of these blacks will be of essential benefit to themselves and the colony. The large tracts of pasture that have so long been deserted owing to their murderous attacks on the shepherds will now be available. A very sensible relief will be afforded to the flocks of sheep that have been pent up on inadequate pastures—a circumstance which has tended to impoverish the flocks and keep up the price of butchers' meat.

Thanks to Mr G. A. Robinson, who must surely be generously rewarded by a grateful Colony, we now want only increased immigration, the abolition of the Colonial Office sale-of-lands measure and the restitution of the system of granting farms on equitable quit-rents to give full elasticity to the Colony's natural spirit of development and enterprise.

[Found—these pages of what is apparently part of a personal letter, or a copy of one—folded between the last leaves of *The Savage Crows* manuscript.]

. . . and is she still alive today in what would now be, the seasons being naturally the reverse of ours, that balmy southern autumn? I have wondered this ever since finishing my chronicle. Travelling down to Westbury last Tuesday to address the Mission Society I caught a glimpse of green sward just outside Trowbridge which put me in mind of the hinterland of Bruny—of the sloping meadows of Kelly's farm where the recalcitrant Truganini and her friends truly tested my patience with their flirtations so many years ago. Returning home to Bath that evening I sought this little piece of Antipodean landscape once more, but in vain. Perhaps it was the slant of the road or the noon light striking the meadow-tips that teased my sensibilities and half convinced me that over the next rise lay my first small establishment and beyond it the green sea.

Truganini, of course, has been in my mind lately for other reasons. Last month, as you know, the British Association for the Advancement of Science held its meeting in Bath, the 'Queen of Cities', a great honour for the city and for those of us members who reside here. On this occasion I mentioned her role in my journeys and it was one of the most satisfactory and successful meetings the Society has held. (The only drawback was naturally the unfortunate and melancholy accident to poor Captain Speke in the Dark Continent.) On the occasion of the meeting my esteemed friend Lady Franklin visited me, also the Arctic traveller Sir John Richardson and Lady Richardson, Sir John and Lady Lubbock and Doctor Davy, brother of the inventive Sir Humphrey. McDouall Stuart the Australian explorer spent a day with us at *Prahran*, and other scientific friends visited us. Indeed, it was one of the most delightful social gatherings I have experienced in a long time. Everyone present admired the Giani portrait of Rose and me which we had commissioned in Rome after our marriage in 1854. I am sufficiently easily flattered at my age to take comfort in such kind remarks, as I am in the interested attention some friends in the British Association and the Ethnological Society have shown in the manuscript of *The Savage Crows*. Lady Franklin, who with poor Sir John (to be so sadly taken among the Arctic ice packs not a decade later!) visited Flinders Island in 1838 while I was Comptroller, has been especially encouraging. She tells me (with the secretive air of the *confidante*) that I may yet be honoured by H.M. for my many explorations and benevolence among the aboriginals. Naturally I do not deem myself worthy of any more kudos than I have already achieved. My reward came from serving the Almighty and the Mother Country as I saw fit. Besides, McDouall Stuart tells me there is a lobby in Cabinet definitely averse to giving knighthoods to 'colonials'. Downing Street is believed equally apathetic. The Palace is also more excited, I hear, by good works in Africa, the Orient and the Arctic, finding these places more 'adventurous', an attitude I cannot share having experienced more than my portion of dangerous perils in the Royal service while some of those bumped-up, be-knighted clerks were sipping tea in the Raj!

Excuse my digressions. I was mentioning Truganini, or as I later christened her, Princess Lallah Rookh (I changed most of their names when I took control: Hannibal, Napoleon, Leonidas, Achilles, Washington, Neptune, Bonaparte, Arthur, Alexander and Alphonso sounded so much more euphonious and dignified than either their native or vulgar 'whiteman's' names). She continued to strain my good nature while, alas, retaining her special place in my attentions both during my command at Flinders Island and later during my Prefecture at Port Phillip. She would never have been charged with murder, for example, indeed the unfortunate deaths of the two sealers would not have occurred had she not been prey, as usual, to the unwise influences of men. As it was she absconded in New Holland with Wooraddy and Umarrah and was with them when they killed the sealers trying to entice her away at Westernport. Suffice it to say that she learned a good lesson from this folly; her acquittal and placement in my charge showed her the generosity of the British legal system (albeit a colonial version), her obligatory viewing of the executions served to stress the severity with which that system—the envy of the civilized world—regards crimes of atrocity. She was much affected as Wooraddy and Umarrah (incidentally, the first persons hanged in Melbourne) climbed up on the scaffold with some difficulty because of their pinioned arms. Umarrah was crying but Wooraddy, the stoic, uttered nothing. Truganini was amazed enough at the crowd of approximately six thousand people which had gathered for the event but never had I seen her so confounded as when the chaplain said, 'In the midst of life we are in death', and the hangman signalled to the puller below and the drop fell. (Unfortunately the drop descended only halfway and the natives twisted and writhed convulsively to mounting exclamations from the crowd until an alert member of the audience had the presence of mind to knock away the obstruction, thus clearing the fall. Umarrah died instantly but Wooraddy struggled for some five or six minutes.)

Maria and I took Truganini with us back to Van Diemen's Land and oversaw her welfare for a time but the illness which was to eventually overwhelm my first wife's fortitude had begun its depradations and after selling my land grants and taking stock of my various pecuniary rewards from the Government we were pleased to depart the Colony for England.

To conclude my friend, I trust that your company will treat my poor manuscript generously and that the hoped-for success of *The Savage Crows* will enhance both our reputations. One other thing: do you think the dedication 'To Truganini, the Princess Lallah Rookh' might be received a little askance by certain persons in the Association and elsewhere? If so, please replace it with 'To Lady Franklin'.

Your obedient servant,
(as ever)
G. A. Robinson.

15

Tallarook

DAYS NOW BEGAN in strange ways, damp dawn fogs dense enough to close airport and harbour traffic giving way to humid warm mornings acrid with the odour of brake linings, carbon monoxide, rubber tyre particles and other carcinogens. A broad-headed ginger tomcat tiptoeing along his kitchen window ledge suddenly jumped in and sprayed his breakfast table for him. Cornered against the stove it stood its ground pugnaciously, like a bulldog, neither hunching nor spitting but defending its new territory with gurgling growls and spasmodic twitches of a stumpy tail. He slammed the door on it in fear and when he opened it the cat had gone, leaving its stink on the breadboard—just the sort of disgusting thing they'd warned Jimpy would do before they'd had him neutered, coming groggily home from the vet's in a cardboard Karry-Kat and walking gingerly across the lino, stiff in the back legs, finally sitting, squatting rather, on his cute little furry painful orange empy scrotum. Now he can come inside, Mum said, and he won't get into fights and come home with tattered ears and, indeed, hadn't he been a faithful little pet to Geoff and him? Doggishly following them to school, sleeping on the bed-end, all for one meal of liver or whalemeat a day and all the water he could drink, preferring it to milk unlike Shep the Border Collie bought from 'Petland' where the proprietor lied about his distemper shots, so shortly he drooped about the yard with pus-filled eyes and snapped listlessly at Geoff whereupon he was 'sent to the country', as the family euphemism went, to live with imaginary dog-lovers of great kindness and many sheep-filled acres.

Emotion-charged zoological days in the suburbs! The panic in his mother's voice, ringing Hallstrom's in the middle of the 1958 Golden Anniversary Sales Conference to announce: 'Junior's fallen into a cup of black coffee! Hot Nescafé! What will I do?' (Have a cup of tea instead?) But his father was too furious at the interruption to the 1958 Golden Anniversary Sales Conference to be flippant about the budgerigar's accident. V.I.Ps from head office were in attendance. The slump in epoxy resins was under discussion. Nevertheless he dined out on the story for the next year or so. And the budgie, weepingly rinsed under the cold tap and fortified with an eyedropper of Dewar's, rallied around, opening little warty eyes and croaking, 'Today you'll use a Hallstrom product, my name is Junior Crisp, I love Mummy, Tie me kangaroo down sport', and other clever sayings before shitting a long pale streamer into her hand out of shock.

Mornings moved erratically into afternoons in leaps and bounds of depressing and curiously interconnected events and incidents. The papers told fascinating tales of disease and death. Surveys of complete towns carried out by anxious heart researchers on grants showed that 83 per cent of males over the age of twelve had unattractive cholesterol levels. Coffee and bacon regularly consumed together at the one meal predisposed the breakfaster to one of the nastier cancers. (The adjacent fried eggs, of course, assisted coronaries.) Two people had been found suffering from a new clinical disorder called metageria or premature ageing. Both had 'a bird-like appearance', were tall and thin, with prominent hooked noses. Their skin was mottled and pigmented. Diabetes and diseased blood vessels developed early. There was a loss of fat from the arms. (His skinniest feature!) It was believed the condition was inherited. Study of further cases might throw new light on the perennial question of why the body aged.

All food, bar organically grown fruit and filtered rain water, killed one. The air was poisonous and the lungs of city dwellers so withered and black thoracic surgeons were hard pressed to guess whether patients had smoked eighty a day or none at all. And breasts were being sliced regularly off the wives of the leaders of the Free World. But all was not lost. He read that the blind could now learn to read through their navels, via electronic scanners, masterpieces in miniaturization. A tiny television camera mounted on a pair of spectacles transmitted signals through a transformer to a metal pad worn across the lower abdomen. Each signal triggered the movement on the pad of minute metal reeds, half the diameter of a hair, which pressed against the skin to form the exact image or word being read by the camera. According to an expert in the field of navel reading, 'The area around the navel is ideally sensitive, making it relatively easy for the blind to recognize letters and images.'

Another medical optimist announced that death all boiled down to heredity. It was all in the genes, he said, and Crisp, perversely hankering after longevity above all else, added his parents' ages at death, divided by two and despaired. Visions of his own death were constantly with him, and not one of them a 'good' Hemingwayish death either, but after the fashion of Murray Crisp's, a lonely, not unexpected, but nevertheless terrifying occlusion on the toilet seat in the dead of night, the fall to the cold tiled floor, the hammering on the bathroom door, the towel rail pulled from the wall and the striped pyjama pants still around the icy blue ankles in the morning. And the toilet unflushed and rank. Better the mundane but dignified Last Speech of Jean Crisp, fighting to connect just enough cerebral circuits within the bloody pounding flood to announce the whereabouts of the breakfast beans.

Afternoons slipped crazily into evenings. A smiling man, middle-aged, with spiky, home-scissored hair, tapped on the door at dusk, leant slantingly over the threshold.

'Good evening,' he said. 'Beg your pardon but I have a message that could save your life.'

'Is this a religious call?' Crisp asked suspiciously. The man's general dinginess and lack of symmetry seemed to indicate this was the case.

'I bring some useful advice for today,' the man said, waving a bunch of yellow leaflets. His smile approached vacuity. He peeled off a leaflet and pressed it on Crisp.

'I'm agnostic I'm afraid.'

The man smiled relentlessly. 'Over seven thousand Australians will die of heart disease this year. Beg your pardon, but you might be one of the victims.'

Good God! 'Thank you, I'm busy,' he said, taking the leaflet and moving to close the door. But the smile seemed to be wedged in it, benign but forceful and exposing a set of dark-gummed dentures.

'According to the findings of the scientists heart disease is caused by too much cholesterol in the blood. To keep the amount of cholesterol low we have to stop eating animal fat.' His breath hit Crisp, sweet and lolly-sucking, a musk-aniseed mixture. 'The Bible agrees with the scientists here. Leviticus 7:23-27. John 6:1-13. Mark 5:11-13. God promised freedom from illness to everybody who obeys the simple rules laid down in His word. Exodus 15:26. Leviticus 11:1-47. Exodus 23:25. Psalms 105:37.'

'Not interested, sorry.'

Abruptly the man dropped his smile, slapped the bundle of leaflets against a palm. 'Yet the churches have twisted everything God said to mean just the opposite.' Indignant clicks sounded in his dental work.

'Acts 20:30. Jeremiah 8:8. Zephaniah 3:4 and so on. Check the facts sir, check the facts. They teach you may eat and drink anything you like but God said, "All day long they insult Me by eating pork and other forbidden foods." Isaiah 65:3-5. "Those who eat pork and forbidden meat will be destroyed together." Isaiah 66:15-17.'

'Thank you. Goodbye.'

'Just a second sir. They teach the soul is immortal, but the Bible says only God has immortality. One Timothy 6:16. And what about Ecclesiastes 9:4-10? "The dead know nothing, they have no part in anything here on earth any more." Or John 5:28-29? One Thessalonians 4:13-18? "I will raise them to life *on the last day*." The last day has not come yet sir, therefore *all the dead*, Holy Mary and the saints included, are still dead and in their graves . . .'

Crisp shut the door, backed away from it in shock clutching the yellow pamphlet. The voice droned on through the door. 'What about supernatural manifestations as seen in Fatima, Lourdes et cetera? Beware of counterfeits! The Sunday is the mark of a religious-political power. The Papacy! . . .'

Nothing ventured, nothing gained. Thick-headed, depressed, Crisp nevertheless essayed forth in the mid-morning, puffed up the hill to the shops, bought a bag of fruit and, shining an apple on his chest, sauntered towards the harbour to try to clear his mind for the thesis, meanwhile playing peculiar games in his head. (Unless I reach that kerb before the next car passes I'll have a heart attack!) Stepping out briskly to beat it, heart pounding on cue, experiencing the sweet momentary relief at winning that particular race at least.

'Watch your step, mate,' said the corner fruiterer, arranging oranges in his doorway as Crisp strode past, wheeling suddenly to avoid the indicated dog droppings and pulling a knee ligament. 'Fuckin' Labrador just did it,' the fruiterer said.

'Thanks.'

'Bloody mongrel. Hey mate, what you want to buy apples at Tony Conte's for? I got better fruit.'

'Next time,' Crisp promised, limping off.

The fruiterer adjusted his bananas. 'They shit anywhere they like. No one does nothing.'

Further along at the Caltex service station, as he passed with his apple bag, a queue of unusual vehicles was lined up by the petrol bowsers: seven identical wheelchairs carrying nodding grey geriatrics and chronic invalids in checked dressing gowns. Seven nursing aides stood idly by, smoking and chatting, while their charges had their wheelchair tyres inflated by the garage attendant. Pale sunlight gleamed on chromium spokes and footrests, fell on pallid foreheads and age-spotted hands. The patients were not speaking to each other but slumped in their chairs as the garageman scurried from one wheel to another, dragging the air-hose after him, applying it with a *phsst* to one valve here, another there.

'That'll do you for a few weeks,' he said finally, straightening up. The hose sprang back into its base, the aides finished their cigarettes and moved towards their patients. They set off in single file along the pavement, their outing over, their hard white tyres rolling soundlessly down the hill to their 'home'. *Eventide? Sunset?* One of the nursing aides, a sallow girl with short legs, bent over her lolling patient and shouted in her ear. 'All pumped up, eh Mrs Cleary?'

You read that they treated them like vegetables in some of those places, doping them up so they were trouble-free and inanimate, feeding them sparrow-sized meals, charging a fortune from guilty and grateful relatives, usurping their complete pensions. Even, he'd read, on hot days stretching them naked like frogs on the lawn and hosing them down. Better to go quickly with an excreta-induced chest spasm on the dunny seat or from a burst brain at forty-six. Perhaps even to drown with sand and weed in the lungs at seventeen, though he wasn't convinced about that. Nothing more dreadful than the death of the young, no sound as chilling as the wails of bereaved mothers. Chasing after them with cameras and microphones when their four-year-olds died from sandhill cave-ins or swimming pool drownings or discarded refrigerator suffocations or freak Christmas peanut inhalations, Crisp the budding TV reporter hadn't wanted to catch them, hoped they'd hide inside and send out red-eyed husbands to say piss off you jackals, you shit-eaters, and meanwhile the boys from the afternoon papers slipped inside anyway and got the baby snaps from the album and the studio portraits from the mantelpiece.

Wendy's face swam over all these imaginings, cupid-lipped, soft-cheeked, Wendy asthma-stricken, stifling in her own mucus, rolling (in frozen frame) over the Whale Beach cliffs in the school bus, gravely following slobbering sausage-fingered retards and their gift ice creams into old panel vans. Changing her first nappies he'd been amazed at the perfect neatness of her tiny mandarin segments, opening and closing with her wriggles and kicks, and when once he'd bent to kiss them she had arched her chubby back, gurgled happily and miraculously pissed in his eye. Violators would find liberal humanitarian Crisp a black-blooded fascist-father seeking punishment corporal, capital and eternal; alongside him Zeus would have been a bleeding-heart piker and Prometheus would have copped it sweet.

But she would leave him anyway, his only trace of her (pilfered on the last visit) her old feeding spoon, round-bowled and with a panda on the handle.

He was sweating from the sun and the exercise. He removed his windcheater and tied it around his waist, rolled up his shirt sleeves. The right arm was scarred jaggedly at the elbow—no heroic injury, the result of slipping on the quarry-tiled patio at one of David Appleyard's Sunday afternoon parties and tearing it on a wrought iron railing. He hadn't even been drunk, he'd slipped heavily and foolishly on a pickled onion or something, but Appleyard's fetish for order and decorum had registered a demerit. He hadn't been asked again. Even as Lola Appleyard was staunching the wound, dabbing it with Mercurochrome and providing Band-Aids, he had felt the transient nature of his visit. Among the favoured producers and administration heavies he had been momentarily accepted at the Commission because of some fleeting curiosity about his intractability, his informed and aggressive interviewing techniques. This had soon palled, he'd discovered, but on that Sunday afternoon he'd drunk numerous nervy clarets in the sun, made several forthright opinions in exalted company to make up for the patio stumble, had even caused some noted wits to laugh once or twice. But he had overstayed of course, still drinking wine well after sundown, and for some now unfathomable reason had been making a tipsy red-headed actress choke with laughter by reading to her an old Fantale chocolate wrapper (souvenir from some film night with Anna?) discovered in his jacket pocket:

ROCK HUDSON. This handsome six-foot four-inch giant's husky good looks and steadily improving acting have made him the world's No. 1 male actor. Born Roy Fitzgerald in Illinois in 1925, Rock was a truck driver until 'discovered' by agent Henry Wilson. After a series of 'pretty boy' roles Rock hit the top in *Magnificent Obsession*, hasn't looked back since.

'Steadily improving acting!' the actress shrieked.

Appleyard, nattily dressed in New York casuals purchased on a recent trip, had wandered up to them during the merriment collecting dirty glasses, adjusting scattered savouries, flicking peanuts into his mouth.

'What's so funny?' He smiled aggressively.

'Listen to this, David—"Rarely off the top box office stars' list, popular William Holden was born in Illinois in 1916. He burst on to the screen in *Golden Boy* in 1939 and won an Oscar for his acting in *Stalag 17* in 1953. An inveterate world traveller, Bill makes Europe his headquarters these days, rarely returns to Hollywood." '

'Collect those things, do you?'

'I just found it in my pocket. I wonder who writes that stuff?' Crisp crumpled the wrapper and dropped it in an ashtray. The actress had stopped giggling, was anxiously arranging a shawl around her shoulders, rounding up her cigarettes, lighter and beaded bag.

Appleyard said, 'I wonder if you'd mind going now? Lola and I have a busy day tomorrow.'

Up in the power lines ahead of Crisp a flying fox dangled electrocuted, stiff as a board. It had chosen to hang simultaneously from two closely parallel wires strung near its fruit-laden Moreton Bay fig tree and now, the life scorched out of its furry, foxy body and leathery bat wings, it would hang there rigidly until removed by a linesman. Its body was much bigger than those of run-of-the-mill bats. The summer he and Anna first lived together they'd been wakened by the screeching, fighting and flapping in the trees beyond *Cardigan* and had been bewildered for a week or so by the big, night-flying 'birds'.

Dreaming out the bathroom window one tepid night, brushing her hair, dabbling in the hand basin, feeling the breeze, she shrieked, 'They're huge bats! Vampires!' She was naked and suddenly goose-fleshed.

'Aha, show them your cross.' Though a professed agnostic (or humanist, as she called herself) she wore at the neck a tiny cross that had been her Catholic mother's and her grandmother's and so on back into the vast aeons of Yugoslav and Austro-Hungarian time. 'Got any Transylvanian ancestors?' he joshed.

'Funny.'

He joined her at the window, patted her round European buttocks. 'They're just flying foxes,' he soothed. The animals wheeled and flapped against the navy-blue backdrop of the Harbour Bridge and the city's buildings and he said, 'Amazing, all that jungle wildlife not a mile from the G.P.O.'

She shivered and pulled on her pants. 'Imagine getting one in your hair!' For several nights she insisted on sleeping with the windows closed.

Crisp turned off the main road and headed for the nature reserve on the headland. His knee twinged where he had twisted it avoiding the dog turds. The body's crumbling was proceeding apace, degeneration in every limb and organ. The joints went first and hadn't grey hairs been sneaking around the edge of the head and materializing at the throat and chest? He was puffing up a small steep hill. Joggers pounded past him breathing regularly and efficiently, their rubber soles making little squeaks of fitness and energy on the asphalt. Time was when he could have beaten the lot of them, whippet-thin and speedy, expending his sixteen-year-old's sexual energy in mile and half-mile races, racing every Saturday afternoon in silk shorts light as air, nylon jock, red singlet Number 101 and a pair of running spikes handmade from kangaroo skin. With enough left over for the Saturday night dance, vigorous girl gropings and swigs of warm beer from the bottle in the back seat of Harley Onslow's parents' car. And home like Cinderella by midnight with shin soreness from the running track, an aching, thwarted groin and a mouthful of Juicy Fruit to chase the beer from the breath.

So after a couple of years of Saturday night 'lover's nuts' who could blame him (though plenty did) for being so enthusiastic about the habit when he and Jane, his first serious, *mature* girlfriend, actually *did it*, pulling out quickly the first time before thinking *Jesus!* and leaving it in thereafter, snuggling under her eiderdown with the chair under the bedroom doorknob, *Australia's Hour of Song* on high volume and her mother playing bridge two rooms away. The days when nervous tension made it go up instead of down.

'I thought it had a bone,' she whispered. 'I really did.' And *macho* Mr Seventeen, sliding in for his umpteenth burst of rapid fire, pulled her pink shoulders close and chuckled, 'Heh, heh.'

An oil spill had stained the rocks at high-water mark along the bottom of the cliff. Gingerly, favouring his aching knee, Crisp picked his way down steps cut into the rock-face to the harbour. At the water's edge a wide rock pool with a sharkproof fence had been built back in the days when this part of the harbour was clean enough to swim in. He stepped along the rocks, peering into the oily shallows. Could anything live in this? Even the seaweed looked lifeless. Through rainbow smears at the shoreline the faintest of movements caught his attention—an undulating, the slowest of slitherings, was occurring at the edges of his vision. Squatting down he saw several, then scores of slowly shifting blobs. Glossy black, like shapeless oil globules, they glided over the bottom of the pool, seemingly grazing on grease, science fiction sea-slugs big as milk bottles. Adapting to their environment? Nourishing themselves on pollution ready for the big takeover when all human lungs had collapsed together from a surfeit of brake linings? Soft-bodied like his childhood silkworms, so soft you didn't quite know if you were touching them or not, munching away regardless on their mulberry leaves in the shoebox with the airholes punched in.

The stuff of nightmares, like his old teaque dreams. (As he grew older he had found another way to survive the teaques' rapacious hunger. Apart from sacrificing Harley. When they flummocked towards him belching their rancid breath, rasping against his legs, he'd lie down right where he was in the dream and instantly fall asleep, waking in his real bed with a high sense of victory. This almost hypnotic ability he had refined down to a matter of seconds. Here they came, heaving their jelly-flesh over the sand, poised to eat him. Click. There he was in the sleep-out, his box of comics under the bed and the moonlight coming through the fly-wire and striking the porcelain pot under little Geoff's bed. Beside his bed-head was his watch with the luminous dial and his Benson and Hedges cigarette tin full of foreign coins.)

Then he had somehow had the knack of avoiding trouble.

Edgily, Crisp circuited the pool, then climbed up another flight of irregular stone steps and walked around the headland, keeping to a narrow path worn into the hillside. Every so often he passed a cave or a pair of caves, natural rock formations some of whose frontages were blocked in, with wooden or iron doors, air vents and an occasional rusted tin chimney jutting obliquely from the rock roof. During the thirties' Depression homeless men had been cave-dwellers here, living in the damp among the funnel-web spiders, catching fish from the rocks, trapping the odd rabbit and plodding forth each day up into the North Shore to plead for work: a spot of weeding or firewood chopping and hopefully a pinched parsnip or two from the bank manager's garden.

Old Pop Crisp, struck dead on the bowling green at seventy-nine (not a foot from the jack), had taught him an old Depression verse, plonking him on his long bony knees while he prodded him in the chest to get the beat and reciting:

There ain't no work in Bourke.
No lucre at Echuca.
Damn all at Blackall.
Things are crook at Tallarook
(or Muswellbrook).
Got a feed at the Tweed.
No feedin' at Eden.
Everything's wrong at Wollongong.
Might find a berth in Perth.
In gaol at Innisfail.
Got the arse at Bulli Pass.

'Oh, don't say that word Pop!' his mother said every time. Talk of depressions depressed her. Pop would just laugh, sitting there exuding his elderly smell of nicotine, singlets and dandruff.

Now skylarking kids trod the unemployed's paths around the headland, at night possums scratched at rubbish baskets, and middle-aged men liaised, their current model sedans nosed into the bush, with secretaries or each other. Joyriders of some resourcefulness would push Falcons and Valiants over the cliff, setting them first on fire and sensibly retaining the licence plates. Recently a Greek cab driver had been stabbed to death there and rolled under the wire fence of the adjoining coal depot. Very mysteriously, his cash bag was untouched and his taxi found in flames on the other side of the harbour. Crisp passed the spot now. It had been marked with an X on photographs in the afternoon papers. They had the theory that the murder had been committed by 'the Greek equivalent of the Mafia'. He knew someone once, personally, who'd been murdered. Back in Perth. Gerald Nairn, an agricultural science student, he'd run 440s against him in 1958 or 59. Poor Nairn, sleeping on the back verandah of his boarding house near university when a complete stranger tippy-toed up in tennis shoes and put a rifle to his head because he couldn't live with his own hare-lip. Even though he was God, said so in court, he still couldn't live with his hare-lip because of childhood teasing and sexual rebuffs. So he shot Nairn, a fifty-year-old account executive who answered his 3 a.m. doorbell, a bookie, a barmaid and the vice-president of the Swanbourne golf club. The bookie and the barmaid (who were in each other's company looking at the ocean) survived the shots through the car's steamed-up rear window; the golf club vice-president, like Nairn asleep in bed, lost the best parts of his brain and vegetated expensively for five years. Only the account executive and poor Gerald Nairn—not a bad sprinter at his peak—died on the spot.

But there were many other violent deaths of friends or acquaintances. Everywhere he looked. He made a rough chart in his head. *Deaths, in order of age:* Marilyn Stonor, taken to the movies twice, the Australia Day carnival once, kissed three or four times at age fifteen (head severed five years later by Cessna propeller after rushing from just-landed aircraft following argument with grazier husband); Brian 'Stal' Rowlings, muscular rower and footballer, school classmate, aged fifteen (self-inflicted .22 rifle shot to the head after illicitly borrowing father's car and running it into stationary dry-cleaner's van); Clive 'Rags' Schupp, handy centre-half-forward and boxer, aged seventeen (electrocuted by fallen power line on way home from football training in windy winter dusk); Peter L'Estrange, attendee of same first-year psychology tutorials, aged eighteen (motor accident); Gordon Palmer, Commission trainee cameraman, aged nineteen (light aircraft crash in Indian Ocean while covering search for missing crayboat); John Hassett, neighbour, aged twenty (motor accident); Andy Melrose, former classmate, aged twenty-one (motorcycle accident); Graham O'Halloran, John Marshall and Tony Vanderpost, journalists, aged twenty-four, twenty-six and twenty-five (ambushed in jeep by Vietcong on outskirts of Saigon even while yelling frantically '*Bao chi! Bao chi!*—Press! Press!'); Kevin Henderson, drinking companion and journalist, aged twenty-eight (swept away by flash flood and mudslide after party in Kowloon); Maureen Donnelly, TV researcher, slept with once after party, aged twenty-eight (suicide—wrists); June Hancock, magazine journalist, beautiful rosy complexion, platonic friend, aged twenty-eight (suicide—overdose); Nigel Hurst, John McKinlay and Peter Burkitt, journalists, aged twenty-nine, thirty-two and thirty-eight (severed head, severed femoral artery and brain injuries respectively, received from broken, spinning shards of helicopter propeller blade while guest of oil company's PR department aboard off-shore oil rig in Bass Strait. All enjoying sunshine on rig's flight deck when helicopter mislanded thirty yards from them); Paul Samuels, TV scriptwriter, aged thirty-four (motor accident); Margaret Ivanoff, feminist friend of Anna (motor accident); Tony Butterworth, *bon vivant* and Parliamentary press secretary, aged thirty-five (choked by lump of beef in windpipe during Friday luncheon to celebrate the fall of Saigon); Michael Giambazzi, TV producer, aged fifty-two (washed overboard from sloop off Broken Bay) . . .

And one omitted of course. Harley Onslow, aged seventeen, drowned. *Drowned* for Christ's sake! Just a dream surely. He's only playing funny buggers and any moment now will surface from the waves like a smart red-haired shit. And if not I'll search for him and persevere until I find him. Resuscitate him using approved 1959 Royal Lifesaving Society methods. Extract weed from mouth and throat with index finger. Ensure no dentures to block breathing. Turn patient on his stomach. Kneel at his head, facing down his body. Lay his head on its side on his folded arms and commence pressing firmly and rhythmically with the hands just below the shoulder blades. One, two, three. One, two, three. Swing back and forth to this count, pressing firmly and regularly. If patient doesn't respond give him the newfangled 'Kiss of Life'. For this method the rescuer turns the patient on his back. If the rescuer prefers (in the case of a male patient) he may forgo the lip contact of the mouth-to-mouth position for mouth-to-nose resuscitation. In any case *do* hurry up, bring him round, tend any welts from marine stingers with methylated spirits (wet sand is a useful substitute). Walk him up to the clubhouse, administer a cup of tea, then pack him off home in a blanket.

Down the hill and past the coal depot he trudged, eyes searching once more for any grim traces of the late Greek taxi driver. None were visible amongst the skid marks and oil streaks on the bitumen. (A bachelor, the papers said, with no family here and a quiet fellow, boarded with a Leichhardt family, no drinker but liked to gamble in a small way at the Athenian Club. Once part-owned a greyhound with several wins to its credit but sold his share to a countryman in 1973.)

Alongside the coal depot in a small white-fenced enclosure was a slab of rock on which the Port Jackson Aborigines had many centuries before engraved a drawing of a big fish—probably a shark from the shape of the dorsal fin—with a man inside its stomach. More recently a European, possibly from the Department of Main Roads, had traced around the engraving's outline with thick white road-marking paint. In the rock's depressions were slick pools of coal-dust blackened rainwater and two sodden Kentucky Fried Chicken boxes. (In farthest North Queensland Anna and he had visited a remote Aboriginal mission run by the Lutherans north of Cooktown, travelling there in a Land-Rover through jungle and stream and over soft dangerous tracks of brown loam. At the mission all the Aborigines made their boomerangs, message sticks and spears on mechanized lathes in a large, well-equipped workshop, hundreds a day, and for a price they'd engrave your name on one, using electricity.)

Bumping back to Cooktown Anna had stroked his vacation beard and her breasts had jounced unceasingly for thirty miles. She had a way of walking, straight-backed, head high, that he admired and she blushed when he complimented her. A funny thing about her: her ear lobes contained little lumps; squeezing the lobes he'd feel tiny hard spots hidden in the plumpness. They slightly embarrassed her.

'I don't like baring my ears,' she said. 'It makes me feel vulnerable.' Jane, on the other hand, had virtually no lobes at all, the ears curving down gracefully into the sides of her head. It made it uncomfortable for her to wear ear-rings but otherwise she couldn't have cared less.

'Bing Crosby's got ears like mine,' she told him once, and when they saw *High Society* he observed that indeed he had. Both Jane and Anna had admired *his* ears, despite their tendency to project a long fair hair from the centre of each auricle.

'Nice,' Anna had remarked, snuggling in with her nose one Sunday morning early in their relationship. They were lying on a blanket in the park reading the papers and munching peanuts. She inserted a nutty tongue tip in each of his ears. 'Leathery but nice.'

How different they were, Anna and Jane. Anna, the voluptuary, would lie on top of him, along him, dangling breasts on his skin while he drowsed, cheekily kissing him to action with soft and well trained orifices, scuttling backwards to the foot of the bed to launch hungry attacks. They made love in unlikely places, later discovering stains on divers surfaces and fabrics. She called them 'maps of Tasmania', apt enough considering his other passion, and, nude and pink-blotched, would call gaily from making coffee in the kitchen, 'I'm leaking like a sieve.' Her nose was aquiline (Jane's was a pert snub job), with narrow nostrils through which her breath whistled softly in sleep and passion. She had been known to moan and sob and call for God (and, in Yugoslav, her mother) and he could not forget her seagull cries in the dark. In their tiny bedroom the frayed net curtains had drooped from the window pelmet over the bed and once during their threshing he'd caught a toe in the curtains and brought them down on top of them, curtain-rod and all.

'You make the earth tremble,' she said solemnly.

'You make the heavens open,' he offered, and they writhed in the tangled curtains and bedclothes, caressing and laughing until tears came.

I wonder who's trembling her now.

Sex with Jane, after Wendy's birth, had first been an anxious and deadening ritual of foams and jellies, then, with the advent of the contraceptive pill, an even more tense affair as she, rattled and disorganized, forgot to take it. (Then, too, he'd shied distastefully away from condoms.)

'Motherhood isn't very sexy, is it?' she murmured one night, an apologetic moistness in the eyes, seeking rebuttal. Beyond their bed Wendy slept in her little cream bassinet. Teddy-bear transfers frolicked across its sides. The room smelled of baby powder and oils and the warm, pervading presence of infant flesh. The effect of Jane's nightdress, blue and lacy, was offset by the breast pads and maternity bra. Her hair was shiny nut-brown and fluffy from shampooing and she had made up her face. A dab of beige powder masked a blemish on her chin.

'Of course it is,' he lied, fondly and sadly, and began gently to stroke her. Around the straps and nipple flaps. A tiny sound came from the bassinet, a gurgle, and Jane clutched at her breasts.

'I'm leaking,' she whispered. 'That's all it takes. If she makes one sound they just pour it out. They've got a mind of their own.'

It tasted curiously sweet but you couldn't live on it forever.

Down streets, a short cut through a harbourside park and fatigue and the sun overcame him. He lay on a sloping lawn by a bowling green, stretched out on his back, closed his eyes. Blurred voices sounded up from the green. 'Good girl Iris!' a woman called and there was the light clapping of two or three pairs of hands. The child-feeling of lying on grass swept over him, the sun on the skin, the brain emptying and filling, sifting everlasting snippets of trivia and reabsorbing them: *Chester Gould draws Dick Tracy and B. O. Plenty's pop-eyed wife is Gravel Gertie . . . I've got the bell-bottom blues 'cause my sweetie is a sailor . . . Bud Abbott is the thin one and Lou Costello is the fat one . . . Maureen O'Hara is very pretty with nice red hair . . . Four hundred years ago on a remote Bengali beach a man swore on the skull of his father's murderer . . .*

An American came home to dinner with Dad at short notice and Mum had to spread the meal around. Short, sandy hair, rosy cheeks, an amazing accent. 'This is wonderfully hospitable of you,' the American said, and won Mum around. 'This is Stephen, he's doing well at school.' 'Is that so? Nice to meet you, Stephen, or do I call you Steve? Well here's a little problem for you, Steve, what's three nines?' Three multiplied by nine? Mind turned embarrassingly, idiotically blank, fazed by the accent and the excitement of meeting a real American. Hours passed. Everyone in room, city, country hanging on his utterance. Tears coming fast but averted by fast-thinking American. 'Say, do you play sports, Steve? Terrific!' Remainder of evening he was in the American's thrall, hanging about the conversation dressed in a succession of cowboy suits and football togs. 'I'm a registered Republican,' the American said. 'I believe your parties are a little different to ours.' 'Oh, the Liberal Party recognizes the importance of business,' Dad said. 'Square dancing has caught on here like wildfire,' Mum said. 'We love it.' Dad said with a laugh, 'Ross Warner, our top dance caller, makes more than Prime Minister Menzies.' 'It's so kind of you to have me in your home,' the American said. His hair and clothes were different, his shoes were heavy and round-toed and later he sent Mum a thank-you bouquet of flowers. 'What a lovely gesture,' she said. 'You can't beat the Yanks for manners,' Dad said. 'I meet a lot of them these days.'

His parents gave a party and he was woken by tiptoeing and shooshing guests peeping in at Geoff and him sleeping. He lay doggo during the whispered admiration of their inert forms but when the adults had gone back to the party he crept down the hall towards the laughter and there was Harry Dengate the lawyer with his pants rolled up and his, Stephen's, waterproof sou'wester perched on his bald head, singing in an eye-rolling mock falsetto:

I don't care if it rains or freezes,
I am safe in the arms of Jesus.

I am Jesus' little lamb.
Yes, by Jesus Christ I am!

On the way back to bed he went to the lavatory and someone had pissed all over the seat.

Dad returned from a business trip to the Eastern States with a present—a pair of Phantom Ranger jeans. The first Phantom Ranger jeans in W.A.! With the Phantom Ranger's masked head on a star background stencilled on the reversed denim of the front pockets. Wore them proudly to school, kids very impressed right up to nine o'clock when he went to the lavatory before assembly and the zipper broke at the first tug. Stood in assembly on school verandah with fly open amid girls' giggles. Flew home crying to resume khaki Yakka shorts. Flyless but trustworthy.

'Ladies, afternoon tea is served,' announced a voice on the bowling club's sound system and Crisp stood up, brushed the grass from his clothes and put on his windcheater. He picked up his bag of apples. White clad, broad-hipped and bow-legged figures meandered to the edges of the green. Crisp sauntered past the clubhouse, separated from the matrons by a low wire fence. In his hearing one said to another, 'How's Mavis bearing up?'

'You know Mavis,' came the answer.

He headed back to *Cardigan*. Of course, he reflected, the person who had decorated that Aboriginal rock carving had probably had the best intentions. (Embolden it, give it some oomph, show them what the old witchdoctor had been trying to say with his shark carving back in 1312 or whenever.) They'd had the best intentions when old Truganini died in 1876, too.

Well remembering Billy Lanney's fate she had begged the doctors and scientists not to mutilate. 'Bury me proper', she said, enough of Conciliator Robinson's religion having rubbed off on her. The gentlemen of the Royal Society were once more clamouring for a body, in the public interest. Oh no, the Government had been adamant, no more body-snatcher's carts, so this time the coffin was locked in the gaol and next day buried in a secret grave observed by the Premier and the Colonial Secretary. A funeral of dignity and decorum. No possum skin rugs and Union Jacks by request. Five husbands, scores of lovers and numerous rapists gone before her, slaughtered, hanged, syphillitic and tubercular; even Conciliator Robinson (the self-aggrandizer, the cop-out, the *petit-bourgeois* paternalist. '*I am the Father!*') ten years mouldered in Bath's quiet soil. The last of the Tasmanians now buried in a plain wooden casket marked 'Truganini, died 8th May 1876, aged 73 years'. So, the old coquette laid peacefully to rest, extinction officially observed, time was ripe to pay belated tribute to her race's admirable traits. 'Essential nobility' was very popular, 'tragic stoicism' another favourite. Dignified breast-beating was permitted in the letters columns of responsible newspapers. So vigorous was support of the lost Aboriginal cause that only resurrection would satisfy its new worshippers. Out came Truganini, exhumed, tidied up, lacquered and stapled to the museum wall.

Inside the flat again he paced and sat alternately, agitatedly tore cuticles with his teeth, stared vacantly out the lounge-room window, unable to work, to concentrate on any subject for longer than a minute or two. (No glare flashed from the out-of-season daisies today—their leafy stems hung haggardly over the garden edge.)

Things get bad and then worse. Memories crowd and fears impinge and pretty soon there are pains beneath the breast-bone (Is this it? Finally?) and a pressure in the forehead and temples (Perhaps the brain first—a victory for the maternal genes!) Complications become so oppressive something must give. But look on the bright side. Where? Surely not at parents, wife (ex), daughter, lover (ex), friends dead and alive, health, finances, work, state of nation, international affairs, world climatic instability and the anticipated melting of the Polar ice cap. Disorder and unhappiness are all about.

(But consider the lot, say, of the widow of Haji Abdus Shahid of Sylhet, Bangladesh, 'gifting away' her small daughters aged eight and six for ten taka each so they can avoid the small foxes feasting on the wide selection of unclaimed humans lying on the local railway junction waiting for the temple pickup truck. While officials smuggle fish, rice and powdered milk over the border to the Indians in exchange for those necessities of life—lipstick, cigars, toothpaste and *Time* magazines.

Or imagine, for that matter, the state of ten-year-old 'Danny' Das, sleeping on the phlegm-spattered kerb of Jawaharlal Nehru Road, Calcutta, in the fire smoke, cow dung and carbon monoxide. Waking each morning by the steps of the Roxy Cinema to lead his blind grandmother forwards to the gutter, to pass her a tin of water and watch her pour the water on her feet and clean them. Then lead her back to the cinema wall—she leaving a fading trail of damp footprints—arrange her mat against it and help her down by the elbow. Alongside his two younger brothers, both coughing in the sun, the youngest sitting watching his spit fall in a waving tendril on the cinema steps. His grandmother scratching at her head lice with both hands. Chasing up a trace of food for all of them before setting off to tout: 'You want girl? I get you beautiful girl. You watch two girls nekked? Kashmir girls. They do everything. You watch. You want massage? They massage you everywhere, on all your parts. Oh yes sir!' While visiting people from Developed Countries grimace in pity and distaste—'I shut off when I see beggars using kids. I mean you could go mad if you didn't shut off'—'Danny' Das is safe under his country's expensive nuclear umbrella.)

Crisp thought, I have considered them and their *real* suffering only increases my chaos.

He must get out of *Cardigan*'s confines, escape spartan bachelor routines, views from the lavatory and the smell of cat piss. Flee from the thesis, the delving into dusty reputations and the navel-gazing self-absorption of the old and mad. At this rate he'd be undertaking mucus-free diets and administering thrice-a-day enemas before long. (Only yesterday he'd caught himself checking dormant hæmorrhoids with a hand mirror.)

Away, away on his own colonial odyssey.

16

The Mutton Bird King

MIND AGITATING on several levels next morning, Crisp showered, shaved (how hairy his nostrils were becoming! Brown antennae peeping out to right and left easily avoided the razor's corner), dressed, packed an overnight bag, ate a Vogel's bread peanut butter sandwich, caught a taxi to the airport and, using a slightly dodgy credit card, took an economy flight to Melbourne. *Cardigan* could not hold him now.

After an hour's delay he took another flight to Launceston, arriving just after noon. He carried his bag over to the inquiry counter. 'Flinders Island,' he said. 'When does the next plane leave?'

The clerk rustled through his schedules. 'Three hours time, 3.15.'

Crisp waited in the airport cocktail lounge drinking glass after glass of the local beer, folding and refolding drink coasters in his fingers until the damp cardboard fell apart. An ashtray before him became gradually heaped with paper pulp. The barman, white shirted and with a clip-on bow-tie, did a quick supercilious trick, plonking another ashtray on top of the full one, turning them upside down, leaving the clean one in its place. But he said nothing about the coasters.

Crisp was finally prepared. He found a phone booth, obtained a dollar's worth of change, a Hobart telephone directory. He thumbed through the Ks, found six Katers. One was an electrician, another a marine engineer; the third entry was for a Doctor M. P. J. Kater and provided numbers for his city surgery and home address.

Beer bubbled in his stomach and he belched into the dead mouthpiece. He felt vaguely nauseous, atwitch with nervousness. It cost him some effort to ask the operator for Doctor Kater's surgery number, to listen to it ring, to ask the receptionist if he could speak to the doctor, an urgent personal matter, yes he'd hold on. He wanted urgently to urinate, his bladder throbbed.

'Yes, who is this?' The voice was deep and fruity. An important voice. Definitely that of a man with ancestors.

'Ah, I'm ringing on behalf of my organization. We're involved in historical research. Setting the record straight. Certain anthropological aspects. I'd like to ask you some questions, Doctor, if you don't mind.'

'Who am I talking to? Are you a patient? I'm a busy man.'

'Crisp's the name. I'm operating under the auspices of a government grant. Intrigued by your family, Doctor, by your ancestors and their role in the last days of the Tasmanian Aborigines. Very prominent role, finger on the pulse of the colony and what-have-you. Important Establishment figures.'

'Never heard of you, I'm afraid. Perhaps you could write me a letter. I have a waiting-room full of patients.'

'No time for that, Doctor. I have a plane to catch. Just one question but please elaborate if you wish . . .'

'I must go.'

'Doctor Kater, what did they do with the head?'

'I beg your pardon?'

'Have you got it? Is it still in the family, among the heirlooms? Auctioned at Christie's like Napoleon's wizened genitals? Is King Billy grinning up on your mantelpiece? Or was the skull presented to the Royal Society? The Royal College of Surgeons even? A lot of professional kudos in such a presentation.'

'Get off this line!'

'And Doctor, who got the arms and legs?' He was shouting. Airport strollers were glancing towards the phone booth. 'It strikes me there would be enough skin there for several tobacco pouches!'

The line was dead. He discovered his head was pounding and replaced the receiver in an instinctual motion blurred to his eyes. His vision was masked by a grey film, of rippling effect, like peering through a wet window. Spots juddered around the window's rim. He found the lavatory, shut himself inside a cubicle and, a finger down his throat, effused a bowlful of alcohol, bile and other bitter curds.

The flight to the island was over quickly, not forty minutes. Below him it stretched surprisingly wide and long, high mountained and khaki brown. Many inlets and bays glistened along its coastline, patchwork fields clustered inland. As the plane taxied to the tiny airport shed Crisp suddenly felt the need to be undertaking a specific task, for appearances' sake. There were problems in just aimlessly materializing somewhere. Research, naturally, research for the thesis. An all-encompassing excuse.

He hired a ten-year-old Falcon with no handbrake from the general store, tried to check into the single hotel (its eighteen beds were booked out to a party of amateur gemmologists from Melbourne) and was diverted to a sprawling old guest house thirty miles northwest along narrow dirt roads. There he and a blue-haired old woman, the proprietor's mother, were the only guests. The tall thin proprietor introduced himself as Trevor Gaebler, a former linotype operator from Launceston, and went out in gumboots to milk the cow. Log fires burned in the sitting-room and dining-room. A roast was cooking in the oven, his wife (Call me Betty) said, and showed him to a high-ceilinged, wood-panelled room containing a deep double bed and a bookcase of *Reader's Digests*. He lay on the bed, sinking spongily into the thick eiderdown. An electric generator hummed somewhere in the yard. Outside there was also a constant dull thudding on the ground and a freshening wind which was forcing its way through invisible cracks to stir the net curtains.

He considered the fact that within the day he had reached one of the world's most remote places—an island of extinct people. He had escaped to the arse-end of the Earth. No one who knew him knew he was there. Strangely, this didn't afford him the relief he had expected and, alone in the darkening room, the restlessness of the curtains making shadows on the walls, he cried for several minutes.

A knocking came on the bedroom door. 'Tea's on the table,' called the Gaebler woman. 'Don't let it get cold.'

The thudding outside was kangaroos, he discovered. At dusk they appeared out of the bushes in their hundreds, Gaebler told him, right up to the front porch, ate the bran and pollard from the hens' bins. He took a shotgun to them periodically, for dogs' meat. They came in handy as bait for his craypots set just offshore over the hill.

Slaughter everywhere, Crisp thought.

'One thing's for sure,' Gaebler said, 'the old Abos didn't become extinct out of starvation. A century later, farms, guns, all that and the bloody island's still plagued with roos.'

Gaebler's old mother sucked her soup, broke some bread into it. 'They died of broken hearts,' she said. 'Pined away for their homes like animals in a zoo. My grandad had them working for him in Burnie. Lovely crochet work some of the women did, fine eye for detail.'

Gaebler offered, winking edgily at Crisp, 'People say they refused to breed. Apologies to the ladies, but they reckon from the moment they landed here they wouldn't have a naughty.'

Up early, stiff-backed from the over-soft mattress, he was served a huge country breakfast—three eggs, a chop, bacon, toast and marmalade—and set off in the Falcon, following Gaebler's instructions, to find the remains of the old Aboriginal settlement. Along the road a mile he plunged the car through a deep puddle, fifty yards on it faltered and stopped. He got out and lifted the bonnet. Crows grated in trees above him. He wiped the ignition points dry with a sheet of newspaper from the floor of the car, began to crumple the paper in his hand. A heading from the paper's editorial caught his eye: 'OUR PERIPATETIC PRIME MINISTER–Enough is enough. Though the Prime Minister undoubtedly has an Aristotelian image of himself, his custom of strolling in Lyceum while at home the economy crumbles about our ears . . .'

The car started, he drove off again. Flattened kangaroo bodies lay along the road and in the water-filled trenches at its sides. Patches of fluff, paws, tyre-tracked skin, were imprinted into the earth. On the graded embankments beside the road fat crows flopped, their job made easy, sated with flesh.

He found the site of the settlement, on a hillside spotted with cow-pats and bounded by a great prickly thicket of red berries and four-inch thorns singing with crickets. The Aborigines' old chapel sat in a valley overlooking the sea. A sign said it was being refurbished under National Trust supervision. Crisp left the car and walked through a graveyard towards the chapel, passing a big tombstone yellowed by lichens. The stone was erected by Private Patrick Monaghan of the Kings Own Light Infantry in memory of his drowned wife and children. One of the guards sent to watch over the Aborigines' languishing?

Crisp passed smaller rough stone memorials. One, erected by the Historical Research Association, said:

Manna-largenner
Last Chief of the Portland Tribe
Died December 4, 1835.

Another, a grey plaque, was erected by the Junior Farmers of Flinders Island 'To commemmorate approximately 100 Tasmanian Aborigines buried in this vicinity 1833-47'. (Manna-largenner, the only one to get his own individual memorial. Dying with a theatrical twitch or two of his well-trained shoulder towards the homeland?)

He reached the chapel, peered inside the door. Building materials were strewn over the floor, heaps of old handmade bricks were arranged against the walls. Empty cigarette packets, a workman's sandwich crusts, lay in the rubble. At the far end of the chapel among the debris a cow stood masticating. The sun came in the unglassed windows, and the sound of the crickets in the prickle bush. He didn't know what he was expecting but there were no ghosts, anyway.

What was he looking for? He turned the car around and drove back along dirt and gravel tracks for many miles to the west end of the island, away from habitation. Rain squalls hung in the grey stringy clouds over the straits but here it was sunny with a gusty wind. Walking down to the sea, Crisp stepped cautiously along a natural path of buffed oval rocks, round as eggs, each stained orange, yellow or leaf-green with lichens.

A thudding startled him, then came a scrambling and an excited bark and a wallaby bounded past him into the undergrowth followed by a Disneyish English sheepdog, shaggy and lolloping. The animals vanished. He sat on a rock streaked with bright fungus and opened the lunch Betty Gaebler had packed for him: thick lamb and pickles sandwiches in greaseproof paper, two slices of Swiss roll, an apple, a Thermos of white coffee. Keep up this diet and physical survival at least was unquestioned! Munching a sandwich he looked about him, at the headland and scattered inlets stretching away on both sides. There was no sign of habitation, no beer cans or plastic detergent bottles. The coast seemed unseen by human eye, unmarked by man. In the sand tiny crabs rolled spitballs in front of their nest holes, pelicans and cranes fished in the shallows.

A sudden wind gust brought quick sheets of rain and rainbows flashing against the mottled basalt cliffs; he sheltered under an overhanging conifer, crouching in its dead needles. The sheepdog joined him, flopping wetly beside him, sniffing at his lunch. He gave it a sandwich and poured coffee. The rain passed over the island but he remained where he was, sipping the hot sweet drink, the pine needles cushioning him from the ground. *There's peace here*, he thought, *and order enough for anyone, but still they died. What else does happiness need? Only truth, freedom and protection from inclement weathers. That's where they missed out.* At his elbow the dog lay thoughtfully chewing a heap of kangaroo turds. Crisp was no less confused.

The Gaeblers had been settled on the island long enough to know a few tales. Oh yes, they said over dinner, between spoonfuls of home-made mushroom soup. 'More characters around these parts than you can poke a stick at. Inbreeding does it,' Gaebler asserted. 'Mind you, the young ones are starting to leave home, marry on the mainland and spread the nuttiness around a bit. Not as crazy as they used to be.'

His wife said, 'Take old Freda Cubby. Black as the ace of spades. The soul of discretion all year until the end of the birding season. Every year the same thing, she comes in from the rookeries, drinks the season's wages in scotch and lime and passes out naked on the porch of the C.W.A. hall. Seventy if she's a day and in late April it's getting mighty nippy around here.'

'Too cold for me,' muttered Gaebler's mother. A speck of mushroom remained on her lower lip. 'You won't catch me out without a spencer.'

Black eccentrics. Rookeries. A tremor of excitement began in Crisp. He asked Gaebler, 'Are these people mutton birders? Straitsmen? The descendents of sealers and their stolen Tasmanian women?'

'Sure. That's them. Cape Barren Island's their headquarters. Now it's the season they're all scattered about the Straits' islands—Big Dog, Cat Face, Preservation, Gun Carriage. Catching birds, living in little tin sheds. Rough sort of life.'

The way before him was clearing. Things fitted suddenly into the requisite slots, round pegs into round holes. Light appeared at the end of tunnels. *The answer*?

'How do you get there? Who can take me there?'

'You want to go to one of the birders' islands?'

'Yes, tomorrow.'

'It's easy enough done. Hire a fishing boat, they're all in port at the moment. Or Ted Carew'll take you over to Cat Face in his powerboat. I'll ask him.'

'Good, good.'

'Yes, Cat Face would be your best bet. That's the Blue Plum's island. See the Plum, he'll help your research.' Gaebler smiled enigmatically into his soup.

'The Blue Plum? Why do they call him that?'

'You'll know when you see him. His real name's Leo Raintree.'

In his room the curtains were drifting in the draughts. Full-bellied, he climbed in under the eiderdown with a *Reader's Digest* from the bookcase and, feeling more purposeful than he had for months, was able to concentrate on a story of a humble scientific saint making wonderful progress on infantile cancers.

Ted Carew's powerboat bounced across the sound. Crisp sat midships clutching a seat strut to anchor him down as Carew gave it full throttle into the snappy tides. Spray streamed down the perspex cabin shield. Carew suddenly slowed the boat's speed, pointed out beyond the perspex to the open straits.

'Plenty of abalone out there,' he said. 'Beds and beds of it. I know where it is.'

'Where is it?' Crisp asked politely, standing and gazing out to sea.

'Wouldn't you like to know?' Carew chuckled. He was a squat man ferociously amused by life. 'Wouldn't you just like to know?' Fiercely he gunned the engine and the boat ripped through the low waves.

They came up to Cat Face the back way, around the ears and right cheek, approaching the island on a narrow sandy bay somewhere near its chin. Carew coasted the boat in gently through the shallows. 'Sandy bottom but one or two rocks,' he pointed out. 'You'll have to wade in from here.'

The water looked very shallow, deceptively so, as Crisp discovered on jumping over the side with his pants rolled to the knees, his desert boots in one hand. It rose to his thighs, half-submerging his overnight bag (carrying a sweater, a couple of his exercise books and one of Betty Gaebler's massive picnic lunches). His bare feet squelched on kelp and layers of shells.

'Watch your step.' Carew smiled broadly and reversed his boat twenty yards, then faced it out into the sound. 'I'll be back to pick you up.' The motor burbled healthily and ambiguously. 'Take it easy with the Plum.'

Crisp waded ashore through the kelp feeling less a Crusoe than a sodden travelling salesman, again confused and feeling at some physical disadvantage in his soggy clothes. He sat on a mound of dry kelp, rolled down his pants and put on his boots. Blowflies rose from the weed—it was strewn with bird heads, feet, stringy intestines.

Fifty yards up the hillside from the bay two small buildings squatted close together in the grey dirt. One was a shack made of galvanized-iron sheets, whether rusted or painted with red-lead it was hard to tell at the distance. From the other, a rectangular grey shed of cement blocks, a radio blared a jingle for petrol. As he trudged up the hill carrying his bag a grubby baby appeared in the doorway of the cement shed, dropping its bottle in surprise at the sight of him and vanishing inside. Abruptly the radio's noise stopped. A column of cloyingly sweet smoke rose from this shed's chimney and was blown off into the Straits.

Crisp walked up to the shed and the baby appeared again in the doorway, grimy-mouthed and playing with a bird's foot. Crisp poked his head inside. The atmosphere was steamy and brilliantine-sweet. Feathers and greasy tussock-grass covered the floor. In a corner, sitting around a boiling copper, were two women, one brown-skinned, the other white. The brown woman was scalding plucked bird corpses in the copper and passing them to the other, who rubbed off the clinging down-feathers with a piece of hessian sack. Their faces were smudged with grease. Despite the humidity the white woman kept a cigarette going in the corner of her mouth. Neither looked up.

'Good morning. Is Mr Raintree about?' He shuffled damply in the doorway. The baby, presumably the white woman's, had the bird's foot in its mouth and surveyed him intently.

'Up birding,' the brown woman eventually said, assessing him but still not looking at him. She was snatching the scalded birds from the copper with bare hands. 'Plum's up birding up the rookery up the hill.'

The white woman did not speak. As he hesitated in the doorway she put out a hand and turned up the volume on the radio. He turned and left, almost stepping on the baby's bottle which still lay among the feathers and tussock-grass.

'Thanks.'

He squinted up the hillside. A small collection of people could be seen high up amongst the tussock-grass, bent double most of them, then straightening up and moving upwards away from him. He left his bag beside the shed and set off towards them, limping heavily up the hill, tripping over grass clumps and sinking into burrows. Nevertheless he almost ran, as far as that was possible, so anxious was he to reach them, to find the Blue Plum. *The questions he had to ask him! The unique opportunity that had presented itself!* The sun emerged from a steel-and-purple cloud bank but the wind gusts kept it cold and blew at his back and shoved him upwards.

They had seen him coming now and paused in their ascent. Three men and two boys watched him clamber up the slope, puff up to them. They carried long wooden spits across their shoulders, all of them, strung with mutton birds, threaded on to the spiked spits through the soft under-beak. A ginger cat was with them, tail frisking, looking strangely out of place. While they waited for him to reach them they put down the spits and lit cigarettes, the boys too, and one man used the breather to urinate. Two of them had knitted woollen caps; they all wore ragged pullovers, dirt-blackened sandshoes and their pants tucked inside their socks.

The oldest and biggest man had the darkest skin Crisp had seen outside African documentaries. He was about fifty, tall and plump, with a broad forehead and features, short and tightly curled negroid hair and round glossy cheeks. His eyelids and lips were tumid, his eyes mere slits within the flesh folds. The overall impression was one of roundness and blue-blackness. He was obviously the Blue Plum and was aptly nicknamed.

'Morning,' Crisp panted, trying to avoid breaking an ankle in a bird burrow. He addressed the Blue Plum. 'Mr Raintree? Crisp's my name. I'm doing some research on mutton birding. I'd be grateful if you could help me.'

'Research? They're always doing fuckin' research, bandin' birds, lowerin' the bag limits.' The smooth moon face looked exasperated. 'Another government man, are you sport? Upset about *Puffinus tenuirostris* eh?' He pinched his cigarette dead with black banana fingers and stuck it behind a tiny curled ear.

'No, oh no.' Definitely the wrong ploy. 'I work for myself, you see, writing about the history of Tasmania and so on.' He did not say, *you may be the link in it all, the whole business, the bridge between the past and a longed-for tranquil future.* Even the solution to other problems. Instead he said, 'I believe you have an, er, interesting background, fascinating ancestors.'

'You could say that, sport. You could definitely say that.' Suddenly he smiled and shook Crisp's hand. 'I'm the Blue Plum. So was my old man and his before him. When I go young Victor will be the Blue Plum.' Here he ruffled the hair of a slight dark boy of about ten who stood nonchalantly by puffing a cigarette. 'Call me Plum. I'm only Raintree to the authorities.'

Crisp was excited, delighted at his change of mood. 'I'd like to watch you work, talk to you about certain matters. Without getting in your way, naturally.'

The Blue Plum was generous. Expansive. 'You're most welcome.

Be my guest. And meet my rookery hands—Simon, Cyril and Angus.' Respectively, they were a small wiry white man with a turned eye, an olive-skinned young man with broad Aboriginal features and another boy, fair-headed, a year or so older than Victor. They nodded at Crisp expressionlessly. The man with the wall-eye pulled his cap down over the tops of his ears.

'You wouldn't think we're all related, would you sport?' The Plum laughed. 'Oh, we're an amazing race.'

The small boy Victor sidled up to Crisp as the party moved up the hill. 'A bloke got bitten by a copperhead the other day,' he said. 'Here, poke your arm down this hole and get a mutton bird.'

'Not on your life.'

'Scared are you? You a mainlander? From Tasmania?'

'Even more mainland than that—from Sydney.'

'Shit-a-brick. Want to see me get a bird?' The boy dived down on the tussock-grass and plunged his arm down a burrow in the hillside. He was prone, up to the armpit in the hole, his face in the dirt. Out he came with a furious struggling bird bigger than a gull though downy in patches and still a fledgling. It squawked a high cry and flapped untried wings. Victor Raintree, the next Blue Plum, swung it through the air by its head as his father was doing. (The Plum was casually breaking birds' necks every minute or so like a schoolboy flicking his necktie.)

Victor's bird presented a little trouble, however, 'Break, break!' he screamed, whirling it around his head. The bird screeched louder, its wings beating against the boy's angry brown face. Suddenly (but to Crisp's eyes in slow motion) the head came off in the boy's hand and the bird's body flipped high into the air.

'Shit! Shit! Shit!' Victor yelled. He had bleeding scratches on his hand, peck marks on the wrist. The ginger cat sniffed at the truncated bird not yet ten seconds dead.

'Do that again and you'll have a week in the pluck-house,' the Blue Plum boomed down on the boy. He scooped up the corpse and impaled it through the neck on his own spit. 'Mark my words.'

As always routines, proficiency at a task, fascinated Crisp. (Am I actually a practical man underneath? he'd thought before.) Even observing the bizarre cottage industry of Cat Face Island, the grisly and squalid processes of mutton-birding, brought on the old pleasantly numbing sensation (along with the conservationist's vague liberal/

urban distaste for the slaughter of animals, granted). The efficiency of the operation was amazing. A regular Henry Ford factory line. When the Plum, Simon, Cyril, Angus and young Victor had a spit-load of birds, sixty or so strung along their shoulders, they'd carry them down the hill and place them on a wooden rack outside the cement processing shed. Here it was Victor's job to remove each still-warm body from the spits, hold it by the legs and squeeze the sweet bloody stomach oil out the gullet into a 44-gallon drum. The drum already brimmed and glistened with streaky red liquid.

He was an extrovert, the junior Plum, throwing himself into his work, milking away at the plump bellied, lolling headed corpses, banging them against the side of the drum to shake off the drips.

'Why aren't you in school?' Crisp asked.

'Ha. Got the birding season off, haven't I? Get every season off school. Didn't you know that?' He threw each squeezed body through a small opening a foot square, into a tiny dark room. 'The pluck-house,' he announced. 'That's the part that shits me off, the pluck-house. I'm allergic to it, gives me bronchitis.'

Down on his knees in the grease and gizzards Crisp peeped into the opening, squinted to make out a human head and shoulders in the blackness. The smell, the sense of claustrophobia, were overpowering. His pupils adjusted, he saw an old dark man sitting on the floor chest-deep in feathers. His hands, protruding from the wall-to-wall feathers, were plucking still more from the birds Victor had thrown in, working quickly, methodically, and then passing each plucked bird through a hessian flap-door into the scalding-room. Where the women sat around their steaming copper like comic-book witches.

'Morning,' Crisp greeted. Inanely. It was actually now afternoon, not that it made any difference to the man in the feathers in the dark. But he felt he should say something to cover the intrusion. Anyway, the old man ignored him, dropping his chin low on his chest, almost sinking into the feathers.

'Who's that?' he whispered to the boy, withdrawing his head. 'What a job!'

Scarlet mucus gushed into the drum. Victor kneaded another belly. 'Grandpa Raintree,' he said, off-handed.

'Your father's father?'

'Yeah, Grandpa.'

'I'd gathered he was dead, that he was the Blue Plum before your father.'

'He *was* the Plum.' The boy gave a frown of exasperation. 'Until he got too old.' He dashed a body against the rim of the drum. The beak struck metal with a small *tink*. 'You've got to be on the ball to be the Plum.'

'But what does the Blue Plum do?' Crisp had to ask though he thought he might know.

'He doesn't do anything special. He just *is*.'

He sought refuge again in technical processes, mustn't overdo things in the beginning, arouse antagonisms, traditional islanders' suspicions. What happened to the plucked, scalded birds now? he asked Victor. What was the next stage in the procedure? The boy showed him. When the women had finished scalding them (severing heads and legs along the way) they pushed them through another sack flap-door into the shed's third room where they were cleaned and laid to cool on racks. Here the birds were finally dressed, spread flat like kippers and packed in casks of brine. The drums of stomach oil ended up as suntan lotion, pharmaceutical and cosmetic products; the feathers filled mattresses and sleeping bags for campers.

'Remarkable,' said Crisp. The debt bathing beauties owed the squawking fledgling of the sooty-petrel. Greasing themselves with its glandular secretions to avoid crow's feet and unglamorous pallor.

'The market price is forty bucks a hundred birds,' Victor said. Businesslike and brisk. 'We'll get eighteen thousand this season, six hundred a day. Not bad for a month's work.'

The birders came down the hill for lunch, setting down their spits on the rack by the pluck-house. The women scampered from the scalding-room to the tin shack, returning with sliced bread in waxed wrappers, cans of sardines, a jagged-topped tin of apricot jam. Amazingly (to Crisp's eyes), the pale-skinned woman scooped out a billy-can of boiling water from the copper and threw in a handful of tea. Sure enough the brew was oily, cloudy, supported several floating feathers. He was grateful for Betty Gaebler's Thermos, offered the coffee and sandwiches around, but they preferred their tea and sardines. (Only Victor accepted a slice of Swiss roll.) There was no talking, everyone squatted on the scalding-room step or on their haunches in the dirt outside. Blinking against the light Grandpa Raintree emerged from the pluck-house, thin and withered, one hand curled around a cigarette. He wore a greasy green sweater stuck through with feathers and tightly belted khaki pants. Age greyed his skin. He drank some tea and munched listlessly on bread and jam, leaning against the shed wall. Down flecked his knotted white hair.

The other men lit up cigarettes, sighed and stretched out. Simon-with-the-wall-eye scratched his groin. The baby toddled forward with a jammy crust and sat on his legs, jigged up and down in play. Simon stroked its wispy hair, blew smoke towards the bay.

'You a writer are you?' he asked. Avoiding Crisp's eye even with his own wandering one.

'Yes he is.' The Plum answered for him. 'He's interested in our way of life.' He grinned enigmatically, to himself or the others Crisp couldn't tell. And frowned with it.

'Not much to it,' Simon muttered.

'Quite wrong,' the Plum said loudly, drawing up his bulk. Rigid-backed. 'You're wrong there, Simon.' Grinning ferociously now he reached over and helped himself to one of Simon's cigarettes, lit up thoughtfully. Simon subsided in silent distress. 'We're a whole new race,' the Plum announced. 'I've been told that by experts. Museum and university men.'

'Oh, Plum,' murmured the dark woman. She squirmed in embarrassment, screwing a twist of bread wrapper in her hands.

'Shoosh, Ivy! Don't get your tits in a knot.'

Ivy flustered in agonies around the lunch scraps. Victor snickered, 'That's right Mum.' The Plum nonchalantly backhanded him across the ear.

'You're going the right way for the pluck-house, sport.' The boy sulked off down to the shore, restraining himself proudly from rubbing the throbbing ear.

'Named him after Victor Mature,' the Plum said. 'The Hollywood star. Me and Ivy saw *Demetrius and the Gladiators* once in Launceston.' He snorted. 'Boy thinks he's a fucking star sometimes.' Then a look of scholarship played over the globular countenance. He was back on *the* topic. 'What I mean to say is we're a whole new human population brought into being by hybridization.' He pronounced the word carefully and apparently from memory. 'You wouldn't credit the number of anthropologists interested in us.'

Here Crisp was nodding in an interested fashion, screwing the top back on the Thermos flask, when the Plum asked sharply, 'Where's your notebook? You'd better take this down for your write-up.' In his bag he found the exercise book, a bit soggy, and a pencil. He looked attentive, poised over the book.

'Write this name down. Norman Tindale. You've heard of him of course. Top anthropologist, researched into my old man for months on end. Gave me a good going-over too, when I was a kid. He worked out what I am. Know what I am?'

'Tell me please.'

'A fourth generation cross. Tasmanian Aborigine on both sides. American nigger and a touch of Polynesian on my old man's side. Also Irish. On my mother's side Australian Abo twice and Scottish. Glasgow actually.'

'Very diverse.'

'Oh yes, they were a wild bunch in those days,' Between his fat eye folds he glinted. 'Fucked about a lot.'

By this time the others had hauled themselves up from the dirt, grunting and sighing, picked up their spits and set off again up the hill. Silent Grandpa Raintree creaked off to the pluck-house (driven by the passive slave-genes of Alabama ancestors?) to sit amid the feathers. The women tossed the lunch garbage in a fly-blown hole behind the shed and returned to the copper.

'Did I get you right?' Crisp wondered. 'You said you were all related.'

'Very true. We must be. Only seventy of us left. We don't marry much outside. Causes one or two problems with the whiter ones—funny eyes like Simon's, the odd hare-lip. But we're strong as mules.' Teeth short and stained showed when he smiled. 'We've got hybrid vigour, sport.'

Crisp found himself jotting down disjointed words and phrases: *fourth generation, hybrid vigour,* meanwhile staring entranced at the animated patent-leather visage, the creased neck fat crowded upward to the neck and shoulders. Ambrosia wafted from the frayed sweater, the stained pants—certainly a death-smell but one of pleasant associations: summer sun-baked days, bikinied girls, youth, health.

'You're wondering about my colour. Me and Victor being darker than the rest. And my old man of course. It's a matter of breeding, naturally. The Raintrees breed dark, always have. Abo genes are strangely recessive generally. Overtaken by the European. You see half-caste kids with yellow hair and grey skin running round Australia.

Freaks. Well we breed dark. Having the African blood helps. A good mix: African-Tasmanian-Australian. Plus the tranquillity of your Polynesian. The cunning of the white adventurer, the pirate, slaver, sealer, the convict runaway. That's why we produce the Blue Plums. Nearly always a Raintree though I had a third cousin, a Dunlap, black as pitch, was a Plum for a while.'

'If you don't mind me asking,' Crisp was very deferential, 'what exactly are the advantages in being the Blue Plum?'

A peculiar transformation overtook the shiny face. Deep corrugations of amazement gathered in the forehead. The Plum grabbed Crisp's unsuspecting wrist in a sharp pressure. Squeezed it, shook it vigorously. All the time a look of the wildest frustration was in his eyes. Crisp thought, Great Christ—what do I do now?

The Plum cried, 'You ask me that! You ask me what's the advantage in being the Blue Plum! With me sitting here talking nicely to you . . .' He uttered several words of gobbledegook—'gunmer-yer-trowl' or somesuch—and then took some deep breaths of self-restraint. 'Isn't it obvious, sport? The Blue Plum is the one who communicates.'

Carried forward by rapid wind gusts, purple cloud banks covered the sun, darkened the island, changed the bay from shallow green to lead. Waves began, and choppy tides collided sharply, tossing up spiteful spray plumes. Savagely bright rainbows snapped on and off whenever the sun flashed momentarily. Heavy, widely spaced raindrops fell on the sand.

'Sou'easterly,' the Plum said, inhaling the wind.

Bad weather?'

'Right.' He got heavily to his feet, dislodging a flat stone with his shoe. Anaemic mites, shrimp-looking, skittered frantically for cover. 'You might be stuck with us. If this gets bad Carew'll never bring his boat out.' He gave a sudden and gentle smile. 'Timid bugger, Ted. Doesn't like to get his Johnson wet.' Sheets of cold rain arrived as he spoke and a fetid wind brought the smells of the rubbish hole and the vegetable combustion of the weed heaps.

God Almighty! Various emotions immediately struck Crisp. Anxiety. Excitement. Frankly a certain degree of bourgeois distaste at the immediate residential prospects. And people will worry, he thought. Altered plans always brought on insecurity, anger, disorientation and burnt dinners. But again he realized, with a cold shock, that no one really knew and so how could they care? Only the Gaeblers and they would hardly turn a hair.

He ran for shelter to the door of the scalding-room. Again the baby was on the floor, this time asleep on its knees bottom-up amongst the debris. The women still sat around the copper, silently working in the sweet steam. They ignored him of course, scrubbing away at the plump white corpses with their pieces of sacking.

'Raining cats and dogs,' he announced. He couldn't have felt less significant. Rain drummed on the tin roof at the world's end.

The others tramped slowly and soddenly down the hill from the rookery carrying spitloads of limp, bedraggled birds. Victor darted about in the rain, hair frizzed and streaming, draining the body oil into the drum, flipping the bodies through the pluck-house trapdoor.

'Grandpa'll be shitty,' he giggled. 'Wet birds are a bastard to pluck. Slippery as buggery.'

Aimlessly, Crisp hung about, in people's way. They bustled through the processing of the final haul, the men helping in the scalding-room, steam rising from their dripping bodies. Urgings came from the Plum. Playful whacks on the back. 'Come on you boongs,' he shouted, gleaming in the dampness. 'Bloody lot of slow wankers.' In the *mêlée* the baby woke, sat up flushed and screaming with a feather on its cheek. 'Come on me little possum, come to Plum.' And he swooped on it, hoisted it in his fat arms, pressed it to his glistening neck creases. Crooning soft growls of gibberish through his jaunty short teeth. 'Oh, who's my tiger? My little possum-boy?' Swinging it shrieking to the ceiling then abruptly holding it quizzically at arm's length. And tossing the giggling child to its mother, he called, 'Hey Edna, Tiger's shat himself.'

They moved through the storm's sludge to the tin shed—the living quarters. The Plum unlatched the wooden door and ushered Crisp inside. The others followed, so what with Simon, Cyril, Angus, Victor, Ivy, Edna, the ripe-diapered baby and old Grandpa Raintree shuffling inside in their saturated clothes as well as Crisp and the massive Plum, the single room was packed to the gunwales and stuffily, tropically malodorous, Crisp found himself pressed against the rear wall. He had no choice but to sit where he was—on a narrow camp stretcher—with his legs drawn up to his chest.

'Home sweet home,' boomed the Plum, gesturing as expansively as was possible in the circumstances. Ivy and Edna disappeared behind a blanketed-off corner with the baby; the men stood or sat where they were and peeled off their wet clothes, kicked them into the doorway, fumbled around naked for dry ones in kitbags and cardboard suitcases. Dimpled and bouncing, the Plum rumbled about the shed in a pair of grubby orange underpants, found two plastic mugs and a bottle of hospital brandy. He loomed black and quivering over Crisp. 'Say when,' he ordered, filling the mugs.

Sitting there across from him, squatting rather, all big breasts and stomach not three feet from him, the Plum reminded Crisp more than ever of some African potentate from the travelogues, a 300-pound chieftain being weighed in gold offered in supplication by his faithful starving subjects. From their poor melted-down trinkets and tooth fillings. A ceremonial spear would look well in his fist, a touch of leopard skin not amiss. And various jungle teeth would set nicely against the blue-blackness. The Mutton Bird King.

Mugs of the brandy went down, sharply and acidly. Body heat filled the shed. The birders slumped on their stretchers sipping sweet sherry and flipping through magazines. Victor read a comic, moving his lips. Expressionless, Grandpa Raintree sat against a wall in striped wincey pyjamas with a bottle to his mouth. A stormy mid-afternoon light still came through the small windows on each side of the door but the women were lighting two kerosene lamps at a narrow table. Rain thudded outside and drummed on the roof and walls of the shed. Inside, the lamps discharged oily smoke and, reaching into the shed's farthest corners, illuminated pictures—cut from the *Women's Weekly* and *Australasian Post*—decorating the walls. At Crisp's cheek Princess Anne was juxtaposed with Sammy Davis Jr and Muhammad Ali. Over one bed was a violently coloured picture of Jesus in the temple: a white and angelically boyish Jesus telling the money-lenders where to get off.

'Good wrecking weather,' the Plum said into his brandy mug.

'Heh heh.'

'Nice strong rip-tide. Good little shoals off Cat Face. Inter-island trader comes off here of a Wednesday.'

'Those were the days, eh?'

'Wonder what she's carrying this trip?' Those stubby teeth showed between the lip pads, grinned evilly. 'Old Dad wields a good lamp, brings 'em in like a sheep-dog. Simon tends to rush it, hurries the flashes.'

'Really? Ha, ha.'

The Plum reached over without getting up from his bunk, hauled in a handful of Crisp's still-damp sweater with swollen fingers, breathed brandy fumes into his face. 'I know this won't go no further, sport. Strictest confidence. It was a Blue Plum got the *Britomart* you know. Lured by false lights on to Goose Island.

'Is that so?' Jolly adventures in the Straits. He was being had. Or was he? The face, the clever eyelids, the fat quirky cheeks, the whole man had wily ways. Devious wisdom.

'Looted, scuttled in the Green Hole. Captain, crew and passengers all despatched. Buried or ended up in craypots some of them.' The plastic mug went up to the lips again then the Plum sat up straight, stretched and got to his feet. 'But the old man had his day, I'll give him that. He brought the *Southland* aground in 1922 off Gun Carriage. None of us've beaten that.'

While Crisp was considering this intelligence, mulling it over in the brandy-clouded brain, the Plum stepped over the reclining Cyril and Simon, took a seaman's lamp from a shelf above the table and walked out into the storm in his orange underpants. The wind slammed the door shut behind him. In his corner Grandpa Raintree looked up from his bottle and spoke.

'Not worth a cunt full of cold water,' he announced in a high, dry voice—and resumed drinking.

Edna and Ivy served dinner: mutton birds (one each), bread, jam, tea. The birds, Crisp reasoned, were inevitable. He'd have to try one sooner or later and while not looking amazingly appetising sitting there cold as plaster, pale and naked on plastic plates, they resembled chickens enough not to be completely repellant. Edna handed him his meal wordlessly.

'Thank you Edna. Much obliged.' His mind was simultaneously on other things but the brandy had a foothold. 'I'm very grateful for your hospitality.'

She acknowledged this with a cautious sniff. But topped up his brandy beaker before serving the others. They fell to, busily if not enthusiastically, chins and lips soon shining with grease. The baby waved a drumstick in its hands.

He began eating, too. Really, he considered, I don't care what it tastes like. Beyond caring about such unmeaningness. Least of my problems. It's all just fuel. Actually the mutton bird tasted most unlike chicken—oily, salty and over-fresh. He washed down each fibrous mouthful with brandy. Blotted the flavour with bread.

'Mm, interesting taste. I understand some Tasmanians swear by it. They canned it during the war and marketed it as squab-in-aspic.'

Simon's wall-eye glanced maliciously. But his face and other eye remained vacantly oblivious. Munching occurred without further discussion. Heat and a sweaty negativeness filled the shed. Thumpings and rustlings sounded at the door and the Plum swung inside, streaming and puffing.

'You're here for ever, sport. It's blowing a bloody gale.' He kicked his sodden Y-fronts across the fuggy room and towelled himself dry. Sitting on his bunk grossly naked he said no more until he'd worked his way through two mutton birds and a pile of bread. Then he reached out his empty mug, clasped it in shiny swollen fingers. 'Who does a man have to fuck to get a drink around here?'

Crisp leaned back against the magazine cut-outs, head swimming. *The Plum's mission accomplished?* The women had turned on the transistor radio, picked up faint Dixieland jazz from the mainland. *Which mainland? Which country? Planet even?* The baby was asleep and now Edna and Ivy were also passing around the sherry, tapping feet to the music. Victor had his *Phantom* comic propped up against the jam tin by one of the lamps and his cigarette smoke drifted in the lamplight. How cynical, worldly the boy was! Little Wendy getting *The Magic Pudding* at bedtime and saying parentally inspired prayers. '*Thank you for the world so sweet*' . . . et cetera. Whereas wiry black Victor already knew, even here at the end of the world, who was up whom in this life. Like his father.

But . . . were people at this minute drowning in the shoals in the maelstrom? Sturdy immigrant crewmen roused from sleep, alcoholic card games, buggery and knifings by the grinding of metal on reef. Floundering a lifetime away from Oslo and Bremen, lured to gagging deaths by a crazy hybrid.

Suddenly, from the corner of the shed, came a growling. It was Grandpa Raintree. 'Trowl-yer gun-tool,' he said. 'Berg-ner fart-boon.' Or something like it. The old man rose to his feet with difficulty and, clutching both his sherry bottle and his pyjama pants, stumbled outside.

Eyes widened around the room. There were hisses of exhaled breath, knowing glances passed. The Plum shrugged meaty shoulders. 'Greg-ler gun-yer,' he muttered. 'Silly old bastard.'

Unreasonable fears began inside Crisp, along with a spiky discomfort in the stomach and gullet. He passed a hand over his forehead: he was sweating heavily. A trickle ran down his chest. His heart shuddered against his rib cage. There was a thought-flash. *I'm going to die here! Me, too!* He pushed himself off the stretcher, got up shakily, tried to salvage some oxygen from the fusty air. He inhaled sharply and immediately the old post-meningitis pains sped up his spine. Clumsily he rushed for the door, climbing and falling over languid bodies, out-stretched twitching limbs. Simon burbled something unintelligible as he stepped over him. Asleep with his wall-eye open.

'The bog's out the back,' the Plum yelled. 'You'll know it when you fall in it.'

Cold air rushed at him; winds coming directly from Antarctic oceans buffeted him, fizzed through the tussock-grass behind the huts, howled up the hillside. Momentarily the rain had stopped. The sky was black, moon and stars smothered by cloud. He could not see the sea, only the dim silhouettes of the sheds and the blurred mass of the hill rising up now before him . . . He paused, steadied himself with several shallow breaths and abruptly realized he was poised on the brink of the shit-pit. There was a plank across it for squatting. Stepping quickly back and lurching off again up the hill, he fought to clear his head. Vainly. Winds blasted the pit-smell into his lungs—the sweet and purulent ordure of mutton bird eaters. Down on his knees Crisp collapsed among sodden hillocks and tunnels, tussock-grass prickling his palms, the winds shrieking over his back and neck and driving his hair over his eyes. So violent was the vomiting, however, and the nature of the bloody, squalid images that accompanied it, that these discomforts went almost unnoticed until his body was drained and he hawked useless drops of spittle on to the grass.

Hollow, spent, he got to his feet and continued, slithering and falling, up the hill. Grabbing clumps of grass to save himself from tumbling. Tripping in bare nest-holes, snatched up again by the wind and driven forwards and upwards. He made the crown of the hill at last, sagged down on a narrow flat piece of ground, bare and muddy, and turned and faced the bay. The wind in his face was welcome even in its ferocity, piercing his brain and air passages, scouring the bile from his chin. The huts lay below him; only the tin living-quarters was faintly visible, from its dim kerosene light. Crisp concentrated on the bay, the headland, squinted out into the black shoals. He drew on dormant boy-scoutish resources of night vision, an acuteness of hearing. Seeking silhouettes: the uptilted bow, the acutely-angled mast. And death-yells of terror.

There were sounds, finally, heard above the beating of the wind. Small cries. Disturbances of the air. But Crisp, straining into the darkness, saw nothing. He could not define the sea from the land or the sky from the sea. Again came the sounds, closer now and louder. A concentrated agitation was in the wind, like a crowd's combined gasp of despair.

Crisp strained to listen. Immediately a scratching occurred to his left, at first slow and soft but gradually becoming frenzied. His spine turned to cold metal, breathing ceased in fear. The same noise struck his attention to his right. And below him. And then, helped by a momentary abating of the weather, it was all around him and he saw the cause. Cleaving in from the sea were clouds of birds, each homing in silently on the wind to its own burrow. To feed its fledgling. The parent mutton birds were returning to the nest to find in most cases an empty burrow. And scratching and searching in desperation.

Different deaths. Muddy-legged, his bad knee paining, ice-cold, scratched on the palms and wrists from panicky grabbings, he slid, stumbled down the hill again, setting a diagonal course to avoid diving headlong into the cesspit. The old bird holes on the lower levels were water-filled; in one of them he sunk a leg up to the calf. *Meanwhile, raddled old Poles bugger each other safely through the shoals.* The brilliantine aroma of boyhood barbers' shops struck him at that moment and he found himself hard up against the back of the processing shed. The cement wall was warm to the touch. He fumbled around to the door. In the scalding-room there was a big fire going under the copper. Steam clouded the room. The warmth drove pins-and-needles into his cold skin. He took off his wet boots and hovered over the light and heat of the fire. Feathers stuck to his soggy feet.

A rasping cough, curtained-off from him, startled him. Then an arm pulled aside the sacking flap-door and eyes stared out at him, opalescent, from the blackness of the pluck-house.

'For Christ's sake get in here out of the cold,' ordered Grandpa Raintree, drawing his pyjama coat tight at the throat. 'Colder than a nun's tit.'

The old man crawled backwards into the black feathery hole. Crisp, long since bereft of independence, followed, crawling forwards.

Flapping shut behind him the sacking obliterated the firelight. It was dark as the womb. Or tomb, depending on the point of view. More accurately the womb, because of the warmth and layered feathery softness. Grandpa Raintree's voice came out of the darkness.

'Get your back against the wall,' he said. 'Warm as toast. Want a drink?'

'I'd rather not.' He squirmed up to the warm brick, spreadeagled himself against it to absorb some heat.

'Warmest place on Cat Face, this. Comfy. Private. None of them silly bastards farting and having nightmares from the booze. No crying babies.'

'It's certainly all that. But I didn't realize you *chose* the pluck-house.' How to put it delicately. 'I imagined it was sort of a retirement job.'

'Ha. What sort of fool would I be at seventy-eight out in the weather poking me arm down holes? I come out to eat, piss and shit. The rest of the time I'm in here having a nice warm holiday. Leo's welcome to the grafting.'

'Grafting?'

'The bullshit. Dealing with people. The Blue Plum's a ratshit job these days, no mistake.'

'I don't follow.'

The old man adjusted his feathers around him. Crisp could hear the rustling, like the circular scrabbling of a weary dog.

'In the old days it was something to be the Plum—the blackest, toughest bastard in the Straits. To have the Tasmanian blood and all that. There was all sorts of funny business he was in charge of, with the law miles away.'

'Like wrecking?'

'Oh well, a bit of this and that.' There was a sneezing, then a snorting laugh from the old man. 'Oh, we took a few risks in them days. It was a trial just living around here then. Everyone knew where a few bodies was buried. No tasks to be done now but. Nothing left. Us Straitsmen are out of date. You know what the Plum's main job is now? Where all his energy goes?'

'Tell me.' So not on waving cruelly false beacons. Or even on mutton birding.

'Talking to the Government. Grafting. Dealing with the Aboriginal Affairs Department on our behalf. Us quaint and unique Straitsmen. The blackness comes in handy. The certified Tasmanian blood . . .'

'But what's the Blue Plum deal in?' But Crisp, above anyone, already knew.

'Guilt, of course. Fuckin' guilt. There's money in it boy, and a new tractor or abalone boat when you need it.'

Hemmed in by warm walls of feathers Crisp drowsed off, or imagined he'd just drowsed, dreaming briefly of Jane, who became his mother, who was alive on Cat Face leading a solitary but contented life. Movements and conversation woke him, coming from the scalding-room next door. Waking in the pitch blackness, dull behind the eyes from stale air and cheap brandy, he thought it still night and was astonished to push aside the flap-door and discover Ivy and Edna stoking up the fire in broad daylight. They showed no surprise at seeing his head pop out, tousled and feathered. The baby, already dirt-caked, said 'Dadda!' as he crawled from the pluck-house. The wool of his sweater was stuck through with feathers. Others were itching his skin inside his shirt and pants. He found his boots, stained with damp, and put them on.

'Morning,' he greeted the women, giddy with the activity and glare, blurry with the night's recollections. 'How's the weather?'

'Wind's dropped,' Ivy said. 'Bit of cloud. Rookery's half flooded.'

'Where is everyone? The Plum?' His stomach prickled for breakfast. His mouth was arid and sour. But otherwise things could be worse. The women looked at each other. Edna had a new pink sty growing in the corner of one eye that she was embarrassed about.

Ivy said, 'Loadin' crates of birds on Ted Carew's boat.'

Outside the air was fresh, stunningly cold after the shed, making his nose and eyes run. No handkerchief: he blew his nose carefully on the sand. The high storm tide had scoured all the kelp and debris from the beach, leaving it white and slick. At the edge of the bay, in the lee of the headland, Carew's powerboat was drawn close inshore. Five or six crates were stacked in the stern. The men were lounging on the shore, squatting on their heels, smoking and drinking from cans of beer, Grandpa Raintree and Victor, too. A small snatch of laughter blew away in the breeze. He strolled towards them, not exactly happy but more disburdened, slowing his stride to one of relaxation. Carew's boat was in the edge of his vision. Carew himself was sitting on a flat rock with a can to his lips.

Crisp called, 'Hello there!' as he came up to them, scuffing through the tight wet sand. Carew mumbled something to the others—it sounded like 'ten-ther plow-bom'—and there were several smiles.

The Plum's face was wide and meaty with cheer. This morning he wore a checked shirt rolled to the elbows, voluminous shorts and a woollen cap. He was barefoot. 'Morning,' he answered and tossed Crisp a can of beer. 'How'd you sleep?'

'Fine.' He guessed he had. Gingerly though, he sipped the beer—the liquid seemed to immediately hit the pit of his stomach, form gases, spread to extremities. He belched loudly, like a bark.

Crisp said goodbye. Victor said goodbye, the others nodded mutely. The Plum said, 'Back to civilization, eh. More bangs than breakfasts on the mainland, I've heard. A new car every year and men my age wearing makeup.'

Crisp smiled. 'Something like that. Thanks,' he said.

The Plum tossed his empty can into the sea. 'No thanks necessary. Just a day on Cat Face with the crazy men.' But as Crisp took off his boots to wade out to the boat the Plum sharply clasped his elbow with those black banana fingers. 'You could do us a favour, sport,' he muttered. 'Know anyone in the media?'

'Sure.'

'Tell them about us. It'd make a good programme. Approached from the right angle.'

From Carew's boat Crisp looked back at Cat Face. The men had left the beach. The only person visible was the baby, a small blob in the doorway of the processing shed. He waved and it disappeared. Smoke rising from the scalding-room chimney dispersed almost immediately.

He stretched his legs for his pants to dry in the air, plucked stray feathers from his sweater, scratched various itches. One itch persevered, became a peculiar tingle just below his left armpit. He took off his sweater and shirt and investigated: two small brown creatures were half burrowed into his skin.

'Christ! What's this?' He tried to brush them away. Unsuccessfully. Anxiously.

Carew looked across quizzically from the wheel. He removed his cigarette from his mouth, handed it to him.

'Just ticks. Burn them off. But don't leave the heads in, they're the poisonous part.'

He cauterized the insects. Eventually they released their hold, desisted from tunnelling into his flesh. He singed his chest slightly in the process, flicked their dry-shelled bodies overboard with repulsion and great relief, then searched his body and clothes for others. His hands were trembling; a small amount of his blood was on his fingers and beneath his armpits. As he was putting his shirt on again—the southerly breeze goosefleshed his back and chest—Carew asked nonchalantly, lighting up another cigarette, 'Well, how was the island?'

He straightened his clothes, prepared himself for homeward journeys. 'It was worth the trip,' he said.